Regency Society

D0465762

PREJUDICE *in*
Regency
Society

MICHELLE
STYLES

MILLS
BOON
&

Published in Great Britain 2014
by Mills & Boon, an imprint of Harlequin (UK) Limited,
Eton House, 18-24 Paradise Road, Richmond, Surrey, TW9 1SR

PREJUDICE IN REGENCY SOCIETY
© 2014 Harlequin Books S.A.

An Impulsive Debutante © 2008 Michelle Styles
A Question of Impropriety © 2008 Michelle Styles

ISBN: 978-0-263-25013-8

052-0415

Harlequin (UK) policy is to use papers that are natural, renewable and recyclable products and made from wood grown in sustainable forests. The logging and manufacturing processes conform to the legal environmental regulations of the country of origin.

Printed and bound
by CPI Group (UK) Ltd, Croydon, CR0 4YY

Born and raised near San Francisco, California, **Michelle Styles** currently lives a few miles south of Hadrian's Wall, with her husband, three children, two dogs, cats, assorted ducks, hens and beehives. An avid reader, she became hooked on historical romance when she discovered Georgette Heyer, Anya Seton and Victoria Holt one rainy lunchtime at school. And, for her, a historical romance still represents the perfect way to escape.

Although Michelle loves reading about history, she also enjoys a more hands-on approach to her research. She has experimented with a variety of old recipes and cookery methods (some more successfully than others), climbed down Roman sewers and fallen off horses in Iceland—all in the name of discovering more about how people went about their daily lives. When she is not writing, reading or doing research, Michelle tends her rather overgrown garden or does needlework—in particular counted cross-stitch.

Michelle maintains a website, www.michellestyles.co.uk, and a blog: www.michellestyles.blogspot.com. She would be delighted to hear from you.

An Impulsive Debutante

MICHELLE STYLES

Chapter One

'I kept my promise, Father.' Tristan Dyvelston, the new Lord Thorngrafton, placed his hand on his father's grave and his fingers touched the smooth black marble, tracing his father's name. He glanced down at the weed-infested grave.

'Your brother has died,' he said solemnly, repeating the vow he had made on this very spot ten years ago. 'I have returned to take the title. I will be above reproach now. But while my uncle was alive I wanted him to think the worst about me and to fear for the future of his beloved title.'

He bowed his head and stepped back from the grave. One part of his oath was complete.

The late morning sunlight broke through the cloud and illuminated the ruins for a single glorious moment, making it seem like he had stepped into one of John Martin's more evocative paintings. Tristan tightened his grip on his cane. Here was no picture to be admired. The scene showed how much had to be done. How much would be done.

He was under no illusion about the enormity of his task. His parents' graves lay under a tangled mass of nettles and brambles. In the ten years since he had last been here, the entire churchyard had fallen into decay, echoing the state of Gortner Hall, some fifteen miles away. He would put that right, eventually. His uncle was no longer there to object.

He traced the lettering on his mother's grave. How would the county greet the return of the black sheep? He had heard the tales his uncle had spread—the gossip, the scandal and the plain twisting of the facts. His uncle had sought to deny him everything but the title and the entailed estate, a dry husk, long starved of any funds. Tristan took great pleasure in confounding his expectations.

The clicking of a gate caused him to turn. Irritated.

A blonde woman with a determined expression on her face tiptoed into the churchyard, glanced furtively about and raised a shining object into the air. The sunlight glinted on it, sending a beam of light to dance on the yew trees. Tristan relaxed slightly. She was not someone he had ever encountered before and therefore was unlikely to recognise him. But there was something about the way the petite woman held her head that intrigued him.

Why would anyone come here?

She wrinkled her nose, fiddled with the object again and finally gave a huge sigh of satisfaction. 'I told Cousin Frances that a moonlight aspect would work better than a Gilpin tint, and I was correct. She will have to retract her scornful words. The church could be romantic in the moonlight. One would have to imagine the hooting owl, but it could be done. It could be painted.'

Tristan jumped and considered how best to respond to the statement. Then he gave an irritated frown as he realised that the woman was not speaking to him. He regarded her for another instant as she peered intently at the object in her hand. He gave a wry smile as he realised the object's identity—a Claude glass, a mirror that prettified the landscape and allowed the viewer to see it at different times of the year, or hours of the day, simply through changing the tinted glass. It all made sense. She had come in search of landscapes.

If he was lucky, it would be just the Claude glass and a few ladies to coo and ahh at the ruins. If he was unlucky, they would have brought their watercolour paints, brushes and easels, the better to capture the romantic ruins. He lifted his eyes towards heaven. God preserve him from ladies wielding Claude glasses, their pursuit of culture and their self-righteous indignation that others should not share their same view of the world, interrupting his first chance to pay his respects to his parents. Tristan frowned. Not if he acted first.

'Precisely how many more of you are there?' he asked, making sure his voice carried across the disused churchyard. 'How many more are there in the horde?'

The woman spun around, her mouth forming an O. She had one of those fashionable china-doll faces—blue eyes and pink cheeked in a porcelain oval. The lightness of her complexion was highlighted against the darkness of the yew hedge, giving her almost an angelic appearance, but there was a sensuousness about her mouth, a hint of slumbering passion in her eyes. Her well-cut walking dress hinted at her rounded curves as well as revealing her tiny waist. A temptress rather than a blue stocking.

'You are not supposed to be here,' she said, putting her hands on her hips and gesturing with her Claude glass. 'Nobody ever comes here. Cousin Frances told me emphatically—Haydon Church is always deserted.'

'Your cousin was obviously mistaken. I am here.'

'My cousin dislikes admitting mistakes, but she will be forced to concede this time.' The woman hid her mouth behind her hand and gave a little laugh. 'She much prefers to think that since she has her nose in a book all the time, she knows rather more than me. But she can be blind to the world around her, the little details that make life so interesting and pleasant.'

'And you are not? Looking at the world through a mirror can give a distorted view.'

'I am using both my eyes now.' She tilted her head to one side. 'Are you up to no good? Cousin Frances says that often you meet the nefarious sort in churchyards. It says so in all the novels she reads. It is why she refused to visit.'

'But she thinks it deserted.'

'Except for the desperate. Are you desperate?'

'I am visiting my parents' graves.'

'You are an orphan!' The woman clasped her gloved hands together. 'How thrilling. I mean, it's perfectly tragic and all that, but rather romantic. What is it like not to have family considerations? Or expectations? Is it lonely being an orphan?' Her face sobered. 'How silly of me. If it wasn't lonely, you wouldn't be visiting your parents and attempting to derive some small amount of comfort from their graves.'

'There is that.' Tristan allowed the woman's words to flow over him, a pleasing sound much like a brook.

She came over and stood by him, peering at the ground. 'You should tend their graves better. They are swamped in nettles and brambles. It is the right and proper thing to do. An orphan should look after his parents' graves.'

'I intend to. I have only recently returned from the continent after a long absence.' Tristan stared at her with her ridiculous straw bonnet and cupid's-bow mouth. Right and proper? Who was *she* to lecture him?

'That explains the entire situation. You had expectations of another's help, but that person failed you.' She gave him a beatific smile. 'Orphans cannot depend on other people. They can only look to themselves.'

'How very perceptive of you.'

'I try. I am interested in people.' She modestly lowered her lashes.

He straightened his cuffs, drew his mind away from the dark smudges her lashes made against her skin. 'How many more shall be invading my peace? Ladies with Claude glasses have the annoying habit of travelling in packs, intent on devouring culture and the picturesque.'

Her pink cheeks flamed brighter and she scuffed a toe of her boot along the dirt path. 'I am the only one. And I have never hunted in a pack. You make society ladies sound like ravening beasts, longing to bring men down when, in fact, they are the ones who provide the niceties of civilisation. They make communities thrive. When I think about the good works—'

'Only you? Are you sure that is prudent?' Tristan cut off the discussion on good works with a wave of his hand.

Even though Haydon Bridge was rural Northumberland, the woman did not appear the sort who would be allowed to roam free and unaccompanied. Her pink-and-white-checked gown was too well cut and her straw bonnet too new and finely made. Her accent, although it held faint traces of the north-east, was clear enough to indicate she had been trained from an early age by a succession of governesses.

'I am able to look after myself. I know the value of a well-sharpened hat pin.'

'You never know what sort of people you might meet.'

'It is the country, after all, not London or Newcastle.'
Her cheeks took on a rosy hue and she lowered her tone
to a confidential whisper. 'I am aiding and abetting a
proposal. At times like these, positive action is required,
even if there is an element of risk.'

'A proposal?' Tristan glanced over his shoulder, fully
expecting to see some puffed-up dandy or farmer advancing towards them. 'Tell me where the unfortunate man is
and I shall beat a hasty retreat.'

'Not mine. My cousin's.'

'The one who is mistaken about graveyards,' Tristan
said, and struggled to keep his face straight. It made a
change to speak about things other than the state of
Gortner Hall's leaking roof, the fallow fields and the other
ravages that his uncle had wreaked on the estate.

'That's right.' There was a sort of confidence about the
woman, the sort that is easily destroyed later in life. 'All
Frances ever does is read Minerva Press novels and sigh
about Mr Shepard's fine eyes and his gentle manner. What
is the good with sighing and not acting positively? She
needed some help and advice.'

'Which you have offered…unasked.'

She held up her hand and her body stilled; an intent expression crossed her face. 'There, can you hear it?'

The sound of a faint shriek wafted on the breeze. Tristan
lifted an eyebrow. 'It sounds as if someone is strangling a
cat. Is this something you are concerned about? Should I
investigate?'

'My cousin Frances, actually. She is busy being rescued
from the Cruel Sykes burn.' She tilted her head, listening
and then gave a decided nod. The bow of her mouth tilted
upwards. 'Definitely Cousin Frances. We practised the

shriek a dozen times and she still managed to get it wrong. She needed to gently shriek, and to grab his arm, but not to claw it. I do hope she has not pulled him in. That would be insupportable. Truly insupportable.'

'All this is in aid of?'

'Her forthcoming marriage to Mr Kent Shepard.'

The woman drew a breath and Tristan noticed the agreeable manner in which she filled out her gingham bodice. But he knew she was also well aware of the picture she created. A minx who should be left alone. Trouble. He would make his excuses and depart before he became ensnared in any of her ill-considered schemes.

'Cousin Frances has to get engaged. She simply has to. Everything in my life depends on it.'

'Why should it matter to you?' His curiosity overcame him.

'I was unjustly banished.' The woman wrinkled her nose. 'It was hardly my fault that Miss Emma Harrison kissed Jack Stanton in a sleigh in full view of any passing stranger.'

'Jack Stanton is well able to look after himself.' Tristan gave a laugh. His impression had been correct. She was the sort of woman to stay away from. Trouble with a capital T. 'I hope your friend was not too inconvenienced, but she picked the wrong man to kiss. Jack is a good friend of mine and not given to observing the niceties of society.'

'Do *you*?'

'When the occasion demands. I was born a gentleman. But Jack…is immune to such stratagems. It is amazing the lengths some women will go to.'

'It all ended happily as they were married, just before Christmas.' Her eyes blazed as she drew herself up to her full height. 'You obviously do not know your friends as well as you think you do.'

'I have been travelling on the Continent. But if it ended happily, why were you banished?'

'My brother Henry was furious. He turned a sort of mottled purple and sent me out here to Aunt Alice until I could learn to keep my mouth quiet. "Lottie," he said, "you have no more sense than a gnat," which was a severely unkind thing to say.'

'And have you? Learnt to keep your mouth quiet?'

'Yes.' Lottie Charlton looked at the elegantly dressed man lounging against a yew tree with exasperation. Who was he with his dark eyes and frowning mouth to sit judgement on her? He was not her brother or any sort of relation. She snapped the Claude glass shut and took as deep a breath as her stays would allow her. 'I have, but Henry refuses to answer any of my impassioned pleas. He ignores me. And Mama is being no help at all. She keeps going on about her nerves and how unsettling family disagreements are, but she refuses to do anything.'

'And you dislike being ignored, forced to the margins.'

Lottie retained a check on her temper—barely. They were not even formally introduced and already this man had picked her character to shreds. 'This is my best chance, my only chance, to get back to Newcastle this season. I know it is. My dream of a London Season has vanished for the moment, but there are appearances to maintain. And some day I shall visit all the great cities— London, Paris and Rome. I plan to be the toast of them all.'

'How so? Haydon Bridge is very far from these places.' The man lifted one eyebrow, seemingly unimpressed with the brilliance of her scheme.

'I am well aware of geography.' Lottie pressed her hands together. She had to remain calm. 'Aunt Alice will have undying gratitude to me if I arrange this marriage between Cousin Frances and Mr Shepard. Mr Shepard has been making sheep's eyes at Cousin Frances for weeks now, and the only thing Cousin Frances can do is blush and readjust her pince-nez.'

'And you are an expert in these matters.' His eyes travelled slowly down her and Lottie fought against the impulse to blush. 'You look all of seventeen.'

'Twenty in a month's time. My sister-in-law sent me the Claude glass for an early birthday present. It is quite the rage, you know.'

'Nineteen is not a great age.' A smile tugged at his mouth, transforming his features. Darkly handsome, she believed it was called, like one of those heroes in Cousin Frances's Minerva Press novels. 'When you are my age, you will see that.'

'And your age is?'

'Thirty-one. Old enough to know interference in matters of the heart brings unforeseen consequences.' The words were a great finality. Lottie frowned and decided to ignore his remark.

'I helped to arrange several proposals last season in Newcastle. Proper ones as well, and not the dishonourable sort.' Lottie resisted the urge to pat her curls. 'I can number at least seven successful matches that I have helped promote.'

'Including the one that sent you here.'

'If you are going to be rude, I shall leave.' Lottie lifted her skirt slightly and prepared to flounce off. The man made her brilliant stratagem sound like a crime, like she was intent on ruining someone. Newcastle was not London, but at least there remained a chance of meeting someone eligible. It was the most prosperous city in the whole of the British Empire, everyone knew that. 'You

must not say things like that. I *have* helped. Martha
Dresser and her mother showered me with compliments
when I brought Major Irons up to snuff.'

'Don't mind me. It is one of my more irritating habits.'
A slight smile tugged at the corner of his mouth, making
him seem much younger. 'Your scheme appears to be full
of holes. And I doubt you would know the difference
between a proposal and a proposition.'

'I know all about those. One learns these things, if one
happens to possess golden curls, a reasonable figure and
a small fortune in funds.'

'I will take your word for the funds. I can clearly see
the other two.' His dark eyes danced. 'I agree that they can
be a heady concoction for some men.'

'Yes, I know.' Lottie began ticking off the points. 'One
has to be wary of the inveterates who stammer out
marriage proposals at the sight of a well-trimmed ankle,
the cads who try to get you into corners and steal a kiss,
the let-in-pockets who only have an eye to one's fortune
and clearing their vowels. I have encountered them all. But
I am quite determined to be ruthless. Mama wants a title.'

'A title can be a difficult proposition. What makes you
positive that you can snare one? What sort of mantraps do
you intend on laying? It can take great skill and cunning
to succeed when so many are in pursuit.'

Impossible man. He made it seem like she was some
sort of predator. Lottie stuck her chin in the air and
prepared to give the *coup de grâce*. 'I have rejected Lord
Thorngrafton. He positively begged for my hand last
November.'

'Lord Thorngrafton? The elderly Lord Thorngrafton?'
The man went still and something blazed in his eyes. The
air about him crackled.

'Not so very elderly.' Lottie kept her gaze steady. She refused to be intimidated. As if the only titled men who might be interested in her were on their last legs or blind in both eyes! 'Around about your age and you are hardly in your dotage.'

'When did he propose to you?' The man leant forward, every particle appeared coiled, ready to spring. 'I would like to know. It is most intriguing. I have been on the Continent until recently and am unaware of certain recent events.'

'Shortly before Christmas.' Lottie gave a small shrug and wished she had thought to bring her parasol. She would have liked to have spun it in a disdainful fashion. 'However, I do not think the proposal genuine as Mama never remarked upon it. I rather fancied it was the sort where the gentleman expects you to fall into his lap like a ripe peach, perfect for the plucking and tasting, but easily forgotten.'

'You'd be right there.' The man's eyes became hooded and his shoulders relaxed. 'I do not believe Lord Thorn-grafton intends to wed any time soon. I should not try any of your tricks with him.'

'Are you acquainted with Lord Thorngrafton? Is he another of your friends that you have misplaced while you were on the Continent?' Lottie narrowed her eyes, peering at him more closely. Silently she cursed her wayward tongue. He did look like Lord Thorngrafton, if she half-closed her eyes. But this man had a wilder air about him. She would swear that he moved like a panther that she had once heard about at the Royal Zoological Society in London. 'You look somewhat similar—dark black hair, same eyes, but he was shorter, more squarely built. He had fat, doughy hands and he spoke with a slight lisp.'

A muscle twitched in the man's jaw and a cold prickling sensation trickled down the back of Lottie's neck. What had Lord Thorngrafton ever done to this man?

'We are acquainted. Relations.'

'And you are?' Lottie clutched her reticule tighter to her bosom. She knew the information should make her feel more secure, but somehow, it didn't. The man knew both Jack Stanton and Lord Thorngrafton, but that did not mean a thing.

'Tristan Dyvelston,' he said and his dark eyes flared with something.

Tristan Dyvelston. The name rang in Lottie's ears. She glanced about her and the giant yews began to press inwards, hemming her in. The notorious Tristan Dyvelston. Cousin Frances, in one of her more expansive moods, had whispered about him and the scandals he had left in his wake. She peered more closely at the weed-choked graves and picked out the Dyvelston name. The tale on balance was true. Why would anyone pretend to be Tristan Dyvelston? Even after ten years, the wisps of scandal clung to his name. A scandal so great that Frances only knew the barest of details.

She made a pretence of straightening her skirt. Life's little problems were never solved through panic. She had to find a way to retreat in a dignified manner. She doubted if society's rules and niceties would constrain Tristan Dyvelston. He would take, and pay no regard to the consequences. That was a woman's job—looking towards the consequences of her actions.

'But he went to the Continent, pursued by several angry husbands.' The words slipped out. She wet her lips, drew a deep breath. 'Are you funning me? Who are you really?'

'Tristan Dyvelston.' A faint hint of amusement coloured his dark features. 'I have returned…from the Continent. It is no longer necessary for me to be there.'

'But the scandal.' Lottie made a small gesture. 'The shame, the dreadful, terrible shame. Those poor women. Cousin Frances was most particular on the shame.'

'She knew what she was on about, the lady I left with. And I use the word lady lightly.' Tristan Dyvelston's mouth turned down and his face took on the appearance of marble. 'No husband pursued me. I believe he was thankful to get rid of the encumbrance of his wife. The affair cooled before we reached Calais. Last seen, the woman in question had found solace in the arms of an Italian count.'

Lottie measured the distance between herself and the gate. She wanted to appear sophisticated and unconcerned, but if she was caught here alone in the company of a notorious womaniser, any hope of regaining a social life would be gone. She might as well learn to do tatting and resign herself to looking after Henry and Lucy's children. She had to leave. Immediately.

'An Italian count—imagine that. Really, it has been very pleasant speaking with you, but I must be going…'

'And here I thought we were having a pleasant conversation.' He took a step closer to her. A smile tugged at the corner of his mouth as if he understood precisely why she had decided to depart. 'I regret that I disturbed you.'

'You didn't. I have seen all that I came for. I will return one day with my paints. There is a certain melancholy air about this place.' She cautiously took a step backwards, then another; her foot slipped and a bramble snaked around her boot, holding her fast.

She attempted to free herself but only succeeded in catching the skirt of her dress. And it would have to be her new checked gingham. Fine lawn. Easily torn. She could hear Frances's clucking and Aunt Alice's sighing now. Then there would be explanations, ones she did not want to make. The dreaded Carlotta would be used in terrible tones. Carlotta—a name more suited to her aunt in Alnmouth than her.

Lottie shivered slightly and redoubled her efforts, wincing as a thorn pricked her through her glove. Her reticule with the Claude glass dropped to the ground with a slight crash. Lottie cursed under her breath. Everything was going wrong.

'Allow me, Miss Lottie.' Tristan Dyvelston bent down, and his long fingers caught her ankle, held it firm, while his other hand freed her from the bramble. He handed her the reticule and Lottie clutched it to her bosom. 'No harm done and no need for unladylike utterances.'

'You know my name.' Lottie stilled, the reticule dangling precariously from her fingertips.

'You said it earlier.' He stood up, but did not move away from her. 'You should be more cautious.'

'Is this a warning?' Lottie's heart began to pound in her ears. He was very close. Earlier she had failed to notice the breadth of his shoulders or his height. She wondered how she had failed to do so. Wondered briefly what it would be like to be clasped in his arms, and she knew this was why he had his scandalous reputation.

'An observation from one who has lived a bit longer than you.' He looked at her. 'I have met women like you before. They need to learn life's lessons.'

'And do you propose to teach me them?' Lottie crossed her arms and forced her back straight. She gave her curls a little toss. They were back on familiar ground. She had endured such propositions before, although none given in such a warm voice. She supposed he practised it, but a small part of her wanted that voice to be just for her.

'Do you wish me to?' His eyes blazed with an inner fire.

'Forgive me, but it is dangerous thing to do—provoking a man when you are quite without a chaperon.'

'Forgive me, Mr Dyvelston—' Lottie inclined her head '—we travel in different circles, but that line has been tried on me at least four times. You are not the first to use it and no doubt will not be the last. I may give the impression of being a silly blonde, but I am not. I might be not as sophisticated as some, but I can take care of myself. I have no intention of learning life's lessons from one such as you. Or indeed any of your kind.'

He raised both eyebrows. 'You speak in a very forthright manner for one who is barely out of the school room.'

'Men such as you are an occupational hazard.' Lottie smoothed the folds of her dress. A cold fury swept over her. Why was it that men expected women to swoon when confronted with something? Or to recoil in horror? Flirtations were fine, but men always went that little bit beyond. She cleared her throat and assumed an air of haughty superiority. 'The agreed answer is that I am quite satisfied with my life at present, so thank you for the honour, but no. I shall wait until I receive the perfect proposal.'

The corner of his mouth twitched upwards as if her words amused him. Amusement! How dare he!

'And having received this set-down, I am supposed to walk away, and not gather you up in my arms. Is that what they taught you?' He paused and his hand brushed her gloved one, sending tingles throughout her body. 'Or would you rather a demonstration?'

'A demonstration?' The word emerged as a high-pitched squeak. Lottie held up her reticule like a shield. But she was torn between the knowledge that propriety demanded that she should flee, and the desire to stay and

see what he might do. What would it be like to be held in
the arms of a man who knew what he was doing? 'I have
no wish for you to demonstrate *anything*.'

'Don't you?' The words wrapped around her like a
silken rope and held her.

Slowly Lottie shook her head, but she watched Tristan
Dyvelston's smile increase. Lottie took two steps backwards. Perhaps she had made a mistake. The sound of
Frances's shriek was far too distant. She had been overconfident. 'I will be going now. Straight away.'

He threw back his head, and his laughter startled a
wood pigeon out of a tree. Broke the spell. He had
intended on frightening her. She wanted the earth to up
and swallow her. She had been naive.

'I fail to see the amusement in this.'

'Your expression is that of an outraged kitten with
spiky hair.'

'My hair is not spiky.' Lottie opted for an expression of
haughty disdain. 'I have had odes written to my hair. Lord
Thorngrafton sent me an ode about the gold in my curls.'

'Not from me. Never from me.' The colours of his eyes
changed and she wondered that she had thought them deep
black. They appeared full of hidden lights, shifting,
dancing. Never the same, but spellbinding to watch. 'I never
write odes to hair. Never write odes at all if I can help it.'

He crossed the distance between them in one stride. His
hand brushed her curls. 'Definitely not spiky. I retract.'

'Oh.' Lottie put a hand against her throat. Her heart had
begun to beat very fast. She parted her lips and closed her
eyes. What would it be like to feel his lips against hers?
She had only been kissed twice last Season, and neither
time had been what she would qualify as a success. They
had been somehow dissatisfactory, particularly after she

had learnt that Lieutenant Ludlow had gone around trying to catch Caroline, Diana and Leda under the mistletoe as well. She waited, lips pursed and poised.

'Virtuous virgins hold little attraction, even those with strawberry red lips. You may lower your mouth, Miss Lottie, and next time, wait.'

Lottie opened her eyes and hurriedly lowered her chin. She could feel the heat beginning to rise on her cheeks. A mocking smile twisted his mouth and his face became like carved marble.

'Do they indeed?' she asked in her frostiest tone as she drew her body up to her full height.

'Too many complications. Too many considerations.' He gave an elegant shrug of his shoulders.

Lottie released the air from her lungs. She should be relieved, but a small stab of regret ran through her. She had wanted to experience his arms holding her. 'You make me sound positively frumpish. Highly unattractive.'

'Not plain. Just a young lady who is far too aware of her charms and wants to play games, dangerous games that lead where neither party is prepared to go.' His eyes darkened. 'Women such as you provide complications, complications any sensible man would be well advised to give a wide berth, if he wished to retain his place in society. Even among my kind, we have a certain honour. I prefer someone who knows how to play the game.'

Lottie inclined her head. 'Goodbye, Mr Dyvelston. It has been enlightening.'

'Until we meet again, Miss Lottie.'

'I doubt that very much.'

'One never knows. When you are older, perhaps…'

He captured her hand, raised it. His lips brushed the exact point where her glove gapped, and touched her naked flesh for the briefest of instants. It seared through her.

Lottie jerked back her hand, and fled to the echoing sound of laughter. She ran straight into Frances, who wore the look of a disgruntled hen as she squelched along the lane. Her straw bonnet dripped muddy water.

'Ah, Cousin Carlotta, at last we discover you.'

'I was regarding the old church through my Claude glass.' Lottie held up her reticule with a smile. How many times had she told Frances that she hated the name Carlotta? And how many times had her cousin ignored the request? Her hand went around the reticule. She winced as she realised that she had dropped the Claude glass and returning to the ruins was impossible. Not while Tristan Dyvelston was there. 'The moonlit aspect was quite unusual. I shall have to show you some time.'

'You mean now?' Cousin Frances held her hands as an alarmed expression crossed her face.

'Impossible, Fanny dear, as you appear a bit damp and I have no wish for you to catch a chill.'

'I hate the name Fanny.'

Lottie gave a small smile. 'I always have difficulty re-membering that.'

'We thought we heard voices, Miss Charlton, just now.' Mr Shepard's Adam's apple bobbed up and down. He appeared to have a very damp, dead sheep look about him and Lottie was positive that she detected a tinge of pink to Frances's cheeks. 'Yours and someone else's.'

'Yes, a male voice, Cousin, and yours answering him.' Frances gave her a piercing glance. 'Is there anyone of our acquaintance there?'

'How did you find the bridge at Cruel Sykes burn?' Lottie asked quickly. They had to get away from here before Mr Dyvelston appeared with a sardonic twist to his lips. When Frances was in one of her moods, everything would come out. Then she would never get back to Newcastle. 'Was it easy to cross?'

'Wet,' Frances replied. 'Very wet. Cold and slippery.'

'Miss Frances fell in.' Kent Shepard puffed himself up. 'I had to rescue her.'

Lottie did not miss the slight change of name. Some good had come of this afternoon after all. Her scheme showed definite positive signs.

The golden portals of society and triumph beckoned. Tristan was wrong. She glanced behind her at the seemingly empty churchyard, biting her lip. As long as her little encounter went undiscovered. It had to go undiscovered. No one would believe that a notorious rake like Mr Dyvelston had gone to the churchyard of his own volition. He supped with the devil, according to Cousin Frances.

Why was it that the attractive men were always among the most unsuitable?

Lottie gave automatic answers as the conversation turned towards pleasantries about the weather. Her hand went to the place his lips had touched her wrist. She shivered involuntarily. She had had a lucky escape. Mr Dyvelston represented danger and she had best remember it. She would lead the sort of life that her mother and Henry wanted her to, if only she could return to civilisation. It was her destiny. She knew it.

Tristan watched her go. He heard her bright laugh and artless explanation and then turned back to his parents' graves. A small case winked up at him. He reached down and pocketed it.

There was very little point in going after the woman

now. Tristan closed his eyes. He had lied when he'd said that Lottie's hair was ordinary. It was the colour of spun gold. He could see how men could have their heads turned. But there was something else about her. Something that called to him.

'We will meet again, Lottie, you and I. And on my terms,' he said, fingering the Claude glass and staring down at the village. 'But first I need to determine who the false Thorngrafton is.'

Chapter Two

'I had expected my sister to be here.' The sound of Henry's pompous voice greeted Lottie as she entered Aunt Alice's house. 'You know, Aunt, what sort of mischief Lottie can get into when left to her own devices. It is precisely this sort of thing that I warned you about.'

Her aunt's soothing reply was muffled behind the door to the parlour.

Typical, Lottie thought, the one time her brother decided to make the journey here, she was out, gallivanting across the country with an ungrateful Cousin Frances. It could have been worse. Frances could have spotted her with Mr Dyvelston. But Frances showed a singular lack of interest in her whereabouts or in the church. And nothing had happened, nothing at all.

Lottie's fingers explored the underside of her wrist. The imprint of his touch still burnt her flesh. What was it about that one particular man? Was it the danger he represented?

'Do you have any idea of when she might return?' Henry's pompous voice brought her back to reality with a bump. 'I have business to attend to and cannot wait around for ever. The train leaves for Gilsland in two hours. And there is not another one until morning.'

'Henry, is that you? Are Lucy or Mama with you?' Lottie called out as she removed her gloves and bonnet with trembling fingers. Why was her brother here? Had something happened? She would be brave.

'Ah, Lottie, you make an appearance.' Henry turned from her aunt and Lottie was surprised to see how fat he had grown. 'Come and greet me. What do you have to say to your brother?'

He had a well-fed look like a trained seal. If anything, the last five months had made him sleeker and fatter. She noticed he wore normal clothes and not mourning ones. Lottie gave a sigh of relief, thanking God for small mercies.

'You should have sent word, and I would have been here.'

'I had expected you would be here, doing your needle-work or making another one of those pincushion mottos that you and my wife are enamoured with.'

'Why?' Lottie blinked rapidly and refused to let his cutting words hurt. She would have been here, sitting, doing needlework if only he had let her know. 'We keep different hours in the country. I went for a stroll with my cousin. The fresh air is reputed to be good for most constitutions. You should try it some time.'

Henry harrumphed. 'I suppose there is no harm in a quiet walk.'

'Now, tell me, Henry what is the news?' Lottie came forwards and caught her brother's hands. 'How are Mama, Lucy and the children? They send letters, but it is not the same as hearing it. I do miss them so. Do say they are all well and that you are not here because of them.'

'Lucy sends her regards. The children are well, or so Lucy tells me.' Henry's face softened. 'Mama has gone to Gilsland Spa for the waters.'

Lottie concentrated on her aunt's patterned Turkey carpet. It could be that this was her best chance, far better than the marriage plans for Frances and Mr Shepard. She had to show that she had learnt from her exile. 'Is my dear sister-in-law planning to come out to Haydon Bridge? There are some fine walks around here. I can tell her the legend of Cruel Sykes burn and she can look for the blood in the water.'

'Yes, Carlotta and I went to the Cruel Sykes burn today.' Frances nodded and her cheeks flamed to a bright pink. 'It is quite a pleasant walk. I nearly fell in the burn, but Mr Shepard rescued me. Fished me out.'

'I had no idea that Mr Shepard had accompanied you.' Aunt Alice's voice was chilling. 'Who arranged this?'

'He did not accompany us, exactly, Mama. We met him on the pathway and Carlotta suggested that he walk with us for a while.'

'One can hardly be rude to one's acquaintants, someone one has been formally introduced to.' Lottie shifted uneasily. Perhaps she should have discovered Aunt Alice's feelings towards Kent Shepard first, beyond noticing the warmth with which he was greeted at church.

'Niece, are you going to explain further?' Her aunt tapped her fan against the small table. 'Is this some new scheme of yours? Why precisely did Mr Shepard join you and my daughter? Had he experienced difficulty with one of his cows? Goodness knows I have tried many topics with Mr Shepard but he always returns to his irksome cattle and their breeding.'

'Our paths crossed,' Lottie said, trying to forestall more

of Frances's confidences. From the thunderous look on Aunt Alice's face, she was beginning to think that perhaps she had been mistaken. Perhaps Aunt Alice had not wanted the match for Frances. 'And I…that is…we suggested that he might like to join us. He appeared quite willing to do so and in a jovial mood.'

'Yes, yes, Carlotta made the suggestion. Mr Shepard is very good at rescuing, Mama.'

'Ah, and did he rescue you from the burn as well, Carlotta?' Her aunt gave her an icy stare, one that caused her to shift uneasily in her boots.

Suddenly Lottie was very aware of the glaring and obvious flaws in her matchmaking scheme, fundamental flaws that she should have anticipated. She could not lie, but to tell the full truth would invite disaster. She had no wish to explain about Tristan Dyvelston, and the kiss on her wrist.

'You might well ask that, but the truth is…'

'Niece, none of your smoked gammon and pickles for me. You appeared to have outgrown the tendency once you were away from your mother and under an altogether steadier influence. Did or did not Mr Shepard fish you out of the burn?' Aunt Alice raised her spectacles. And her piercing gaze appeared to look into the depths of Lottie's soul. 'You are rather less damp than my daughter. Your clothing shows no sign of being rumpled.'

'No.' Lottie kept her chin high, but she swallowed hard. How was she going to explain this away, particularly as Henry had put Aunt Alice into one of her moods? 'He did not.'

'He couldn't.' Frances gave a high-pitched giggle that echoed around the room. 'She wasn't there.'

Lottie heard her aunt's little screech of horror and

wished the floor would open up. Why had she ever considered that today could be called a good day?

'Was not there?' Her aunt's voice sounded like a church bell tolling out a funeral march. 'Why not there? You depart together. You come back together. But Lottie was not with you at the burn when Mr Shepard oh so gallantly fished you out.'

'Lottie, what were you doing?' Henry thundered. 'Are you up to your old tricks? I warned you.'

'I had gone to look at the old church's ruins with the Claude glass that Lucy sent me as an early birthday present and I could have sworn they were right behind me.' Lottie opened her eyes, and used the slightly singsong voice she adopted whenever her mother accused her of anything untoward. 'It was only when I arrived that I discovered my mistake. They had taken the turning to Cruel Sykes burn. Seeing that I was there, I had a look about the church… Cousin Frances had extolled its virtues as a…subject for a watercolour…'

She glanced between Aunt Alice and Henry to see if they were going to accept the story. Cousin Frances made encouraging noises about the Claude glass.

'Mr Shepard and Cousin Frances soon caught up with me.' Lottie wiped her hand across her mouth and hoped. 'And that is all to the story. A simple misunderstanding.'

'Carlotta Charlton,' her brother thundered, 'how could you do such a thing!'

'We were right behind Lottie. Only but a moment, once we realised there had been a mistake,' Frances agreed, nodding vigorously, impressing Lottie with the way she entered into the spirit of the thing. Perhaps she had mistaken Frances's intentions. Perhaps they could become friends. 'Mr Shepard thought he heard voices. Lottie's and a man's.'

Lottie put her hands over her ears and turned her head away as everyone began to speak at once. No, definitely not friends.

'That settles it, then.' Her brother's tone boomed out over the rest.

'Settles what?' Lottie asked into the sudden silence.

'Haydon Bridge has singularly failed to curb your wayward tendencies.'

Lottie curled her fingers as she tried to suppress the wave of hurt that washed over her. 'I think you are being harsh, Brother. I have led an exemplary life. Ask Aunt Alice, or Cousin Frances.'

'Carlotta Charlton, you have been attempting to do mischief, serious mischief.' Henry stabbed his forefinger into the air. 'I told you at Christmas, I have had enough of your minx tricks! You treat your reputation with a casual contempt and a woman without a reputation might as well not live. Polite society certainly will not recognise her.'

'I…I am entirely innocent,' Lottie said through gritted teeth as Cousin Frances gaped, opening and closing her mouth like some demented cod fish. Right at that instant, she was not entirely certain whom she hated more— Cousin Frances, Mr Shepard or Tristan Dyvelston.

'It is no matter.' Henry brushed an imaginary speck of dust from his frock coat. 'Mama is determined that her daughter will marry a title. There is no reasoning with her. You know what she is like with her enthusiasms.'

'I am hardly likely to catch an aristocrat in Haydon Bridge.'

'True, true.' Henry gave an exaggerate sigh. 'Mama has been bending my ear about the very subject. I had hopes when she left to take at the waters at Gilsland Spa that she would be distracted, but her experience has only served to renew her determination. She has sent me letter after letter on the subject. Hardly a post goes by without yet another epistle arriving.'

'Do you mean to send me to London?' Lottie felt the room tilt slightly. Perhaps today was not terrible after all. Perhaps everything was a blessing. She attempted to keep the eagerness from her voice. 'I know I have missed the Queen Charlotte Ball, but a number of events remain in the Season. Mrs Fullen did say that she might be prepared to sponsor me and she is the sister of Lady Rowland. She knows the patronesses of Almack's.'

'Lucy considers otherwise. She thinks Mrs Fullen exaggerates about her connection with the patronesses.'

'Lucy forgets what Mrs Fullen did for Ann Mason only two years ago. Lady Rowland is a respected member of the *ton*, Henry. I read her antecedents in *Burke's Peerage, Baronetage and Knightage,* and if she is in Burke's…'

Henry held up his hand. 'I am unprepared to countenance you set loose in London. Lottie, you would be ruined within moments of stepping on a dance floor. Were very nearly, by all accounts, ruined by an unknown man in a deserted churchyard. You have no sense with men, Sister.'

'Then Newcastle? You are taking me back home.' Lottie refused to let the disappointment of London bow her spirits. Once she returned to Newcastle's society, she could work on her mother. Mama would realise the true importance of having a London Season to securing a title.

'Gilsland Spa where Mama is taking the waters.'

'Gilsland?' Lottie's heart sunk. 'What is at Gilsland? *Who* is at Gilsland at this time of year? It is fine for Mama, but does she intend to marry me off to some gouty lord or a creaking count from some unknown European principality?'

'Lord Thorngrafton currently resides there. He has taken a suite at Shaw's Hotel, as have several other members of the aristocracy. Mama has sent a list of the titled currently residing there. The prospects quite excite her and I must say that they make for quite intriguing reading. I had never considered Gilsland Spa as a possibility before.' Henry puffed his chest out. 'I am given to understand that Lord Thorngrafton was very interested in you at an Assembly ball last autumn, Lottie.'

Aunt Alice gave an audible gasp and Cousin Frances's eyes gleamed as Lottie gave a sigh of relief. Here at last was an opening.

'I believed Lord Thorngrafton's attention was of a dishonourable nature than honourable.' Lottie settled on the horsehair sofa, crossing her ankles and arranging the folds of her gown. If she could turn Henry's attention away from Lord Thorngrafton, she might be able to return to Newcastle after all. It was a matter of persuasion, applying the right sort of pressure. He would yield.

'Our mother believes otherwise. She has had a conversation with the man in question and he remarked on your fine eyes and how much he admired them.'

'Lord Thorngrafton spent most of last November speaking to my bosom. I do not believe that he once noticed my eyes.'

'Carlotta!' her aunt shrieked. 'Unmentionables in front of Frances! Cover your ears, Daughter!'

'I have done so, Mama.'

Lottie crossed her arms and glared at them. 'It is true.'

'Mama stated in her letter that he asked after you particularly.' Henry's eyes narrowed. 'Do not play the sly puss with me, Carlotta. I have it on good authority that Lord Thorngrafton is possessed of a more than agreeable fortune. He saw the possibilities of railways, long before I. He is a business associate of Jack Stanton, a partner in some of his ventures. And you know how rich Stanton is. I have done some investigating.'

'So rich that Mama would have happily forgone a title.' Lottie made sure that her smile was sweet. 'Letter or no, Lord Thorngrafton is up to no good. Why should a titled gentleman possessed of an agreeable fortune wish to ally himself with our family?'

Aunt Alice began to fan herself rapidly at the outburst as Henry's face turned a sort of mottled purple.

'Explain yourself!'

'I simply feel there are other better places where I could go.'

'You do, do you?' Henry jabbed his finger at her. 'Let me tell you this, Miss Butter Would Not Melt in Her Mouth! Should you fail to bring Lord Thorngrafton up to the mark, I will marry you off to the next person who asks. In fact, I am tempted to marry you off to the next person—Lord Thorngrafton or whomever—after this latest outburst. I have it on good authority that Mr Lynch is currently on the lookout for a wife, or should I say nurse-maid, for his brood of seven children.'

Lottie stared at her brother in horror. He could not do that. Could he? She fought against the panic that swept over her, struggling to breathe against the confines of her corset.

'Where is Mama? Let me speak to her. You cannot do that, Henry. I forbid it. Mama will be distraught when she learns of your unkind and uncharitable attitude.'

'Mama is at Shaw's Hotel, waiting for your arrival. And despite Lucy's misgivings, I must conclude that it is the best place for you. You will catch a titled husband there, so help me God.'

'Why are you doing this, Henry?' Lottie asked in a small voice. 'Why are you doing this to me?'

'My sister's marriage is a matter of business. You have two weeks, Lottie. I am not an unkind man, but it is all the time I wish to be away from my family. You and our mother together…'

'But…but…'

'Perhaps we send for Mr Lynch now?'

Lottie stared at her brother. Once she had thought him a god, but now she knew he was a hard, unfeeling monster. He did not care for her future happiness, merely for what prestige or power her marriage could bring to him. What business opportunities might arise. Her value on the marriage market. Lottie refused to cry or give way to temper. That, she knew from bitter experience, would not help the situation. She had to be calm. Somehow, she would find a way.

'I will go,' she whispered.

'Good.' Henry turned his back on her. 'Now, Aunt, may I have another of your esteemed muffins?'

'Lottie, dry your eyes.' Cousin Frances patted her shoulder. 'Things like this are always happening in my Minerva Press novels and they turn out all right in the end.'

Lottie gave a small hiccup. Somehow, Cousin Frances's sudden solicitude made everything worse.

'Time to wake up, Lord Thorngrafton.' Tristan strode across the darkened room, pulled apart the curtains and let the fresh air enter the wine-soaked room. 'Or should I say, Cousin Peter? I had wondered who I might find at Shaw's and had suspected that it might be you.'

The prone figure on the bed groaned, mumbled a few incoherent words before pulling the pillow over his head. 'Go away. It is the middle of the night.'

'Time to be up, Peter. Three o'clock in the afternoon. Play time has finished.' Tristan controlled his fury at his first cousin. 'Quit your shamming or you will have cause to regret it. Can you give me any reason why I should not summon the parish constable?'

At the mention of the parish constable, the man sat straight up. His florid complexion paled as Tristan regarded his first cousin with a dispassionate eye. There was a vague family resemblance, but nothing remarkable.

'You…you…you are supposed to be on the Continent. Or, better yet, dead in some alleyway.' Peter's hand trembled as he passed it over his eyes. 'I was sure you would never return to England. And Uncle swore it when I changed my name from Burford to Dyvelston.'

'Changing a name and being acknowledged as his heir does not change the order of succession, Peter.'

'I know that, but…'

'I returned, Cousin, as I promised I would.' Tristan stared at him. 'I always keep my promises…unlike some.'

'Allow me some moments to dress. This is quite a shock to me. You here. Alive.'

'Not as big of a shock as it was to me to discover that Lord Thorngrafton had been responsible for a variety of actions. What amazes me is how brazen you have been about it.'

His cousin stood up and started to dress.

'Don't begrudge me, Tris,' he said. 'I thought you dead. I was sure you were dead. Uncle Jeremiah swore it as well. He told me that you were seriously ill in Florence…or was it Venice? Don't matter, but I didn't expect you to appear.'

'Reports of my demise were premature.' Tristan paused and brushed a speck off his frock coat. 'And never call me Tris. It implies a familiarity that does not exist between us.'

'But I am your heir. There ain't no other and if you were

dead...' Peter ran his hand through his hair. 'Be fair, Tristan. Uncle's obituary, of course, made the papers and everyone naturally assumed that I would be the one... Who am I to dissuade them?'

'And who are you charging all this to?' Tristan made a sweep of his hand. 'The best suite at Shaw's is ruinously expensive.'

'You need not worry. I only borrowed the title.' Peter shook his head. 'I am not that let in the pocket. And one has to speculate to accumulate.'

'Good use?'

'Exploring business opportunities...' Peter gave a prac-tised smile. 'I have a plan about lead mining, and I just need a little capital. There is a piece of property.'

'And it has nothing to do with the card game I heard about being arranged at Mumps ha' not a mile from here. Or the two aged widows Lord Thorngrafton pursued without success last month.'

Peter winced and ran his hand through his hair, making it stand up on end. 'You heard about that.'

'Certain parties were keen to inform me of this devel-opment once I enquired. I am not without friends, Peter.' Tristan regarded his cousin. 'I warn you, Peter, the current Lord Thorngrafton will be above reproach, his name un-blemished. I intend to restore the estate to its former glory, to undo the damage our uncle did.'

'But...but scandal dogs your footsteps.' Peter blinked. 'It is why you went to the Continent. You killed a man.'

'He failed to die.'

'But you shot him.'

'For cheating at cards. I had had too much to drink and my aim was less than true.' Tristan gave a cold smile. 'It has improved. Now your exploits are at an end.'

'You remind me more and more of Uncle Jeremiah! He had the same aptitude for a chilling phrase. The same ice-cold eye.'

'Shall I forget we are related?' Tristan asked, raising an eyebrow.

'Please, Tristan, for old time's sake, let me do this one thing. I have prospects. There are three youngish widows whose heads are turned at the thought of a title. Then there is this businessman, whose mother is impressed with titles, but if I can persuade him to invest in the old lead mine, it will return a thousandfold…' Peter laid his hand on Tristan's shoulder. 'When we were young, we used to help each other out. I helped you escape to the Continent. You can't deny it. You owe me, Tristan. I was the one who aided you and Suzanne. Made things possible.'

Tristan regarded his cousin. Peter's body was already starting to run to fat and his face showed a certain thickening. Perhaps the widows and the businessmen deserved what they got. But neither was he ready to forgive Peter's observation. He and his uncle did not share a temperament.

'You did indeed. Perhaps I do owe you for that. I recall precisely why I was there as well.'

'A simple misunderstanding.' Peter held up his hands and began to speak very quickly as he dressed. 'It is my best chance of getting the readies I need. I have spent time conversing with the businessman's mother. She is here taking the waters. He is coming to visit and bringing his sister.'

'His sister?'

'She has a small fortune in funds… A week—that is all I want and then I shall never trouble you again.' Peter's eyes grew crafty.

'Who exactly is this businessman?'

'Henry Charlton. His sister is mad for titles.' Peter gave a laugh. 'I had thought to seduce her last November, but she slipped through my fingers. Then her mother appears here, an odious woman with aspirations, and informs me of her daughter's fortune in funds.'

'You tried to seduce a number of women last November.'

'Yes, but they knew what they were on about.'

'As long as you are sure. Virgins and the like can lead to unforeseen complications.' Tristan paused. 'We leave now.'

'This very instant? But it will take me a time to pack and it is past checking out. I will have to pay for tonight's room.'

'That is your problem.'

Peter's eyes grew crafty. 'You will need a place to lay your head. Stay here tonight. One night and see if I can't persuade you to invest. For days gone by. Please.'

Tristan regarded his cousin, with his face pleading. 'I want no more of this deception. You will put matters right.'

'If I must…' Peter's face showed signs of clear relief.

'I positively insist. You will follow my lead. Do not attempt to cross me, Peter. The next time, I will forget that you are kin.'

'Have you memorised the list I gave you, Lottie, so you will know which gentlemen to dance with?' Her mother grabbed Lottie's elbow as they descended the stairs at Shaw's Hotel the next evening. 'You must make sure that you speak very loudly to Lord Crawley. He is as deaf as a post. And Sir Geoffrey Lea…'

'Mama, I have read the list and committed it to memory. You have asked me this twice already.' Lottie fought the temptation to roll her eyes heavenwards.

'I know how inattentive you can be, Carlotta. This is a serious campaign. I had expected you two days ago.'

'Aunt Alice sends her apologies, but the packing took time.'

'Not when I do it.' Her mother gave a loud sniff and muttered something about the incompetence of sisters-in-law.

Several hours at Shaw's Hotel and Lottie come to the conclusion that her options were limited. Nearly every person she had encountered was well past the age of fifty or appeared to be suffering from a weak chin and watery eyes. Or both. The only possible glimmer of an idea she had was to steer the men towards other women. If they all found wives, she would be free.

'But Mama, the men here are more likely to want a nurse than a wife. I will make a very bad nurse.'

'A young titled widow is always in demand, Lottie. You can marry for other things later.' Her mother caught Lottie's chin between her thumb and forefinger, twisting Lottie's head to the left and right before releasing it. 'Your looks should hold another five years at least. Plenty of time. You need to think towards the future. I would see you married well.' Her mother went down the stairs with a determination that Wellington would have admired.

'Are you sure this neckline is not a touch too low?' Lottie asked Henry as they followed in her wake. 'Mama appears to have forgotten the lace. Perhaps I ought to go back.'

'You never bothered about such things before,' Henry said. 'I feel certain that Lord Thorngrafton will appreciate the...dress. Or one of the other gentlemen. I dare say Mama was correct. There are any number of titled widowers here.'

'They are all about one hundred years old except for Lord Thorngrafton, and I warned you, Henry, about him.'

'You appear to know a great deal about Lord Thorngrafton all of a sudden.' Henry frowned. 'And he has yet to make an appearance.'

'We encountered each other last November. Martha Irons saved me from disaster with her timely swoon.' Lottie demurely lowered her eyelashes. 'But my lace, Henry. Is the neckline not a bit daring? The dress is two seasons old.'

'It looks lovely from where I stand.' The low rumble of a voice washed over her. Lottie froze as she felt a hot tide of red flush her face. He was not supposed to be here. He was supposed to be safely in Haydon Bridge or wherever rakes went. Certainly not here.

'Are we acquainted, sir?' Henry's voice had become frigid.

'Tristan Dyvelston.' Tristan's voice was cool. 'Perhaps, Peter, you would be so good to introduce us.'

'My cousin, Henry, my cousin.' Peter Dyvelston, Lord Thorngrafton, came forward and caught Henry by the arm. 'It was my mistake. Tristan, I told you about Henry Charlton and his charming sister, Miss Charlton. Where is your delightful mother? I was looking forward to speaking with her again. We had such an amusing conversation the other night.'

Lottie stared at the impeccably dressed gentleman standing next to Lord Thorngrafton. Her pulse began to race and she struggled to remember how to breathe. She had told herself that she had been mistaken, that Tristan could not be that handsome. But her memory had lied.

He was far more.

The darkness of his frock coat contrasted with his face, and his cream trousers skimmed his figure. But what was he doing here and in the company of Lord Thorngrafton?

He had given the impression the other day that he had very little to do with the man. Lottie tightened her grip on her fan and hoped that he would not make any untoward remarks about their last meeting.

'I am delighted to make your acquaintance, Mr Dyvelston.' Lottie held out a gloved hand, prayed that his lips wouldn't brush it, then prayed that they would.

Chapter Three

Tristan regarded the trio in front of him. The mother and the brother were types he was used to, but Lottie Charlton in an evening gown was a piece of shimmering blue confection. The form-fitting bodice bowed out at her waist and her petticoats swirled about her ankles in a sea of white foam. Tristan wondered if his hands could span her waist or would there be a gap? Would her flesh feel as warm between his fingers as her wrist had felt against his mouth the other day?

Her ear bobs swayed gently and her blonde ringlets were artfully placed on the top of her head. No expense had been spared. She was obviously angling for a husband, but which one of the geriatrics did she want? And what would happen if she knew his title? Would she use their earlier meeting against him? A pulse of anger ran through him. He would not be so easily ensnared into marriage.

'I am delighted to make your acquaintance at long last, Miss Charlton. I was confused as to your identity.' Tristan bowed low over her hand. His breath touched the thin kid of her glove, though Lottie drew back before his lips encountered her palm. But he had seen the slight flaring of her nostrils. 'I have heard a great deal about you from my cousin.'

'What are you doing here?'

'Lord Thorngrafton has taken a suite of rooms here and my cousin is permitting me to share them.' Tristan watched the comprehension grow on Peter's face. The masquerade would continue for tonight, until the precise nature of the situation was clear. It paid to be cautious.

'How did you get here?' Lottie asked in a furious undertone, pointedly ignoring his arm. 'You were in Haydon Bridge looking after your parents' graves and hopefully feeling remorse at the state you allowed them to get into.'

'I could ask the same of you.' His eyes stopped at her neckline and flicked up to her generous mouth. 'What did you come in search of? A husband? Your gown is admirably suited for the hunt.'

The corners of her mouth turned down and her blue eyes took on a mulish expression. 'You do take the strangest notions into your head, Mr Dyvelston. Do you always give lectures in this manner?'

'My cousin is here but for a short while.' Tristan gestured towards where Peter stood, rapidly expounding on the virtues of lead mining in the district to Lottie's brother. An unforeseen complication, but one he intended to his advantage. If Lottie discovered his true status, would she tell her mother about the incident in the cemetery? Would the mother use it as an excuse to ensnare him? He refused to take the risk. Peter would keep silent, he was certain of that. 'I do not feel that he would be good husband material.'

'And is there anyone you recommend in his place?' Her tone was light, but her eyes narrowed as she fluttered her fan.

'I have not been here long enough to advise properly,' Tristan said, allowing his eyes to dance.

'You should not assume, then.' Lottie snapped her fan shut. 'I declined your cousin's offer before Christmas.'

'So you did. I had forgotten.'

'I am here because my brother brought me.' Lottie risked a glance at Tristan's unyielding profile. It irritated her that he thought her so blindingly obvious in her husband-hunting. And if he had made that assumption, how many of the other guests had also come to the same conclusion? Her mother could be terribly indiscreet. 'My mother is taking the waters. She swears that they do her nerves a power of good. She enjoys the company.'

'The sulphur water at Gilsland is renowned as is its matchmaking Popping Stone. I believe the numbers are about even.'

Lottie gritted her teeth. 'My mother desired a bit of company. I shall not be following the footsteps of Sir Walter Scott.'

'Did everything work out as you had planned for your cousin?' he asked in an arch tone, seemingly amused rather than quelled by her remark. 'Is your aunt pleased with your interference in matters matrimonial?'

Lottie examined the pattern of the carpet. He would have to bring that up. 'I maintain hopes, but I misjudged the situation slightly. It was felt that perhaps I was better off departing as Mama was desirous of me arriving here. I am to be the belle of tonight's ball, so I understand.'

'Ah, you are here for the matchmaking.'

'No, I am here to prove to my mother and brother that I can be trusted. I wish to make my mark in London.'

'Do you think you will be able to? Many young ladies vie to become to the Incomparable, the Diamond of the Season. The vast majority are condemned to be wall-flowers.'

She glanced up and noticed that his dark eyes were fringed with impossibly long lashes, the sort of lashes that were wasted on a man. But his gaze held no malice, only concern. A queer trembling overtook her. He, a near stranger, cared. 'I think there are other places where I stand a better chance of achieving my goal.'

'And the goal is…'

'To make a brilliant match.' She threw back her shoulders and made sure her eyes danced. 'And you do not need to worry. I have no designs on your virtuous name. Mama is insistent on a title.'

'That fact relieves me no end.' He gave a short laugh.

'I thought it would.'

'Who are you hunting?'

'Mama has made a list, but I fear she has not consulted Burke's recently and is doomed to disappointment.' Lottie rubbed her eye, relieved to be explaining the problems. Tristan Dyvelston, at least, was a sympathetic ear and he might have a solution to her problem. 'I distinctly heard Lord Foster mention a wife and she has him down as a widower. I am not sure if she has been careless or if she simply made a mistake. These things can happen even in the best ordered of campaigns. But it doesn't really matter as I have no intention of marrying, simply demonstrating to Mama that I can behave properly. There will be no scandals clinging to my skirts.'

'Sometimes scandals happen whether one is trying to avoid them or not.'

'What does it feel like to be on the outside of society, Mr Dyvelston?' Lottie tilted her head to one side, making her smile sweet.

His eyes became a deep black as the barb hit home and he inclined his head. 'It is a cold and bleak place, Miss

Charlton. You would not care for it. And yet women are easily banished there. Too easily.'

Lottie grasped her fan tighter and struggled to breathe against the tightness of her corset.

'No, I probably would not, but then it is unlikely I shall have to encounter it.' She gave her ringlets a little toss. 'I plan to be at the very heart of society. It is my natural place.'

'Are you determined to marry a title, then? Against the odds?'

'It is as easy to love a titled man as an untitled one.' Lottie glanced over her shoulder and dropped her voice. 'One of Mama's little sayings, and it does seem to mean so much to her. She has aspirations.'

'So your sights are set on Thorngrafton, as much as you try to deny it. I will warn you for the last time, Miss Charlton, my cousin is not to be trusted. Please consider long and hard if he does make an offer.'

'His title includes a baronetcy, one of the original ones purchased from Charles I, or so Henry says.' Lottie tapped her fan against her mouth, suddenly aware that she had perhaps revealed too much. 'It is an honourable title, but I hope to do better. I want to convince Mama that a London Season is what I need.'

'Then why are you here?'

'Because I have yet to convince my brother.' Lottie held up her hand. 'I know what you must think of me. Cold-hearted, unemotional and obsessed with titles, Mr Dyvelston, but may I remind you that you are hardly a person to be sitting in judgement.'

'I never judge my fellow human beings, Miss Charlton.' A dimple flashed in the corner of his mouth. 'Particularly when the person in question is as refreshing about her intentions as you.'

Lottie's breath caught in her throat. Why couldn't Tristan Dyvelston have a title? It would make life much simpler. She would not have minded setting her cap for him, despite saying otherwise. He was exciting, different. He did not melt at a flutter of her eyelashes, and, more importantly, he did not treat her as an inanimate object or speak exclusively to her breasts. 'I hardly see any point in pretence, Mr Dyvelston.'

'Will you save a waltz for me?'

Lottie turned her face towards the corniced ceiling as she tried to resist the sudden quickening of her pulse. A waltz in his arms. 'If you like…'

'Lottie, do hurry up. Lottie!' her mother called. 'There are a number of people who are desirous of meeting you.'

'One should always be careful about whom one meets in a hotel, Miss Charlton.' His eyes held something hidden. 'There can be no telling if they are the genuine article or not.'

'One should be careful about whom one meets in a ruined churchyard, Mr Dyvelston.' She tilted her chin upwards and prepared to sweep away.

'One meets all the best sorts of people there.' His voice held a note of amusement that rose around her and held her spellbound.

'Lottie, why do you dally?' Her mother's voice resounded across the foyer, recalling her to her duty. 'There is someone here who insists on making your acquaintance. I am certain you will find him most agreeable.'

'My mother calls. She will wonder why I have been detained.'

'Do not let me keep you, Miss Charlton. I have no wish to cause a scandal.'

'I thought that was what you did best.'

'You mistook me. My scandalous days have long past. I lead a sober and uneventful life.'

'Mr Dyvelston.'

Lottie picked up her skirts and hurried over to her mother. She stopped short as she saw the wizened man that her mother was sitting next to. Her heart sank. Sir Geoffrey Lea. The name that was proudly written below Lord Thorngrafton's. He was over seventy. How could her mother do this to her?

She forced her shoulders to stay straight, refusing to glance back at where Mr Dyvelston stood.

Why were men such as he always dishonourable and forbidden?

Tristan bided his time during the early part of the evening, observing the current guests of Shaw's Hotel, waiting and watching. They were a mixed group and, as far as he could tell from the accents, not from the general vicinity. It was becoming clear why Peter had been able to carry off his impersonation.

Many of the men were elderly and comfortable in their own self-importance. He felt sorry that Lottie Charlton was going to be sacrificed to one of them. But he had to trust that her family would not marry her off if she objected.

He watched as Lottie's blue gown with its swirling lace flashed by and heard her laughter float out over the crowd. A number of matrons and their other less well-endowed daughters clicked their tongues, but Tristan sensed a sort of desperation in her moves as if she was determined to show that she was having fun. He had been tempted to confess the truth about his title and watch her face. But there was also the mother to consider. One false step and he could find himself shackled.

'Congratulate me, Thorngrafton.' Sir Geoffrey Lea, one of the more decrepit denizens of Shaw's came up to Tristan.

'My cousin—' Tristan gestured towards where Peter stood, speaking about his lead mine to any who would listen.

'Is plain Mr Dyvelston. Being adopted does not mean inheriting the title.' Sir Geoffrey tapped his nose. 'I am not past it yet, whatever anyone might say. Took me until I saw you to put my finger on why I did not trust him. I dare say that most people have forgotten which cousin would inherit, particularly as your uncle was so marked in his preferences. Won't enquire into the game you two are playing either, it is not my place. But your cousin will not get the Charlton heiress. You may inform him of that.'

'I never intended that he should.' Tristan tightened his jaw. The elderly gentleman made Lottie sound as if she was some sort of bone to be fought over. He had forgotten quite how depressing the English marriage market could be. 'I have my reasons, Sir Geoffrey, please respect them. I ask this as a gentleman.'

He held out his hand and, after a moment, Sir Geoffrey took it.

'I shall keep your identity secret while you are at Shaw's, Thorngrafton. I give you my word. We are both men of honour.'

'Thank you.'

'There was bad blood between you and your uncle. Shouldn't happen in families, but it does.' Sir Geoffrey gave a wheezing laugh. His watery eyes narrowed as he peered at Tristan. 'You are like your father in many ways, but I see your uncle as well. You had best be careful. You know how life treated him. A pity—he showed such promise at Eton.'

'What should I be congratulating you for?' Tristan said firmly, drawing the man from his reminisces. He refused to be compared with his uncle. He knew what a bitter and twisted man his uncle had become.

'Pipped your cousin at the post. Pipped everyone. That's what. I have spoken to that vision's mother.' Sir Geoffrey used his walking stick to indicate where Lottie danced with an elderly man. 'She is as charming in person as she is to look at. A true picture, an ornament worthy of appreciation. Her mother assures me that she is an excellent nurse.'

'Does she, indeed?'

'She also assures me that her daughter is every bit as virtuous as she is good-looking. She will make an admirable wife. I shall have to make a visit to the Popping Stone with that gel.' Sir Geoffrey gave a wheezing laugh.

'And virtue is important to you, Sir Geoffrey? I would have thought conversation, wit and a general attraction.'

'Virtue is everything. Without virtue, the woman has nothing.' Sir Geoffrey thumped his cane on the floor.

'Except a fortune in funds.'

'The fortune allows me to overlook other certain less favourable aspects about the match.' Sir Geoffrey cleared his throat. 'Did you know her paternal great-grandfather was in trade? A grocer!'

'I had no idea, but the family, I believe, has high aspirations.'

'It is true.' Sir Geoffrey nodded and a twinkle came into his eye. 'She will make an admirable companion for my waning years, don't you think? Quite a well-turned ankle. It will show them at the club that I am not past it, that I can still attract the fillies.'

'Some might entertain that notion.'

* * *

A huge bubble of pleasure coursed through Lottie. She had forgotten how much fun it was to waltz, polka and generally be the centre of attention. True, Shaw's Hotel was not London or even the Assembly Rooms in Newcastle, but there was dancing. Ever since the five-piece orchestra had begun to play, she had had no time to sit down. One after another the gentlemen had begged for the favour of a dance. Lord Thorngrafton had staked his claim to the Sir Roger de Coverley before disappearing to converse with Henry about lead mines.

Her only disappointment was that Tristan Dyvelston had not come near, not once. She had seen him following her with his eyes, and twice he led other ladies out onto the dance floor. Stately widows with well-upholstered bosoms and braying laughs, the sort one might dance with if one was looking for a wealthy wife who would not be picky about his lack of a title.

Was that in truth why he was there? That he was seeking a wealthy wife? It made a certain amount of sense, but it annoyed her that he had made remarks about her husband-hunting.

She redoubled her efforts to be charming and to forget him, but it appeared her body had developed an acute awareness when he was around. Each time she circled the floor, she wondered what it would be like to have his hand on her waist, clasping his fingers instead of her partner's.

'Shall you dance with me next?' a bewhiskered elderly gentleman asked. 'Your mother has proclaimed how divinely you waltz.'

'This waltz is already spoken for.' A shadow loomed over her.

Lottie glanced up into Tristan's darkly intent face. Her body tingled as her breath caught in her throat. 'Is it?'

'You agreed to waltz with me earlier,' he said. 'Have you forgotten?'

'So I did. I cannot think what might have come over me.' Lottie tried to ignore the frisson of pleasure that rippled through her. She wanted to waltz with him. She wanted to forget everything else, to forget her future. She simply wanted to dance and take pleasure in the moment. 'Shall we waltz then, Mr Dyvelston? They are playing one of the Strauss waltzes.'

'It is not one of the most fashionable, but it has a pleasant enough melody.'

He put his hand on her waist and they started off. Somehow, dancing with him was different from every time she had danced before. His steps were perfect—not overly showy like a dancing master's or clumsy. She concentrated on his shoulder rather than on his mouth.

'Where did you learn to waltz like this?'

'In Vienna.'

'One day, I should like to travel. I have only been as far as Yorkshire. Mama does not believe in foreign travel, but I think it must be tremendously exciting.' Lottie was aware she was babbling, but it kept her mind off the gentle pressure on her waist and how their bodies fitted exactly, moving in time with each other.

She looked down at the smooth floor. Less than a week ago she had had no idea of his existence, but by ten o'clock this evening, she could think of nothing but him. She wanted to say that it was Cousin Frances's scandalous tales but there was something else that drew her to him. She had seen the way he'd looked at his parents' graves.

'You are not attending me, Miss Charlton,' he said. 'I

just gave you a witty sally about Vienna and you remain silent. Not even a smile passed your lips.'

'I shall try harder.' Lottie glanced up into his face and saw the crinkles around his eyes. She swallowed hard and struggled to think beyond his hand upon her waist. 'Was there something in particular that you wished me to be amused at? Repeat it and I will attend. You will find me the perfect conversationalist from now.'

He gave a husky laugh and she felt his hand tighten, pull her closer so that their bodies collided. His breath fanned her ear. 'Sir Geoffrey Lea. He was in a very self-congratulatory mood.'

A stab of fear went through her and she missed a step. Her fingers clutched at his shoulder as if it were a life raft as the ballroom tilted sideways. Her slippers skidded into each other. 'Sir Geoffrey? Congratulations?'

'He is very pleased with what he has done. Matrimony.'

Lottie looked wildly about her and tried not to panic. She had to remember to breathe, and not to give way to wild imaginings. Such things were for Cousin Frances, not for her. Her mother would not have done such a thing without speaking to her.

'Is there some problem?'

'He figured highly on my mother's list. My mother's list of eligible men.' She struggled to draw a breath and found she could not. Her fingers curled around his arm. 'Please say his congratulatory mood had nothing to do with me, that he has found some well-endowed widow of about fifty. I saw him with my mother earlier. He is more than three times my age.'

'I would say that is an accurate assessment.'

'You are not providing much comfort, Mr Dyvelston.' Lottie tried to draw a deep breath and mentally cursed her corset and the need for a fashionably tiny waist. She should not have insisted that they be done up so tightly. She had to do something or she would faint. She swallowed hard.

'You become pale. The air in here is close.' His arm came around her, an iron band of support. Lottie leant back against it, grateful. 'I must insist we go outside.'

'A breath of fresh air would be helpful, Mr Dyvelston.' Lottie concentrated on putting one foot in front of the other as she leant on his arm. Around her the sound of the waltz swelled, mocking her.

How could she have taken such pleasure in such a transitory thing?

Her life teetered about her, threatened to collapse. Mama would insist and Henry would agree. He had already begun to make noises about the expense of staying here and how he longed to be back within the bosom of his family. And she would be sentenced to a life of misery.

Tristan threw open the French doors and led the way out onto the terrace. The blackness of his hair and coat mingled with the darkness that surrounded him.

The cool air rushed out to meet her, caressing her fevered skin. In the distance she could hear the River Irthing. Above her were the first faint glimmerings of stars. The whole world was at peace. She was aware of Tristan coming to stand by her. Not touching her, just standing close enough that he could act if she fainted. Lottie pressed her lips together. She would not faint and give way to her feelings. Such things were for women like Frances. When one fainted, one lost all control. She drew in another breath and concentrated on the shadows in the lawn.

'Have you recovered, Miss Charlton?' His hand hovered at her elbow. 'We may go in if you like. I am certain no one noticed us coming out here. Your virtue is quite safe.'

'Who has Sir Geoffrey found to marry?' she asked in a strained voice as she dug her nails into her palms. 'Exactly which widow will look after him in his declining years?'

She glanced up and saw the sombreness of Tristan's face. Slowly he shook his head and his eyes showed pity. 'The woman in question is no widow.'

She clutched the balustrade, forced her lungs to strain against her stays. 'Does it have anything to do with me?'

'Would it matter if it did?'

'Several days ago, I played a game, Mr Dyvelston, an innocent game.' Lottie looked out into the blackness. She could make out the vague shape of the trees. 'I sought to help my cousin to become engaged to a man whom I felt she had affection for. This afternoon, my mother gave me a list of eligible men, men I have no affection for, but one of whom I am supposed to marry. It is my task.'

'Does affection have anything to do with marriage? I would have thought security and status were high on your list.'

Tears pricked Lottie's eyelids. She blinked rapidly. He was being kind. It had been a long time since anyone had been kind. She wanted him to be cruel or to laugh at her. Anything but be kind. He knew what her mother and Henry had planned for her. It felt as if great prison doors were swinging shut.

'I used to think, like my sister-in-law, that security was important, but then I saw how happy Emma Harrison was…is and knew I was mistaken. Emma waited years for the love of her life. She is adored.'

'Is being adored something you wish?'

Lottie nodded mutely. She half-turned and her cheek encountered the starched front of his shirt. She rested her head, listening to the reassuring heartbeat, the steady thumping. His hand went under her chin and raised it so she could look into his eyes. They were larger than she remembered, warm. She could drown in eyes like that.

'Lottie, you must be strong.'

'I will try.' She gave a slight sniff.

'That's my girl.'

She knew that propriety demanded that she move away. She was anything but his girl. She was nothing to him. She was about to be promised to Sir Geoffrey Lea. Sacrificed on her mother's altar of social ambition. Ever since she had made her début, she had paid attention to the consequences. But for what? To be married to a fossil, a man older than her late father. To submit to his horny-handed embrace. Fate was cruel and she wanted to cheat it.

Her feet stayed still as he placed a strong hand on her shoulder, drawing her closer. She struggled to breathe, to remember her name, to remember anything beyond the shape of his lips. She raised a hand in mute appeal. Touched his shirt front.

He lowered his mouth, captured hers. A featherlight touch that rapidly became firmer, deeper, called to her. She felt her body arch towards his, wanted it to continue. But he lifted his mouth and regarded her.

His face was all shadows and angles. Moonlight shone down, giving it another glow. In the distance she could hear the faint strains of a polka, but much closer she heard the pounding of her heart. Her tongue explored her aching lips and a sigh escaped her throat.

His arms tightened about her again, held her there against the length of his body. A fiery glow built inside her. She was alive in a way she would never be again, if she were married to Sir Geoffrey Lea or whichever other titled fossil her mother might discover.

'Kiss me again,' she whispered, pulling his head down to hers. Whispered against his firm mouth, 'One last time. No one is here. Tomorrow will be too late.'

Her hands came up and clung to his shirt front. He lowered his mouth again and pressed kisses along her neck and then returned to recapture her mouth. This time the kiss was harder, more insistent. Penetrating. Sensation coursed through her body in hot pulsating waves.

Her body collided with his as the meeting of lips stretched. His hand tangled in her hair, holding her face. A warmth grew deep inside Lottie, melting her limbs, forcing her to seek the support of his body. Her breasts strained against the confines of her corset. Ached. She felt the material give and his cool fingers slide against her fevered skin. Her entire world had come down to this one moment, this one point in time. She sighed and parted her lips, drank in the scent of him. His lips trailed down her neck, tasted her skin, and began to slowly travel lower.

'Unhand that woman, you…you cad!'

The words pierced her inner core. Lottie froze, hoping they were directed at someone else. Tristan raised his head, looked over her shoulder towards where the voice resounded. He put her away from him. Lottie looked up at him, unable to turn around. His face changed, became hard, but his arm remained about her, holding her. She resisted the temptation to bury her face in his shoulder. Both enormity of what she had done, what she had been discovered doing, and the knowledge that if it had continued for much longer, she would have been powerless to stop it, weighed in on her.

'Is there a problem, Sir Geoffrey?' Tristan said, drawling the words.

Lottie flinched and moved out of the circle of his arms. He made no attempt to keep her in them. She turned and looked back towards the French doors. Sir Geoffrey stood there, leaning on his cane, surrounded by other figures. How long had they been standing there? How much had they seen? She glanced down to where her bodice gaped open, brought her hands up and tried to rearrange it. Her curls tumbled in disarray about her shoulders, the artful hairstyle her mother's maid had arranged earlier this evening gone in a moment's passion. She winced, knowing the wanton picture she must make.

'What is going on here?' Her brother's voice floated over the rapidly increasing crowd. 'Oh my God, Lottie, what have you done?'

'He has seduced her.' Sir Geoffrey's voice boomed out over the rest. 'He coldheartedly took her innocence and virtue. Look at her state of undress.'

'It all depends on your definition of seduction.' Tristan's voice dripped with ice.

'Mr Dyvelston was helping me because I felt faint.' Lottie forced the words from her mouth. She looked up at Tristan for confirmation. His eyes blazed black. 'I needed a breath of fresh air. Nothing happened.'

'It looked rather different to me,' Sir Geoffrey thundered.

'I kissed her, yes. I overpowered her.' The words exploded from Tristan Dyvelston.

'Did you kiss this man, Carlotta?' her brother asked. 'Did you allow him to kiss you?'

Lottie's tongue explored her lips—full, swollen and aching for the pressure of his mouth once again. She dreaded to think what the front of her gown looked like. They had been caught. Denial was impossible. Everything appeared to be happening from a long way away. She nodded as she crossed her hands over her chest. Waited.

'Charlton, our bargain has ended.' Sir Geoffrey's voice resounded across the veranda. Strident. Furious. 'She is damaged goods, sir. Given towards lewd and licentious behaviour. I wish you luck in finding a husband for that baggage. No gentleman will have her. Thank God I discovered what she was like before I married her. She'd have run away with her dancing master, soon as look at you.'

Lottie heard the swell of voices rise around her, echoing Sir Geoffrey's harsh sentiments. Everyone speaking at once. Ruined. She was ruined. The dreaded consequences that Lucy had so confidently predicted for her all those months ago had happened. There would be no London Season. No triumphant return to Newcastle. Nothing, all because she had not been able resist the temptation of Tristan Dyvelston's mouth.

'I…I…' Lottie put a hand to her head and groped for words, something that would explain it all and that would restore everything to its natural order. Her mother and Henry had to see that it was not the end of the world, that she was still an asset to the family. In time, she might once again have marriage prospects.

She scanned the rapidly expanding crowd for a friendly face and found none.

'What do you intend to do about it, Dyvelston?' Sir Geoffrey shook his stick at Tristan. 'You have ruined this young person. Taken advantage of her youth. The tales they whispered about you were true, even though I have always vigorously denied them. No son of your father would behave in such a libertine manner.'

'Do? Why should he do anything?' Lord Thorngrafton

came forward. 'All he did was kiss the girl. She asked for it. There was that incident in Newcastle—'

'Stay out of this, Peter!' Tristan Dyvelston thundered. 'You have done enough damage already.'

'Lord Thorngrafton is right. He simply kissed me. Nothing more.' Lottie hated the way her voice shook. She tried for a smile. She might be ruined, but Tristan should not be held entirely to blame. 'Might this whole thing be…?'

The faces turned towards her were less than encouraging. Several of the old ladies lifted their fans to gossip behind. The tale was already being embroidered. By morning she'd be a harlot and there would be no hiding from the scandal.

Lottie took a step backwards, encountered the railing. The enormity of what she had done washed over her. She had kissed a man, passionately kissed him, without expectation or forethought. A huge gaping hole opened in her middle. She wished she could turn back the hands of time.

'Oh dear, oh dear, whatever shall we do? All the love and attention I gave her and she repays me like this.' Her mother stood next to Sir Geoffrey, white-faced and wringing her hands. Her ample bosom trembled as she raised an accusatory finger. 'Carlotta, look what you have done to the family. To me. It is not just your reputation you have tarnished. You have shamed the family.'

'I didn't mean to.' Lottie held out her hands and willed her mother to smile at her, to make some small sign that she would stand by her. Her mother buried her face in her hands and the sound of sobbing increased.

'You only have yourself to blame, Mother.' Henry put a hand on their mother's shoulder and turned his furious gaze on Lottie. 'You encouraged her far too much. I knew one day she would go too far and she has. You have disgraced us, Carlotta.'

Lottie kept her back straight. She had to get through this somehow, and then she'd decide what she could do. Perhaps there was a way to hush the whole thing up. If only everyone would stop yelling at once.

'He has ruined her, I say. I demand to know what he intends to do about it!' Sir Geoffrey drew himself up to his full height. 'I may be old, sir, but I am not without influence. I will have it known that you are debaucher of virgins, a man not to be trusted. What are you going to do? Are you totally devoid of honour?'

Tristan stared at the elderly man as the diatribe washed over him. He knew Sir Geoffrey was correct. Doors would be closed to him. He'd spent ten years in the wilderness. He did not intend to go there again. He glanced at Lottie Charlton. At first she had winced every time someone said something, but now she stood, straight, not moving a muscle. It would not just be he who was ruined, but also this woman.

He gave an ironic smile. He should have remembered his own advice—virgins were complicated. He should never have tasted her lips. He wanted to taste her skin again. He wanted her lips to softly yield under his again.

'Marry her. I will marry Miss Charlton.'

The veranda went silent.

'You are going to do what?' Mrs Charlton squeaked and began to furiously wave her fan.

'As I have ruined her, there is only one course open to me, I will take the responsibility and marry her. My honour demands it.'

'I knew you had it in you, Dyvelston,' Lottie's brother said, clapping him on the shoulder. 'There, Mama, problem solved. Dyvelston will marry Lottie. We will have a quiet wedding and no one in the business community will turn their faces from us. While Dyvelston might not be what we would have wished, he will at least do the decent thing.'

'I am so grateful you solved the problem, Sir Geoffrey.' Mrs Charlton grabbed on to the elderly man's arm. Her plump face was very close to his. 'Eternally grateful.'

Sir Geoffrey patted her arm absentmindedly. 'My pleasure.'

'Where will the marriage take place?' Henry Charlton's eyes became crafty. 'It is all well and good to agree a marriage, but does he have any intention of actually marrying her? I know how these rakes operate. When do you intend to marry my sister?'

Tristan rubbed his chin. He could see Mrs Charlton's eyes gleaming. How much did she know? How much of this had been planned? 'I don't want banns. It might cause talk.'

'Let it be a special.' Mrs Charlton's eyes lit up. 'I always wanted my daughter to be married by special licence. So much more status than an ordinary license.'

'Oh, yes, Mama, a special licence would be splendid.' Lottie clapped her hands, like a child in a sweet shop. 'What a wonderful idea. Can you arrange that, Mr Dyvelston?'

'No special,' Tristan said through gritted teeth.

'What are you saying?' Her bottom lip trembled like a child who had sweets taken away from her. Her blue eyes shimmered with tears. 'We are going to marry, aren't we? An ordinary licence, then.'

Tristan looked at where Lottie stood. It would be easy to indulge her when she looked at him like that. He wanted her to go on looking at him like that for the rest of his life, but he was a realist. Lottie Charlton, through no fault of her own, had all the hallmarks of a spoilt child who would grow into a spoilt woman. He knew what sort of trouble a woman like that could cause, if left unchecked. He would marry her, but she needed to be taught a lesson. If he confessed now who he really was, he would always wonder.

Had tonight's events been fabricated for her benefit? Did she really know who he was and was that the reason she had kissed him so passionately? And asked him to kiss her?

He needed to know; until he discovered the truth, he would keep his identity a secret.

'Gretna Green is but a few miles from here.'

The entire crowd fell silent.

'You mean to elope?' Mrs Charlton's shawls quivered. 'You are proposing to elope with my daughter.'

'It is the most sensible solution in the circumstances,' Sir Geoffrey said, giving a decisive nod. 'I will vouch for this man's honour, madam.'

'My sister is to elope? Married under Scottish law?' Henry Charlton's face expanded and he bore a distinct resemblance to a walrus. 'Do you know what you are on about, man?'

'I have agreed to do the decent thing and marry the woman, but it will be at Gretna Green, and not in some church wedding.' Tristan straightened his cuffs. 'It will save gossip.'

He took great pleasure in watching Henry Charlton's mouth open, but have no sound come out. Three times he started to say something, but somehow the words would not appear. He tried jabbing with a finger. 'You…you bounder. You will create a scandal if you marry her in that fashion.'

'I have agreed to marry your sister. I am hardly a bounder. And there is already a scandal of sorts.' Tristan gave a shrug. 'I am sorry if the terms of my offer are not to your liking, but there they are. You must decide which is the greater scandal—your sister unwed but kissed, or your sister married at Gretna Green.'

'But…'

'You must decide. Or, better yet, let your sister decide. It is her life and reputation we are discussing.'

'I suppose you do have a point.' Henry Charlton gave a harrumph. 'Carlotta?'

Tristan watched Lottie. What would she do? Would she risk it? A wild exultation grew within him. The risk. The gamble. What would she choose?

'Thank you for allowing me to make the choice, Henry.' Lottie came forward and tucked her hand into Tristan's. He glanced down at her, impressed with her dignity in the face of her brother's blustering and her mother's shrieking. She appeared to have accepted her fate. 'Mr Dyvelston is correct. Banns and the like will simply point to a harum-scarum marriage. I will make a runaway match. Far more romantic.'

Chapter Four

'Not the watercolours, Lottie. And only one satchel, you heard Mr Dyvelston.' Lottie's mother hurried into the room where Lottie sat packing. 'You will need a complete new wardrobe now that you are married. I dare say that he plans to buy it. It is the best way.'

Lottie tucked the watercolours and brushes into her bag. The first words her mother had said to her were a complaint. 'I heard Mr Dyvelston the first time, Mama, and I intend to paint on my wedding trip. I am being practical.'

'You have dashed all my hopes and plans for your future.' Her mother gave a loud sniff. 'And now all you can talk of is painting. Have you no consideration for my nerves? For what you have done to your brother? To me? You were supposed to wed a titled man. It was to be the culmination of everything.'

'I am getting married, Mama. He is connected to a title.'

'Yes, but will anyone know? I should never have let Sir Geoffrey sway me. I should have insisted on a proper marriage.' Her mother buried her face in a handkerchief. 'Lucy warned me that you would come to a bad end with your tricks and you have. You are a lucky woman that Mr Dyvelston turned out to be a gentleman. Goodness knows what you were thinking…Sir Geoffrey had made an offer for you. How could you do this to me?'

Lottie slammed another pair of stockings into the satchel. She refused to dignify her mother's remark with a reply.

'Well, Carlotta, what do you have to say for yourself? How can you explain away what you did? The man has no title, nothing to recommend him. Why did you kiss him?'

'You were quite prepared to marry me off to Jack Stanton.'

'Lottie, you ungrateful child!' Her mother gave a sharp intake of breath, went white and she waved her hand in front of her face, choking. 'My medicine, Lottie.'

Lottie rushed to the washstand, picked up the small vial, pulled off the stopper and held the smelling salts under her mother's nose. Her mother inhaled deeply; gradually, her colour returned to normal. Lottie breathed again. 'Are you better, Mama? I did not intend to give you another attack. You should take more care.'

'Me? You are the one who should have been cautious. I had everything arranged.' Her eyes narrowed. 'You threw it all away, you ungrateful spoilt child. Well, young lady—'

'I am marrying Mr Dyvelston, Mama.' Lottie fastened the satchel. She adjusted her pelisse and bonnet. It made a charming picture over her paisley silk afternoon dress. The cut was fashionable and Lottie had made sure the corset was laced extra tight in order to show off her waist. She wanted Tristan to look again at her with those smouldering eyes.

'Neither of us planned it, but it will save me and the family from ruin. I cannot undo the past. And Tristan does have connections, Mama. He is Lord Thorngrafton's cousin.'

'Lottie, Lottie. I cannot help but worry. Though Sir Geoffrey says that this is the best way and I must trust him.'

'And it saves the expense of a London Season. You might remind Henry of that, if he intends on huffing and puffing.'

Her mother gave a loud sniff. 'Yes, I suppose Dyvelston is doing the decent thing. But I care about my daughter's future. You were given every advantage.'

'I believe in my case, if I fail to marry, the advantages will mean nothing. I will be ruined, Mama. And won't I spend my life repenting that as well?'

'Oh, you young creatures are all the same. You think you know everything.' Her mother threw up her hands and Lottie wondered if she was going to have to retrieve the smelling salts again. She shifted uneasily, hating the disloyal thought, but she had seen how her mother had used the attacks before. 'A man should respect his wife. If you keep giving in to your passion, it will be the road to ruin. Your poor papa and I had a good marriage based on mutual respect and duty.'

And what about love? Or desire? Lottie stopped the words and allowed the remainder of her mother's diatribe to flow over her. She did not love Tristan, but she knew that there had to be more to a marriage than respectability. And she certainly did not want a title if Sir Geoffrey Lea was offering it. She was not a pawn to be sacrificed for her mother and brother's social ambition. She would lead her own life.

'You are not attending, Carlotta.'

'Mama, it is time to go.' Lottie leant forward and kissed her mother's cold cheek. 'I am getting married today to a good man. I can sense it in him.'

'Lottie, Lottie. There is more to being a good man than a pair of broad shoulders and a smooth dancing step.' Her mother's hands grasped Lottie's upper arms and she made a clucking noise at the back of her throat. 'You are such a child, Lottie. I blame myself. There is so much I should tell you, warn you about. Men do not like wanton creatures. They use them and discard them. When I think of your poor dear departed papa…'

'Papa would have wanted me to be happy.' Lottie stared at her mother, seeing for the first time the attempts to hold age back, the slightly over-garish jewellery, the petulant expression. Then she shook herself, hating the disloyal thoughts. Here was her mother, the woman she should revere above all others, but who had wanted to sell her for a title and reflected status. 'It was all he ever wanted. It is why he worked so hard. He wanted to give us everything we wanted.'

'Happiness is a fleeting thing. Security and connections are all.' Her mother shook her head and buried her face once again in a handkerchief.

'It just happened, Mama.' Lottie touched her lips, remembering the sensation of Tristan's lips against hers and knew that she would yield again.

'That is no excuse. I trust you will remember where your duty lies. A woman must take responsibility for a family's status. Remember that and behave accordingly, if nothing else. Try to grow up, Lottie…before it is too late.'

'Mama, I will be a good wife.' Lottie curled her fingers around her satchel. 'I will make sure the marriage prospers.'

She marched out of the room, head high and shoulders back. She would show her mother that her dire predictions were wrong. She would make this marriage a success.

Lottie sat opposite Tristan in his borrowed carriage and watched the sunrise begin to appear on the horizon. Her bonnet had slipped over her nose and the wild exhilaration she had felt as she'd waved goodbye to the assembled throng of people had vanished. Her back ached and her feet were numb.

What had she done? Had she done the appropriate thing? She had done the only thing.

Each turn of the carriage wheel took her farther away from her mother, her family, her former life and closer to Gretna Green and marriage, marriage to Tristan. She would snatch a sip from the cup of happiness. Somehow. She refused to believe her mother's dire predictions about marrying for passion.

The carriage hit a rut, and her shoulder met the side of the carriage with a thump. Lottie winced at the pain, stifled the gasp behind her gloved hand.

'Careful.' Tristan, from where he sat, put out a hand to steady her. The touch of his hand burnt through the thin material of her dress. 'You don't want to injure yourself.'

'I will be fine.' She sat up straighter. Her hands curled around the edge of her seat, holding her there. 'I was unprepared. The road to Gretna Green is heavily rutted.'

'It is a well-travelled route.'

'Yes.' Lottie agreed. Well travelled. As if she needed reminding how many people went there to get married because they had to or because their families objected. Some might call it wildly romantic, but the doubts had started to circle around the edges of her brain. The Tristan

Dyvelston who sat opposite with his top hat, black frock coat, cream-coloured trousers and hands lightly resting on a cane was very different from the excitingly attractive man who had kissed her earlier. No less handsome, but somehow more reserved, as if he were waiting and watching for something. Self-contained.

Lottie searched her mind. What did one say politely to the man who was about to become one's husband, but appeared now more than ever to be a stranger? And in such a fashion? How could she explain that she was terrified of what the future might hold?

She had no wish to appear a ninny or a brainless fool. She thought of topics like the weather or music, only to reject them. Some were too impersonal. Others far too personal. It was difficult, particularly as she simply wanted to curl up next to him and feel his arms about her. The silence seemed to hang between them, growing with each turn of the wheel until it was a palpable living thing that threatened to crush her.

'Wasn't it kind of your cousin to lend us his carriage?' she said, finally, in desperation.

'My cousin?' He raised an eyebrow and his face did not invite further enquiries. 'What does my cousin have to do with this carriage?'

'His arms are on the carriage door,' Lottie said, sitting up. Her hands adjusted the ribbons of her bonnet and tension appeared to ease from her shoulder. Finally a subject they could discuss—social niceties. 'I noticed it when we got in. Little details make the world go round. It eases social tensions, if one does not have to explain everything. It is something one learns rapidly when you are required to do as much visiting as Mama and I.'

'I had not considered that.'

'It was obvious to any who had eyes. Why else would someone paint their arms on a carriage unless they wanted to be noticed? Unless they were proud of the title?'

'Why indeed?'

Tristan's hand tightened around his cane and his mouth became a thin white line. Was he ashamed of borrowing his cousin's carriage? Was he worried that others would mistake him for his cousin and cause embarrassment? How awful would that be—to be mistaken for a peer when one wasn't.

Lottie folded her hands on her lap and crossed her ankles. Considered the possibility and decided against it.

Anyone who had met the two would know they were different. Tristan could never be Lord Thorngrafton. They had similar looks, but their temperaments were not at alike.

She never would have allowed Lord Thorngrafton to take her in his arms or even escort her outside into the darkness for a breath of fresh air. The air of a snake hung about him. He had presumed much last November and acted as if she was a naive miss who had no idea of what going to see etchings entailed, as if his title and status was all the reassurance a woman needed.

Lottie concentrated on taking a deep breath, and not letting her fury at the memory overwhelm her. But he was to be family now and she needed to be charitable. She might have mistaken him, but in any case, when they next encountered each other, she would be married and related to him. Family was different.

But she could not expect Lord Thorngrafton to apologise. It was up to women to mend bridges. And at the same time she would make Tristan see that there was nothing to be ashamed about when it came to using family connections. It was positively *de rigueur*, according to Mama.

'When did your cousin inherit the title?' she asked, assuming the voice she used for the more important At Homes when she wanted to make a suitably genteel appearance. She would find a way to build the bridges without revealing her distaste for the man.

'I doubt we will be seeing my cousin often.' Tristan's tone was less than encouraging. 'The present Lord Thorngrafton inherited the title within the last year. I was travelling on the Continent at the time.'

'But he is family.'

'Yes, of a sort. The old lord was my uncle.' The merest hint of a smile touched Tristan's lips. 'One cannot pick and choose one's family as easily as one's friends.'

'That is why family is all the more important.' Lottie batted her eyes and made her voice sugar sweet. It was obvious to her that there had been a quarrel between Tristan and his cousin. Perhaps she could do something to get them to make up. It was never good to quarrel with those who might be in a position to help you. 'Friends may come and go, but families are always there.'

'You are not encumbered with my relations.' Tristan's reply was crushing. He tilted his hat over his eyes and stretched out his legs as if to indicate the conversation had ended and the topic was no longer up for discussion.

Lottie looked out of the carriage window at the darkened countryside sweeping past and felt the prick of tears. This ride was not going as planned. He was not behaving how he ought. She swallowed her annoyance at Tristan's obstinacy and tried again. She had to explain why this overture from his cousin had to be treated with respect and gratitude. Why it was the only way. Anything to keep her mind off the closeness of Tristan and how she wished he'd take her in his arms and tell her not to worry.

'But he is your cousin, and titled,' she said, trying again. This time she ran a hand down the horsehair seats. 'It was very kind of him to lend us his carriage and driver. Most unexpected and done with such grace. Does he do this sort of thing often?'

'Kindness had nothing to do with it.' Tristan lifted his hat and peered at her. His dark eyes flashed with some barely suppressed emotion, but then he leant forward and touched her hand briefly. The tiniest of touches, but one that made her heart pound slightly faster. 'Lottie, my cousin Peter has never done anything for the benefit of others. It is part of his creed.'

'I suppose you are right. You have known him longer than I have.' Lottie resisted the urge to put her glove to her cheek and savour the lingering imprint of his fingers. 'He must have been pleased that you were finally going to settle down.'

'I expect he was.' There was a note of surprise in Tristan's voice. 'I had not considered it. He is probably pleased to see me gone from Shaw's. I was not adding to his general state of well being. Destroying his ambiance, as he put it to me before we came down to dinner. I believe he rather wished I had stayed on the Continent.'

'I am certain you are wrong.'

'I know I am right.'

Lottie shifted, sliding slightly on the horsehair seats. He was not making this easy for her. All she wanted was some reassurance that he would make his peace with his cousin. And maybe, one day, when Tristan and she had children, his cousin would ease their way in society. Lottie drew in a breath. Children. Babies. Lying in Tristan's arms.

Suddenly the carriage appeared to shrink, to push her closer to his chest, his lips. This topic was supposed to keep her mind off such things, not bring it back to his kisses.

'The carriage is very new,' she said, searching for another topic, one which did not lead her thoughts on such dangerous paths. 'He obviously thought enough of you to lend it. He trusts you.'

Tristan's hands tightened on his cane. 'You are very observant, but your conclusions are wrong. Neither of us trusts the other further than he can toss him. There is much that lies between my cousin and me. He wished me gone with all speed.'

'I try to be observant.' Lottie cleared her throat, pleased that she had found a subject they could converse on, a chance to show off her social skills without suddenly blurting out that she wanted to be kissed or held. Already, she could imagine introducing him to her friends: my husband—not only is he handsome but also a cousin to a lord. Martha, Caroline and the rest would forgive the elopement once they had met him. 'It makes it easier when I go calling. Fifteen minutes is barely any time and the hostess is often tired of repeating the same story over and over again. It saves idle chit-chat or speaking about the weather. Some days it seems I never speak about anything but the weather. There is only so much one can say about the rain.'

'Is there? I never participate in At Homes if at all possible.' A shudder went through him. 'On point of principle.'

A sudden pain coursed through Lottie as her future plans crumbled to dust. Not participate. But the After the Marriage calls were some of the most significant calls a woman could ever make. She might not be having the wedding of her dreams, but she thought she'd at least have the calls and the attention. She had dreamt of making such calls ever since she had first been allowed to participate in At Homes.

'But you will have to.' Lottie leant forward, placing her hands on her knees to keep them from trembling. 'We will need to make calls when we get back to Newcastle. The After the Marriage calls are a necessity, or how else will anyone know that we will continue to see them socially? And all of my friends will be anxious to meet you. I dare say they will be quite green with envy. Pea green.'

'We won't be living in Newcastle.' Tristan regarded the woman sitting opposite him. Her head was full of society and outward appearances. At Homes. Dances. Positions. Furthering her status at the expense of others. She had to be made to realise that there was more to life than such things. He wanted to glimpse again the woman who had berated him for not looking after his parents' graves.

'Where? London? Or on the Continent? Paris, maybe? I do think I would quite like Paris and its salons.'

'Not there,' Tristan said firmly, gritting his teeth. He would test her, and she would learn the lesson. He would reach the woman from the cemetery.

'Where will we be living?'

'My uncle left me an estate—Gortner Hall. I have a fancy to settle down. It is up in the North Tyne Valley, about fifteen miles from Haydon Bridge.'

'Then I will be expected to make calls on the various ladies who live near there.' Lottie folded her hands in her lap with maddening complacency. 'It will be expected. You will have to go calling with me. There must be someone I know from Newcastle who could smooth our way…'

'No one of any consequence lives near.' Tristan paused. 'It will not be expected. It is the country, not the town.'

'Aunt Alice and Cousin Frances are bound to know several.' Lottie waved a dismissive hand. 'Aunt Alice knows positively everyone in the Tyne Valley. She can offer introductions. It may be the country, but there is always somebody. Calling and socialising is what makes the world go around.' Lottie sat up straighter. She shook out the folds of her dress. 'It is the lifeblood of the community. I plan to play my part as your wife. I will show them the right and proper way to behave.'

'I have been on the Continent for years. And as your cousin quite rightly pointed out to you, I led a somewhat scandalous life in my youth.' Tristan struggled to maintain his temper. He would give her one more chance. 'I am uncertain how many might wish to acknowledge me.'

'Oh. How truly thoughtless and terrible of me.' Lottie sat back against the hard seat and her face crumpled. She reached out and touched his hand. 'No doubt we shall meet them in due course and convince them of our worthiness to be befriended.'

'It may take some time.'

'But working together, we will convince them in the end. For our children's sake.' Her cheek flushed scarlet. 'You have proved your worth to me. You have saved me from ruin.'

'It was something any gentleman would have done.' Tristan shifted slightly. His plan would be harsh, but it should work. She had a good heart.

Lottie drew a shaking breath. Why was he making it so difficult? Tears pricked at her eyelids. He had to understand what she was attempting to do and why. He had to accept her apology. She would try much harder in the future, truly she would, but right now she needed reassurance—reassurance he appeared reluctant to give.

'Not anyone. I can name a half-dozen officers who would not have done what you did. They would have left me to my fate.'

'I kissed you. It very nearly went much further, Lottie.'

'You saved me from a life of cats and skirts being subtly drawn away. I do not think I would care for being my mother's companion either—fetching and carrying all the time. We would have driven each other mad within a fortnight.'

She stuffed her hand against her mouth and looked out of the window at the grey landscape. Yesterday on the train coming to Gilsland Spa everything had seemed so fresh and new. She had never imagined that she would be sitting here, facing an almost complete stranger on her way to be married.

'Yes, in due course, we will encounter the neighbours.' Tristan reached forward and caught her hand with his, interlaced his fingers with hers. The slight pressure sent tremors along her arm. 'Try to sleep now, Lottie. It has been a long day and we won't be in Gretna Green for a few more hours.'

'As long as that?'

'Would it be easier if I came over and sat next to you? You may put your head on my shoulder.'

He moved over and sat by her. The pressure of his leg against hers somehow made everything appear better. He wasn't angry with her. He did not blame her for what happened. It was not what either of them had anticipated, but she would do her best. Surely being married to him would be pleasant. A great wave of tiredness washed over her. It seemed liked for ever since she had kissed Aunt Alice and Cousin Frances goodbye. What would Frances say when she learnt her cousin had married the notorious Tristan Dyvelston? She gave a small sleepy smile and settled her back more firmly against the seat. There was at least that.

'I will close my eyes for a moment. It is really quite pleasant to be able to lean against someone. Comforting.'

His arm came around her and held her. 'It will work, Lottie. You must see that.'

The sun had risen and the road teemed with carts, carriages and various livestock by the time the carriage reached the outskirts of Gretna Green. Tristan's muscles ached from the journey and his arm had gone to sleep. However, Lottie had snuggled close. Her warm body touched his. He looked to where her red lips had parted, soft and inviting. Her lavender scent rose around like a perfumed cloud.

It had taken a vast reserve of Tristan's self-restraint not to pull her more firmly into his arms and make love to her in the carriage.

He forced his body to wait, to remember that she was a virgin and unused to such things. He would have the rest of his life to get to know her.

But first he had to be certain of why she had married him so quickly, why she had agreed to his suggestion. Did she know his true identity? Had she seen this as her only remaining chance to fulfil her mother's expectations and marry a title? He was under no illusions how powerful an incentive such expectations could be, but he wanted to know that she had married for the man, not the status. He had to know.

The carriage slowed down to a crawl and the noise of the town resounded in the enclosed space. They had arrived in Gretna Green and Tristan knew he had to act, he could no longer afford to sit and cradle his wife-to-be. He gently eased the sleeping Lottie from his shoulder and banged on the roof with his cane. Instantly the carriage halted. Tristan stepped out and closed the door behind him.

'Market day, my lord,' the coachman said, coming down to stand beside him. 'There are drovers and farmers all along the road. I am thankful today is not a hiring fair as the town must heave then.'

'I can see the carts and the cattle. The drover's bellowing echoes off the carriage walls.' Tristan stretched, trying to clear his mind. Today he needed all his wits about him.

'Where are we headed for, my lord? The headless cross? A quick marriage and then back to London?'

The coachman's voice jerked Tristan fully awake. 'Robinson, we had words earlier.'

The burly coach driver's cheek tinged pink. 'That we did, sir. I had forgotten. I don't understand the ways of the aristos, that I don't.'

'You are not paid to.'

'But what do you want me to do now?' Robinson rubbed the back of his neck. 'Are you going to marry her, like? You can always send her home.'

'Of course I am. I am going to marry the girl, and I am going to tame her.' Tristan glanced over to where Lottie softly slumbered, her red mouth now pouting slightly and her golden curls tumbled about her face. He had to admire her irrepressible spirit. 'I have to know, Robinson. I have seen too many women forced into marriages against their will. I have seen what it does to them, what it does to their husbands. She must want to marry me for me.'

Robinson gave a long whistle. 'It never did your uncle any good.'

Tristan's jaw tightened. 'That marriage brought misery to everyone.'

'What am I to do, sir? I mean, it is not right leaving you alone like this here. The London dockyards are refined compared to this place.'

'You are to put us down, that inn will do.' Tristan pointed towards the disreputable-looking coaching inn. 'Then take the carriage back to London. Wait for my word. We will take the train to Hexham. I have sent word to Mrs Elton at the hall. There will be a cart for us at the station.'

'As you say…sir.' Robinson's voice betrayed his uneasiness.

'You need not worry. I am well used to looking after myself.' Tristan reached into his jacket pocket, pulled out several notes and handed them to Robinson. 'These will see you to London.'

'And beyond.' The man gave a soft whistle.

'I want you to leave directly, Robinson. No hanging about.' Tristan looked pointedly at Lottie. Lottie stirred slightly in her sleep and murmured something indistinct.

Robinson ran his finger around his collar.

'It is the part of the plan I am uneasy about, sir. The lady is Quality. You can see it from the cut of her clothes and the way she speaks. She could be in danger.'

'Nothing is going to happen, Robinson. I promise that.'

'It is not you that I am worried about. It is that lass. How will she react? Someone ought to watch over her, like.' Robinson assumed a pious expression that was at odds with his former occupation as a boxer.

'Hopefully, she will reject temptation and obey my instructions, but if not, her lessons in life and treating people properly begin now. The ride in the carriage convinced me of it.'

'If that is what you want.' Robinson resumed his place, grumbling about the swells and their peculiar ideas.

Tristan stepped back into the carriage and smoothed a damp curl from her forehead as the wheels began turning again. 'Time to wake up, Lottie. We are nearly there. See. It's the headless cross.'

She wrinkled her nose and pushed at his hand.

'It is far too early for such things, Cousin Frances.' Her eyes flew open and widened at the sight of her hand clutching his. Her cheeks took on an even rosier hue. And she rapidly dropped his hand. 'Oh. It's you.'

She sat up and began to rearrange her dress and bonnet.

'Did you have a pleasant slumber?' Tristan asked.

'I fear I fell asleep on you. Our limbs became entangled and I may have mussed up your shirtfront. You should have woken me. It was presumptuous of me.' She clasped her hands together. 'Do say that you forgive me. Please do.'

'We will be married today, Lottie. Man and wife. No one will say a word if you fall asleep on my shoulder.'

'I suppose not.' She bent her head so that all he could see was the crown of her straw bonnet and its elaborate blue ribbon. 'I keep forgetting. It is all very sudden. It is the best thing. I know it is the best thing.'

'Good.' Tristan lifted her chin so he looked her in the face. For an instant he drank in her luminous beauty. Then he hardened his heart. He wanted her beauty to be more than skin deep. He wanted her to want him for more than a title and his worldly goods. He had to carry out his experiment. He had to show her that there was more to life than social calls and pincushions. Life was to be lived, and not reflected in a Claude glass. 'I want you to stay here while I procure us a room.'

'Here? In this carriage? On my own?' The words came out as a squeak. Her eyes widened and she clutched her reticule to her chest. 'I have never been left in a coaching yard on my own before.'

'You will be quite safe in the coaching yard…as long as you remain there. No one will harm you. Your dress is of a certain quality.' Tristan forced himself to walk away from her, not to take her by the arm and lead her to another inn. He had to do it, for the sake of their future.

Chapter Five

Lottie watched Tristan walk away from her. She half-raised a hand to beg him to stay or at least to take her with him, but he never glanced back. She gazed about the coaching yard where several drovers discussed cattle in heavy Scots accents. The smell of manure and sweat seeped into the carriage. Lottie put her handkerchief over her nose and hoped the inn would be better than its yard. 'This is a fine mess you have landed yourself in, Lottie Charlton. What happens to you now? Why did you let him go like that?'

'You will have to get out, miss.' The large coachman with the broken nose opened the carriage door. 'Orders is orders. It ain't my business to contradict Lord Thorngrafton. He says to me, leave when you get to Gretna Green.'

Lottie blinked. 'Excuse me? Why? Mr Dyvelston is getting a room. Surely you may wait a few moments. I wish to stay in the carriage, away from the gaze of ordinary bystanders. It wouldn't be proper for me to wait in the yard on my own.'

'I am only a coachman. I know nothing about the ways of gentlefolk.'

'Your master will understand if you wait. You must wait.' Lottie tried to give her words all the imperiousness of her mother, but she heard the undercurrent of desperation.

'I need to leave.' The coachman's countenance took on a mulish expression. 'My…master said that I needed to be in London with all speed once I had brought you to Gretna Green. He didn't say nothing about waiting until that there gentleman procured a room. He told me, go once you get to Gretna Green.'

'Can't you wait until Mr Dyvelston returns? Please? For my sake?' Lottie pressed her handkerchief more firmly to her mouth and willed Tristan to return. Her whole body tensed as she peered out of the carriage door into the crowded yard: drovers, farmhands and the odd woman, but no broad shoulders encased in a fine frock coat. Her insides shook at being cast amongst those people. 'I beg you to reconsider.'

The big man shook his head. 'It wouldn't be proper, like. I have me orders. I like my job, miss. I won't jeopardise it for no one.'

'Why not? Mr Dyvelston charged you to look after me. I am sure he did. You cannot intend to leave me here with those ruffians.' Lottie bit her lip, aware that the words had come out more harshly than she had intended. But he had to understand that she had been cosseted and looked after. She was of gentle birth.

'No, he didn't, like.' The coachman lifted a bag from the back and set it down on the muddy cobblestones. 'This is all there is, miss. I am sure he will return in a few moments. If you please, miss. I am on my way to London to wait for Lord Thorngrafton's instructions. It is a week's journey in good weather and I'd like to get on my way.'

'But you have been driving through the night. Surely

you will need time to rest. Mr Dyvelston will return in a few moments.' Lottie clasped her hands together. 'I beg you. Have mercy.'

'That is true and you should be safe in that time. I want to be well into England afore I do that. If you please, miss....'

Lottie looked at the single bag. Her mother had said that she would send her things on. It appeared that Tristan had not bothered to pack a trunk or even a bag. She reached down and picked the satchel up. The yard blurred for a moment, but she stiffened her back. Regained her composure. She would be fine. Tristan would return before she knew it. She held out her hand and the coachman helped her from the carriage. 'Thank you. It is very kind of you.'

She reached into her reticule and drew out a halfpenny. 'This is for you.'

'It's all right, miss, Lord Thorngrafton pays me well, so he does. Best of luck.' The coachman twisted his hat. 'Begging your pardon, but this here is from Lord Thorngrafton…in case you change your mind. In case…'

Lottie regarded the bank note with a sinking heart. Lord Thorngrafton must believe that Tristan was planning to abandon her. 'Don't you trust Mr Dyvelston?'

'I trust him all right, but…just the same. Best to be prepared, miss.'

'I couldn't, really.' Lottie turned her face into her handkerchief.

'Take it, miss, for my sake. Lord Thorngrafton has a right temper if his will is crossed.'

Her throat closed. She had wronged Lord Thorngrafton last November. He had thought about her comfort and had not been sure of his cousin. He had sought to protect her. She fingered the note and placed it in her reticule. 'You must thank Lord Thorngrafton for me. I will thank him myself when I can.'

'As you wish, miss. God speed.' The coachman touched his hat and went back to his place.

He snapped the reins and the carriage started to move. It made its way through the jumble of carts and horses, rolling away from her. A single tear ran down her cheek, but she pushed it away with impatient fingers.

Lottie stood there, her head held high and her fingers clutching her satchel and reticule in the centre of the yard, aware that people were looking at her and her much creased clothes. Aware that she had rapidly become an object of interest and curiosity. Lottie tightened her grip. She refused to stand there, being gaped at like some spectacle in a diorama or other cheap entertainment. She had to act.

She walked towards the inn and peeked into the public room, hoping to discover the familiar shape of Tristan's shoulders or his top hat floating above the crowd. The entire room appeared full of farmers, day labourers and drovers. High-pitched female laughter came from a dimly lit corner where Lottie could just make out a flurry of petticoats and entangled limbs. She stared for a heartbeat at the brazenness of it. The stench was worse than the yard. Lottie gave a soft cry and buried her face more firmly in the handkerchief.

'Is there something you want, dearie?' an old crone asked, leering at her with a one-toothed smile. 'Sell your ear bobs, or your pretty hair? I pay top price for golden curls like yours.'

'Not my hair. Not my ear bobs.' Lottie blanched and rapidly made her way back into the coaching yard. She heard the crone's laughter chasing her as she went.

Lottie paused by the stable entrance and tried to get her breath as she scanned the yard for any sign of Tristan. But it remained stubbornly free of her future husband. She closed her eyes and wished. Opened them. Nothing. The sun beat down on her bonnet and her shift stuck to her back. Maybe Lord Thorngrafton's surmise was correct and Tristan did not intend to come back for her. He had only taken her here to abandon her to her fate. He would then claim she had run away and he'd be free to live his dissolute life.

Abandoned at the altar to a life of sin.

Cousin Frances had taken great pleasure in describing several Minerva Press novels where this was a main feature. The villain lures the heroine with blandishments, only to abandon her after he has had his wicked way with her, forcing her into a Life of Degradation…if it were not for the hero.

Lottie gave a tremulous smile. She had to think logically. Tristan had not had his wicked way with her, beyond the kiss they had shared on the terrace. If he had been planning to abandon her, he would have done so then, instead of taking her here. She had to be logical, and not give way to panic.

A sob built in her throat and she muffled it with the handkerchief. She refused to give way to wailing here despite the longing in her breast. She scrubbed her eyes with the now-crumpled handkerchief, replaced it in her reticule and took a fresh one as she made a slow circuit of the yard. When she returned to the stables, there was still no sign of Tristan. It was as if he had vanished.

Had something happened? Had some evil befallen him? An ice-cold hand went around her heart.

She counted to thirty and then thirty once more. Looked

again hard at the door Tristan had disappeared through. Tristan failed to appear.

She bit her lips and attempted to think clearly as a pain pounded against her eyeballs. Something had happened to Tristan. She had to find where he had gone and determine if he did intend to marry her. She would search for him, all day and night if she had to, and, if he remained lost, she would return to Newcastle, much chastened, hoping for charity. She would use Lord Thorngrafton's money to purchase her train fare back to Newcastle. The first thing she would do when she did arrive home would be to raid her savings and send the money back to Lord Thorngrafton. It would be the polite thing to do, and she would not mention the scoundrel-like behaviour of his cousin.

Henry and her mother might not be pleased to see her, but they would not turn her from their door. She was certain of that. She was part of their family, in spite of everything.

She cringed, thinking of the words Henry would use, and how Mama would cry and how Lucy would look and sigh. Behind her skirts, everyone would whisper that she had deserved it, that pride came before a fall.

Emma Stanton had had it lucky, looking after her mother. Lottie caught her lip between her teeth. She wished she had never made fun of her last Christmas. Social success was such a transitory thing. Maybe Emma would be kind and send a list of books for her to read in her exile.

But somewhere deep inside her, a little voice told her that Tristan would look after her. She had to trust him. He had no reason to abandon her like this.

'Where is the market?' she asked an elderly lady with a well-lived-in face. 'I wish to find a constable. I have lost someone. He needs to be returned to me.'

The lady appeared surprised to be addressed. 'Lost someone? A man? Mother Hetts is good at finding men for pretty doves.'

'Yes, my fiancé appears to have gone missing.' Lottie was unable to prevent the slight catch in her throat. She swallowed hard before she continued in a steadier voice, 'It is imperative I find him. I am worried that something might have happened to him. It is unlike him to leave me for so long and in a place like this.'

'Men are like that, pet. They come. They go. You will find another soon.' The woman's eyes roamed over Lottie's dress. 'Particularly in them there togs.'

'I don't want another. I want to find my fiancé, Tristan Dyvelston. I thought the parish constable might be able to help.'

'His box is that way. But you won't be catching him in his box today, mind. Market day, me pet.' The old woman's eyes grew crafty. 'Of course, I could be wrong. It might be best to check. Make sure you take the third turn on your right. It will take you straight there. Otherwise it is a long ways around and there are bad folks about.'

'Thank you, thank you.' Lottie pressed the woman's hand. 'I really appreciate your kindness. I am sure I will find him now.'

'I hope you do, pet. There are them that don't.' The woman smiled, a cruel smile. 'You can always come back and finds me. I will offer you a good home. You come back here and tell that there landlord Mother Hetts will give you a place to rest your pretty golden head.'

Lottie stepped over a pile of muck and turned her back on the woman and crowded yard, hurrying away from that evil place as quickly as she could. She would not think about 'them that don't' and 'a good home'. She could do this. She was capable. It would be no worse than going for a walk in Haydon Bridge. She would find the constable and explain. He could discover Tristan's whereabouts while she waited. She would be safe.

The market-day crowd jostled her, but she kept on walking, relieved to be taking action instead of standing there panicking. She released her breath and tried to ignore the stares, acutely aware that her paisley dress was more fit for carriages than walking. Several women wrapped in woollen shawls and carrying baskets stared at her and put their heads together, whispering and pointing.

A carriage with a young girl and her mother in it swept past, splashing mud on the hem of her gown. Lottie gave a small cry and jumped back. Then she stooped and tried to wipe it off as men stopped and stared. A man said something unintelligble, but Lottie shook her head. She glanced back over her shoulder towards the inn, but it had been swallowed up by the crowd. She couldn't go back and she had no guarantee that Tristan would even be looking for her. Once she found a constable, things could be put right. All this unpleasantness would be a bad dream.

Several of the market goers jostled her. Lottie continued on, holding her reticule close, trying not to think about the beggars and thieves. She saw the opening, more of an alleyway than a street. She hesitated, then chided herself for being a ninny. The elderly woman had been quite specific with her directions. She plunged into the narrow street. It was imperative that she find the constable as quickly as possible.

'Going my way, my pretty dove?' a gin-soaked voice asked. 'See here, Fred, a fresh dolly bird has flown into our nest.'

* * *

'Ain't never been paid to do this before.' The innkeeper looked skeptical, but he pocketed the coins that Tristan pushed forwards on the bar.

'As long as it is done tomorrow morning, I don't mind.' Tristan pressed his hands against the bar and leant forward so that he was close to the unshaven jowls of the innkeeper. 'I always pay my debts, keep my promises and never forget a favour or an injury.'

'You had that look about you.' Sweat broke out on the innkeeper's face. 'I will do what you ask. And your lady friend, she is your wife, isn't she? I run a decent establishment.'

Tristan glanced around at the bar where a motley group of farm labourers, card sharps and ladies of the night were arranged. Blue smoke hung in the air. In one corner, a woman warbled a forlorn song. 'Your opinion and mine may differ as to decent.'

'Are you saying that I cheat my customers?' The man wiped his hand across his forehead. 'I ought to have you thrown out of here.'

'But you won't. I paid in advance and far more than that room is worth.'

The innkeeper licked his lips. 'That you did, that you did, and I don't say nothing to a paying customer.'

'It is how I want it.'

A moment of unease about the deception he was playing on Lottie passed over Tristan, but he pushed it away. He was doing what was right. One short sharp shock for Lottie Charlton and their married life would be far happier. It was easier if she learnt lessons now, before it was too late.

Tristan went back to the yard, filled his lungs with clean

air and swore. Loud and long. No blonde in a paisley silk afternoon dress, straw bonnet with a satchel by her side. No woman of quality waited there.

Tristan pressed his lips together. He had expected her to be there—spitting fury with her eyes perhaps to be left in the yard on her own, but to be there. He tried to think clearly. Robinson would have obeyed him. He would not have taken her with him. Tristan swore again, wishing he had told Robinson to stop and explain once he had left the yard. A mistake, but one he could not undo.

He had been gone longer than he anticipated, but not that long. She had gone. He had been mistaken.

A hard tight knot came into his throat. He had counted on her being different. He did not think she would have abandoned him so easily, not after the stand she had made at the hotel. He gave one more sweeping glance of the yard. Next time he would remember about the perfidy of women.

'Lost something, pet?' an elderly woman crooned to him. 'A trinket? A pretty little dove? I know where you can find another. Mother Hetts knows everything about little doves, she does.'

'There was a woman here. A blonde woman, well dressed. Do you have any idea where she might have gone?'

'Can't remembering having seen anyone of that description.' The woman gave a shrug of her thin shoulder and her watery eyes turned crafty. 'Then my memory ain't what it used to be. Lots of folks searching for things today. Always asking Mother Hetts if she's seen this or that. Can't be expected to remember. It's market day.'

The old woman gave a cackle, reminding him of a demented hen. The crackle went straight through him. He swung back and advanced towards the woman, whose crackling abruptly ceased.

'You know something. Where did she go?' Tristan advanced towards, his hands flexing at his sides, longing for something to hit. 'Would a coin help to recover that memory of yours?'

'May do? May not?' The old woman rocked back and forth. 'It is amazing what silver coin can do for my memory.'

Tristan reached into his pocket and fished out a shilling, holding it beyond the reach of the woman. 'The truth. Quickly.'

'I sent her to the parish constable...if she can find him. Mother Hetts looks after the little doves, she does,' the woman said, holding her basket in front of her face. 'She was looking for someone who was missing. Right concerned she was. Nearly in tears. Poor little dove. Are you lost?'

Tristan tossed her the coin. She caught it with expert claws, tested it as Tristan's insides twisted. He had not considered the possibility that Lottie might wonder about his whereabouts and worry. He had to find her and quickly. There was no telling what trouble she might encounter.

'Bless and keep you, sir. You are a real gentleman. If you don't find her, I can always get you another pretty dove.'

Tristan pushed past a cart and horse blocking the entrance to the yard, and went out into the street. His blood pounded in his head.

She had to be there. She could not have gone far. That old crone would not spend for ever in the yard. He must have missed Lottie by a matter of moments.

Only farm labourers, cattle drovers and a few women wrapped in shawls and carrying baskets lined the streets. There was no sign of Lottie's brightly coloured straw bonnet anywhere.

He fought against the sudden stab of concern.

Lottie had gone looking for him. He would find her more than likely with the parish constable. He would keep her safe. Then they would marry. All would be well.

A woman's scream rent the air. Tristan raced towards it.

'Let me go.' Lottie twisted away from the evil-smelling man and screamed again. Her sleeve tore slightly as she elbowed the man hard in the stomach. His hands loosened as he doubled over in pain.

'Why did you have to do that? I didn't mean no harm, did I, Den?' the rough unshaven man said to his companion.

'No, Fred, you didn't,' the companion said, sticking his hands in his pockets and giving a low whistle.

'I doubt the truth of that statement.' Lottie kept her nose in the air; her stomach was in knots as she struggled to breathe. She wished her corset was not so tight, then she would have been able to run, but as it was, she could not draw sufficient air.

If she walked quickly, perhaps she would come to the constable's box…if it even existed, if the woman had been correct in her directions, something Lottie was beginning to have her doubts about. She should have never gone down this alleyway. She should have never trusted that old woman. She should have stayed in the coaching yard until nightfall and then demanded the constable be brought to her. That would have been the sensible thing to do.

Her slippers resounded on the cobble stones. Only a few more steps and she'd be back in the open. She'd be safe. One more step. Lottie resisted the temptation to turn around and see where the men were. The back of her neck pricked, but she forced her feet to move. They had to let her go.

'Playing hard to get, me little golden-haired beauty? Thinking yourself all prettified in those togs? Above the likes of me and me pals? Way aye, I have the measure of you.'

Rough hands grabbed her waist again, dragged her back into the alleyway, away from the light, and back into the dark. The scent of alcohol wafted over her. Lottie gagged and kicked backwards. But the man had lifted her off the ground and her slippers only encountered thin air.

'Not this time.' He wiped a dirty paw down her face. 'You won't get away so lightly, but I likes it when they plays rough, I do.'

'Let me go, you—you monster!'

'We will go somewheres quiet. You, me and Den. I knows a good game we can play.'

'Unhand me this instant or I will call the constable.' Lottie fought against the hands, saw her handkerchief, reticule and satchel fall to the ground and with them all her money. She gave a little cry of despair. But the arms continued to hold her tight. She kicked backwards and screamed.

'And what is the constable going to do about it, my pretty?' His companion laughed. 'See here, Fred, see if you can wake him from his box. Or is he snoring his head off?'

Lottie's throat went dry as she prayed for a miracle. She should never have gone off out of the yard. She should have stayed and waited. She whispered a prayer.

'The lady is with me and not with you.' Tristan's voice cut through the man's banter. 'Release her. Or I won't be held be responsible for what happens.'

Lottie froze as hope bubbled up inside her. Tristan. He

was here. He had not abandoned her. He had found her. She turned her head towards the sound, hoping against hope that it had not been her imagination. He stood at the entrance to the alley, large and solid, formidable, his lips turned down in a furious expression.

'Tristan! I am here! Thank God you are all right. I thought something must have happened to you.' Lottie struggled against the imprisoning hands. 'Help me.'

'I said let the lady go.' Tristan advanced forwards. 'I am in no mood to repeat myself. No mood at all.'

'Why should I?' The man stood there, hands imprisoning her. 'I caught her first. Prove she's yours.'

'In the interests of your long-term health…release her.' Tristan's voice was calm and cold as if he were passing the time of the day. 'A friendly warning, if you like.'

'How so?' the man's companion asked. He advanced towards Tristan, brandishing his fists. 'Fred found her, plying her trade. You best be about your business, you jumped-up Englishman. I'm a professional boxer, like. My punch is harder than a sledgehammer. Den Casey, Sledgehammer of the North, they calls me. Won five straight.'

A loud thwack resounded in the street as Tristan's fist connected with the man's jaw. The man tumbled backwards, lay on the ground. 'Remind me not to bet on any of your fights, then.'

'Den down?' Lottie's captor looked at his prone companion and back at Tristan. 'The Hammer is on the ground. Dead to the world. Felled with one punch. I ain't never seen the like.'

'Who is next?' Tristan straightened his stock. 'I want the lady released. Unharmed. Immediately.'

'It were only a bit of sport, your worship. We did not mean no harm.'

The hands were withdrawn so suddenly that Lottie stumbled forwards and encountered Tristan's hard body.

She gasped slightly at the sudden contact, but her feet refused to move as her entire body trembled. Safe. She longed to lay her head against his broad chest. Her knees refused to support her. She clung onto his arm and pushed all thoughts about what might have happened to her had Tristan not come by when he did out of her head.

'I…I…' Her throat closed and she found it difficult to speak. She swallowed and tried again, her voice barely audible. 'I should have stayed at the inn. I went looking for you. I was worried that something might have happened and that was why you didn't come back. I wanted to get help.'

'Are you unhurt?' His arm went about her waist, supporting her. Lottie gave into temptation and rested her head against his shoulder, felt his strength. She closed her eyes and breathed in his crisp, masculine scent. She was safe. He put her away from him and looked her up and down. 'Have they harmed you?'

'My…my reticule has vanished.' Lottie straightened her bonnet and shook out the folds of her gown. She glanced at the rip in her sleeve, winced, but it could be mended. 'My bag.'

'Give the lady back her reticule. And her bag,' Tristan said in the same deadly quiet voice to the man who was standing over his fallen companion, staring at them with fearful eyes.

'Look what you done to our Den. There ought to be a law.'

'There is and you are on the wrong side of it.'

'What you mean? The wrong side?'

'I have no little doubt the constable will be interested to learn of your whereabouts.' Tristan held out his hand. 'The bags. Now. And I might allow you to go.'

There was a shuffling of feet and her satchel was held out. Lottie curled her fingers around it, hugging it to her body. She opened it and saw everything her mother's maid had packed remained there.

'And the reticule.'

Much shuffling of feet and the reticule appeared. Lottie gave a small cry of joy.

'Is everything there, Lottie? Check it.'

Lottie opened it with trembling fingers and gave a little cry of delight. Lord Thorngrafton's money was there. 'It is all there. They took nothing.'

'You see, like I said, your worship, it's all a big mis-understanding. We was just taking her…'

'You were not just taking her anywhere. Next time, when a lady protests, you leave her alone. Do you understand me?'

'We didn't mean no harm like, your worship.' The thick-set man held up his hands and backed slowly away from Tristan. 'We didn't know the lady was with you, like. It was just a bit o'sport. She seemed up for it, like.'

'I was not! I never!' Lottie balled her fists. She glanced up into Tristan's face, but all she saw was cold fury. At her? At the men? She tried to breathe. 'I would never. I was trying to get to the parish constable's box.'

'There ain't no constable's box around here.'

'I asked…the woman said…' Lottie paused. Tristan had to believe her. 'I thought something had happened to you. I wanted to make sure you were safe.'

His dark eyes stared at her for a long moment, searching her face, looking for something. The stern planes of his face did not change as he raised a single eyebrow. 'The lady says you were mistaken.'

'Maybe.' The man flushed and ran a finger around the neck of his shirt. 'Could have been. It were Den that—'

'Definitely mistaken.' Tristan's voice could cut through granite. 'You owe the lady an apology. The lady is my fiancée and deserves your respect. It is only the fact that it's my wedding day that puts me in a good mood.'

'I am…am sorry, your worship.' The man stumbled backwards, fell over his prone friend and scrambled to stand up again, touching his cap as he did so. 'I don't mean no harm like. I, that is we, had no idea. Many happy returns on your marriage.'

'Off you go.' Tristan gestured towards the prone figure of Den. 'Take your friend, he is cluttering up the pavement.'

'Right you are, your worship.' The man hoisted his friend on to his shoulder, and began to walk away, complaining loudly as he went that he did not mean any harm and how he was always hard done by.

Lottie's body began to shake. She wanted to sink down to the ground and weep. Tristan's arms came around her and held her against his body until the shaking passed.

'You are safe now, Lottie,' he said, his breath ruffling her bonnet. 'I am here.'

'Yes, you are.'

'And we are going to be married in a few moments.'

This was not supposed to be what her wedding day was like. She had had it all planned right down to the white silk dress, fashionable bonnet and veil and orange blossoms. Instead she had ended up brawling in an alleyway like a fishwife. She had been taken for a lady of the night.

Lottie moved backwards and Tristan's hold loosened. She wrapped her arms about her waist and attempted to control the shivers that now racked her body. She did not want to think about what had nearly happened to her. She took a deep breath and regained a small measure of control.

'Thank you for saving me,' she said when she trusted her voice would not quaver. 'Those men had evil intentions. I am sure of it. If you had not—' Her voice broke and she could only look up at the hard planes of his face, hoping he'd understand what she meant.

'You are safe with me now. Think no more about them.'

'I made a mistake. I should never have listened to that old woman's directions.' Her voice held a pathetic quiver. She fumbled for her handkerchief, discovered she had lost it. With angry fingers, Lottie brushed away the tears. 'None of this was supposed to happen.'

He inclined his head, but his dark gaze searched her face. 'Did those men do anything to you?'

'They pawed at my dress and my face, but I will live.' She brushed a speck of dust from her sleeve, a small act, but one that did much to restore her confidence. She would not think about what might have been, but about the future. From now on, it would be the future she faced. And she would refuse to let Tristan leave her again like that. 'It is most aggravating to be touched in that familiar manner. Most unexpected.'

'The streets are unsafe for a woman dressed as you are. Gretna Green teems with drunks and ne'er-do-wells today. Far more than I thought possible for such a town.' His face turned grave. 'If you had stayed where I told you to, none of this would have happened. Why did you leave the yard? You were safe in the yard. You had no cause to go.'

'The coach driver went off. I was left alone. I became frightened and tried to find you. I went into the inn, but there was no sign of you. A woman offered to buy my hair.' A shudder went through Lottie at the memory. 'I couldn't stay there. I became worried, certain something had happened to you. I went to find the parish constable.'

'It took longer than I anticipated to arrange the marriage and our accommodation. I had not thought to be gone so long.' His fingers curled around hers. He brought them to his lips. Then let go. 'I regret that.'

Lottie resisted the temptation to put her hand to her face and savour the touch. Was it an apology? She did not want to ask. All she knew was that he had not abandoned her. She hated her earlier thoughts.

'If you had not come when you did…' Another shiver convulsed through her.

'Forget the unpleasantness ever happened. It is over, truly. I swear it and I keep my promises.' He put his hand on her shoulder and looked at her with an intense expression. 'Remember that. If I say I will return, I will return. I will protect you.'

'Do you mean that?' Lottie asked in shaking voice.

'As best as I am able.'

'That is good to know.'

'And now if you remain willing, the blacksmith awaits.'

'The blacksmith?' Lottie tilted her head and tried to quell the sudden butterflies in her stomach. 'We have no horses that need shoeing.'

'We have a marriage that needs forging. It is where all the best marriages take place in Gretna Green, or so I am reliably informed.'

'We are not marrying in a church?' Lottie regarded her hands. 'I had always imagined that I would be married in church.'

He shook his head. 'We are marrying in Gretna Green, under Scottish law. Two witnesses are all the law requires. The blacksmith is waiting for us. All you have to say is that you don't want to, Lottie, and I will personally put you on a coach back to your mother and Newcastle.'

'No, I will marry you…even if it is a blacksmith's shop.' She drew a deep breath. Her wedding would bear no resemblance to the wedding of her dreams. A blacksmith's anvil and a torn dress. But it was a better prospect than the future those men had planned for her. 'Like you, Tristan Dyvelston, I keep my promises.'

He curled his fingers around her gloved hand, raised it to his lips. 'Thank you for that.'

Lottie allowed her footsteps to match his. She was getting married. It might not be the wedding she dreamt of, but she was determined to be the right sort of wife. She would make him see that she could be helpful. It was the details that counted. She gave one last backward glance to the alleyway and turned her face to the sun. Her footsteps faltered. 'Tristan, what sort of ring?'

'The blacksmith will take care of it. He is used to weddings. He informs me that he has already performed two this morning.'

'You mean it isn't going to be a gold ring?'

'Is a gold ring a requirement for a marriage in Scotland?' His gaze narrowed. 'Is it ever a requirement?'

Lottie wet her lips and said goodbye to the last of her dreams. 'I had only wanted to know.'

Chapter Six

Lottie twisted the iron band about her left ring finger, rather than look at her new husband where he stood speaking to the blacksmith. The ceremony had gone quickly, squeezed in between a horseshoeing and mending a plough. Nothing fancy. Simple and ordinary.

Her face burnt from the heat of the fire and her ears rang from the clanging of the hammer against the anvil. A quick brush of his lips against hers. Very correct. Very polite, but nothing more. But she wanted more. She wanted him to kiss her like he meant it, like he wasn't marrying her simply because he had to, because society forced them. Lottie concentrated on the iron band. Slowly she drew on her glove, hiding the ring, but her hand remained heavy with the unaccustomed weight.

'Shall we depart, Lottie?' Tristan said, coming over to her; the blacksmith started striking the anvil with his hammer again. 'Unless you want to stay and see the horses being shod, there is nothing here for us.'

Lottie shook her head and allowed Tristan to lead her from the shop.

'So we are married. Forged as it were.' She gave a small laugh once they had returned to the street. It looked as it had when they had entered the shop—people were still hurrying by, intent on their shopping, the mud still lay in pools. Nothing had changed. No one noticed what had happened to her. 'I had never thought about it. My friends will be all agog when I write. One only ever hears about going to Gretna Green to get married, and the precise details are never spelt out.'

'Yes, we are married. The ceremony was perfectly legal.'

'I never questioned it.' Lottie glanced quickly up at her new husband. His face was remote and held little of the warmth she had glimpsed last evening. She wondered how she could get it back. If he had looked like that, then she would not have been tempted to make this marriage. She wanted him to smile down at her, to do something to show that this marriage was more than an inconvenience caused by her own indiscretion. 'We have both been saved from ruin. The marriage will be a nine-day wonder, if that. Undoubtedly someone somewhere will do something worse and it will be forgotten.'

'I am no stranger to scandal but I had no wish to be outside society for ever. It is not good business.' His eyes showed no signs of softening. 'Neither of us had any choice in the matter, Lottie, but we do have a choice about the life we lead. Shall we look to the future, rather than live in what might have been?'

'The ice-cold wind of disapproval.' Lottie adjusted her bonnet and ignored the rip in her sleeve that appeared to grow each time she moved her arm. She hated the thought of being dressed like this in public, but there was nothing she could do. She had to hope no one would notice. She moved so her arm was next to Tristan's, hiding the worst. 'I need to know, Tristan. Why did you marry me, since you had already experienced society's disapproval?'

'Once you ruin a virgin…there is very little way back.' Tristan ignored her invitation to take her arm and stood staring down at her. His voice did little to restore her confidence.

'And did you want a way back?' Lottie asked. She wanted to believe that there was more to this, that he had wanted to marry her.

'I am no cad. And perhaps I no longer wanted to be an orphan.' A cold smile touched his lips. 'Does it matter about the reasons? We are married now, and we will go forwards without scandal. I will lead the sort of life my father had envisioned for me. Upright. Solid. The sort of life I intend to lead now that I have returned to Britain.'

'You appear to have made a number of promises to your father.'

'They were all part of the same promise. My father and my uncle were not friends.' He gave a bitter laugh. 'I wanted to torment my uncle.'

'And what did your uncle predict?'

'That I would come to no good, that I would blacken the family's name and die in an unmarked grave.'

'It is hard when families fight, particularly if one of them is titled.' Lottie placed her hand on his arm. 'Didn't your mother try to help? Or your aunt? It is the duty of the women in the family to mend quarrels.'

'My uncle's wife was concerned with…other matters and my mother died when I was three.' A flash of pain crossed Tristan's face and Lottie's heart constricted. In that instant she caught a glimpse of the young boy Tristan must have been. How truly awful to have this long-ago quarrel blight his life. 'I doubt she could have mended this quarrel, but I like to think she would have understood.'

'I am sorry. I lost my father when I was twelve. I cried for days on end. Buckets and buckets.'

'My father died when I was seventeen. I had stopped crying then.'

Lottie bit her lip, aware that she knew very little about the man standing next to her, very little about the man whose bed she would now share and whose table she would grace. She had always thought that she would have a long and proper courtship, but it had happened a different way. They would get to know each other in time. And some day, she would make him see that making social calls and being part of a community was important. It gave meaning to people's lives. It enabled people to help each other and to help their families lead better lives.

'We shouldn't be talking about sad things on our wedding day.'

'You are quite right—we should only speak of happy things.'

'It is the polite thing to do.'

'And you always do the polite thing.'

Lottie tilted her head. 'Whenever possible. It saves making a spectacle.'

'Then we had best move as we are beginning to make a spectacle.'

Tristan put his hand under her elbow and guided her away from the blacksmith's shop. Lottie saw the curious stares from several women. With his other hand he carried her satchel as they walked slowly through the streets of Gretna Green. The market crowd had dispersed somewhat, but the streets still heaved with people. Twice, Lottie had to walk around a drunk lying the gutter.

'Where are we going now?' she asked as he strode along, not looking left or right. 'What happens next?'

'You are my wife and I shall take you back to the inn where hopefully the innkeeper will have prepared rooms for us.'

'Do we have a private room?' Lottie asked. She attempted a smile. She did not want to think about what men and women did in bed at night. She heard whispered rumours from the servants, and once at Martha Dresser's house had come across *Aristotle's Complete Master Piece* in a box of books that belonged to Martha's grandmother. They had spent a half-hour giggling over the pictures before they'd been discovered and had their ears boxed.

'Is that important to you?'

'Yes.' The word came out a squeak. The thought of being with her husband for the first time in a room crowded with strangers had no appeal. And yet, she could not bring herself to explain, to confess to her complete ignorance about lovemaking beyond the few kisses she had shared. 'I know they must be at a premium, but somehow I don't fancy sharing a bed with a stranger.'

'And what would you call me?' He gave a short laugh, but his eyes were sombre. 'We are very much strangers to each other, Lottie.'

Lottie tucked her hand more firmly into the crook of his arm.

'My husband.' The words sounded new and exciting, but more than a little dangerous. 'I see no point in being old-fashioned and calling you Mr Dyvelston like Mama did with my father. It sounds so cold and formal. I…I want something more from our marriage.'

'Somehow I can't imagine you calling me Mr Dyvelston…ever.' A tiny smile on his lips. 'Tristan will suffice.'

Lottie tightened her grip on her reticule. Exactly who was her new husband? She had seen his controlled fury at the men earlier. She knew very little about him, about his prospects. And he appeared content to ignore Lord Thorngrafton's generosity to them. No, not content, but determined. But that was a problem to be solved later.

'And at least you call me Lottie. I loathe and detest Carlotta.'

'I will try to remember that, Carlotta.'

Lottie started and then she saw the devilment in his eyes. She aimed a kick at him, which he neatly sidestepped.

'But the rooms—will I be expected to go into a public room? It wouldn't be seemly.'

'My finances can stretch to a private room at that inn. I thought it would be better as we did marry this afternoon.'

'You never said about money.' Lottie stopped in the street, her slippers skidding into each other. Marriage meant sharing a bed. She forced her mind from that. 'You never agreed to a settlement with my brother. Will we need to ask for Lord Thorngrafton's assistance? You did borrow his carriage.'

'I have enough. I have no need for Thorngrafton's charity,' he said and his eyes slid away from her.

A pain gathered behind Lottie's eyebrows. He was trying to hide something from her. Had she fallen into a trap? She had not even thought about money; she had only thought about the shape of his lips and how they fit against hers. Mama had always told her to be sensible about men and she had failed, failed utterly and miserably. And now she was going to a mean inn for her wedding night. Her only comfort was that she remained respectable—barely.

'What is the estate you inherited like? Is it in good repair?' She placed a hand on his arm. 'Please, I want to know. Is it a place to raise a family?'

He looked down at her and his black eyes flared with some unknown fire, a spark of something that ignited a glow within her. And she knew she had asked the right words. Then the mask came down.

'It was a prosperous estate once, highly productive, but it has been neglected for many years. It has fine views of the river, a series of follies in the garden. It was quite well thought of in my grandfather's day.' Tristan looked ahead, rather than down at Lottie with her brave face and slightly torn dress. She had been battered more than he had intended before they were married, but here she remained firmly fixed on their social status. There were flashes in her of genuine concern, but he had to be sure. Too soon and he'd never know. Patience brought rewards. 'My uncle took a perverse pride in letting me know about its neglect. How the fields were fallow, and how the garden had become choked with weeds.'

'Neglect of good land is a crime.' Lottie turned her gaze upwards and a furious expression came into her eyes. 'Why would anyone do that? Was it because of a will? Was the estate stuck in chancery? Why didn't anyone stop him?'

'It belonged to him. What do you know about estates and chancery?' A faint smile touched his lips as he realised a way to turn the conversation on to less rocky shoals. 'I thought you were a city woman.'

'I may look like just a pretty face, Tristan, but Mama was determined that I learn…as she was determined that I fulfil my destiny and marry a title or, failing that, someone very wealthy.' Lottie paused and gave tiny shrug.

'Not that it happened, but I needed to know something so I wouldn't be a ninny. My skills can be put to good use.'

'I think you are anything but a ninny.' Tristan resisted the temptation to draw her into his arms and confess. How much did she truly know?

'I thank you for the compliment.' Lottie gave a little wave of her hand. 'I know my limitations. I am not a blue stocking like Emma Stanton, nor am I the excellent house-wife that my sister-in-law is. But I plan to be a social asset and help further your standing in the community.'

'Whatever that is. I don't recall ever worrying about it before.'

'What did you do before you returned to England?'

'I gambled and led a disreputable life.' Tristan stopped and considered what to say. How much to reveal. How much to keep hidden until he was certain of her motives. 'Most of your cousin's stories contain an element of truth in them.'

'Are you ashamed of the life you led?' she asked. The rim of her bonnet shadowed her face, making it impossible for him to determine her expression.

'Should I be?' He raised an eyebrow and turned their footsteps once again towards the inn. He would tell her the truth and then see her reaction. 'You probably think me wicked but, no, I am not ashamed. I did what I did for a purpose and I kept my promises.'

He waited for the gasp of horror, but instead she tight-ened her grip on his arm. A tiny furrow appeared between her brows. He resisted the temptation to smooth it away.

'Some people like my cousin would say yes, you should, but I am not sure. Keeping your promises is im-portant.' She looked up into his face and he received the full blue gaze of her eyes. 'Does that make me wicked as well? Everyone says that I am, but I don't see it that way. My intentions are good.'

'I cannot change the past, Lottie. I did what I did to survive.' Tristan stopped by the inn's stables. He grasped her shoulders. 'Trust me?'

'But…but…' She pressed her hand to her lips, squared her shoulders. 'I will trust you. You are my husband. I am sure you have done your best and will look after me.'

A twinge of guilt passed over Tristan. What would she say when she actually knew what he had done? He dismissed it. His experiment would work. 'I will do well by you, Lottie.'

The smoke-hung public room fell silent as Lottie entered it. The crowd of drovers, workmen and ne'er-do-wells stared at them. Lottie shrank back against Tristan's arm. She turned her face towards his frock coat, breathed in, tried to rid her nostrils of the awful stench. He put a hand on her shoulder and lifted her chin as his dark eyes searched her face.

'Do I have to go through there? A woman tried to buy my hair! She appeared quite put out when I refused to sell it. Apparently golden curls are all the rage. I could get a good price for them, but they are mine.'

'If you want to get to the room, you will have to go through the throng, but I will be with you.' He touched her golden curls, a light touch, but one that sent a quiver arching through her. 'There should never be a need for you to sell your hair. Or your ear bobs. Trust me to provide for you.'

'How did you know she asked about those?'

'It stands to reason.' He gestured around the public room with its curling smoke and clanking tankards. 'In a place like this, people are looking to buy and sell whatever they can.'

'Do we have to stay here?'

'I have paid for the room.'

'I had rather thought it would be like the coaching inn that Mama and I stayed at when we went to Yorkshire once.' Lottie attempted a brave smile as she groped for a clean handkerchief, but could only find the crumpled one from earlier. 'Large clean rooms and an apple-cheeked proprietor. This inn has probably not been cleaned since the Jacobite rebellion. The ceiling is positively black with smoke.'

'I regret that it is not up to your standards but it is where we are staying.'

'It is not what was I was expecting.' Lottie tried to keep her skirts out of the unidentified puddle on the floor, but failed. A small cry of distress escaped her lips. 'It was my best afternoon dress.'

'The room is better than this.' His fingers tightened on her elbow.

'Have you seen it?'

'Dyvelston!' A voice hailed Tristan from a corner table. 'Here you are. Just the man for a game of cards.'

'A friend of yours?' Lottie asked, and her forehead puckered. Her husband was a gambler. He had to be if he was being hailed with such familiarity in an inn such as this one. She should have expected it, but she knew how much her father had hated cards. How he blamed them for his brother's downfall. For some men, cards was more than a pleasant pastime, they were a way of life, a religion.

'He is someone I knew once.'

'From your dissolute days.' Lottie strove to keep her voice light. 'Are you going to have a game of cards?'

Tristan paused, frowning.

'I will see you to the room. You need not worry about that.'

'And afterwards?'

'We are newly married, Lottie.'

'That is no answer.'

'It is all you will get.' He started towards the stairs. 'Are you coming with me or do you wish to be accosted by another buyer of hair? Or an owner of a nanny house?'

'I will come.' Lottie skirted around a second unidentified puddle on the sawdust-strewn floor and hurried after Tristan, reaching him just as he opened a door to the upstairs.

She followed Tristan up the stairs, along a narrow passageway, and then up another narrow flight of stairs. She tried to push away her fears. Tristan was taking her to their room. He had not abandoned her for a game of cards. Henry would have done that. Lucy was often left on her own. Ignored. Lottie wanted more from her marriage than Lucy had. She was determined to show Henry and Lucy that she could make a success of things.

Tristan opened the door and turned to her with a grim smile. 'How do you like the accommodation?'

Lottie started. She had expected a large poster bed with a roaring fire and a wash basin. This room was mean with bare floors and furniture that looked as if it had come from the early part of the last century. The sagging bed with its stained, greying coverlet took up a large part of the room and appeared to grow bigger with each beat of her heart. She would be expected to share it with Tristan.

For the first time in her life, she was alone in a bedroom with a man, a stranger. Lottie struggled to breathe. No, not a stranger, her husband, the man who had held her in his arms last evening. What would he expect of her?

Suddenly the public room was not as frightening as here.

Lottie wished she had had Lucy to ask about it, and Mama had been no help. All she had said was that all men were beasts and want to have their own way; women had to preserve their dignity. Beasts. Rolling around on that bed? Lottie winced, not liking to think of fleas or other insects lurking. She had enough to worry about without wondering if she would be bitten alive. She swallowed hard and risked a glance up at Tristan. His eyes were hooded, but watching her, his entire body stilled, waiting.

'You say nothing, wife. Does it measure up to your exacting standards?'

Lottie held back the arched remark she was about to make. This room was not his fault. It was quite probably the best he could afford. If he had known about Lord Thorngrafton's money, then perhaps he would have procured a better room, but he hadn't. And she had no wish to mock him. 'The room will be lovely for the night, I am sure.'

'It is a place to stay.'

'Yes,' Lottie said around the increasing lump in her throat. With every breath she took, it became harder and harder to pretend that this room was fine. Harder and harder to ignore the bed looming in the centre. 'No doubt your house will be better than this.'

'It may be. It may not be.' Tristan gave a little shrug. 'It has been vacant for years.'

Lottie did not dare reply. She wanted Tristan to take her in his arms again. She wanted it to be how it was last evening. She knew if his lips were against hers, she would not have to think or to worry.

'Is there some problem, Lottie?' Tristan put a hand on her shoulder, drew her to him. He pressed his lips to her temple. His breath against her cheek sent a pulse of warmth throughout. 'Confide in me. What troubles you? Why don't you like being here with me? Alone. You appeared to like being on the terrace with me last evening.'

'Nothing troubles me.'

She turned her face upwards and met his mouth. Their lips touched, parted and she tasted him. A jolt ran through her, igniting her insides. She moaned slightly in the back of her throat, felt her body begin to arch, and stiffened, stunned by her reaction. His hands dropped away. The kiss ended as air rushed between them. He regarded her with a question in his eyes, but made no move to touch her.

'Lottie, sweet Lottie.'

Lottie pressed her hand against her stomach, willed that the melting sensation would go away and tried not to think about what was to come. She knew her face flamed. What could happen if Tristan did not respect her?

The thoughts circled and circled in her head, making her dizzy. She had to find a way to breathe, to regain control of her thoughts and desires.

A distinct smell of wood smoke and cooking pervaded the room, gave her an excuse. 'Is there a possibility of food? I barely had anything for supper last night. I feel a bit faint.'

It was better than the truth. She knew she had done something wrong, but she had no idea what she had done. Why he had put her away from him.

'I will go and check.' Tristan's hand grasped the door. 'It will give you time to change, and to get comfortable.'

'Can you send someone to help me?'

'To help you?'

'I need a maid. I cannot undress myself.' She gave a small shrug.

He looked puzzled, then his face cleared. His voice

became velvet soft. 'Unable to undress? Shall I play a lady's maid?' He came back over to her and trailed a hand along her shoulder. 'I have had a bit of experience in how ribbons and laces become undone.'

Him? He thought her a strumpet. Her mouth went dry at the thought of his undoing her clothes. She remembered her mother's other words. A lady did not show passion. A lady submitted. Surrendered.

She had no wish to repel him. She knew she was not ready to give away her soul. Last night at Shaw's, his kisses had awakened something deep within her, a sort of hunger. But she wanted him to respect her. She was his wife, not his courtesan. She doubted if it would be possible to be both as much as she might like to be.

'My corset ties at the back. It can be very tricky. A serving maid would be best. More dignified.'

'If you wish, I only made the offer.' His voice lost its warmth and became correct. 'I have dealt with ladies' laces before…in my misspent youth.'

'Your misspent youth? It is different for a man. No one expects…no one makes comments…' Lottie watched him. Would he help her? What would it be like to have his long fingers stroke her skin? To feel his mouth move on hers like it had last night? She daren't ask in case he refused. She knew she was babbling, but anything to stop this growing dread inside her. What would he think of her without any clothes on? She hated her toes. Would he like her toes? Blind panic filled her. She knew nothing about lovemaking and he was an accomplished rake. He was used to women who knew how to please a man.

'Lottie, sweetheart, tell me what you want. It is our wedding night.' His voice played like silken velvet over her skin.

'It would be useful to have someone.' Lottie began to pace the room, unable to stand still, unable to think. 'Is there anyone at Gortner Hall? I shared a maid with Mama and then Cousin Frances and we helped each other. It was not ideal, of course, but I made do. It does not have to be a French maid. Any girl would do. I could teach her to do my hair. I am sure I could.'

She knew she was babbling and watched his eyes grow cold and his hands fall to his sides.

'I will send one of the serving maids with some bread and cheese. She should be able to help.' He bowed and closed the door. 'I will return shortly. That should give you enough time to make yourself decent.'

'Decent. Yes, I will be decent.'

'And, Lottie, there is no need to panic. I will send the maid. Remember to breathe while you wait.' He touched his fingers to his temple. 'It always helps.'

'I am not panicking.' She paused and smiled. 'I have no desire to faint.'

'That is a start.' He closed the door softly behind him.

Lottie breathed again. She would have time to get her nerves together. She would make sure that she did not give in to her passion. She would be dignified. Tristan would respect her for that. Men wanted wives that they could respect, who could help them. She had to remember that. She listened to the sound of his boots going down the stairs. The despair inside her increased with each step.

Had her passion doomed the marriage before it had started?

Tristan sat nursing his second pint of bitter. The inn-keeper had doctored the beer to a black sludge that gave no pleasure. He would give Lottie a bit of time before he returned to the room.

All around him, the dice rattled and the smoke swirled. Several ladies plied their trade. It was hard to imagine a more disreputable place, but it served its purpose. However, he wondered if he had made a slight error.

He had seen her face drain of colour when he suggested his playing the lady's maid. Silently he cursed her mother or whoever had told her about the facts of life. He had never lain with a virgin before, and most in particular had never lain with one who was his wife.

He had a responsibility to awaken her properly, to teach her about passion, and that meant going slow, and not forcing her here where the memory might be distasteful. Tristan regarded the bottom of his pint glass. He had to decide where it would be. He had to balance his desire against the need to make sure her first experience went smoothly. A great deal of responsibility rested on his shoulders. He was determined that his marriage would be a passionate one. He'd felt the passion in her earlier when they'd kissed.

Tristan gave the remaining dark liquid a final swirl. He was not ready for this. He tried to think about his other piece of unfinished business—his cousin, and how he could ensure Peter remained true to his word.

'Thorngrafton, it is you.' A large hand pinned him to his stool. 'I told Saidy that you weren't answering to Dyvelston any more, not since your uncle kicked up his heels. That was why you ignored him. It is amazing what some forget.'

'McGowan.' Tristan nodded as he finished his drink. The only thing he could be grateful for was that McGowan had failed to accost him while Lottie was there. He needed her to remain in ignorance for a few days longer. His experiment had to succeed. 'Is there some particular reason you are in Gretna Green?'

'Passing through, but I am most surprised to find you in a hellhole like this one. I would have thought you were more accustomed to staying at the finer coaching inns.'

'I have my reasons.'

'And it doesn't have anything to do with the beautiful blonde you were with—a real looker, that one. Golden curls, blue eyes and curves. You can pass her along to me when you've finished with her.' McGowan gave a coarse laugh.

'She's my wife.'

'Please give *Lady* Thorngrafton my compliments.' McGowan's leer told Tristan that he did not believe a word. 'Do she have a sister or three?'

'I will see that she gets your compliments.' Tristan gritted his teeth. He had no intention of explaining his actions to McGowan, an acquaintance from those long-ago days when he had taken great pleasure in making sure his name was as scandalous as possible. The difference between them was now marked. Once McGowan had been considered handsome, but now he showed the signs of overindulgence and too much high living.

'How came you to be let in the pockets?' McGowan fingered his chin. 'The last I heard you had done very nicely out of railways. One of the railway kings.'

'People talk too much, but I have no money worries.'

'Then why are you here? In this inn?'

'I have my reasons.' Tristan turned back to the barman, motioning for another pint. 'Allow me to pay for the next round.'

'Do you have time for a game of cards?' McGowan

persisted. 'For old times' sake. I can remember how you and I would play until the dawn broke. You always knew when to stop, though. You had the coolest head I have ever seen.'

'You still play cards?'

'Avidly—you should have seen the money Saidy won off some high-flaunting lord lately returned from India. The nabob thought he were a king at cards, but we got his vowels in the end.'

'I will watch you play.' Tristan smiled as an idea on how to teach Peter a lesson came to him. Simple. Neat. It simply took a cool head and a steady nerve. The same approach he had to use with Lottie. 'There is a proposition I wish to put to you and Saidy. A little job that will put your…skills to good use, but you will be amply rewarded.'

'You interest me greatly.'

Dearest Henry and Lucy,

I cannot tell you what a splendid wedding Tristan and I had. You have never seen the like! You would have been so proud. My step never faltered and I said my vows so all could hear.

Lottie turned her face away from the letter and wiped a tear. She would allow no blotches on the paper. They would never know her wedding was anything less than marvellous. The shame would be unbearable. With a shaking hand, she added a few more lines enquiring about Mama's nerves, and her nieces and nephews. Then she sealed the letter and handed it to the serving girl.

'Will that be all, ma'am?'

'Your assistance is no longer required.' Lottie took the last few coins from her reticule. 'You have been most helpful. This should pay for the stamp as well as a little extra for your trouble. I do appreciate your help with the dress.'

The girl made another curtsy and left. Somewhere in the distance a door banged and loud footsteps sounded on the stairs. She hurried to the bed, dove in and pulled the sheets up to her chin.

'Where are you, Tristan? Why did you leave me alone?' she whispered and willed the door to open and her husband to appear.

Nothing.

A second set of footsteps came up the stairs, and several drunken voices argued about how much money was left in their purse and whether or not one or two of the lovely ladies downstairs would care to warm their beds.

Lottie clutched the sheet to her, and looked wildly about the room for a poker, for anything to defend her honour with. Her whole being longed for Tristan to appear and to cradle her. But when no one entered the room, she forced her hands to relax.

Her last waking thought before sleep overtook was that Tristan had not bothered to return. He was not interested in her. She wiped away a few tears and refused to cry. Crying only turned her nose red.

How everyone would laugh if they knew—the incomparable Lottie Charlton spending her wedding night alone in a filthy flea-infested coaching inn, fearful of drunken drovers and abandoned in favour of a card game by a husband who had married her out of duty. Married in a torn dress, a crushed bonnet and with an iron ring for a wedding band.

This was not how her life was supposed to go—at all.

Lottie slammed her fist into the pillow and resolved that, somehow, she would triumph. She would make this into a glorious match, if she could only figure out a way. She wanted a different way. She deserved better. She would find that way.

Chapter Seven

'Oy, you in there, get up. We need the room. You only paid until morning. It's first light now!'

A steady pounding on the door opposite them woke Lottie from her slumber. She pushed at the unaccustomed weight of an arm around her middle and suddenly realised that yesterday had been no dream. She was married. And Tristan was in bed with her. Not only in bed, but her bottom was snuggled up against him in a suggestive manner and her whole being infused with the warmth of him as his breath tickled the nape of her neck.

He must have come in some time in the night. And so great was her exhaustion that she hadn't woken. She should have done. Lottie bit her lip, regretting her late-night thoughts, regretting her damp pillow.

Had he noticed?

She resolved to be a better wife. She would give him no cause to run away and play cards. Her mother must have been right and her passionate response to his kiss disgusted him. She longed to have been wrong.

Half-turning her head, she caught his deep dark gaze

watching her. The sight took her breath away and took all thoughts from her head. She could only drown in his eyes as deep hunger grew within her.

'Good morning,' he said, running a finger down her arm and sending a warm sensation pulsating through her. 'You were sleeping like an angel when I came to bed.'

'There is someone banging on all the doors,' Lottie said, hanging on to the last remnant of common sense. 'He wants money. Do we owe him money?'

'He won't come in here.'

'I rather think he means business. He will kick the door down.' Lottie fought against the tide of rising panic that threatened to engulf.

'He wouldn't want to damage his own property.' His breath tickled her neck.

'Tristan!' Lottie covered her ears with her hands.

'If you insist, I will see what can be done to preserve your sensibilities.'

Tristan removed his arm and stood up, totally unconcerned about his nakedness. His skin gleamed golden in the morning light. Lottie looked at his chest with its sprinkling of dark hair and then forced her eyes higher. She had been sleeping with a naked man and had brazenly pushed herself up against him. Was she a wanton creature?

He pulled his trousers on, and did up the buttons.

'How can you be so casual about this?' Lottie clutched the sheet and raised it to her chin. 'We will be disgraced! He is only next door. I am sure of it!'

'The room! Or more money!' The pounding increased. 'I will have the law on you.'

'We will leave in less time than it takes to get the constable!' a man shouted back. And a woman's voice hurled abuse at the innkeeper.

'Quit your blathering! You will wake the dead!' another yelled.

'Are you telling me to get the constable? I will and I will have every man Jack of you out of this inn. This here inn is a respectable place.'

Lottie regarded the door with horror. What was happening out there? Was the innkeeper demanding money from everyone? Was she going to be treated like some wastrel?

'Please, Tristan, I beg you—do something.' She made a little gesture as insults were exchanged between the innkeeper and the unknown guest. 'I am not decent. Goodness knows what sort of mood the innkeeper will be in when he knocks on our door. Please, Tristan.'

'Relax, Lottie. I have taken care of matters. We are safe, but if you are worried…' He opened the door, and stepped outside, closing the door behind him. 'Is there some problem?'

The reply was muffled, but the knocking ceased abruptly and the innkeeper went off, grumbling. Lottie rested her head against her chest. She was safe. She was not going to face the humiliation of being thrown out of the inn without any clothes on. But would the innkeeper come back? She tucked a strand behind her ear and tried to collect her thoughts.

Tristan came back to bed and put his hands on either side of her face. 'He has gone now, Lottie. You can stop trembling with fear. You won't have the innkeeper barging in.'

'The shame of it. I couldn't stand the shame.' She concentrated on taking steady breaths. 'That poor couple. Do you think they had just married?'

'I have no idea. They have nothing to do with me. I did not want you to be fearful of the innkeeper.'

'Thank you.' Lottie watched the muscles ripple on his shoulder and her lips ached.

'Perhaps I should have come back to bed earlier. Then you could have expressed your gratitude more properly.' He trailed a hand down her arm. 'But it is too late for regrets. We have to move. The day is wasting.'

'Where are we going?' Lottie asked quickly. If his hand continued to stroke her arm, she would lose all power of movement. All her resolutions would be forgotten before she had even risen from the bed. 'What are your plans?'

'To Gortner Hall, the house I inherited in the North Tyne Valley.' Tristan withdrew his hands and stood up. He picked his shirt up from the end of the bed. 'Where we shall spend our days.'

'There is to be no wedding trip, then?' Lottie hated the plaintive note to her voice. She knew their wedding was unorthodox, but she had thought they might have a trip, go somewhere before she was buried in the country. Even Henry had taken Lucy to France. A week in Calais. She was going nowhere. There were no doubt some who would say the punishment was justified, but she had always dreamt of a splendid wedding trip.

'I had not planned to marry. There are things that need my attention. The estate was left vacant for a long period. There is much to do. It will be restored to its former glory.'

'Lord Thorngrafton's coachman has gone.' Lottie wrapped her arms about her knees. She had to be practical. She had to put aside her girlish fantasies, even if it pained her to do so. She had not married a fairy-tale prince; she had married Tristan, a man who had inherited a small, vacant estate. In time, things would improve. She had to be practical, but there remained a little piece of her that wished she didn't. The sooner they arrived at Gortner Hall, the better. A long, low wail resounded through the room and gave Lottie an idea. 'Shall we take the express? There is one that runs to Carlisle. I overheard Henry speaking about it the other night at dinner. The speeds are incredible—over forty miles per hour in some places. The first-class carriage has real armchairs.'

Tristan's hands stilled on his shirt buttons and his face once again wore his remote look. Lottie shifted slightly. Had her tongue run away with her again? What was wrong with the train? It was surely practical. She had not suggested buying a new carriage.

'That train costs large sums of money. A third of a month's wage for a labourer.'

'But you are not a labourer.' Lottie swallowed hard and struggled to breathe normally. What was Tristan saying? How poor were they? 'You are a gentleman. You were born one.'

'You have not seen what needs to be done on the estate.' He gave a slight shrug. 'My hands will soon become as rough as any farmer's.'

'You are not suggesting we walk all the way there?' Lottie strove for a laugh.

'Walking is one way of travelling. Country folk do it all the time.'

'Yes, but—' She thought about her slippers and wished she had brought her boots. She had never considered the possibility of walking. Surely he had to be joking. Her slippers would not make it and her feet would be cut to ribbons. If they were going to walk, she'd need stout boots. A train journey would cost less than stout boots. It had to. 'Gortner Hall is…in the North Tyne and we are in

Scotland. It took us all night to drive here from Gilsland and we travelled with fast horses. How long would it take us to walk that distance and more? A day? Two?'

'Don't you fancy a night or two out on the open countryside—you, me and a friendly haystack?' His dark eyes danced as he expertly did up his cravat. He had once again become remote. It was as if suddenly there was a wall between them.

'Surely we are not reduced to begging.' The blanket she had been clutching to her chest fell unheeded as Lottie realised the potential. Begging. Being classed as a vagrant. Maybe if she was very unlucky, being thrown in the stocks. She would become one of the despised. There had to be a way of avoiding that fate. 'My settlement…we can borrow against that. It will be more than enough to take the first-class express.'

'I have no idea what your settlement will be.' Tristan finished dressing. The golden god of this morning had vanished and in its place was the remote man from the carriage, the one who had left her standing in the inn's yard. 'Your brother and I did not have time to discuss it. I have no doubt your brother will be fair when the time comes. Until my banker tells me it is there, Lottie, I have no wish to borrow against it. It is a good way to end up in Newgate or one of the other debtors' prisons.'

Lottie put her hand to her head. Her stomach reeled. Debtors' prison. The workhouse. She busied her hands with retrieving the thin blanket. Tried to concentrate on breathing. She could not borrow trouble. 'Have you been in one before?'

'Yes.'

The single word fell between them. Lottie put her hand to her mouth and tried to prevent the gasp. A debtors' prison. Her husband. There should be some polite remark to cover the incident, but her mind failed her. 'You have been? Were you there long? Was it as awful as they say?'

Tristan became made out of stone. Then his eyes creased and he stroked her hair, a simple touch, but comforting. Lottie resisted the urge to turn her face to his palm and rest her head.

'I was visiting a friend who had fallen on hard times. It is far from a pleasant place, Lottie.'

'You mustn't tease me like that.' Lottie released a breath and offered up a small prayer. Her husband wasn't a feckless fortune hunter. He had gone to visit a friend.

'You should believe better of me.'

'Why?' Lottie bowed her head. 'Why should I?'

'Because…I am your husband.'

'Trust is something that is earned.' She clasped her hands together. Her heart pounded in her ears. Tristan had to understand. She enjoyed expensive things, but she also understood the value of money and how quickly wealth could be lost. 'I have learnt to be cautious. Far too many men see a wealthy woman as a way to end their debts and continue with their debauched lifestyle. A debutante rapidly learns or faces the consequences.'

'You were not cautious the other night.'

'That was different.' She waved her hand. 'Other considerations were in the forefront of my mind.'

'And now you find out what I am like.' He rubbed his thumb against her mouth, a featherlight movement that sent ripples of sensation flickering throughout her body. 'I will be beholden to no man, Lottie.'

'I have some money. We can send a message to Henry…'

'I have no use for your money. Charity is nothing I have ever looked for.'

'Being proud is one thing, but this is different. I am your wife.'

'You just gave me a lecture about imprudent husbands and fortune hunters.'

'But there are certain standards one must maintain.'

'Must one?' He raised an eyebrow.

'Yes.' Lottie heard the desperation in her voice. He had to give in. He had to see. 'It must be miles to Gortner Hall. Days. Days we would waste if we walked.'

'I have enough to get us back to Gortner Hall.' His eyes were cold. 'We will take the parliamentary trains. There is a connection at Carlisle. We can get off at Hexham and catch the coach. I purchased two tickets yesterday. I thought it best to be prepared.'

A parliamentary train. One of the trains Gladstone had ordered to be run along each railway line once a day and stopping at all the stations. Lottie's heart sunk.

'But it is so slow, little faster than a stage coach, and it is all third class. All wooden benches and a tin roof.' The words escaped from Lottie's mouth. She winced as a muscle in his jaw leapt. 'Surely we can take the express. How much more expensive is it?'

'There is nothing wrong with being ordinary, Lottie. Keep your money for when it is truly needed.' He pushed the reticule away, but tugged her towards him. Her unresisting body fell into his as his arms went around her. 'It is about time you realised this. You married me. You did not marry someone like Sir Geoffrey who maintains a private railcar for his journeys. The parliamentary train with all its stops will get us there in good time.'

'I never wanted to marry him. Ever. He was old, older than Mama.' Lottie gave into temptation and placed her head against his shirt front, listened to the steady thumping of his heart. 'That was my mother's desire.'

'And what was your desire?' His fingers tilted her chin upwards and she wanted to drown in the warm pools that were his eyes. Lottie felt a tide of heat wash through her body. 'Shall we find time to explore it?'

His lips touched the corner of her mouth, one tantalizing touch. Soft. Calling to her. She lifted her arms, placed them around his neck. Held him.

Somewhere far away heavy footsteps pounded on the stair, recalling her to where they were and what might happen if she was not careful.

'It appears that I have already explored it. I followed my desire rather than my mother's. I married you.' Lottie pushed herself away from his body. She forced her legs to carry her to where she had neatly placed her clothes last night. She rolled up her stockings, slipped on her petticoats and finally held out the corset. All she would need was to be entangled in Tristan's arms and for the door to come crashing in. For the parish constable to be standing there. She had had enough embarrassment for one week.

'Was that all you wanted—to be married to a young man?'

Lottie ignored the comment and concentrated on tying the drawstring of her petticoats. 'It would appear you will have to help me to dress if we are to leave this room and to catch the parliamentary. And I shall pack away two of my petticoats as there is bound to be little enough space on the parliamentary.'

Tristan stood very still, but his eyes burnt with a fire as if he had watched every movement and memorised it. Lottie felt the tide of a blush wash up her cheeks as she remembered some of the illustrations from *Aristotle's Complete Master Piece*. Did men like to watch women dress?

'I am only doing this because we have an innkeeper breathing down our necks.' Tristan gave the back of her neck a kiss before he rapidly laced up the corset. A warm glow infused through Lottie. It would be easy to turn and to be in his arms again. 'I would far rather spend the morning with you in this room.'

'You should pull the corset tighter.' Lottie took a deep breath in. If she concentrated, these ripples of sensation would fade.

'You will do yourself injury.'

'What is a little pain compared to fashion?' She gave a laugh. 'I thought you liked my narrow waist. I felt your hand on it when we danced. It is one of my best features.'

'What is fashion compared with pain? We are at an impasse, Lottie, and as I have to lace you, the corset will stay loose.' His fingers spanned her waist. 'Your waist is small enough.'

'When I get my new lady's maid…'

'If you get her—who knows, you might enjoy my services.' His breath tickled her ear.

A shiver went down Lottie's back as his voice held her. The temptation to lean backwards into him nearly over-powered her. Instead she pulled her dress over her head and stood while his firm fingers fastened up the back. When he had finished, his fingers trailed along her collar-bone. She held herself stiffly, refusing to give in to the sensation. 'The parliamentary.'

'I see you are determined to catch this train.'

'The innkeeper is determined to be rid of us and you delight in teasing me.'

'That much is true.'

'And if we miss this train, we will have to wait for the next one. We don't have the money for that.'

Tristan looked at her with hooded eyes. 'Do you know how much money I have, Lottie?'

Lottie drew a deep breath. She knew when she could not change things. She would have to make the best of it. Just as she had at Christmas when she was sent away or last birthday when she had been given a set of improving poems rather than the tortoiseshell combs she had longed for.

'If we must go, it is better to go now,' she said brightly. 'And who knows, I might enjoy the parliamentary. I have never been on one before. When I went to Haydon Bridge, I took the express.'

'The parliamentary is an experience.'

'My only wonder is how you managed to stay at Shaw's. My brother was at pains to point out the expense to my mother and me. Several times in the course of the afternoon and at least once more at supper.'

'Ah, Lord Thorngrafton managed that.' Tristan's eyes slid away from her. 'The suite was rented in his name.'

'But you are unkind about your cousin.' Lottie clasped her hands. Tristan had to lose his unreasonable prejudice towards his cousin. 'He obviously wanted to promote you in society. He had no cause to befriend you.'

'This much is true. My cousin did appear rather put out that I had arrived. He thought me safely on the Continent, lost for all eternity, never to set foot in England again.'

Lottie wrinkled her nose. 'You really must refrain from disparaging him. It would be dreadful if it were ever reported back. He…he even gave me money.'

'Why would he do that?' Tristan stilled. A watchfulness came about him.

'In case I changed my mind—at least, that is what his coachman said when he handed me the bank note.'

'The coachman told you this.' Tristan's voice was ice cold. 'What else did he tell you? What did Lord Thorngrafton want from you? What was the payment to be?'

'He did not inform me.' Lottie kept her head up. How could she tell Tristan that Lord Thorngrafton had thought his own cousin would abandon her? How could she divide the two further when she knew how important it was that they have good relations with him? She gave a laugh that sounded more like fingernails grating on a slate. 'Perhaps he entertained notions of me becoming his mistress in gratitude. His intentions were far from honourable last autumn. I know this. A woman can tell.'

'And you thought my intentions were honourable at Shaw's? Was that why you went out on the terrace with me?'

'I didn't think at all.' Lottie knew she had to be truthful. She could not lie to Tristan about that. 'For the first time in my life, I forgot to think about the consequences.' She paused and continued in a very small voice, 'If I had, perhaps we would not be here.'

'Perhaps.' Tristan reached down and picked up the satchel. He paused, his back towards her. 'Would you become Lord Thorngrafton's mistress? He has the reputation of being an excellent lover. The life of a mistress can be exciting to some women.'

'How can you say such things! I am your wife!'

'Lord Thorngrafton is…unique,' Tristan replied. 'Some women are entranced by a title.'

'All the more reason for not antagonising him. But rest assured that had I wanted that outcome, I would not have waited until now…until after my marriage to his cousin.'

Lottie reached for her bonnet and fastened it with expert fingers. She attempted a bright smile, but inside her blood boiled. Lord Thorngrafton held no attraction for her. The only man who had ever made her melt was standing before her, being annoying. It was as if his touch had been infected with some loving disease and all she could crave was another touch of his hand, another smile. These things had become necessary to her. And she would die before she ever admitted it. Before she would admit his failure to come to her bed last night until after she was sound asleep had hurt.

'Why did you tell me now about the money? Why didn't you tell me earlier?'

'I was ashamed.' Lottie twisted the iron ring about her finger. 'I thought you might think that I had no faith in you. That I had begged him for the money and was planning on running away at the earliest opportunity.'

'And why did you tell me just now?'

Lottie turned her head. She couldn't confess her reasons, not to him. They were too new and raw. She could not risk his mockery. 'Shall we depart? There is only one parliamentary per day.'

'You are a puzzle, Lottie Dyvelston. I would have expected you to be in tears.'

'Some things I can change, and others I can't. It is up to me to know the difference, as my old nurse used to say.' Lottie glanced back at the pillow, grateful that, after her sleep, her eyes betrayed no sign of redness. It would not do to have Tristan know that she had shed tears over him on their wedding night.

Lottie gave one last look at the mean room. There was nothing except the rumpled bedclothes to show they had ever been there. She was a married woman. She had spent a night with her husband, the first of many to come. But now she had to face the parliamentary and her fellow passengers.

Chapter Eight

Everyone crowded towards the doors when the parliamentary arrived in Carlisle, pushing past and not really caring that others might want to get off. A rather large lady elbowed Lottie in the ribs with a basket and then glared at her as she started to protest.

Lottie stepped gingerly down from the train, one of the last to disembark. Her bottom ached from the short time she had spent on the overcrowded wooden benches. She had carefully kept her skirts away from the other passengers and had declined any overtures from their fellow passengers.

'How long do we have to wait?' she asked Tristan as, with a great roar, the train chugged away, leaving them standing on the platform. She fumbled for her one remaining handkerchief. She regarded the soot-spotted cloth with distaste and put it back in her reticule.

'About two hours,' he said, checking his fob watch. 'The parliamentary to Newcastle leaves quite late in the day.'

'Isn't there a train before then?'

'Not a parliamentary.' Tristan gave her a dark look.

Lottie straightened her shoulders and took a breath. She would be dignified. 'What will happen when we get to Hexham?'

'We will find transport somehow. There has been talk of building a railway up the North Tyne, but nothing has come of it yet. There are still many more profitable places to build.'

'Then we shall have to hope there is transport.'

'I did send a letter to the hall. There should be transport waiting for us.'

'A carriage?' Lottie sent up a prayer for a well-sprung carriage, one like Lord Thorngrafton's with deep seats and a roof to keep the rain out. Not a bone-shaking pony cart that was exposed to the changeable English summer weather like the one she'd had to use at Aunt Alice's.

'Whatever Mrs Elton can arrange. It won't be the last word in luxury.'

Lottie mentally whispered goodbye to the carriage. She had to think positively—it could be worse. She had to believe in the word—transport. She lifted her chin. 'As long as I don't have to walk, I will be fine.'

'I will do my best.' Tristan put his hand under her elbow and led her to the third-class waiting room. It did not have the armchairs or the fire that the first-class waiting room did, but it was clean and neat. Respectable, but barely. 'You may wait here, if you like.'

'Where are you going?' Lottie fought to keep the note of panic from her voice.

'I am going to try to find a newspaper. W. H. Smith recently started a newspaper train to Carlisle and I would like to have a look at one of the London papers.' His eyes crinkled at the corners. 'Can I trust you to stay here in the train station? Unless you would like to tramp around the streets of Carlisle with me?'

'You pointed out before, my dress is not made for walking.' Lottie gave a shiver. She had no wish to be stared at from carriages. What if she encountered someone she knew? How they would all laugh at her. Lottie Charlton… Dyvelston, not dressed properly. She could not take the humiliation.

'If that is what you want…'

'I have learnt my lesson.' Lottie looked around the small waiting room. Several men in ill-fitting frock coats and tight collars sat reading papers, and in a corner some children played a game of marbles. Peaceful. 'It appears to be safe enough. I want to rest for a little while.'

The pads of his fingers brushed her chin, a featherlight touch, but one that stilled her, left her longing for more. 'I will keep you safe. Trust me on this.'

'You earned my trust yesterday,' Lottie whispered back. Her mouth ached for his kiss. The heat began to rise on her cheek at the boldness of her thought. Even thinking about kissing her husband in public showed how wanton and wicked she was becoming.

'Thank you for that.' He raised her gloved hand to his lips and was gone.

Lottie pressed the glove against her mouth and stared after him. Her whole body tingled, remembering what it was like to wake up in his arms. Tonight, surely, he would find time for her and she would be able to control her passion. He would not be disgusted with her behaviour again. She would not give him any excuse to leave her.

She settled down on one of the vacant benches to wait. She smoothed her dress and winced slightly at the stains and mud that were now engrained on it. No one would ever think that it was this season's silk paisley. It far more closely resembled a cast-off to a second housemaid. She gave a wry smile. At least no one would say that she shouldn't be in the third-class waiting room.

The time dragged and she began to amuse herself by making up little stories about her fellow passengers. Anything to keep her mind off Tristan and the shape of his mouth. It seemed impossible how important he had become to her already. And he was a good man. Against the odds, she had found a man who was honest and true.

'Pretty lady, can you help?' A hand tugged at her skirt. A young girl about eight stood there. Her young brother clung to her hand and regarded Lottie with big eyes in a tear-streaked face. 'Our nurse is missing.'

'I am not sure if I can do anything.'

'Please, miss, please help. You have a kind face. We are lost.'

Lottie regarded the children. Their clothes were well made but dirty and the little boy's trousers had a rip in one knee. Tracks of tears showed on the girl's face. And the boy's face was smudged with coal dust and mud as if they had scrambled about the railway yard.

'I will do what I can.' Lottie looked towards the door and wished Tristan would arrive back. 'What does she look like? And where did you lose her?'

Both children began to talk at once, chattering about this and that and how they were chased. Lottie held a finger to her lips, waiting until they fell silent. 'Please, I will help. We shall have to find the stationmaster. He is probably in the first-class waiting room. I am sure your nurse is looking for you both right now.'

'A guard told us that we couldn't go there. He called us urchins. Chased us away. And a bad man came and tried to capture us.' A single tear ran down the girl's face.

'He was going to take us away and put us in a pie,' the

little boy said. 'And I would never see Nurse or Mama or Papa again.'

'Hush, Charley.'

'But you said, Verbena. It is why we hid in the coal pile,' the boy protested.

Lottie shifted uneasily. She remembered all too clearly her experience yesterday. There were other worse things that could happen to children. She regarded the door and willed Tristan to return, but the doorway was vacant. She pressed her hands to her mouth, thinking. She had to do something. 'I will do the best that I can to reunite you with your nurse. She will be looking for you on the platform. I am sure she will.'

The children's faces cleared and the boy shyly placed a kiss on her glove. 'Thank you, pretty lady.'

'First shall we clean your faces? Make you more presentable?'

'Please, we have lost our handkerchiefs.'

Lottie took out her handkerchief and began to wipe the coal from the boy's chin. He gave a grateful smile. She handed it to his sister, who scrubbed her face before holding it out.

'Keep it. You have greater need than I do.'

She took the pair by the hands and began to look. The nurse would be frantically searching. No doubt she would discover her or someone else on the platform.

Except for a pile of luggage and a porter, the platform was empty. Lottie stamped her foot in frustration and wished she had waited for Tristan. She had to think clearly.

It was possible she had made a mistake and that perhaps the children were meant for the first-class lounge and had become confused. The nurse might have fallen asleep and the children wandered away. It had been known to happen.

She had done it once as a little girl and had been discovered crying in a livery stable.

She lifted her head and turned the knob and took the children in. A steward with a disdainful look blocked her way. He curled his lip as he looked her and the children up and down.

'Here, what are you doing with those filthy children? You are only allowed in this here room if you are a first-class passenger. I will need to see your tickets.' The steward's expression indicated that he doubted Lottie or the children would possess such a thing.

'I am looking for their nurse,' Lottie answered. 'They may have become confused and entered the third-class waiting room by mistake.'

The steward began a long lecture about the rules and regulations of the railway company and how she would have to comply. Lottie resisted the temptation to roll her eyes heavenwards. Did she look like riff-raff? At that moment, a soberly dressed elderly woman with a worried expression came up with the stationmaster. When the children saw her, they gave a glad cry and rushed into her arms.

'Bless you, my dear,' the woman said to Lottie. 'I have searched everywhere for them. They are a pair of scamps. I only took my eyes off them for an instant and they were gone. Vanished into thin air. Their mother would have been beside herself with worry. She suffers dreadfully from her nerves.'

A lump grew in Lottie's throat as the children began to talk at once. Tristan would understand why she had left the waiting room, she was sure of it. The children were so delighted to be reunited with their nurse.

'It was my pleasure,' she said when the children had finished telling their tale.

'Would you like something for your trouble?' The woman reached into her reticule.

'Nothing, thank you.' Lottie kept her back straight. No one had ever offered her money before. She had only done a good deed. 'The children's smiles are enough reward.'

'If you are sure…' The nurse held out a coin. 'You have saved my job. I shouldn't like to think what would be said.'

'Quite sure. It was my pleasure and I believe the pair have learnt their lesson.'

The two children nodded vigorously.

'If you insist, but…' The woman shook her head. 'The master won't like it. Nor will my lady. They like to help those less fortunate than themselves.'

'I do insist.' Lottie turned on her heel and started back towards the door. With any luck, Tristan would not have returned and she could explain the story with a light laugh. She intended on leaving out the bit about the offer of payment. There was no need for Tristan to know about that. She knew she had done the correct thing. She stubbed her toe on the edge of the carpet and nearly fell.

'I am so sorry,' she said. 'I was thinking about other things.'

A fashionably dressed mother and daughter drew their skirts back as if she might contaminate them. Lottie's heart lurched. The pair could have been her own mother and her six months ago—wrapped up in their own self-importance, blind to the world around them. She wondered if those two had even seen the children and thought to stop them.

She gave her head a slight shake. The blindness and stupidity of people. A cold shiver ran down her back—how many things had she failed to see? How many things had she missed because she was too busy looking towards the best social advantage? Thankfully this time she had noticed. She shuddered and kept on walking.

'The nerve of some people, Mama.' The younger of the pair waved her fan. 'Some people think they own the railway and the station.'

'They don't know their place, dear,' the mother replied in a strident tone. 'This waiting room is supposed to be for gentle folk. Such a display of ill breeding.'

'I doubt you would know any,' Lottie muttered under her breath.

'Were you speaking to my daughter and me?' The elder of the women looked Lottie up and down. 'You should know how to speak to your betters.'

'I do and when I meet them, I shall.' Lottie lifted her chin and prepared to glide pass. There were shocked gasps from the women and a crowd began to gather around.

'Do you know who I am?' The woman had the same imperious tone that Lottie's mother used when confronted by a hostile shopkeeper.

'Does it matter? The children in question have been reunited with their nurse.' Lottie's stomach churned. Her right to be in a first-class waiting room had never been questioned before. Couldn't people tell?

'And did you know how handsome the reward would be?'

'I guessed.' Lottie gave her best social smile. 'It was very easy to work out that the children were well cared for and would be missed.'

'Shocking! She probably stole the children herself. I wouldn't put it past her,' a portly gentleman pronounced, leaning over to the two women. The elderly woman gave a smile of smug satisfaction as if she knew of her own superiority. 'The steward should be informed.'

'Yes, call the steward, Mama. I wonder I hadn't thought of that. Some people like to give themselves airs and graces. There ought to be a law.'

Lottie stared at the growing throng of unfriendly faces, all looking down their noses at her. Surely they saw her refuse the money. Surely they knew she had brought the children back out of the goodness of her heart.

'I meant their smiles and tears of joy at being reunited with their nurse. Anyone but a simpleton would know that.' Lottie tilted her head higher, ignored the steward who was steadily advancing towards her with a gleam in his piggy eyes. 'If you will excuse me, please, I believe the air is fresher in the third-class waiting room.'

She stumbled out of the first-class waiting room. Her hands were trembling as she leant against the wall and tried to collect her thoughts.

How could people be that cruel?

She put her hand over her mouth and refused to cry. Everything she did was misinterpreted. She straightened her shoulders and resolved never to behave in such a fashion herself.

When she had nearly reached the third-class waiting room, she saw Tristan striding toward her, a newspaper folded under his arm. His eyebrows were drawn together and a look like thunder was on his face. 'You have come from the first-class waiting room. Do not try to deny it. I saw the direction you scurried from.'

'Before you jump to conclusions,' Lottie said, holding up her hand, stopping his words, 'There was a very good reason for me being in there.'

'I have little doubt that you think you had a good reason for being there.' He raised an eyebrow. 'What explanation are you going to give? Were you looking for a comfort-able place to sit? Somewhere where you did not have to mix with the ordinary people.'

Lottie's heart sank and she straightened the folds of her gown before answering. The irony of the situation did not escape her. She cleared her throat. 'Don't you dare try to tell me that I don't belong there. I have had quite enough of that today already. The steward protested in the stron-gest terms when I first went in.'

'Did you go there to prove a point?' He tapped the news-paper against his hand. 'I told you what would happen.'

'To reunite some children with their nurse,' Lottie said through gritted teeth. Then at the slight relaxation of his mouth, she quickly explained the story. Tristan listened, nodding at several points. 'And the passengers were truly horrible,' Lottie said as she finished the tale. 'I shall be pleased to return to third class.'

'What did they do to you?'

'They made it seem like I didn't know my place. The nurse even offered me some money as reward.' Lottie blinked back tears. 'Money? Me? I refused it, of course.'

Tristan put his arm around her and she drew strength from him. 'Some people only pay attention to what is on the outside.'

'But even if my gown is muddy and creased, I look pre-sentable.' Lottie gave a huge sniff. 'It is only a few months old and the cut is highly fashionable.'

He took her chin between his fingers and raised it. 'You look presentable to me, if slightly creased. Do you want to sit in the first-class waiting room? Shall I go and make arrangements? It can be done.'

Lottie shook her head. 'Not now, not when I know what snobs populate it.'

'You have good intentions, Lottie. You did the right thing.'

'I know, but why do they always turn out to be wrong?'

'It is nearly time to board the train, Lottie. Forget about it. They are not important.'

Lottie rested her hand on his arm. 'But they were awful.'

'Now do you see what pride can do to people?' he asked and she could see a strange light burning in his eyes.

'I have never behaved like that.'

'Are you certain?'

Lottie paused. From now, she would make the effort to see the people about her and speak pleasantly without first deciding what their social status was. Her lesson had been a hard one. She would do things because they were right. But she could not explain this to Tristan. He might consider her a monster. And she wasn't that. 'No, never to my knowledge. At least, I hope I haven't.'

Chapter Nine

Tristan surveyed the Hexham railway yard with a frown. He had expected Mrs Elton to send one of the tenant farmers out with a pony cart. Not the lap of luxury, but something.

There was nothing there except a few broken-down farm carts. And Mrs Elton would not have sent one of those. They would take far too long to get to the Hall. He cursed under his breath. There was no use second-guessing the reason. He would have to adapt and cope.

'Is there something wrong, Tristan?' Lottie broke off her farewells with a farmer's widow. 'Something is amiss. I can see it in your face. The train was a half-hour late, but there's nothing we could do about that.'

'It would appear that my earlier presumption was wrong. There is no transport waiting for us. Curious, Mrs Elton is generally very efficient.'

'Perhaps the innkeeper did not send your letter. I did not trust him.'

'That is certainly one explanation.' Tristan scanned the rapidly emptying yard again, but no pony cart or convey-ance magically appeared. And he had no intention of standing about, hoping that one would. 'We shall have to see if the livery stables are open. They will have a carriage for hire. I would like to get to Gortner before nightfall.'

'But won't that be expensive?'

Tristan tilted his head. Lottie had changed since this morning. She made an effort to speak to the people about her and had entertained several children with songs on their journey from Carlisle. How much was show and how much was a true change, he was not certain, but something had happened to her. He knew his plan was working. She was starting to think about others. 'Do you have a better alternative?'

'Mrs Foster's brother is a farmer. He is picking her up. He has the cart with the two white oxen.' Lottie gestured towards the widow, who gave a large beaming smile and waved back. 'Mrs Foster has offered us a place in her brother's cart. They can drop us off at the crossroads to Gortner Hall, if we like. She says it is not a far walk, a country mile or two only. And two more in the back of the cart will not make a pennyworth's of difference. I thought it best to enquire about how one proceeded up the North Tyne Valley as you appeared so vague about it.'

'I am never vague.' Tristan crossed his arms. Irritated. Lottie did not trust his ability. And Mrs Foster had her distances wrong. Gortner Hall was nearly five miles from the Wark crossroads. 'The livery stables will be able to provide something.'

'It is what ordinary people do. Do you think I am so frail that I cannot make the journey?' Lottie adjusted her bonnet. 'A mile or two is nothing to me.'

'It is more than—' Tristan stopped. Lottie wanted to do this. He would let her. It would be a good experience for her. A reinforcement of the lesson. Sometimes, one had to milk the opportunity.

'Don't be mulish, Tristan. I am saving us money.' Her lips turned up in the sweetest smile. 'Tristan, I am being ordinary.'

'Very well, Lottie, if you wish to ride in a farm cart that badly, we will. Go ahead, arrange it.'

'Way aye, it will be a right pleasure, sir,' the plump woman said, coming over. 'Your good wife and I have been exchanging recipes on making jam and chutney. She has some right interesting ideas, like. Elderflower and gooseberry. I had never thought of it, but they would go well together in jam.'

'Indeed?'

'I have always enjoyed helping out in the still room. It is one of my enthusiasms. The still room is a right and proper place for a lady.' Lottie's eyes glowed. 'I found a kindred spirit in Mrs Foster while you took refuge behind your newspaper. She likes to preserve fruit and vegetables. She even told me the best way to make sugared violets. It is a much simpler way than Lucy makes hers.'

'Your abilities never cease to surprise me.'

'I am resigned to my fate now.' Lottie smiled up at him. 'And it will be quite amusing to be the wife of a local landowner.'

Tristan tilted his head, considering the possibilities. Resigned to her fate. A form of words or the truth? Did Lottie know what she was asking? Was it a ploy because she knew he would refuse the gesture and then she would be able to insist on using her money to hire a more expensive carriage? He would play along. Nothing serious would happen and Lottie would learn to listen to him. Mrs Foster led the way to a hay cart where her brother greeted them with a genial wave and readily agreed to take them to the Gortner Hall crossroads. Tristan heard the muttered gasp beside him and the slight hesitation. Then Lottie squared her shoulders, climbed into the cart and patted the hay beside her. Her once pristine dress became covered in wisps of straw, but she appeared not to mind. 'Are you coming, Tristan? It will be fun. And you did mention haystacks earlier.'

'To sleep in, not to ride on.'

'As long as it gets us where we are going, I don't mind.'

He gave an inward smile of satisfaction. He doubted if Lottie had ever ridden in a cart for as long as she would have to today.

'Is the condition of the hall as bad as Mrs Foster says?' Lottie asked as the cart began to move.

'Much worse,' Tristan answered firmly.

'He would know, but I know my late husband—God rest his soul—said that all that estate needed was someone to love it,' Mrs Foster said over her shoulder. 'Mr Foster hated what had happened to it. Once, it was Lord Thorngrafton's seat. The way the old lord treated it after…'

'I think we had best be making a move, if you want to get to Wark before nightfall,' Tristan said, not letting Mrs Foster finish. Lottie did not need to hear the exact details of the scandal from a stranger. She already knew the bare bones, but he would tell her everything in his own time.

'Allow me to help you down.'

Lottie gratefully grasped Tristan's outstretched hand as she clambered down from the farmer's cart. The cart journey had been much rougher and had taken far longer than she had at first supposed. Every muscle in her body ached and at one point she had been sure that her teeth would be shaken loose. Mrs Foster and her brother raised their hands in farewell and started on their way again, seemingly unaffected by the bone-jarring awfulness that was the farm cart.

'I could have done it myself.' Lottie straightened the folds of her dress, picking out bits of straw and hay. Her heart sank as she regarded the windswept crossroads. 'How far is Gortner Hall from here? Mrs Foster said that it would not take very long to walk.'

'Miles. I did try to warn you, Lottie.' Tristan pointed down the desolate crossroad with not a house or horse and cart in sight. 'But you insisted that we accept this lift. It would have been churlish of me to refuse, as you quite rightly pointed out, since the lift was free.'

Lottie swallowed hard. Not even a lone farmhouse where they could beg a cup of tea stood there. It was simply the wild Northumberland moors. Even though it was late May, the wind whistled from the north. Lottie wrapped her pelisse tighter about her and wished the paisley silk had been made of heavier cloth.

Lottie watched the faint dust of the cart with a sinking heart. 'How long will the walk be?'

'Five miles, an hour or two.'

'An hour of walking?' Lottie looked down at her daintily shod foot. She had been so proud of these slippers with their bright blue ribbons when she had purchased them at Bainbridge's in Newcastle last autumn and now they would be in shreds. She should have insisted on buying boots in Gretna Green or Carlisle, on spending Lord Thorngrafton's money, but she hadn't thought beyond the train. 'Surely you must be wrong…Mrs Foster assured me…a country mile.'

'You were the one who insisted on taking up Mrs Foster's offer,' Tristan replied firmly. 'Mrs Foster is a country woman and her notion of distance is somewhat different from yours or mine. I tried to tell you differently, to hire a conveyance, but you chose to believe a stranger.'

'I am not dressed for walking. Something you pointed out to me. Only yesterday.' Lottie fought the temptation to wail. She tilted her chin and glared at his deep black eyes. 'Mama will undoubtedly send several trunks with my clothes and other items from my hope chest eventually, but I was under the impression I was eloping, not marching through the moors.'

The corner of his mouth twitched. 'Are different clothes required? I doubt we will meet anyone along this country lane and, if we do, they will forgive your strange attire.'

'I fail to see what is so funny. Nobody ever instructed me in the proper wear for an elopement. It failed to be included in my social deportment classes.' Lottie started off down the nearest track, tired of arguing with him, tired of being teased. She had been so proud of her coup, of finding a way to save money and it had all gone wrong. She had thought he might pet her and look after her, but he clearly expected her to stand on her own two feet, feet that would be blistered and torn. 'If we are going, I suppose I best begin. Each step is going to take me closer.'

'Are you often like that?'

'If I can't change things, I can make the best of them. Or at least try to. A lady should never show her distress.'

'Do you always live your life through rules?' His eyes danced.

'I like to know which rule I am breaking. It makes it much easier to live up to people's expectations.' Lottie kept her head high. He would be laughing at her now. He seemed to think this whole predicament was a big joke. He was not the person who would be suffering. 'Five miles, you say, and probably not even a cup of hot tea at the end.'

Tristan's hand closed around her upper arm, hauled her back against his hard body. His breath tickled her ear. She stilled as a wave of warmth washed over her. She swallowed hard and tried to concentrate on something other than his mouth or the way his eyebrows arched, but her mind refused to work.

'If you want to go marching off to the Hall, you might enquire the direction. Go that way, and you will only increase the distance.'

Lottie fought against the urge to relax into him and to feel the hard leanness of his body against hers once. All the way in the farm cart, he had sat next to her, his leg brushing hers. Her body tingled with awareness, with the memory of how it had felt to wake in his arms. 'Why didn't anyone come to meet us? This whole thing could have been avoided.'

Her hand lifted up and touched his cheek. He turned his face slightly, brushing her glove with his lips.

'I don't know. There was no time to get a reply to yesterday's letter. If one of the tenants was sent out and preferred to go drinking in the Railway Arms or the County, there will be hell to pay.' His hand moved up to her shoulder, stroked the sensitive skin under her chin, made her lean forwards until their breath intermingled. 'A lady—Mrs Elton does look after the Hall. She will have obeyed my request. It is not a complete ruin.'

'So we will have a roof over our heads.' Lottie glanced up at the sky. All day the grey clouds had rolled in. There was a faint chill in the late afternoon sun that foretold of rain before daybreak.

'A roof over our heads and a cup of hot tea for those who

require it. Or perhaps something stronger.' His hand stroked down her shoulders until his fingers intertwined with hers. 'And a soft bed with clean sheets, lots of pillows and bed curtains to shut out the world.'

'It sounds heavenly.' Lottie concentrated on breathing. Each breath she took, she inhaled more of his spicy scent, which was intermingled with the fresh scent of the hay, an intoxicating aroma that swirled around her and held her fast. Her lips tingled as if he had kissed her. She wanted to be brazen and demand that he kiss her—out here in the open where anyone could spy them.

'Will you come with me? Some day, I promise I will get you a new dress, one far more suited to walking than that one, if you are good.'

'And you always keep your promises.'

'To the best of my ability.' He stood perfectly still, and his hands fell away from her. 'Will you come and be my bride, despite the inappropriateness of your attire?'

Lottie tried for a frown, but the corners of her mouth twitched and a great bubble of happiness burst through her. He did want her for his bride. She glanced up and saw the echoing twitch of his mouth. Their shared laughter rang out and caused several woodpigeons to take off with a noisy clap of wings.

'It would appear I am stuck with you,' she said with a catch in her throat.

'It would appear to be the case.'

He drew her unresisting body to him and lowered his head so that their foreheads brushed. The ribbons of her bonnet loosened and then fell away as he pressed butterfly kisses on her eyelids, her cheeks, the tip of her nose; finally he claimed her lips. Her arms came up and held him there. The nature of the kiss changed and he demanded more, demanded entrance. She opened and tasted the cool inner recesses of him. Molten heat ran through her, causing her body to arch and her breasts to tighten. She pressed closer, wanting, needing something, something only he could give.

'Would you settle for a haystack instead of the bed?' he said against her lips. 'You and I together with the stars for a coverlet.'

'You promised the bed.' Her voice was a raw, husky sound that she barely recognised. The hot pulsating feeling frightened her a little. 'You always keep your promises.'

His eyes searched her face with a dark intensity. She took a half-step backward. 'A bed. My wife insists on a bed.'

'A bed with clean sheets and curtains.'

'It might be possible…if you truly require it.' His thumb traced the outline of her swollen lips, sending fresh waves of molten heat through out her body. She was grateful for the steel bones of her corset as they were the only thing that kept her upright.

'You knocked my bonnet off and it is lying in a puddle,' she said to dampen down her desire.

'Awkward things, bonnets.' A smile tugged at Tristan's features.

Lottie picked up the mud-soaked straw bonnet, held it gingerly away from her body as it dripped. A sense of despair swept through her. The bonnet seemed to echo her current state—once pristine and perfect, but now grubby, soiled without hope of redemption. 'I can't wear that. Even the ribbons will be stained beyond repair. I will have to purchase a new one. This one cost me three guineas.'

'The money is needed elsewhere. You must have other bonnets.'

'It will be days before they reach here, and my nose will freckle before then. I have worked so hard to keep my complexion perfect.'

'You will look sweet with a spray of freckles.' His fingers brushed the bridge of her nose.

'Flattery will not save you. And the thought fails to make me feel better.'

'Isn't that better than trying to make you feel worse?' Tristan picked up her satchel and tied the ruined bonnet to the outside handle. 'I will examine your hat tomorrow. It may not be as bad as you think.'

'It will be worse. Mud-stained straw cannot simply be covered by retrimming. I know hats and their awkward ways.'

'We should go, Lottie. There will not be a horse and cart trundling along here, if that is why you kissed me.'

'It is not why I kissed you.' Lottie stared at him. How could he think that of her? She had been certain no one would see. She was far from being brazen or wanton. She knew that. 'I have lived in the country for the past few months. I know about country roads and how few people travel them. That could take days.'

'Why did you kiss me?'

A tide of heat washed up her face and Lottie turned on her heel. 'You are an impossible man.'

'That is no answer.'

She fluttered her eyelashes. 'So you would carry my satchel.'

Tristan set the satchel down. 'And if I refuse to carry it any further?'

'Are you asking for another kiss?' Lottie's insides trembled. Always before she had been able to play the flirtation games, but suddenly they seemed to matter. She wanted them to matter and to be about more than bandying words. 'I won't be held to bribery.'

'Then I won't be held to carrying this.' Tristan set it down.

'We send a cart for it when we get to the hall. In fact, you could go to the Hall and send back a cart for both the satchel and me.'

'A cart could take days to arrange and you will want to sample Mrs Elton's fruit cake.'

'Mrs Elton?'

'The widow who has been looking after everything for me.'

'Then she can help with my dressing.' Lottie's back became straighter. Maybe it would not be so bad. If Tristan touched her again, she knew she would melt and she was determined to show the proper amount of wifely devotion. Devotion, not passion. There was a difference.

'No, Mrs Elton will be leaving. There is little need to employ a housekeeper at the hall when I have acquired a wife who wishes to wear expensive bonnets.'

'Mama has a housekeeper. She has had a succession of them.'

'Does your mother have a hard time keeping servants?'

'Sometimes,' Lottie said with reluctance. 'She has the tendency to hire the wrong sort.'

'Rather than hiring the wrong sort, you can learn. My mother was always her own housekeeper.'

Lottie stared at him in disbelief. Learn housekeeping? This marriage had brought many unintended changes. 'It will be a change from making patterns with pins.'

He laughed. 'Were you exceptionally fond of pinning?'

'I loathed and detested it,' Lottie said without hesitation. 'It is one of those things I did because it was expected of me.'

'Then it is best to give it up immediately. I will have no pincushion mottos at Gortner Hall.'

'Will I have no help at all? Will I have to do everything? Although I can do preserves, chutneys and jams, I am no cook. I have burnt cakes before.'

Tristan caught her hand and raised it to his lips. 'Ah, Lottie, you do say the sweetest things. If you look at me like that, I am sure I will not beat you for burning cakes.'

'Would you beat me?' Lottie hated the way her voice squeaked. She had never taken Tristan for a wife beater. Had she truly mistaken the man she had married? However, the instant she said the words, his brow darkened.

'No, and neither do I whip or indulge in any such behaviour. Although I know some consider it acceptable, I think men who resort to such measures are cowards, and I am no coward!'

'I never said you were.' A weight rolled off her back. He did not beat women. The words were said purely in jest. There was so much that they did not know about each other. So much she had to learn.

His face suddenly cleared, like the sun coming out after a thunderstorm, warming her all over. 'But what I will do is help you with your corset. I am determined to play a good lady's maid.'

A delicious shiver went through Lottie. She wanted to feel his hands on her, undressing her. A tide of fire burnt within her. She tried to hang on to her mother's words about a wife being respectable. She was his wife, not a courtesan or a mistress.

'I believe we were on our way to Gortner Hall,' she said. 'I would like to get there before it gets too dark.'

'As you wish.'

Chapter Ten

Tristan regarded the darkened house with a frown. The Gothic towers that his grandfather had installed gleamed silver against the night sky. Quite near them a barn owl swept low, pale and ghostly, winging its way into one of the broken windows and disappearing. But the house revealed few signs of human inhabitation.

He had expected Mrs Elton to have one lamp lit at least. The note he had sent before they had left Shaw's had been precise, followed by the one from Gretna Green. He had indicated the date they could be expected. The cart had been an oversight, but he had been willing to believe that one of the farmhands had become drunk and forgotten, but this was inexcusable.

'Is this the Hall?' Lottie spoke, breaking the silence she had maintained ever since they had started down the road. 'It appears straight out of a Minerva Press novel, but somehow it suits you and your reputation. I cannot see you living in a neat and tidy Georgian house or even something from Queen Anne. But it has a certain amount of charm.'

'It belonged to my uncle and I have inherited it.' Tristan

advanced towards the shadowed door, fighting to keep the bitterness from his voice. 'The Duke of Northumberland's remaking of Alnwick Castle heavily influenced my grandfather. They shared a love of the Gothic. The roof badly needs repair, the guttering has seen better days and a family of owls has taken up residence in one of the upper bedrooms, but a few rooms remain habitable.'

'Beggars have little choice.'

'I had hoped you would like it.'

'No doubt in time…when I get used to it. For now it appears awfully big and…well…ruined. Still it has a roof and it can't be worse than that inn.'

'You may be right, but I am at a loss as to why Mrs Elton isn't here.'

'Perhaps your staff believed that you would need to make a run for the Continent again.' Lottie crossed her arms and gave a strangled laugh.

'Mrs Elton knows all about that. There will be some other reason.'

'You mean she doesn't consider you wicked and beyond redemption?' Tristan heard the merriment in Lottie's voice.

'She thinks of me as a little boy in long trousers who had lost his mother.'

'I am sure you were adorable as a little boy.'

'You will have to ask Mrs Elton as I can't possibly comment.' Tristan resisted the temptation to pull her into his arms. He could afford to wait for a few more minutes.

'And you are going to dismiss her because you have married me? Is that fair?'

'She will not starve.'

'You can't do that to people.' Lottie tapped her finger against her mouth and her brow furrowed. 'There must be other ways to make economies. I will go out without a new bonnet, or a new dress.'

'Why such concern for a woman you have never met?'

'Because there are standards to be upheld. The world would cease to function otherwise.' Lottie gave a little laugh, but Tristan saw through the act. Lottie was no snob. Her friendship with Mrs Foster and her concern about two lost children showed that. He knew what she meant, what she was trying to say. He reached over and squeezed her shoulder.

'Mrs Elton will thank you for your concern, once we discover where she is.'

'Please consider it, Tristan.' Lottie's arm dropped to her side and it took all of Tristan's self-control not to swing her into his arms and whisper that Mrs Elton would be well looked after and Lottie might have as many servants as she desired if only she would continue looking at him like that in the moonlight.

'I shall consider your request.' He turned away from her luminous starlit eyes and rapped sharply at the door, but there was no answering sound from within. He reached into the lantern and withdrew a key. The tiny act did much to restore his calm. He had to be resolute and to not be tempted to end the experiment before she had been truly tamed. 'Mrs Elton is usually very efficient. It is unlike her to be away.'

'I thought you recently inherited this.'

'Mrs Elton was my father's housekeeper when I was growing up. After my father's death, my uncle decided to employ her. I know the hours she keeps. We corresponded.'

'And where is the esteemed Mrs Elton? Only the thought of hot buttered toast, fruit cake and tea has kept me going this past mile or so.'

'Was it truly that difficult?' Tristan glanced at Lottie. Her face was slightly pinched with pain and she appeared to be limping. An unexpected tug of remorse hit him. Once they had begun their trek, she had not complained. He had not considered about boots or ladies' footwear until now. He pushed the thought away, surely she would have said something. Lottie had always been vocal about her discomforts before.

'I have had more pleasant days, but I coped.' Her bottom lip trembled and she blinked rapidly, but she kept her back straight. 'I had really wanted hot buttered toast and fruit cake, though.'

'I am sure I can find something. Mrs Elton will have left a cake in a tin. It is odd that she is not here.'

'Perhaps one of the tenants has taken ill,' Lottie said as he opened the heavy door, pushing his shoulder into it as it stuck slightly.

A scent of cold and damp with an undertone of beeswax polish assaulted his nose. On the small table to the right of the door stood a candelabra and a bottle of Lucifer matches. Tristan lit the lamp and scanned the note.

'Mrs Elton's niece has had twins and she has gone to look after her. She trusts I won't be inconvenienced as she expects to return by midday Thursday. Written two days ago. It explains much.'

'What happens now?' Lottie looked about the shadowy hall and shivered. Although it was neat and clean, it had not been redecorated since the war or even before. The silk wallpaper was stained and torn in places, and the white surrounds showed a yellowing that could only come with extreme age. 'Am I supposed to find my own room? Do we have any food?'

She hated the way her voice sounded and resisted the

temptation to cling to Tristan's arm. She also wished that she had not read quite so many of Cousin Frances's books. The memory of them provided little comfort. She was tempted to jump at every sound.

'I am hardly likely to leave you on your own, Lottie. You are my wife.' His smile increased. 'The master bedroom is in good repair. I did spend a few days here, before I went to visit my parents' graves.'

'The master bedroom? Husbands and wives rarely share rooms.' Lottie focussed on the ripped silk wallpaper that hung from the walls rather than on Tristan. They were here. Alone. There was no excuse for him not to touch her. She wanted him to kiss her again, like he had done on the road. But she also knew she was untried. What if she did disappoint? Desire and fear swamped her in equal measure.

'It is well that I do not circulate in the upper echelons of the middle class, Lottie.' His dry voice brought her back to the present. 'I fear the rules would bring out the rebel in me. I will maintain my own separate dressing room, if you require it. My parents always slept in the same bed.'

'Some of us have little choice in the matter, Mr Dyvelston. It is a matter of where we are born, and where we aspire to be.'

'And you aspired to a life of pincushions, shell pictures, visiting cards and At Homes.'

'It is good enough for my mother and sister-in-law.' She held her reticule in front of her like a shield and pretended that her feet did not hurt. She did not even dare sink down on a chair and inspect her slippers. She had felt the cold seeping through during the last part of the walk and was certain a huge hole had developed in her right slipper. How could she have been so stupid to accept Mrs Foster's blithe assurance that it was an easy walk? Maybe for someone in stout boots, but in slippers, her feet ached like fire.

She had kept herself going by concentrating on the journey's end. She wanted a warming cup of hot chocolate or, failing that, tea.

Lottie regarded her hands. That was a lie. She wanted more than that. Mainly she wanted her old life back, the one she'd had before she had met Tristan. She would even like to hear one of Cousin Frances's tales. She had had enough of adventures, but she couldn't go back. She was married. And if she went back she would have to give up Tristan and his kisses.

'Mama and Lucy appear content to prick pincushions and host At Homes. I like watercolours, painting landscapes. It gives me something else to converse about.'

'That, with the greatest respect, Lottie, is not an answer. It should be what you want from life, not what other people want for you.'

Lottie regarded her gloves, picked at a smudge. 'Very few people have ever bothered to ask me what I truly want and even fewer people have listened.'

'I am listening now.' He laid a hand on her shoulder, briefly for an instant. 'Lottie, what do you want from life? What sort of life do you want to have?'

One where I am loved and can love back. The words sprang unbidden to her mind, but she knew could not say them to Tristan. Love had nothing to do with their bargain. He had married her to save them both from the social wilderness. Love and affection played no part. She had to remember that. Maybe in time, they would reach some sort of mutual friendship. Friendship? Already she knew she wanted more than that.

'You promised me…' Lottie felt her throat begin to close. She stepped back away from him. Gave a small yelp as a splinter worked its way through a hole in her slipper. She winced, but resisted the temptation to examine the size of it.

'What have you done?' Tristan's face became hard. 'What are you not telling me, Carlotta? What are you keeping from me?'

'You said that you wouldn't call me Carlotta.' Lottie crossed her arms. This was all his fault, and he did not even care that her feet ached. He had allowed her to accept the lift, knowing full well how long of a march they would have. He had tricked her, and now he was calling her Carlotta. Tears pushed against her eyelids, threatened to spill over.

Tristan put his hand under her elbow. 'Only when you have done injury to yourself and refuse to tell me about it. Now what have you done? You can barely stand up straight.'

'Nothing, nothing at all.' Lottie jerked her elbow from his grasp. She refused to give way to tears. If she did that, she would not be able to stop, and she had no wish to make a scene.

'It looks more than nothing.'

Lottie ignored Tristan's outstretched hand and concentrated on moving slowly towards a chair. Now that they had stopped, her feet seemed to have seized up. It had been fine while they'd been walking. She had simply concentrated on putting one foot in front of the other, knew that there would be no respite and he would not give her any aid if she stumbled. But now, in this shadowy hall with its torn silk wallpaper and dusty pictures, her feet burned and ached. She knew she could not take another step, but she also did not want to give Tristan the satisfaction. He seemed to think she was spoilt and unfit for anything, but she wasn't.

'Nothing that could not have been predicted from my attire.' She gave a shrug. 'I told you that I was not dressed for marching. You knew how far it would be to Gortner Hall and you let me—'

'Sit down!'

'I am fine, I tell you.' Lottie refused to cry. She refused to allow Tristan to bully her. 'I may have lost my bonnet and my shoes may be ruined. I have not begun to examine the tears in my dress. How Mama could ever have considered lightweight silk a suitable costume for an elopement, I have no idea, but I made the mistake of listening to her. Many other people have weathered far worse storms, I am sure.'

Tristan closed his eyes, his hands balled at his sides. Lottie braced herself for an explosion but she would not apologise. She glared at him as he opened his eyes again, matching his dark, intent gaze with one of her own. Slowly, one by one, his fingers relaxed.

'Lottie, please, I beg you, sit down and allow me to look at the damage.' His voice became as smooth as silk, sliding over her skin like a caress. 'I did not think about your shoes. I wanted to teach you a lesson about assuming things and I was wrong.'

'You did what?' Lottie's breath stopped in her throat. Her brow knotted. A lesson? What right did he have to presume to teach her anything? She had thought she was helping! 'You allowed this to happen?'

'I failed to consider the condition of your shoes.'

'You knew I was not dressed for walking long distances.'

'We shall add them to the list of things that need to be replaced.'

'They were my favourite pair.' Lottie gazed down at them ruefully. 'They were beautiful.'

'I shall see what can be done.' He placed a hand on her elbow. 'But right now, my main concern is your feet. The shoes were objects. You are a person and in pain. I never meant to cause you pain. I am sorry, Lottie. Truly and abjectly sorry.'

The quick retort died on her lips. He was contrite? He had apologised? Tristan? She had been prepared to hate him and he did this. Looked at her with such intensity and regret that her heart turned over. And she knew she could forgive him almost anything.

Lottie sank gratefully down onto the small chair next to the table. He knelt beside her and eased off one of her slippers. His face darkened as the stocking revealed the extent of the damage. Lottie stared at the mess of torn stockings and her reddened feet. Tristan's mouth twisted and he shook his head.

'I made it to the hall without complaining.'

'Your feet are bleeding.' He ran a finger along the sole of one foot. Gentle hands removed her stockings. Lottie tried not to wince as his fingers probed. Three blisters had popped. 'When were you going to tell me that your feet were this injured? Or were you enjoying playing the martyr?'

'I thought you might think me spoilt.' She glanced up at the ceiling. 'I wanted to show you that I could enter into the spirit of the thing. Maybe I should have asked.'

He knelt, holding her foot, not saying anything, simply rubbing it between his two hands. She concentrated on the blue-blackness of his hair and the way it curled slightly at the nape of his neck. She resisted the urge to bury her hands in it and to bring his face to hers.

'Tristan,' she whispered, 'are you very angry with me?'

He let go of her foot and stood up. Handed her the candle, seemingly oblivious to her torment. 'Carry this. Keep it steady. Whatever you do, don't blow it out. I have no wish to be plunged into darkness as we go up the stairs.'

'I will try not to drop it, but my feet pain me so. I am not sure how steady I will be.' Lottie regarded the long flight of stairs that seemed to stretch for ever into the blackness. She wasn't sure she could walk even five steps, let alone the whole thing.

'Concentrate and you will keep it steady. I know you can do that, Lottie.'

'You ask too much.' Lottie made a little movement with her hand. Angry tears came to her eyes. He kept asking her to do things, impossible things. Yesterday, he had left her on her own; today, he had made her take a parliamentary, spend time in a third-class waiting room, beg for a lift from a farmer's widow and then walk miles in her slippers. Now he expected her to do more. 'I have tried, Tristan, you must believe that. But here I stay. My legs refuse your command.'

'I did not ask you to walk, only to hold a candle. You must stop assuming things, Lottie. You always make assumptions about people and things.' Without waiting for an answer, he swung her into his arms and advanced towards the stairs. His boots resounded on the marble floor. 'I never wanted to hurt you.'

'You will drop me.' Lottie hastily wrapped an arm about his neck and clung as he began to mount the stairs. He made it seem as if she were featherlight and he had not been walking as far as she had. 'I am going to fall.'

'Not with my arms about you. Keep the candle steady, Lottie, and hold it higher.' His lips were just above her hair. The sound of his heart thumped in her ears.

'Where are you taking me?'

'To the bedroom. I have something there that might ease your aches and pains.' He readjusted his hold on her, moved his arms so she was propped against his chest, but his touch was impersonal.

A liquid fire went through her limbs. She wanted to go there, but not like this. She must more closely resemble a drowned rat or a street urchin. And there would be no one to help with her clothes except for Tristan. Once again she would fail in her duty as a wife. She concentrated on the portraits, rather than on the beating of his heart. This time, she did not want to give him an excuse to leave her.

'Your family?' she asked as many of the portraits had a look of Tristan about them—a wild, untamed look as if they were ready to take on the world.

'The Dyvelstons. I am the last one.' He gave a crooked smile. 'All this history has come down to one person. One unworthy person.'

Her brain buzzed, but she was so tired that she could not think straight. All she could think was that he wasn't unworthy. He had saved her twice. Underneath everything, there was kindness. 'There is your cousin—Lord Thorngrafton.'

'I try not to think about him.'

'But surely your uncle—?' Lottie began, turning her head.

'Hold the candle steady. Do you want to plunge us into darkness? I need to see where to put my feet.'

'I am trying to.' Lottie lifted the candle higher and strange elongated shadows danced in the hallway. Then she stared at the ruined portrait of the woman dressed in clothes fashionable about a decade before. The gilt frame was lavish, but the portrait was slashed from top to bottom several times. 'Who did that?'

'Did you know that you are getting heavy?' He shifted her so that she was no longer looking at the portrait, but instead facing his lips.

'You should let me hobble. I will be too heavy for you. Cousin Frances told me that I look like a stuffed pig.'

'You have walked enough for today. Hold on tight, and you are no stuffed pig. Far too light for that.'

'I will believe you.'

He reached down and opened a door, and, banging it against the wall, he carried her into the bedroom. A large four-poster mahogany bed hung with heavy velvet curtains dominated. To one side stood a birchwood washbasin. The carpet was thick and the walls clean and cobweb free. 'This was to be my room. It is now ours. There are two dressing rooms that connect to it.'

'It is a lovely room.'

'I am glad you approve. It was my grandparents'.' He took the candle from her hand and placed it on the chair beside the bed. 'Release your arms.'

She obeyed him. His hands guided her so that she slid down the contours of his body, her curves meeting the hard planes of his muscles. A tiny spark ignited inside her, but she damped it down, telling herself that he had only wanted to set her down gently.

'And what happens next?' she asked in a voice that sounded unnaturally high to her ears as she sat, balanced precariously on the edge of the bed.

'Your feet are seen to. You should have told me about your footwear before we left Hexham.' He went over to the dressing table and pulled out a canister. 'Ointment. It was given to me by a doctor in Antioch.'

'I will put it on myself.'

'Are you sure you know how to apply it properly?'

A mental image of him stroking her feet, his long fingers curving around her calves and ankles, gliding over them, rose unbidden in her mind, infusing her with heat. She concentrated on a spot somewhere above his head. She would not make last night's mistake. She would show him that she had learnt her lesson. She knew how to behave with the decorum one would expect from a gently reared lady.

'I would prefer to do it myself. I know which blisters are the worst.'

'If that is what you want.'

'It is.' Lottie put out her hand and he placed the cold tin on her palm, then stepped back away from her.

'You only need a little bit.'

She nodded and concentrated on opening the tin, instead of on his lips. Held back the words begging him to stay. She would be dignified about it. She was not going to give in to her passion. If he touched her feet, she was sure to say something vulgar like demanding to be kissed. Her time as a proper wife started now. 'I am sure they are not as bad as they look.'

'It is no bother. I feel responsible.'

'Let me do it.' She put the ointment on her feet, rubbing it in. First one foot and then the other. Tristan had been right. The cool liquid took the fire from her feet. 'You told the truth. They are much better. In a few days, I am sure they will be vastly improved.'

'You seem to be very able and in no need of assistance from me, despite my offer.' He stood there, looking at her. 'Shall I leave the candle?'

'It would be kind of you.' Lottie hated the way her voice had become small. She stood up and held out her hand. 'Goodnight, Tristan.'

He ignored her fingers, picked up another candle and lit it. 'If that is what you want…'

Lottie bit her lip. He was about to leave. In the morning, they would be more estranged than ever. She found her earlier fears had ebbed away. She wanted to be his wife in truth. She wanted his lips to glide over hers and to have that heady fiery sensation fill her again.

She summoned all of her courage. 'Stay.'

'Why?' Tristan watched her with wary eyes. He blamed himself for her predicament. All the words she had flung at him were correct. He had known and had not thought. He had wanted to teach her a lesson, not injure her. He found it too difficult watch her rub the ointment in, knowing she had refused his help. He had never considered her footwear, never considered it at all.

'I can't sleep in my corset.' She stood up. Fiery pain shot through her feet, crippling her, but she ignored it. She started to undo her buttons, twisting herself into a strange shape. Her cheeks were bright pink and her eyes downcast as she worked with a feverish intensity. Was that all she wanted—to be free of her confining garments? 'The button in the middle is a bit difficult.'

'You will do yourself injury…' Tristan barely recognised his own voice as he fought against his desires to tear her clothes from her body and reveal her silken skin, to explore her hidden peaks and valleys until he heard the low moaning in the back of her throat again. But he had to go slowly. A little at a time. *Her* pace.

He forced his fingers to undo the button and to draw back. She said nothing, continued to stand with her back to him as the silk dress gaped and revealed her creamy skin. He had thought when he'd carried her up the stairs that she had understood his need. He had pushed her too hard today, demanded too much of her. He would wait until tomorrow when she was less tired and her feet less painful. He had to be patient, even though his body urged him to take her into his arms…and bury himself within her.

'The first of your buttons is undone.'

'Thank you,' she breathed and her flesh quivered slightly.

'Now keep still, or otherwise you will undo the good that the ointment has done.' He counted the number of buttons and knew he could do this. He had done them up this morning. But somehow, a mean room at an inn with noises about them was very different from the hushed silence of his bedroom.

'I will try to be. I pride myself on being good. Sometimes things seem to happen.' Her voice was small and tight. She trembled, much as a thoroughbred does before a race. 'Sometimes it is very difficult to get my dresses off without assistance. The buttons go straight down my back. I have undone the first few buttons, but the ones further down are impossible.'

'Then I will do my best.'

He leant forward and let his hand slide over her collarbone. Felt her quiver beneath the pads of his fingers. The dress gave way and revealed a creamy patch of skin at the base of her throat. Soft skin that begged to be tasted. Without thinking, his head bent and he sampled the silken softness of her for an instant. Heard her sharp intake of breath, but she did not move away from him.

He risked a glance into her eyes. Waited. Her wide blue gaze stared back at him. She reached out and touched his lips with one finger.

'Lottie.' He took a step closer. Their bodies touched. She turned. Slowly and deliberately she lifted her arms, put them around his neck and pulled him forward. Their mouths touched and her lips parted. He tasted her sweetness, her innocent passion. The way her tongue bashfully entered his mouth and then retreated, only to return. This time more boldly, and to become entangled and to drink deeply. Playful, but unskilled. And all the more enticing for it.

His body responded with all the pent-up energy from their other encounters. Became hard to the point of pain. Urged him to take action, but he wanted to initiate her slowly, to show her what the true sweetness of passion could be like. He had seen what could happen if a woman was not awakened properly. It was one of the reasons why he had avoided the responsibility, but now it fell to him. She was not some courtesan or bored society beauty with an aged husband and well versed in the arts of lovemaking— she was his wife, his innocent wife, and she deserved his care.

Her passion-drugged eyes looked up at him as he withdrew his mouth. 'Is something wrong?'

'Everything is well.' He pushed the cloth from her shoulder and revealed her soft curves, curves that cried out to be savoured. 'I haven't finished your buttons yet.'

'You did promise to be my lady's maid.'

'It may take a great deal of time.'

'I never thought.' Her cheeks flamed pink and she spun around. Tristan allowed himself the exquisite torture of undoing one button at a time. Her gown fell to the floor in a whoosh and he swiftly unlaced her.

As he removed her corset, his knuckles grazed her breast. There was a sharp intake of breath, a stiffening of her spine. Tristan paused, exerted control over his body. His hands ached to caress the two mounds, to feel her nipples between his fingers, to roll them and to hear her gasp of pleasure. But he had to go at her pace.

'I can finish this,' she said with a thickening in her voice that told him she was not adverse to his touch.

'No, no, allow me. I do have some experience with ladies' undergarments.' His hand brushed her fingers from the drawstring. He pushed the petticoat down her body, so that she stood in her chemise.

She gave a small hiccupping laugh. 'You do have the reputation of a rake.'

'Much undeserved.' He cupped her cheek with his palm. 'The ladies understood the game, but they are in the past. You are my present and my future.'

'And now?' The question escaped Lottie's throat before she could prevent it. All the time he had been undressing her, a fire had been building inside her, threatening to overwhelm her senses and good intentions. She had wanted to turn and kiss him again, but had not dared. She wanted to maintain a wifely dignity.

His hands closed on her shoulders and pulled her back against him. Her bottom met his hardness, leaving her in no doubt about his arousal. The sensation thrilled and alarmed her in equal measure. This was the deep, dark mystery.

'You are my wife. You should be in truth. There are none to interrupt us here.'

His wife. The words had a curious echo of her mother's warning. A wife was something different than a mistress. Men had different expectations. Instantly she straightened, held herself away from the tantalising pressure behind her. 'I don't need any more assistance. I can do the rest.'

His fingers turned her body so that she faced him. 'But I do.'

'I have never undressed a man before. I would not know where to begin.' She tried for humour. 'My fingers are all thumbs. I am more likely to strangle you with your stock than unwrap it.'

'As you wish…'

In one motion he had divested himself of his stock and his jacket. His shirt gaped open at the neck, revealing the strong column of his throat. His hands made short work of the buttons and the cloth slipped off his shoulders.

Her breath caught in her throat. All day she had wondered if she had imagined the breadth of his shoulders or how sculpted his muscles were, but now she saw that one brief early-morning glimpse had not been enough. She feasted her eyes on him and the way his golden skin was covered in a light dusting of dark hair, hair that pointed downwards and disappeared into his cream trousers.

A knowing smile crossed his face. She turned her head, ashamed. Perhaps such things were done at night, under the covers, but she wanted to see.

'You may look at me, if I can look at you.' He touched her chin and brought it back so her gaze went to the warm pools of his eyes.

'What do you mean?'

'Very pretty, but unnecessary.' He ran a hand along the lace, his fingers skimming the cloth and delicately stroking the swell underneath, a slow, almost lazy, touch, but one that did strange things to her insides. Instantly her breast responded to the touch, her nipples becoming tight buds, straining forwards, and a primitive longing pulsed through her.

Her hand reached out and touched his silken hair as he rained open-mouthed kisses down her throat. She held him against her skin. His lips went over the shift and circled the outline of her nipples. Circled and tugged, making the cloth wet. A gasp was torn from her throat.

'You seem to have become a bit wet. I should not want you to catch a chill.'

Her nipples were a dusky pink between the now translucent cloth. The cloth rubbed against her, making her breasts seem full and aching, and she knew that she wanted to feel his mouth on her. With trembling fingers, she raised her arms and allowed him to take the chemise off.

'I should not want you to catch cold. All alone in that big bed.' He picked her up and set her down on the bed. The faint traces of lavender and starch rose up to meet her, enveloped her in their softness. He ran a hand over her curves. 'May I join you?'

Incapable of speech, she could only nod.

The bed dipped slightly and his full length came on top of her. Warming her. Pressing her down into the lavender-scented sheets.

His mouth reclaimed hers and this time it demanded a response. A response she was willing to give. Desired.

She feasted on his lips. Their tongues tangled as her body arched and her breasts were crushed against his naked chest. Every piece of her burst into flames, molten to his touch.

Remade.

His fingers slipped down her body until they reached the apex of her thighs where her dusky triangle was, dark against the cream of her skin.

They glided into her crease, into the soft folds until they discovered the hard nub of her. Played and glided, around and round. Exquisite sensations racked her body. She lost all sense of time, all sense of everything except the touch of him against her soft hidden folds, moving along secret pathways of pleasure that she had never even guessed existed. A deep burning ache filled her. She needed something more, something to ease this burning sensation. She moaned, thrashing her head on the pillows, her hands clutching the sheet beneath her.

Her hands pulled at his shoulders, forced him upwards and reclaimed his mouth. Their tongues entangled, but it only served to increase the need inside her, instead of ending it. Her body arched in frustration, pushed up against him. Her curves met his arousal. Felt his hardness through his clothes press into her folds, press against her. Her fingers sought his waistband. She wanted to have his skin slide against hers, to experience all of it. She gave a small cry of frustration as the first button refused to give.

Hands captured hers. Held her wrists above her head. 'Patience.'

'Please.' She thrashed her head back and forth on the pillow, hardly knowing what she was asking, only knowing that she needed him.

'There is no easy way,' he said against her lips. 'I am going to have to hurt you, but it will be only for an instant. Do you trust me?'

She nodded slightly. But every portion of her body ached for him.

He undid his trousers, slid them down. Kicked them to the floor. Loomed over her, golden with a sprinkling of dark hair that, like an arrow, pointed downwards. Her mouth dried as she saw the evidence of his arousal. His masculinity. She reached out a finger and tentatively touched. Velvety hard. Burning silk over iron. She wanted to hold him and caress him. Explore his tantalising flesh.

His hand stopped her quest. 'Later.'

She withdrew her hand, chastened. She had been too bold. She swallowed hard, hating her desire and these sensations that were sweeping through her. She had done it wrong. 'I understand.'

'Sometimes, I forget how truly innocent you are.' His hand trapped hers and raised it to his lips. His mouth suckled each finger. 'I want to make this as gentle as possible.'

'You make no sense.'

'I will.'

He nudged apart her thighs, positioned himself and she felt a burning pain inside for an instant as her body opened up and allowed the length of him to enter. He lay there for a moment, inside her, joined together. His fingers slid over her skin, tracing the outline of her eyes, her nose, her mouth.

'It couldn't be helped. Your maidenhead had to be breached.' His breath tickled her ear.

'Will the pain get better?'

'Yes.' He recaptured her lips, plundering and restarted the fire that flickered inside her.

The aching deep within began again and she lifted her hips, wanting to be closer.

He appeared to understand and together they began to move, faster and faster until she felt as if she were falling. She clamped her mouth shut and stifled a scream. Tried desperately to hang on to her sanity. Failed.

'Did I hurt you much?' Tristan asked as he rolled off her, spent from his exertions. He watched her face for any sign of hidden pain. He'd held out as long as he'd dared, hoping against hope. Then his own desire had overtaken him. Now he looked at her candlelit blue eyes, searched them and saw the smouldering remains of passion.

'A bit at the start.' She squeezed his hand. 'But later it was lovely.'

He pressed his lips to her temple. An exultation filled him. He had done the right thing. He would get the sort of wife he had dreamt of. His experiment was working. Once he was sure, he would let her know the whole truth.

'It will be better next time, I promise.'

'And you always keep your promises.'

His answer was to draw her back into his arms and to stop her laughter with a kiss. Soon, soon, he would confess the truth, but he wanted to enjoy this time with her. He wanted to enjoy her innocence.

And nothing was going to stop him.

Chapter Eleven

'Why didn't you want to tell me who that portrait was? Why did you deliberately change the subject?' Lottie asked as the morning sun peeped through the curtains. She had spent the better part of an hour awake, listening to the steady sound of Tristan sleeping next to her, going over things in her mind and one piece she could not place was the portrait. Why would anyone leave a ruined portrait on the wall?

'It wasn't important,' came Tristan's sleep-laced voice. 'It still isn't. Ancient history, best forgotten. Nothing to do with you or us.'

Lottie brought her knees up to her chest and peeped at Tristan through a curtain of hair. 'I would like to know.'

His finger flicked her hair back, stroked her cheek and sent pulses of sensation coursing through her. 'It is of my uncle's former wife. You won't see it again.'

'Who destroyed it? Your uncle?' Lottie wriggled out of his embrace and sat facing him. 'It looks to be an expensive portrait.'

'You are refusing to be distracted this morning.' His

hand encircled her shoulder and pulled her firmly back against him.

'I should have asked last night, but other things occupied my mind.' She turned her face towards the pillow, rather than face Tristan. Somehow even speaking about what had passed between them seemed wicked.

'My uncle.' Tristan gave a great sigh. 'It was a portrait of his wife. He owned it. You would have to ask him exactly what went through his mind. I had left.'

'But why did he slash it? There must have been a reason.'

'You have been reading too many novels.'

'It is Cousin Frances who reads them.' Lottie propped herself on her elbow and regarded his face. A dimple showed in the corner of his mouth, which showed he was teasing her. Lottie relaxed slightly, pleased that they had reached a point where they could tease each other. 'I simply listened to her graphic tales and this…this house could easily be in one. It has that sort of atmosphere.'

'Does it indeed?'

'Oh, positively, Cousin Frances will remark on it at once when she comes…if she comes,' Lottie quickly amended. 'But how could anyone leave a house like this one to rack and ruin? It must have been well loved once.'

'Too well. My father and mother adored the house, but my father and uncle did not get on. They left when my grandfather died and went to live near Haydon Bridge.'

'You are seeking to distract me with your parents.' Lottie clasped her hands about her knees. 'Why would your uncle leave it like this?'

Tristan sat up and regarded Lottie's rosebud mouth and golden hair streaming out over the pillow. He wrapped his hands about his knees and glanced over at his wife. How much should he tell her? How much did she need to know?

'I believe my uncle never came to this house after his wife abandoned him or so Mrs Elton wrote. We were completely estranged by that point.'

'How sad. He must have been very upset when she left. He must have loved her very much.'

'The only thing my uncle loved was money—the getting and acquiring of objects. He was also devoted to preserving the dignity of the Dyvelston name, keeping it out of the scandal sheets.' Tristan's lips twitched. 'There, he failed.'

'But his wife. What did he feel for her?'

'She was simply a living and breathing object, a trophy in his old age.'

'Much as Sir Geoffrey planned for me.' Lottie brought her knees up to her chest and hid behind a curtain of hair.

'I had not given it much consideration. Sir Geoffrey did not marry you. I did.'

Tristan hoped that would be the end. He had no wish to dredge up old memories about his youthful indiscretions.

'And what she was like—your aunt?' she asked from behind her hair. 'When I meet the neighbours, they are all bound to know and there will be things alluded to. Mrs Foster said something. It will be better if you tell me first.'

'Mrs Foster was an irritant in more ways than one,' Tristan growled. 'I should never have let you accept that lift. I should have known better than to let you speak to her.'

'You are trying to change the subject. Your aunt, not people I might meet on the parliamentary. You must have known her.'

Tristan collapsed back against the pillows and stared up at the bed hangings. How to explain about the beautiful, elusive, treacherous Suzanne? 'Beautiful, charming, much younger than my uncle. Last seen with an Italian count.'

Lottie laughed as she caught his hand and pressed it to her cheek. 'You seem to know a lot of women who were last seen with an Italian count.'

He withdrew his hand. 'Because they were one and the same.'

'You ran off with your aunt. Is it any wonder you are considered to be scandalous?' Lottie sat up, and allowed the sheet to fall to the floor unheeded.

'Hush, Lottie. It happened over ten years ago.' Tristan reached over and pulled her firmly back into his arms. 'It is nothing that concerns you. It was something between my uncle and me. Poor fool that I was—I did not understand how I was used. Both by my uncle and his wife. I was young, naive and totally convinced of my superiority and virility.'

Lottie wriggled out of his embrace and stared at him. 'Your aunt, Tristan? How could you? She must have been much older than you.'

'I never said that I was perfect, Lottie. You knew I had a scandalous past when we met.' Tristan passed his hand over his eyes. He was not ready for this conversation. There were some parts of his life that he had no desire to revisit. 'At the time, it seemed wildly romantic. She was a year old than me and much more worldly. I never considered her to be my aunt, only my uncle's wife. My uncle was aware of the fascination she held for me.' A muscle jumped in Tristan's jaw. 'He encouraged it in the beginning.'

'And he did nothing to prevent it?' Her eyes became wide with amazement.

'It is possible that my uncle felt it the best way to get

a child, one with Dyvelston blood rather than one from some other family. We never discussed it. I am sorry to say that I was not terribly discreet. In my defence, I was young and blind in my arrogance.'

'How did it end?'

'Fate intervened in the shape of a disputed card game, a duel and Suzanne, his wife, elected to come with me to the Continent.' Tristan gave a bitter laugh. 'My uncle did not pursue us. I think he was pleased to be rid of her and her desire for pretty things. They had tired of each other and I was her plaything.'

'But that…that is monstrous… How could anyone be so cruel?'

'It was what my uncle was like. He wanted at all costs to have a son. It became his obsession.' Tristan's face was shadowed and Lottie was certain there was much he was keeping hidden. 'It is not a time I am proud of, Lottie, but it helped shape me.'

'But he did that to the portrait. He destroyed her portrait and he kept it hanging on the wall…for you to find.'

'For me to find, yes, but I chose to ignore it. She means nothing to me.'

A shiver ran through Lottie and she tried not to think of the woman's eyes, staring down at them, and the remains of her smile. 'How awful. He must have assumed you cared for her.'

He shrugged one shoulder. 'Suzanne ceased to matter to me years ago. I had other things on my mind when I was last here.'

'But…but…'

'It is history now, Lottie.' He trailed a hand along her flank. 'A decade ago, and I escaped the worst of it. I had come of age and there was little he could do about it.

Remind me some time to tell you of my other hair-raising adventures. The scandal sheets enjoyed themselves for a few years, until I learnt my lessons and grew up.'

'And like the prodigal son, you have now returned home.'

'That is one way of putting it.'

'Is…Suzanne happy?' Lottie raised herself up on one elbow.

'She is leading a better life in the sunny clime of Italy. Italian counts with castles, money and an entrée to society were far more to her taste than young men with charming manners.' He gave a short laugh. 'A salutary lesson and one not easily forgotten.'

Lottie pressed her lips together. Was that how he had seen her at Shaw's? As someone intent on acquiring the trappings of wealth? Or as someone being sold to the highest bidder to further her mother's ambition? Another Suzanne.

'The scandal is the reason you felt unable to return home until after your uncle's death.'

'I had lots of reasons not to return here.' Tristan came over and smoothed the hair off her forehead. He placed kisses on her nose and her eyelids, soft kisses that filled her with flares of heat. 'But those have all gone. Vanished. We will make our home here—you and I. It is in my blood and I have no wish to leave it.'

'Why did he leave the house to you?'

'Because he did. But enough about history and long-ago scandals. You are here and in my bed. And that is all I need to know.' Tristan began to move his mouth along her bare shoulder, nibbling, calling up the banked fire deep within her. She turned and his tongue plundered her mouth.

It was not until much later that she realised he had never answered her question.

The sun had moved across the room when Lottie next awoke. Only the indentation in the pillow showed that Tristan had ever been there. She looked at the tell-tale streaks of dried blood on her thighs and on the sheets. Winced. Evidence if she needed it of her change from virgin to wife.

She crossed quickly to the basin and washed herself, grateful that Tristan had given her a bit of privacy. Somehow he had understood that she would need to be alone and would need time to make her *toilette*. Only she wished that he had kissed her before he had gone.

Lottie held her mud-splattered dress out with two fingers and decided that she would have to make do with the dressing gown until she could discover if there were any clothes she could make over. The dress needed a good brushing and the stitches had worked loose on the tear. It would never be the magnificent dress it had once been, but it would do after mending. There was no one here to see her except for Tristan and he had already seen her naked. Her face grew rosy at the thought.

A white cotton dressing gown was laid at the foot of the bed. Lottie slipped on a clean shift and then belted the dressing gown around that. She allowed her hair to hang down over her shoulders rather than twisting it into a simple knot.

She picked up a silver-backed mirror. Very much the well-kissed look. Almost wanton. Her mother's friends would whisper in shocked tones if they could see her and the worst of it was that she did not care. Lottie put the mirror down with a thump. She understood why brides had wedding trips. It must be the only time wives could be treated as mistresses.

Mama had been wrong to say that men did not enjoy passion from their wives. Tristan appeared to.

Lottie tapped her fingers together. Her mother had been wrong about many things. The thought failed to pain her as much today as it would have done two days ago. She had Tristan and she was determined to be the sort of wife he could be proud of. Eventually, they would make their triumphant return to society.

She would explain it all to Tristan once she found him.

A banging noise from downstairs gave her some indication where Tristan might be. It felt very strange to be in a house where she and Tristan were the only people. Generally she was surrounded by an army of servants—even at Aunt Alice's there had been three.

Lottie walked down the stairs gingerly. Her right heel still pained her, but otherwise her feet felt far better than she'd thought they would. It was the other parts of her that ached. Places where she never thought she'd had muscles.

She glanced upwards. There was a dark square of turquoise paint where Suzanne, Tristan's former aunt, had been. She thinned her lips. He had been true to his word and removed it. Lottie frowned as a stab of jealousy pierced her. Suzanne was long gone. Tristan had married *her*. They would have a good marriage based on honesty and integrity, sharing whatever the storms of fate had in store for them. She would not desert him.

She peeped into the shroud-covered rooms, looking for Tristan and mentally noting everything that had to be done. A film of dust covered most everything and garlands of cobwebs festooned the chandeliers. A family of starlings had taken up residence in the drawing room, there were definite signs of damp in the dining room and the gilt around the ceiling lay in flaked piles. But for all of the neglect, Lottie could see that it had once been a magnificent house.

It was little wonder that Tristan had been so cautious about money as it would take a fortune, if not two fortunes, to restore the house to its former glory. And it might be better simply to knock it down and start again. She would have to discuss it with Tristan. But in the meantime, there were little things, little touches she could do that would make the house appear more like a home.

The banging increased and there was a smell of bacon. Lottie's stomach rumbled, reminding her that she had not eaten.

She opened the door and stopped in surprise at the scene that confronted her. 'Are you supposed to be here?'

A wizened woman looked back at her as the tiny terrier at her feet gave a sharp bark.

'Who are you?' the woman demanded after she had quietened the dog. 'Does Lord Thorngrafton know you are here? I told him that he was not to bring any of his strumpets here, not if he wanted Mollie Elton to continue as his housekeeper.'

'The house belongs to Tristan Dyvelston.' Lottie kept her chin up and continued on a triumphant note, 'Therefore, I doubt it is any concern of Lord Thorngrafton's if I am here or not.'

Mrs Elton's eyes narrowed and she opened her mouth several times, but no sound came out. Lottie permitted a smile to cross her face. Some people had the insatiable urge to name drop, an affliction that was not simply confined to her mother or her mother's friends. Mrs Elton had to know that Lord Thorngrafton would not simply come to his cousin's house uninvited and certainly he would not bring any of his lady friends here. The notion was laughable.

'If you could manage to find me a bit of breakfast, I would appreciate it,' Lottie said to ease the awkwardness. She knelt down and waggled her fingers at the dog, who tilted its tan-and-white head and then came over to sniff her. The dog lifted its head to Lottie's fingers.

'So that's how it is, is it?' Mrs Elton cleared her throat. 'The dog's name is Joss. He's right picky about those he befriends.'

'He's sweet.' Lottie gave him another pat and tickled him under the chin as the dog lay at her feet. 'Would it be possible to have you fix me a slice of toast to share with Joss?'

Mrs Elton harrumphed, but she put two slices of toast on the range to brown. 'Does Tristan Dyvelston know you are here?'

'Of course.' Lottie waited a beat, beginning to enjoy herself. She would see the woman apologise for her rude behaviour yet. She had to remember that one caught more flies with honey than vinegar. Lottie batted her eyes and adopted her most innocent expression. 'I am his wife. We married at Gretna Green two days ago.'

'I hadn't heard. I have been away. I arrived back only an hour or so ago. I have not had time to sort through the post.' The woman made a clucking noise in the back of her throat as she turned the bread over. She looked Lottie up and down and something in her expression told Lottie that she was found wanting. 'He married you at Gretna Green? Why did he feel the need to do that? Are you in the family way?'

'You will have to ask him.' Lottie adopted her best social stare. Then she held up her hand and showed the iron ring.

'But we are married. It is a legal marriage. I am no strumpet.'

'I never doubted it. And now that I look at you I can see that I made an error. I apologise, Miss…'

'Lottie Dyvelston, Charlton as was.' Lottie held out her hand. She could be gracious, even if she was dressed informally 'We are waiting for my trunks to arrive. It was all very sudden. I didn't think you would return for a few days.'

'That I don't doubt.' Mrs Elton's face creased up and she dabbed a corner of her eye with her apron. 'It's just a surprise that is all. I had never thought Master Tristan one for marrying. Now Master Peter is a different story. He has always been determined to catch himself a wife.'

'I am acquainted with Lord Thorngrafton as well as Tristan. I have never been under the impression that he desired a wife.'

Mrs Elton gave her another queer look before she turned to bang the pots and pans about. 'That somehow was my impression.'

Lottie pinched the skin between her eyes. She knew family retainers were given a bit of latitude, but Mrs Elton was distinctly odd. She decided to try another tactic with Mrs Elton. 'As my trunks have not arrived, and my dress is entirely unsuitable for doing work around this house, perhaps I could trouble you for some clothes.'

'I never thought I would see the day that Master Tristan's wife worked in the kitchen or round the house. The late Lord Thorngrafton's wife never lifted a delicate finger. It ain't right and proper, if you will pardon my saying so.'

'I believe in being practical.' Lottie frowned. She disliked the comparison with Suzanne. She was more than a spoilt rich girl. She had always helped out at home.

'Mama believed that a woman must be useful as well as decorative. It makes it easier to direct the servants if you actually know how to do the tasks.'

'An interesting point of view.'

Mrs Elton handed her a slice of toast. Lottie broke off a small piece and gave it to Joss. The dog gave her fingers a quick wash.

'Ah, Lottie, here I find you.' Tristan came into the kitchen. Lottie felt her cheeks begin to burn. Her entire body tingled with an awareness of him and the way he had held her last night. If anything, he looked more handsome in his shirtsleeves, cream trousers and black boots. His face had a healthy glow as if he had been out walking in the morning air. It frightened her how much she had missed him in the short time they had been apart. How much she had needed to see that glow in his eyes. 'And Mrs Elton, what a surprise. I had not realised you were back.'

He caught up the housekeeper and spun her around. Her white cap with its ribbons went flying as the little dog barked.

'Master…Tristan,' Mrs Elton said in a mock-scolding voice when Tristan had set her down and she had rearranged her cap. 'That was my best cap, that was. With new ribbons and all. You are a caution. Let me have a better look at you. You have married.'

'I have indeed.' Tristan reached out and gathered Lottie to him. 'I had expected my good wife to remain in bed all day. We had a strenuous journey yesterday.'

The tide of red grew higher on Lottie's cheeks and she stepped out of Tristan's embrace. She expected to see disapproval on Mrs Elton's face, but the elderly woman positively beamed at them.

'I woke and was hungry.' She reached down and fed the last of her toast to the dog. 'I came in search of food and you. I met Mrs Elton. There was some confusion at first, but everything is sorted.'

'Confusion?' He lifted an eyebrow and his voice took on a much colder note. 'What sort of confusion?'

'Mrs Elton thought I was one of Lord Thorngrafton's fancy fillies, but I have explained everything. It was, I suppose, an easily made mistake. She was not expecting to see us.'

Tristan's eyes darkened and he shifted his stance. 'Did you now? What did you say to Mrs Elton?'

'I explained about our runaway marriage. She appeared quite overcome by it all. I have made friends with her dog.' Lottie plucked at his sleeve and dropped her voice as Mrs Elton turned back to the range and was busy banging pots and pans. 'I am not sure if she understands that you mean to get rid of her. She did not mention leaving at all. And, Tristan, she has known you since you were in short clothes. There must be a way.'

Tristan stroked his chin and his eyes became misty. 'Lottie, if you will excuse me and Mrs Elton, there is something we need to discuss.'

Lottie bit her lip. She wished she had not mentioned the housekeeping problem. It seemed wrong somehow to get rid of Mrs Elton. The woman appeared so pleased and happy to see Tristan and now her happiness was going to be dashed. But it was better that Tristan made the arrangements. Perhaps he could send her to Lord Thorngrafton— after all, the woman appeared to be fond of him. She would mention it to Tristan at the earliest opportunity.

'I can wait in the drawing room until you are finished. There are probably a thousand and one things that I need

to do. Simple things to make this house more like a home.'
Lottie bent down and gave Joss one more stroke of his
head. 'It was very pleasant meeting you, Mrs Elton.'

'And you, my lady.' The elderly woman bobbed a curtsy.
'I will see if I can discover a serviceable gown or two for
you. We are bound to have some in one of the attic rooms.
It won't be up-to-the minute, like, but it will be serviceable.'

'Oh, I am not a lady. I have no title.' Lottie gave a little
laugh. 'But I am handy with my needle and thread. It is
amazing how quickly a dress can be transformed with a
few tucks and a bit of lace.'

Tristan waited until he heard Lottie's footsteps receding
down the hall. He went to close the door tighter, to be on
the safe side.

'I expect you are wondering what this is about,' he said,
turning to face Mrs Elton, whose face had grown dark.

'Why I should need to know anything is beyond me.'
Mrs Elton gave a loud and long sniff and rattled a pan lid.
'I have only been employed in your family for three generations. Three generations, Tristan Dyvelston, and I
changed your napkins when you were small. Don't you
forget it!'

Tristan put his hands on the shoulders of his old nurse
and looked down at her wizened face.

'I have never forgotten it, and I am grateful, but you
must understand what I am trying to do here.'

'What are you attempting to do?' She cocked her head
to one side. 'Don't you try to pull the wool over my old
eyes. I know your ways of old, Master Tristan. There is
the same sort of look about you as when you stole the
cakes meant for high tea.'

'Hardly that.'

'Out with it.' Mrs Elton gestured with her spoon. 'You are not so big that I can't put you over my knee.'

'I am trying to prevent what happened to my uncle from happening to me—I don't want to be married to someone who only married me for my title and my fortune.'

'Then why did you marry her?'

'We were on the terrace,' Tristan replied carefully. 'She is a member of society. One does not ruin virgins.'

'But you think she is as spoilt as a lace table cloth.'

'I would have never married Lottie if I thought that. I have my reasons for this deception.'

'And you seriously think she knows nothing of this?'

'I am positive of it.' Tristan leant against the sideboard. 'Beyond positive. She believes that Peter is Lord Thorngrafton.'

'I gathered that might be the case.' Mrs Elton gave the fire a poke. 'I am not going to ask what sort of smoked gammon and pickles you and your cousin are up to.'

Tristan rapidly related the details to Mrs Elton, whose expression did not change throughout the recital. 'You can see why I have done it.'

'And when she finds out that you have played flummery with her?'

Tristan stared at his housekeeper. 'I haven't tricked her. I married her. And she chose to believe certain things. And once I am sure of her devotion, I will inform her of my wealth and position. She will be overcome with joy.'

'You may know railways and business, Master Tristan, but you don't know women.' Mrs Elton shook her head from side to side.

'You worry too much. Lottie likes pretty things. She wanted to marry a title. She will be delighted.'

'And I am telling you now, Tristan Dyvelston, you can never predict how a woman will react. You should never have tried this deception. She might feel hard done by and I for one wouldn't blame her.'

Tristan paused. What was between Lottie and him was far too new and fragile. He wanted to savour it a bit longer and bind her closer to him. He had to be certain. He risked losing his heart to a woman who only wanted him for his material possessions.

'I will tell her when I am ready. When I know she is devoted to me and not my title.'

'Sometimes, you have to take a risk, Master Tristan, in love just as you do in business…if you don't mind me speaking plainly.'

'I am determined to have a marriage like my parents. My mother married my father knowing that he would more than likely not inherit the title.'

'That was a love match, that one was.'

'All I am asking you to do is to humour me. Let me be the one to explain everything and in my own time.'

'I won't lie to her. She has a good heart, that one. Real top-drawer quality.' Mrs Elton crossed her arms and glared at him. 'If that is what you are asking.'

'Mrs Elton…'

'And I won't volunteer information either, but I warn you, Master Tristan, this will end in tears and they won't be mine.'

'In my own time, Mrs Elton.'

'You are the master here.'

'That I am.' Tristan turned on his heel.

Chapter Twelve

Lottie lifted the shrouds off the furniture in the morning room. The sofa and the armchairs were highly unfashionable, probably from the reign of William IV or even earlier, but they were serviceable. And a little mahogany desk was placed in just the right position for writing letters.

Opening the lid, she discovered a supply of papers, blotter, a fountain pen and an ink well. She stretched out her hand, tempted to begin writing letters, but stopped and closed the lid down with a banging that echoed around the room.

There was much to explore in the room and how could she begin to describe the house without sounding mean or churlish towards Tristan. He could not help the state of the house.

Above all she wanted to keep busy and to keep from thinking about all the changes that would have to be made because she had married Tristan. Mrs Elton had had no notice. She knew that a good housekeeper could find work anywhere, but one as aged as Mrs Elton? It did not feel right. Lottie began to stack the cloths into a neat pile at one side of the room. With a few improvements, the room could be quite presentable.

'Mrs Elton has agreed to stay and she sends you these clothes.' Tristan strode into the room and placed a collection of clothes down on a chair. 'She thought you might like to change.'

'Agreed?' Lottie lifted an eyebrow as a weight rolled off her shoulders. She liked the little housekeeper. Tristan had seen sense. 'I thought…'

'She would not hear of it. She reminded me how long she had worked for my family.' Tristan gave a shrug and took the dust sheet from her. 'She will stay. It will give you more time to do other things. Young married women have to be cosseted, is her point of view.'

'And do you intend on cosseting me?'

'I doubt you will let me.' He gave a half-smile. 'You refused to stay in bed this morning. I had anticipated that you would remain asleep for the whole day.'

'You were gone when I woke. I went in search of you.'

'And now you have found me. Mrs Elton me told that she will put out some more clothes for you.'

'And a stout pair of boots.'

'That as well. I am determined that your feet be properly shod.' Tristan caught her hand and raised it to his lips. Lottie shivered slightly at the touch, pulled back as his eyes watched her. 'You can have a few days resting and getting to know the house, then, when your feet have fully recovered, I will show you the grounds.'

'Will I have any say in the decoration?' Lottie asked to cover her confusion. What they had done last night needed to stay in the bedroom, not be out here in the open. She was sure of that, of the impropriety of it all. 'Little things could be done to make this place more habitable. We would not need to completely refurnish.'

'Any savings would be appreciated.'

'You sound surprised.'

'If you promise not to fill it with pincushions and have numerous At Homes for farmers' wives, I would very much like you to make my house a home.'

His house, a home. Lottie hardly dared breathe. She wanted to. She wanted to show him how much she could do. 'You always bring it back to pincushions. Do you think it wrong to have an enthusiasm? What do you like to do in the evenings?'

Tristan stared at her. 'I play chess or read when I am at home.'

'I discovered a chessboard.' Lottie tapped her fingers against her mouth. 'Maybe you can teach me to play chess. I know Henry plays occasionally. The rules cannot be too difficult. Henry appears to understand them.'

'It is all right, Lottie, you don't have to learn how to play simply to please me.' Tristan's face became inscrutable. 'You may prick pincushions if that is what your heart really desires.'

'But I want to learn…' Lottie heard the desperation in her voice. She wanted to have a connection with Tristan; if that included learning to play chess, she would. Just as she would learn to make new chair covers and refrain from extravagances. She wanted to make this marriage a success. It frightened her that she was rapidly coming to want his regard. She wanted to see his eyes light up and to hear his laugh. She wanted to be with him. She had to make him understand. 'It will pass the time we have together.'

'We shall see this evening.'

Lottie hesitated and said in a great rush, 'I don't want to have a distant marriage. Mama and Papa were happy. They shared things. They played cards and went to dances at the Assembly Rooms together. Papa used to tease her about that. I think Henry and Lucy are less happy. They have little in common except for the children. If you enjoy playing chess, I would like to learn. No one bothered to teach me. How can I know if I will like something if I am kept in ignorance?'

Her voice wavered as she finished. She peeked at him over her hands.

His face had paled and his Adam's apple worked up and down several times. He started to say something, but stopped. Suddenly he appeared to regain control. He gave her an indulgent smile, like she was someone to be humored. 'I think it is about time you got dressed. Mrs Elton will be happy to assist you.'

Lottie blinked rapidly so that he would not see the hurt. Exactly what did he want from this marriage? 'I will go and change. No doubt the clothes will take some alteration. It is well that I am handy with my needle and thread, particularly as I shall not be spending my evenings playing chess.'

Tristan reached out, but she ignored his hand and he let it fall to his side. His eyes were hooded, unreadable. 'You don't have to do something just to please me.'

'I know, but I did want to learn. It will give me something to do in the evenings. I doubt we will be going to any balls. Or if we do, I shall take a stout pair of boots with me. I will become a regular country lass yet.' She gave a weak laugh at the feebleness of her joke. Tristan's brow became darker and she wondered what she had done wrong and longed to do away with convention and ask him to take her in his arms. Instead, she swallowed hard and wrapped the shreds of her dignity about her. 'I had best make myself presentable.'

She walked quickly from the room before her tongue humiliated her further, before she asked him to kiss her. When she was in his arms, everything appeared fine. It was when they met outside the bedroom that things became more strained. She would show him that she could keep economies and could be an asset as he tried to revive this estate. Then this fragile bond between them could grow. All she wanted to do was have him like her and think well of her. To want to spend time with her, just as she wanted to spend time with him.

Tristan only partly listened to Lottie's earnest money-making schemes as they walked through the grounds two days later with increasing uneasiness at their situation. It was getting harder and harder to tell her half-truths.

He had no need of the schemes. His business was healthy. The estate could be and would be easily restored, but he was impressed that she cared enough to make suggestions. Several of her suggestions, like cutting down stands of mature trees to open the view and selling off the timber, warranted a second look.

Was Mrs Elton right? Would Lottie react badly when she learnt the true state of his wealth? Tristan rejected the idea as preposterous. She would be relieved. Yet he hesitated, unwilling to take the risk.

He became aware that she had stopped speaking quite as excitedly and was staring at him with a quizzical glance.

'You are not attending me, Tristan. And I did beat you at chess last night. Remember?'

'How could I forget?'

'Then attend, please.'

'And after we sell the timber, what do we do?' he asked, enjoying the way the afternoon sunlight caught her curls and turned them to burnished gold. His fingers remembered their silken texture and he itched to smooth them from her face, itched to feel her curves against him and go down the secret pathways of desire with her.

'I have gone beyond the possibility of timber.' Lottie waved her hand. 'You are humouring me, just as Henry does when I try to speak of funds. He seems to think that railway stocks will keep going up and up, but they can't as who is going to be able to afford them?'

'I happen to believe the same as you about the railways. And I am not humouring you.' Tristan touched her hand with his. 'Maybe just a little bit. You are so full of ideas that you are like a bee flitting from flower to flower, rarely stopping to enjoy.'

'I would have preferred a butterfly.' Lottie made a little moue with her mouth and Tristan remembered the slide of her lips against his. He managed to hang on to his sanity and not draw her into his arms. 'Besides, I was not speaking of timber at all. I was speaking about a way in which we could return triumphant to Newcastle and then I spied that hut.'

He moved closer and prepared to lead her away from the shadowy summer house where Suzanne used to entertain her lovers and complain of the boring countryside. He should have thought of it before they turned this way. He was unwilling to seduce her there.

'Shall we go and investigate it? I feel the intrepid explorer.'

'Why should you want to do that? It might be better off sold.'

Lottie pressed her gloved hand against his. 'It will be

amusing to tell my friends about it when we return to Newcastle.'

'We shall be living here.'

She tilted her head. 'Surely you will allow me to visit my mother and sister-in-law? And if we sell that stand of timber, it will provide—'

'Do you always try this hard? Does it really matter if you know everything about this estate today?'

Lottie blinked and a puzzled frown appeared between her eyebrows. 'I wanted to seem interested. I wanted to get to know you and the estate you inherited.'

'Seeming and being are two different things.'

'But I *am* interested.' Lottie rubbed a hand across her eyes. She forced her lips to curve upwards. 'And the hut is intriguing. What do you think it was used for? Smuggling?'

'Lottie.' He moved closer and savoured her fresh scent, her innocence. He knew what that hut had been made for. He closed his eyes and saw every portion of it. The leering cupids, the artfully placed mirror. The peepholes for his uncle's spying. It was not what he wanted for Lottie. 'We have time. You don't have to learn everything in the first week. Your feet must pain you.'

'My feet will be fine. I am excited about what could be done to this estate and how it could be brought back to life. That is all.' Lottie clasped her hands together and her face took on an earnest expression. 'I want to make this marriage a real partnership with no secrets between us. Is that too much to ask?'

Tristan shifted uncomfortably. Secrets. There were beginning to be far too many secrets. He kept finding reasons to put off telling her and explaining. They were growing closer and he had no wish to jeopardise that. He wanted to be certain that her desire for him was more than the duty she felt a wife owed her husband.

'A marriage is a marriage.' His hands closed over her shoulders. 'You don't have to try with me. Be yourself. You don't need to spend time coming up with schemes, plots and plans if you don't want to. The estate will take care of itself.'

'But what should I do if I want to please you?'

'Kiss me.'

She raised herself up on her tiptoes and kissed his cheek. A quick hard peck. A dutiful kiss, not a spontaneous one. 'There, I have done that, now will you take me to see this mysterious temple? There must be a story behind it. It looks so lost and forlorn. I want to be able to tell everyone, Martha Irons especially, as she thinks the countryside is boredom personified.'

'You can give me a better kiss than that. It was like one you would give an uncle you are not overly fond of.' Tristan touched cheek.

'Someone might see.' She lightly danced out of his reach. 'Mrs Elton might be looking from the upper windows.'

'She knows we made a runaway match. We are newlyweds.'

'And of course there is the little girl who does the scullery, and the laundress and…' Lottie began ticking names off on her fingers. Excuses rather than true concerns. Tristan knew it with a sinking heart. She had no desire to kiss him. She was attempting to change the subject. The Lottie of the daytime was not the passionate woman he held in his arms at night, and yet he knew she lurked there, waiting to be unleashed.

'How did you learn about these people?'

'I have eyes, Tristan. I saw them over the past few days, when you were busy riding out on the estate. Mrs Elton does not do her own laundry. Everybody sends it out. And her hands are too smooth to do the pots and pans. It stands to reason.'

'But they are of no significance.'

Tristan waved a hand. Had she guessed how many people were actually employed by the estate? Or had she even considered it? Had she begun to wonder? And why hadn't she asked him about it? How long did they have left together in this innocence?

Tristan knew he was not ready to welcome the world back in, not without knowing how she truly felt about him. He wanted her to desire him all the time, to be passionate, without thinking whether it was the right or dutiful thing to do. Without planning how she would conquer society.

'Tristan, they are servants and servants are people.' Lottie pressed her fingers to the bridge of her nose. It was no wonder that things were in a muddle if he did not know how many people Mrs Elton employed. He shouldn't be arrogant. 'A woman always needs to know the number and names of people in her employ. It is basic common sense. Otherwise she might make a hash of the accounts.'

'I can help you with the accounts, but you are changing the subject. Tell me the true reason. Why do you feel the need to boast and brag about the estate to your friends?'

'Boasting?' Lottie hesitated. 'I want people to hear of your accomplishments. I have no wish for people to pity me.'

'You know little of my accomplishments.'

'Then tell me. I am your wife. There should be no secrets between us.'

'When the time is right.' Tristan's eyes became harder

than black obsidian. 'Not when you want to feed your vanity.'

'My vanity?' Lottie stared at him. 'I am your wife.'

'Then you should kiss me properly, instead of wondering about how to make your life in the country sound more exciting to your friends.'

'Not where the servants might see.' Lottie hoped he'd understand what she was trying to say. 'It is terribly bad form. I don't think I have ever seen Henry being affectionate towards Lucy. Oh, he cares about her, and they have children but I have never seen them kissing…not the way you kissed me.'

'Then Henry is an ass.'

'He is my brother.' Lottie gritted her teeth. 'You should not speak that way about my brother. Only I am allowed to speak about him that way.'

'But the kiss you gave me was more like one you would give your brother.'

She cursed the heat rising on her cheeks, and then she tilted her chin in the air. 'What sort of kiss did you have in mind? Then I will know for the next time and keep it in the repertoire.'

His mouth swooped down and captured hers, plundering it, feasting and calling up all the primitive sensations that Lottie had fought so hard to keep inside her today. His hands cupped her buttocks, pulled her close and left her in no doubt about the state of his arousal.

'Tristan, shouldn't we go somewhere? Somewhere more private?' she murmured against his lips as her eyes flickered towards the house.

His answer was to increase the kiss, to plunder more deeply until her hands curled around his neck and held him there as her back arched towards him. Her breasts swelled and pushed against the cotton. She gave a small mewl in the back of her throat.

He lifted his head, stepped away from her at the exact instant that her bones began to melt and she ceased to care where they were. The cool air rushed between them. His lips took on a cynical twist and his eyes travelled slowly down her form, taking in the state of her clothing.

'Now do you understand the sort of a kiss a wife should give her husband of only a few days? Without being asked?'

Lottie's hands struggled to rearrange her clothes. She wanted her pulse to stop racing.

'I did not want to presume,' she said in a low voice.

'Not presume? You are my wife, my bride!'

Lottie recoiled from the suddenness of his outburst and from the way his eyebrows drew together. Her heartbeat slowed and her breath caught in her throat. 'I am your wife and not your lover.'

'And there is a difference?' He lifted his eyebrow. 'Pray tell me, wife, what have we been doing in our bedroom every evening? Or does that come under wifely duties?'

She bit her lip, not wanting to show how much he had hurt her. Wifely duty—was that all it was to him? 'There are certain expectations…'

'Who has these expectations? Society? Me?'

'I do.' Lottie drew a deep breath, struggled to contain her temper. 'I mean to be a success. And I have noticed that men treat their wives differently from their paramours.'

'You have a lot to learn, Lottie. When two people desire each other, it is natural they should want to touch each other. There is nothing wrong with kissing in the open air.'

Desire, but not love. Lottie put her arms about her waist.

Desire faded, love lasted. And in love was the one thing Tristan was not with her. He might desire her. He might even indulge her, but he was not in love with her.

All the breath left her body as she silently acknowledged that she was falling in love with him. That she loved him. Over a week ago she had not even known he existed and now her whole world was starting to revolve around him and his quest to restore this estate. She wanted to be a good wife, but she also wanted him to look at her with passion. She wanted to be important to him, and not just an object. She wanted this marriage to be a partnership, a meeting of two people who respected each other.

'I understand.' She kept her chin up and did not allow her voice to wobble.

For an instant Tristan's urbane mask slipped and she saw fury. 'You understand nothing.'

'I understand more than you give me credit for.' Lottie kept her back straight and her voice even, despite the knots in her stomach. 'Back at the hotel, you saw me as another Suzanne—a woman whose family wanted to marry her to the first lord who offered. You sought to save me from that fate by kissing me and unfortunately we got caught. We were forced to marry. You played my knight because of your uncle's wife's experience. It had nothing to do with me.'

'No one forced me to marry you.'

'You need not have worried. I would have found a way to avoid Sir Geoffrey Lea.' Lottie paused and summoned all her courage. She had to lance this boil. 'You must stop seeing her in me. Your uncle's wife sounds like a perfect beast.'

'She was spoilt and demanding.' He lifted an eyebrow. 'Has anyone called you that? Have I?'

'I am not spoilt,' Lottie said between gritted teeth. 'I

may like pretty things and enjoy parties, but I am hardly spoilt. I give generously to the poor. I devote myself tirelessly to good works. I even helped out at last year's bazaar and I did not demand the ribbons and bows stall but helped Mrs Hedigan out with her Scents of Araby stall.'

'Are you worried that people think you spoilt? Is that why you are so quick to defend yourself. It is the first time I have ever heard a scents stall used to bolster an argument.' The coldness of his smile increased. 'What else shall you use? Do you give your cast-off gowns to your maids?'

'I shared a maid with Mama. It was what was expected. The maid was grateful for them, I am sure.' Lottie bit out each word.

'You shared a maid. Was that a measure of your economising?'

Lottie longed to throw something. He was laughing at her. Belittling her.

'If you feel that way, I wonder that you married me, spoilt child that you thought I was.' She clenched her fists. Counted to ten and forced her fingers to open one by one. 'Why did you marry me? Was I to be the jewel in the estate? You were going to save me, because you could not save the other woman? I did not need your sacrifice, Tristan.'

Tristan was silent. He stood there, glowering at her while a muscle worked in his jaw. A lump began to grow in Lottie's throat. She wanted him to take her into his arms, but he wouldn't. She turned on her heel and began walking away from him before she made an even bigger fool of herself.

'Where are you going?' he said in an icy voice. 'Our discussion is far from over.'

'There is little point in discussing it further,' she said, after she had regained control of her emotions. She kept her chin high and looked down her nose. 'I am going to write letters, lots and lots of letters.'

'Telling your friends how hard done by you are. What a mistake you made. How you are buried alive in the countryside.' His lip curled back and his eyes had turned glacial.

'No, telling them how wonderful this estate is and how pleasant my wedding trip was.' She paused and drew a deep breath. 'And maybe, just maybe, if I write it out enough times, I will begin to believe it. Good day to you, sir.'

'Wait.' His hand captured her wrist, held her there. She looked at his hand and one by one, his fingers released her. She stood there, rubbing it. 'The hut was used ten years ago by my uncle's wife. It was where she entertained her lovers. It is no place where I would like my wife to be. I never want you to feel sordid and illicit.'

'It would have been helpful if you had told me that in the first place.' Lottie attempted to maintain an icy dignity as a flash of jealousy went through her. Her accusation had been close to the mark. She was a symbol to him, nothing more. 'Far be it from me to disturb the memories of your youth.'

'This has nothing to do with my youth! This has everything to do with you and your need to conform. Your need to find excuses for people's behaviour.'

'How dare you say such a thing! You forget who you are, Tristan Dyvelston!'

'I am your husband and we will live where I say!'

'I was attempting to help! Why do you seek to hide things from me? Maybe if you had told me the truth…'

'Good day to you, ma'am. When you decide to apologise, we can speak.'

Tristan stalked off, leaving her standing staring after him. Open-mouthed. Furious. How dare he suggest that she apologise. She had behaved properly!

Lottie's temper had improved considerably several hours later when she had finished writing her letters to various friends and relatives, telling them about the marriage. With each line she wrote, it became harder and harder to be positive and enthusiastic about her situation. There were only so many ways she could describe the utter horror of the house without it sounding awful.

She chewed the end of the fountain pen and tried again in her letter to Lucy. She described the wonderful battlements on which her nephews would enjoy playing soldiers and how Lucy herself would enjoy strolling in the gardens with its many delights and follies.

She paused and then, gripping the pen more tightly, she wrote: *And, dearest Lucy, Mama is so scatterbrained these days that I fear she will have forgotten to send my trunks. I know how good you were at sending my things on to Haydon Bridge—could you please make the necessary arrangements now?* A problem solved, simply and neatly without having to confess after all.

Lottie tucked a strand of hair behind her ear and began her next letter, the one she had been putting off. She drew out the bank note from her reticule. Placed it on the desk and picked up her fountain pen again.

Dear Lord Thorngrafton, Many thanks.

Her pen paused over the paper, creating an ink blot. She would do this. She would send the money back to Lord Thorngrafton with a pleasant note, inviting him to Gortner Hall whenever he desired to visit. A little pleasantry, but one that could go a long way towards easing tensions between Tristan and his titled cousin. For too long the feud had gone on. She had to show that there was no simmering resentment, and this provided her with the perfect opportunity.

She put the blotter over the paper, folded it with the note inside and sealed it. But where to send it? She frowned. She could hardly ask Tristan. This would be a wonderful surprise for him when she unveiled it. She tapped the pen against the edge of the desk.

Then it came to her—the perfect solution.

Swiftly she addressed the outside to Lord Thorngrafton, care of Shaw's Hotel, Gilsland. If Lord Thorngrafton had left the hotel, he was sure to have provided a forwarding address. Lottie smiled and allowed her shoulders to relax.

The scheme was flawless. She would demonstrate to Tristan that she could be useful. She took her duties as a wife seriously. The social contact was far more than a duty. It was a pleasure.

Lottie remained floating on the air of sainthood when she discovered Mrs Elton in the kitchen. 'I presume there is someone who picks up the post.'

'Way aye, there is, the lad should be coming for it in under an hour, but the master—'

'I have no wish to trouble Tris…Mr Dyvelston.' Lottie gave her best smile. She didn't want to explain about their earlier quarrel. She would be polite, but distant. Mrs Elton had no cause to hear of her troubles. It was far better that the staff were kept in ignorance of such things. She gave a little wave of her hand. 'He undoubtedly has a thousand-and-one better things to be doing than seeing to my correspondence.'

She waited, trying not to hop from foot to foot like a

child. Mrs Elton had to take the letters. The thought of going bonnet in hand to Tristan would ruin the whole surprise.

'Aye, I can see your reasoning,' Mrs Elton said, tightening her shawl about her shoulders. 'He does have a lot on his mind at the moment.'

'There is a letter to his cousin that I am especially anxious to have sent out. There has been much bad feeling between Lord Thorngrafton and Mr Dyvelston; I suspect, left to their devices, neither will make the first gesture of reconciliation.'

'You are a good soul, ma'am. That you are. I knew it the moment you came into the kitchen. Joss is a sound judge of character.'

'Joss is a wonderful dog.'

The small dog gave a little yap at the sound of his name as Mrs Elton's face took on a queer expression, as if she might be about to burst into tears.

'I will see that the letter is sent. You may count on me, ma'am. I have no doubt that it will go a long way towards reconciling them.'

'Do you?' Lottie rocked back on her heels and resisted the urge to pat her hair. 'I do hope so. It is awful to be at loggerheads with one's relations. I want peace and harmony between Tristan and Lord Thorngrafton. It will make it easier in the long run.'

'I do so agree, ma'am.'

Lottie played with the little dog for a few more moments before she returned to the morning room to await Tristan's apology. She would be forgiving with regal dignity. Gracious without being condescending. She would let him kiss her properly as they were indoors and she would make him forget his past.

Lottie picked the perfect spot to wait—the sofa facing the door. The chessboard was ready and waiting. She would offer him a wager, once the unpleasant business of his apology was over.

Twice heavy male footsteps stopped at the door and her breath caught as she lifted her mouth ready for her kiss. But after a moment, they carried on.

When the clock struck nine, she realised that he was not going to come. Lottie rose, enlisted Mrs Elton's aid in loosening her corset and went upstairs. She chose her prettiest shift and left her hair unbound. A golden carpet, he had whispered only last night, running his hands through it. And then she began her vigil again, watching the candle wax slowly drip.

This time, he would appear.

She heard the distinct click of his dressing-room door and the sound of his boots and then his clothes hitting the floor. Every particle of her froze. He would come to her.

She willed him to open the door and stride toward her. Hastily she blew out the candle, readied herself.

Then she heard the creak of the divan in his dressing room. Silence. She waited and waited. Listened to the distant ticking of a clock.

A single tear ran down her cheek as her eyelids fluttered closed. He never came. She had never had a chance to accept his apology.

Never had the chance to whisper her own to him.

Chapter Thirteen

The door to the library was firmly shut. Unwelcoming. Lottie paused and listened for any faint sounds coming from within. Tristan had been excessively polite when she encountered him finishing his breakfast. They had even managed to speak about inconsequential things. Lottie had given him several opportunities and openings to apologise, but he had declined to take them, choosing instead to excuse himself at the earliest opportunity.

Out here in the hallway, faced with a closed door and a day that stretched before her, she knew what she had to do—the unthinkable. She had to swallow her pride and apologise for her behaviour first.

Her peck on the cheek when he had asked for more had been wrong. She should have kissed him. Properly. Without prompting. She should have listened to her body. She should have considered his pride when she mentioned her friends. She had to share some of the blame for their quarrel.

Living like this—alone in this great ruin of a house with the barest of conversations—was not really living, not when she desired more.

She wanted his company. She missed his smile, the way his eyes danced. And how, despite the adversities that life had sent him and his straitened circumstances, he worried about others, sought to take care. He was a man she could respect. A man she desired. A man she loved, even if he did not feel the same.

It was more than she could hope for in a marriage.

It had been stupid and pointless of her to be jealous of some long-ago woman. Changing the past was not a possibility, but she could work with Tristan and, in time, they could grow together and reach an understanding.

She pressed her hands together to keep them from trembling. This was worse than her first ball. She wanted to go back to what they had had before. She wanted to experience that passion again.

Was that so wrong of her?

She went over her speech one more time. She had practised it in front of the dressing-room mirror five times before she knew it was perfect. It had to be perfect. It would be. She took a deep breath and rapped sharply on the door.

'Enter.'

Lottie slowly opened the door. She started her speech and made the mistake of looking at him full in the face. A single lock of black hair dangling over his forehead captured her attention and drove every other thought from her brain. Her fingers itched to smooth it away. It was all she could do to stand and stare at him.

'Was there something you required?'

You. The word leapt to her mind. Hung there. She trembled, worried that she might have said it aloud. Tried to remember her speech, but the words kept sliding away from her and all she could do was stare and mumble slightly. She swallowed hard. 'Tristan, I have come into the room—'

She stopped, her mind once again becoming a blank as he continued to regard her with a stony expression. The temptation to turn around and flee back to her room became overpowering, but she made her mouth turn up at the corners. Hopefully he would understand her unspoken message.

'Do you always state the obvious?' He raised a single eyebrow and her smile faded under the sternness of his gaze. 'Or am I suppose to guess your true purpose?'

'No…that is…I wanted to speak to you about something of great urgency.'

He pointedly rearranged the papers on the table where he was working. A distinct rustle of paper to show her that he was busy, had little time for her. A pang went through Lottie's heart. This was getting increasingly more difficult.

'Do you have another money-making scheme that you wish to discuss? Another way in which you can show off to your friends? Am I going to have to play a game of questions?'

Lottie shut the door with a bang. 'I have closed the door.'

'I can see that.' His hands stilled on the stack of papers. 'A start. You wish to speak to me in private.'

'This is not how this interview was supposed to go.' Lottie gave a small stamp of her foot. 'It is not how I practised it.'

'And what is wrong with it? What small detail? What *duty* have you forgotten?'

'You are not making it easy for me. You were supposed to make it easy for me.'

Tristan stood up. His height towered over her. His dark

hair contrasted with the white of his shirt front. One stray strand looped over his forehead, giving him a boyish appearance. But there was nothing boyish about his guarded expression. 'Should I make it easy for you?'

She moved closer to the table, closer to him. She lifted her face towards him, a clear invitation. 'I have come to apologise.'

His face changed for an instant before the mask went down again. 'What do you need to apologise for? What misdemeanour have you done, Carlotta?'

Lottie winced at the Carlotta. He wanted to provoke her, but she had to take this chance or always wonder what might have happened.

'I should have kissed you properly. I was too far gone in sensibilities. I was wrong.' Lottie stopped. Her brow wrinkled. She had said it and he made no move towards her. Had she left it too late?

'Will you kiss me now?' The words were so softly said that she did not know if she had imagined them.

'Yes.' She took a few steps forward, curled an arm about his neck and brought his head down to hers. His cool lips touched hers. Soft at first, but becoming hard as she teased them with her tongue. His arms came around her and held her. The kiss seemed to stretch for ages. Slow. Satisfying.

'Was this the sort of kiss you had in mind?' she whispered.

'It will do for the starters.' His hands cupped her face. 'I accept your apology.'

'I did say that I would try.' She stepped back, uncertain suddenly. 'Having kissed you, I should leave you to your work. You are very busy with papers.'

'Appearances can be deceptive.'

'Can they?' She struggled to breathe as a delicious pulse of warmth spread through her.

'They can.' He threaded his fingers through hers and pulled her unresisting body back against his. His hands worked on her buttons and she felt her dress begin to loosen. 'Very deceptive.'

He caught her face in his hands. Ran his fingers through her hair. Pressed a kiss against her temple. 'You should not be frightened with me, Lottie. I want to protect you.'

Lottie stiffened. Was Tristan going to carry her up to the bedroom again? What if Mrs Elton or the scullery maid saw? How could she face them? And yet, she knew that she wanted this. She wanted to feel Tristan's body against hers. She wanted to prove to him that she did desire him. 'There is no bed here.'

'We don't need a bed.' He gave a husky laugh. 'Sometimes, I forget how innocent you truly are, sweet Lottie. How much I can look forward to teaching you. Lovemaking can happen anywhere.'

'On the floor?' She didn't want to think how hard the floor was. She didn't want to think at all. She wanted Tristan to kiss her, to hold her. 'Please, Tristan, not the floor.'

'Here.' He lowered his mouth and she felt herself falling back against the table. With one sweeping motion he sent the papers crashing to the carpet.

'Your work!' Lottie turned her head. Paper was now littered all over the floor. 'What can you be thinking of, Tristan?'

'Leave it. Stay there. On the table.' His eyes were smouldering as he pushed her dress down, revealing the cream of her shoulder.

Lottie froze, but she was unable to prevent the warm tingles that were flooding through her. What did he mean to do? She made a little gesture. 'But they are jumbled and you were busy. You will be neglecting—'

'The best place for them. I have more important uses for this table now. You are at the correct height.' His voice was molten honey, flowing over her, lapping at her senses. Lulling her.

Lottie struggled to concentrate. 'Just the height for what?'

'Trust me.' Tristan looked down at her pale oval face, her blonde hair golden against the deep red-brown of the desk. All his muscles tensed. Patience. He wanted to get this right.

She had come to him, had kissed far more passionately than he had expected, but he wanted her to understand that passion was not something that had to be hidden in the dark. He wanted her to surrender to him. Fully. Here. Now.

His hands grasped her shoes, eased them off. One, then the other. He forced himself to go slow. Rolled her stockings down, tracing the outline of her calf with steady fingers, and listened to her intake of breath. He balanced her pink feet on his hands. Small. Vulnerable. A finger slowly touched the now healing blisters. Her foot arched towards him and he placed a quick kiss on its instep. Tasted the smoothness of her perfect skin. His actions had damaged it, but it was healing.

He glanced up. Beyond her feet was the lace edging of her drawers and then the white froth of her petticoat. His body ached with need. He had to go slow. He had to savour this.

'What are you doing?' She raised herself up on her elbows and her hands began to smooth her skirts down.

'Lie back on the table. I want to see how your feet are healing.'

'I could have told you that.' She gave a half smile as her hand tucked a stray ringlet behind her ear. 'Your ointment worked wonders. I have obeyed your instructions.'

'I wanted to make sure. Let me examine your feet.' His fingers encircled her ankle. Held her still. 'Indulge me.'

'Are you sure it is safe?'

'You were the one to close the door.'

Her shoulders relaxed slightly. 'Yes, I suppose you are right.'

He put out a finger and traced the outline of her bottom lip, felt it tremble beneath his touch.

Tristan lifted her right foot and massaged it with strong steady fingers. His fingers circled and stroked and gradually her foot began to relax and her eyes became hooded.

'Tristan, I hardly think a table is the right place for this.' Her voice had deepened to husky rasp. 'There is a sofa over there.'

'It is exactly the right place for what I have in mind. Trust me.'

'I do trust you. You are my husband.'

Tristan raised the foot to his mouth, closed his lips around her big toe and suckled. He heard a gasp of pleasure and reached out to catch her questing hand. Her fingers curled around his as he trailed his tongue down the instep of her foot. He squeezed them as he heard a moan of pleasure come from her throat.

Slowly he put one of her feet on his shoulder. Lifted the other. Trailed open-mouthed kisses from her heel to her toe. Heard her gasp of anticipation as his mouth hovered over her, teasing her toe with his tongue while his hands drew circles on her calves. He stopped. Looked towards her. Her skirts flowed around them and her drawers gaped opened, revealing her dark tangle of curls and her innermost folds—pink, glistening. Tempting him. His groin ached to breaking point.

He caught his breath and feasted on the sight as the urge to take her threatened to swamp him.

His body throbbed with need, but he drew on his reserves of self-control. He had to remember that she was not experienced. He would introduce her slowly to pleasure. Show her what it could be like between a man and a woman. Show her that a wife could experience passion with her husband. That it should be more than simply a duty—it could be the most pleasurable thing in the world.

'Are you finished?' Her voice brought him back from the brink.

'Finished?' He ran his fingers up her calf, under the fine linen, caressing her curves. 'I have barely begun. Now you shall discover what you can do with a table. Why it is more necessary than a sofa or a bed. What its true purpose is.'

'True purpose?' Her tongue ran over her lips, making them glisten.

'Relax and enjoy.' He reached out and touched her hand. 'But if, at any point, you wish to say stop, do so and I will. I want to give you pleasure.'

'Pleasure.' Her husky voice sent a quiver of desire through him. And he barely retained his self-control. 'I will hold you to your promise.'

His fingers travelled up her legs over the drawers, this time, skimming until they reached her warm, moist cleft. He took his finger and very deliberately stroked along its length. Listened to her gasp. Forced himself to wait. To see if she could take more. To see if she wanted more. Her eyes were closed, her mouth full, but she uttered no protest.

He stroked more firmly, deeper. Saw her hips rise and her head began to writhe on the wood as her hands searched for purchase.

He slid one finger in and her body arched to meet him. Tightening around him. Soft. Warm.

He withdrew, bent his head and slid her forward and up until his breath touched her hidden folds. He felt the shiver go through her. His body tensed, waited, as her face was hidden from him in a froth of white. But her only reaction was to tighten her legs about his neck, urge him closer.

His tongue darted forward and lapped at her crease.

She gasped and wriggled as another wave of pleasure hit her senses. He put a hand on her stomach, held her there to allow her time to absorb the sensation. 'Tristan.'

'Do you like this?' he asked as his deep gaze penetrated hers. She could only nod. Every particle of her seemed focused on this one spot. She knew many would be horrified, but his tongue against her innermost folds created a need within her. She wanted more. Her innermost being cried out for more as her body writhed against the silken smooth wood.

'Please.' It was no more than a breath.

He lowered his head and resumed his lazy exploration of her folds and hidden places. Taking her to the brink and retreating. She gave an inarticulate cry and her body bucked upwards as he found her innermost core and suckled. A great molten wave washed through her and her hands clung to the table top as her body arched upwards to meet him, to seek more of the sensation.

Her world exploded.

Her hands gripped the edge of the table, held on as his mouth continued to play between her thighs.

Then, when she felt herself begin to break, he raised his head. Stopped, looked at her. Leant forward. Placed a gentle kiss against her mouth.

'I need...'

'Soon. Soon.' He slowly and deliberately unbuttoned his trousers. Lowered her legs to his waist, put his hands on her hips and brought her forwards. Entered her. Impaling himself. Her body opened for him, lifted up, urged him to drive deeper.

All around her stars burst as he called the rhythm. Faster and faster she felt the table slide under her bottom. She held on to him with her legs. Drove him deeper. Needing him. Needing to feel the length of him. Then, with a great cry, the world exploded for a second time. She heard his cry echo hers as together they reached that exquisite plateau.

He lowered her back down to the table. And she lay there, panting, looking up at the white confection of the ceiling. A deep languor went through her body. She reached out a hand, brought his fingers to her face. Pressed them against her cheek as no words could describe what she felt. She wanted this floating to continue for ever.

He traced the outline of her swollen mouth with his thumb, gathered her in his arms and carried her to the sofa. Tristan sat down with her nestled in his lap. Her head rested on his shirt and her hand played with the buttons.

'Now do you see what a table can be used for?' his lazy voice whispered against her ears.

'I am beginning to understand.' She gave a slight laugh. 'But perhaps I can have a reminder every now and then. From my husband. Tristan.'

Tristan felt the husky laugh go through him. He wanted to shout and dance. He had done it. He had tamed her. She wanted him for herself, not for his title or for his money. His plan had succeeded.

'Do you like it here?'

A crease came between her eyebrows. 'It has potential. Does the sofa have other uses as well?'

Tristan paused. He wanted her again, but he also wanted

her to understand about her misconceptions. How she had to stop leaping to judgements. He wanted her to trust him. Completely. There should be no secrets between them. But how? Would she understand why he had done it this way? Gently he eased her off his lap. 'I meant the house.'

'The house is fine, but I want to be with you, Tristan.'

'We need to speak, Lottie.' He lifted a damp curl from her face. 'About the future. About what happens next. After the honeymoon. After the wedding trip.'

She sat up straight, her hands primly in her lap. Her eyes became troubled. 'To speak? Is there something wrong, Tristan? What have I done? This is our home, isn't it?'

'No, nothing is wrong. Everything is very right.' He gathered her hands in his. 'There are a few things—'

His voice was drowned out by the steady knocking on the door. 'Master, master,' Mrs Elton called. 'A man has come to see you and he swears it is urgent.'

'I will see him later.'

There was some mumbling. 'He says that he is from Misters McGowan and Saidy, sir. Urgent, like. Important.'

Tristan ran his fingers through his hair, glanced back at where Lottie perched. If McGowan and Saidy had summoned him, it was because Peter had not held true to his promise. Tristan would have to make Peter understand there were consequences to his actions.

Lottie would have to wait. He wondered idly what she would look like dressed in nothing but a strand of pearls. They would be his gift to her. A way to explain. An omen for the future.

'I have to go, Lottie.' He kissed her cheek. 'Trust me on this.'

'Go where?'

'Away on business. I should be back within a day.'

Her bottom lip trembled. 'I will miss you.'

'And I you,' Tristan said, looking down at her. She started to rearrange her clothes, but he caught her hands. 'Stay like that until after I have gone. Let me make a memory of you like that. My passionate wife.'

Her cheeks flushed scarlet.

Tristan forced his body to turn and leave her. In a few short hours everything would be clear between them.

'He's in there, or at least I think he is. McGowan and I slung in him there,' Saidy said, jerking his head towards the stable when Tristan arrived at Mumps Ha', the notorious hedge alehouse about a mile from Gilsland. It had lost none of the gloom and secrecy that Sir Walter Scott had noted in his novel about the area. 'Bawling his eyes out like a girl. I would have expected better of a relation of yours, Thorngrafton.'

'Have you harmed him?' Tristan asked, handing the reins of his horse to the waiting groom. The ride from Gortner Hall had taken several hours and the weather had turned nasty. A sharp wind howled down from the north and the alehouse appeared permanently wrapped in mist. 'I told you that I did not want him attacked, and you were only to approach him if he approached first.'

'He came in, all swaggering and puffed up. Throwing his weight around in a manner he had no right to.' Saidy twisted his hat in his hands. 'Even told us that he were you, like.'

'That he should not have done.' Tristan examined his gloves.

'I thought so. I says to McGowan, I says, this here man is our pigeon. That one that Thorngrafton told us to look out. He ain't no right to that name.' Saidy's smile increased, revealing his broken teeth. 'He had the stake, no need for a vowel there. Then the games really began. Fancied himself an expert. And it became right interesting for a while...'

'But have you injured him? I wanted no physical violence.'

'It weren't necessary. Hurt his pride, mayhap, but other than that we obeyed orders. He became overconfident. Thought we were a couple of amateurs. It was like taking bonbons from a girl.' Saidy puffed out his chest. 'He lost and lost badly.'

'Who has his vowels?'

'The vowels are here. Ready for purchase.' The man's face took on a crafty aspect.

'I will pay you for them.' Tristan held a pile of notes out. 'Unless you'd care to play cards for it.'

Saidy's hand went out. He looked at the stables, then back at Tristan. 'Cards? With you? Not on your life. Not after the other night. You know when to stop. A trick I intend to employ more often.'

'I thank you for the compliment,' Tristan said as Saidy handed him Peter's debts. 'It is the amount we agreed... the other night. I trust there are no added extras or incidentals.'

Saidy's face took on an expression of outraged innocence. 'I don't need to count it, you know. We were working for you and you do have a certain reputation.'

'A well-deserved reputation,' McGowan said as he came out from the stables. 'That there punch that you laid on Den Casey is the talk of Gretna Green. He were a champion, he were. And don't deny it were you.'

Tristan nodded. 'I will see him now.'

The stables were little more than a hovel. A figure crouched on the ground, pleading as Tristan walked in.

'You have everything. I don't have anything more.'

'I warned you what would happen if you attempted to use my name.'

'I had a letter from Lottie Dyvelston. Addressed to Lord Thorngrafton. I took it as providence.'

'You had a letter from Lottie?' Tristan started in surprise. What was Lottie up to? 'I don't believe you.'

'She sent the touching epistle to Shaw's and enclosed a considerable sum of money.' Peter gave a watery smile. 'She was under the impression I had asked your coachman to give it to her in case she needed to escape. Yours, I take it.'

'Robinson was in an over-generous mood. And a little over-zealous in carrying out my orders.'

'You should maintain better control of your manservant.'

'Normally I do.'

Peter tapped the side of his nose. 'Ah, but Lottie has very fine blue eyes.'

'I have no wish to discuss the state of my wife's eyes with you. Or with any other man!' Tristan barely retained control of his temper.

'Is your little deception running into difficulties, then, Tristan? Lottie is not feeble-minded. She saw through my stratagem with ease last November.'

'I have no idea what you are talking about.' Tristan crossed his arms. 'I came here to offer you the chance at redemption. A chance to get out of this stinking hellhole and start a new life, away from here.'

'Your wife appears not to know your proper title and begs me to join you at table when next I am in the area,' Peter continued as if he had not heard Tristan speak. 'It would appear that I am not in need of redemption, but you are. You have misled your wife, Tristan.'

'That is the drink talking, Peter.' Tristan tapped the vowels against his thigh. 'I hold your debts.'

Peter's laughter echoed around the stables as he shook his head.

'I fail to see the merriment in this situation.'

'Your wife.'

'My wife?' Tristan stared at his cousin in astonishment. 'What does Lottie have to do with it?'

Peter pressed his fingertips together. 'I am a gentleman, Tristan. And as such never borrow money from ladies. I sent the money back to Lady Thorngrafton with my compliments. Now who is ruined?'

'You sent Lottie the money?' Tristan bit out each word, not able to believe his ears.

'It seemed the right and proper thing to do. A magnanimous gesture to appease the goddess of fortune.' Peter put his hands behind his head. 'I am not without family feeling.'

'You did it to spite me.'

Peter's smile increased. 'That, too.'

Tristan weighed his options. The die was cast. He wanted to be the one to tell Lottie. He might get there before the letter arrived, if he hurried. 'You are incorrigible.'

'I am the only kin you have.' Peter wiped a handkerchief across his face. 'Now, are you going to give me my vowels back? You need me. I will happily explain that I forced you into the situation. Otherwise, what explanation will you be able to offer her?'

Tristan crossed his arms, stared at his cousin. He could not lie to Lottie. 'The truth. She deserves nothing less.'

'But…but…'

'I am going to give you a chance to start afresh, Peter.' Tristan tapped the pieces of paper against his leg. 'Next time, the man you lose to might not be so generous.'

'You are giving them back to me.' Peter's face shone in the pale light. He ran a hand through his hair. 'I never expected it from you.'

'No, I am keeping them as insurance. You owe me first before anyone else.' Tristan felt a pool of cold anger surge through him. Peter had so much, every advantage, and he chose to squander it on this. 'You will not gamble again. You will go elsewhere and start a new life.'

'But…but…'

'Do you have the money to pay me?'

Peter hung his head. 'No. My estates are all mortgaged. I even pawned the family jewels. But you will forgive me. You are my cousin.'

'I did warn you not to use my title. What is mine stays mine.'

'You remind me more and more of our uncle, Tristan.'

'I am not him. His fate is not mine!' Tristan bit out each word. He pressed his hands into his eyes, regained control. 'Peter, I do want what is best for you, so you can prosper.'

Peter hung his head, defeated. 'Where? Where should I go?'

'I will provide you passage to one of the colonies. Prove yourself and you will go far away from here. I am not without mercy, Peter.' Tristan permitted a smile to cross his face.

'And what did you get, Tristan? Was it worth the price?'

'That is for me to decide.' Tristan turned on his heel and left his cousin bleating in the grimy stables.

Chapter Fourteen

Lottie sat on the library sofa with her feet curled under her for a long time. Her body ached from the passion she had shared with Tristan, and she worried slightly about what he wanted to tell her. She had nearly whispered her love for him and for one awful moment had thought she had.

He must care something for her. What they had shared had gone beyond all understanding.

If those men had not come for him on urgent business, perhaps he would have said more. All she could do now was wonder what he had meant about after the honeymoon. This was not a wedding trip. This was where they were going to live—both of them together. He wasn't going to abandon her here, was he?

A small sigh escaped her. Perhaps she had ruined everything and he did not care for her. Perhaps he wanted to escape her. He had been warm and caring before the men had arrived, but then he had changed. It was as if the shutters had come down again, and he wanted to keep parts of his life from her. Was it too greedy of her to want to be involved in everything? She wanted to be his chief confidante, the one he would turn to first. That was the sort of marriage she had dreamt about, one that seemed like a castle in the clouds.

Unable to sit and let her doubts overwhelm her, she began to straighten the library and to plan ways of improving it. The sofa needed pillows and the table legs should be covered.

Her hand hovered over the mess of papers. Tristan had told her to leave them, but that was when… Her cheeks grew hot. Surely he could not have meant these to be left on the floor indefinitely. She picked them up and placed them on the table, making a neat pile. Idly she picked up one and began to read, starting in surprise. She flicked through the next few. They were all addressed to Lord Thorngrafton. Papers that Lord Thorngrafton should have, not Tristan. Or maybe his man of business. It was not unknown for a lord to employ one of his relations to take charge of the day-to-day running of his business so that he could concentrate on those that mattered to him. Lottie pressed her hand against her mouth, comprehension dawning.

Why had Tristan pretended that he and Lord Thorngrafton were not close, when in fact he was his man of business? He had to be. It was the only explanation. It was why Lord Thorngrafton had Tristan at his side at Shaw's Hotel and why Lord Thorngrafton provided the carriage. A tiny pain developed behind her eyes. It had to be the explanation. There could not be any other.

She didn't want to think about Tristan acquiring papers that were not rightfully his, deceiving someone as to his true identity. Tristan had far too much integrity for such a thing. Lottie put her hand to her throat. But that did not explain the queer look he had given her when they'd first met and she said that she knew Lord Thorngrafton. Unless… She dismissed the idea as irrational and the product of a fevered imagination. Tristan would have told her. He would have had to have given his full name to the blacksmith when they married.

She ran out to the hallway and gazed at the portraits. A long line of Dyvelstons. This was no minor estate. And why had the former Lord Thorngrafton left it to Tristan when he hated him so? Had he had a choice? She reached out and grasped the banister, struggled to hang on to the fact that she had met the new Lord Thorngrafton.

Her footsteps echoed down the corridor as she hurried to the kitchens and barged into Mrs Elton.

'You startled me, pet,' the older woman said, smoothing her apron and cap. 'You appear distressed. Master Tristan will be back as soon as he can be.'

Lottie pressed her hands against her stomach and took a deep breath as she fought to keep the nervous tone from her voice. 'I wanted to learn more about Tristan's family.'

'His family, ma'am?' Mrs Elton developed an interest in her apron. 'Shouldn't you ask Master Tristan about them? Begging your pardon, ma'am, but he might be the right and proper person.'

'Tristan has gone off on business and failed to tell me when he might return. I require some information, now.' Lottie paused and counted to ten. 'His father. I wanted to learn more about his father.'

'Lucas Dyvelston?' Mrs Elton's face cleared. 'Mr Dyvelston was a kind master, unlike his brother. He had time for people. It was such a shame that he died so young and his dear wife as well. A tragedy. And such a love story. Tristan was their only child.'

'Exactly what was his relation to Lord Thorngrafton? I know Tristan told me, but I have forgotten.' Lottie batted her eyelashes and gave her winsome smile. 'My mind can be like a sieve.'

'Lucas was the younger brother. He married against his father's wishes and was cut off, but managed to amass a small fortune.'

'Were there only the two brothers in the family?' Lottie made her voice sound light. 'You said—younger brother.'

'Did I? There were three children in the family. Lord Thorngrafton was the eldest.'

Lottie felt certain that Mrs Elton could hear her heart thumping. 'Ah, that explains it. I was wondering where Peter Dyvelston, the present Lord Thorngrafton, fit into the picture. I understand that Tristan's uncle did not have any children.'

'Master Peter?' The woman's eyes flicked about the room and her hands plucked at her apron. 'Now, that reminds me—something did come for you and what with Master Tristan departing and everything, I forgot to give it to you.'

She hurried over to the butcher's block and held up a letter.

'Who could be sending me things?' Lottie turned it over. 'I don't recognise the handwriting.'

'Master Peter sent it. I'd recognise his writing anywhere.'

'Why has he sent me a letter?' Lottie pressed her lips together. First the money and now this. Every single time she encountered Lord Thorngrafton, something went wrong.

'An answer to your letter, maybe?'

Lottie smacked her hand against her forehead. 'Dear, sweet Mrs Elton. Of course. I had not even considered the possibility. That must be what it is. Lord Thorngrafton is being gentlemanly.' Lottie turned the parcel over in her hand. 'And Tristan was wrong. Lord Thorngrafton does want to be friends.'

'Master Tristan and Master Peter were boys together.'

Lottie sat down on the kitchen bench and began to attack the parcel, tearing the letter to reveal the bank note. Was this a hint? Another move in his attempt to make her his mistress? The thought made her flesh crawl. The only man she wanted to touch her was Tristan.

'I shall have to send it back. Immediately.'

'Shouldn't you wait to hear what Master Tristan says?'

'I have no desire to have Tristan find out about this.' Lottie shoved them away from her. 'There are enough problems with Lord Thorngrafton as it is. One simply does not send money like that to a married acquaintance.'

'Maybe Master Peter sent a note. He must have a reason for sending it.' Mrs Elton pressed her hands together. 'You may say many things about Master Peter, but he was never deliberately rude. His heart is in the right place. He used to idolise Master Tristan, follow him around.'

Lottie rubbed her eyes. She wanted to cry. Families and their politics. Tristan's sounded worse than her own. The only thing she was pleased about was that Tristan was not here. He need never know.

Lottie searched through the packaging and found a calling card inscribed: *To Lady Thorngrafton, who has done me much honour by loaning me money, but I am not so lost in feeling to borrow from a lady.*

'Is he mad?' Lottie held the card away from her. 'I am not Lady Thorngrafton. I have never been and will never be. I am married to Tristan!'

'And…' Mrs Elton made a motion with her hand.

Lottie stopped. Stared at Mrs Elton. 'Who is Peter Dyvelston? What relation is he to Lord Thorngrafton?'

'They are cousins. Peter's mother was Lucas Dyvelston's sister. He was born Peter Burford, but changed his name to inherit Lord Thorngrafton's wealth, that portion that wasn't covered by the entail.'

The words hung in the air and Lottie's brain buzzed. Cousins. 'First cousins? And Tristan was the son of the next male heir?'

'Yes.'

'But that would make Tristan Lord Thorngrafton, and he isn't.' Lottie backed away from the table, the full horror starting to dawn on her. Had she made a dreadful error all those months ago? Had she assumed wrongly? 'Is he?'

Mrs Elton nodded. 'I promised Lord Thorngrafton that I would not lie, nor would I volunteer the information, but my lady, it would appear that you have guessed correctly.'

'But why? Why did Tristan…Lord Thorngrafton do this?' Lottie looked at the money. 'What purpose did this whole charade serve?'

'That, my lady, is something that you will have to ask his lordship.' Mrs Elton shook her head. 'I did warn him, you know.'

My lady. Lady. Lady Thorngrafton. She had a title, or so Mrs Elton assumed. The words tasted like bile in Lottie's mouth. She might have a title, but Tristan had lied to her. Deliberately lied to her. How did he plan to keep her in ignorance? Had he truly intended to abandon her here?

'I have been so blind.' Lottie put her hands on either side of her head to block out the echo of Lady Thorngrafton in her head.

What else had he hidden from her?

She paused and wondered how delicately she could ask the question about Tristan's finances. She wanted to rush back to the library and examine his business papers, but that would be prying. Henry had not allowed her to be entirely ignorant of business matters. She could read a balance sheet, but not much else. She had to maintain some sense of dignity.

'Not blind, my lady, simply misled.'

'I don't understand.'

'Lord Thorngrafton had the reputation of being a fearsome card player in his youth, my lady.' Concern creased Mrs Elton's face. 'He keeps hidden what he wants hidden. I did warn him that you might guess.'

'Am I to understand that Lord Thorngrafton can restore this estate without recourse to my fortune?'

'It would not be for me to say, my lady, but I believe his lordship has been very successful in his endeavours. He knew the late lordship's position and knew that he would be inheriting a plundered estate.'

'Do you know what he has business in?'

'Railways. He was much enamoured of the waggon-ways when he was a boy, but I could be wrong. And I ain't said nothing.'

Railways. He was a railway king. Lottie closed her eyes. She should have known something was up when he mentioned Jack Stanton. They were friends, close business associates. She had never even considered the possibility. She had been so quick to label him an adventurer.

'Thank you, Mrs Elton.'

Lottie stumbled out of the kitchen and into the morning room. She sat down on the little armchair and put her face in her hands. Tristan was titled and had money. Everything she thought she had ever wanted, except he had chosen to hide it from her.

He had led her to believe they were penniless. Why had he done that? Why had he deceived her? All the things that he had allowed to happen to her! All the things she had accepted with a cheerful smile, never suspecting that he might be laughing at her.

He had betrayed her trust. And she had believed in him. Her heart still wanted to believe in him.

A cold fury descended on her. She would show him that she was not to be treated in such a cavalier fashion.

The early morning sun's golden rays had reached the top of Gortner Hall's tower when Tristan arrived back. The single shaft of sunlight gave the stone a slight pinkish tinge. A white mist shrouded the walls. A slumbering fairy castle. But was it worth restoring? Would Lottie prefer a new house made to her specifications with all the latest modern conveniences? She could be happy here. He knew she could be.

He'd ask her after he had explained about the slight deception. She would be delighted, he was positive, to know that she had received a somewhat mistaken impression of their finances. He would do it his way and she would understand the reasoning. First he wanted to waken her as she lay slumbering.

His boots resounded in the entrance. Tristan stopped and stared. Lottie was seated at the end of the entrance-way, dressed in her much-mended afternoon dress, with her satchel at her feet and a determined glint in her eye.

'Tristan, you have returned.'

'Don't tell me that you waited up all night.' Tristan attempted a smile, tried to banish the faint feeling of unease.

'I felt it was important.'

'It was kind of you, but unnecessary.'

'I am a considerate person. I am a generous person. Everyone says so.'

'I know, but someone has to look after you.' He reached out and gathered her hands in his, pulled her to her feet. He wanted to smooth away the wrinkle between her brows. 'Aren't you going to greet me properly?'

He captured her cool lips with his. She made no resistance, but her kiss did not hold its usual passion. He let her go and she stepped away from him as if he had burnt her. She put her hands on her cheeks and turned her face away. Tristan frowned as he noticed she wore gloves as if she was about to depart on a round of visiting. A shiver ran down his back. 'Is there something wrong, Lottie? Has something happened?'

'Should there be anything wrong, Tristan?' Her voice sounded tight and high and her eyes were far too bright.

'I am in no mood to play a game of riddles.'

'Funnily enough, neither am I.' Lottie crossed her arms. 'I am not enamoured with riddles and masquerades.'

A wave of tiredness washed over Tristan. He had no wish to start a fight. All he wanted to do was to go to bed with Lottie, sink into her softness. Then when he awoke with her in his arms, he'd explain everything. When she was in his arms, he knew that she'd forgive him.

'Nothing should be wrong.' Tristan rubbed the back of his neck. He wanted the feeling to go. 'I have been up all night, but my business has been resolved satisfactorily.'

'That is good. I am glad.'

She continued to stand there. Did not take the hint that he might like to retire to bed…with her.

'What has happened, Lottie?'

'A letter arrived while you were out. A letter addressed to Lady Thorngrafton.'

'Peter told me that he had sent it.' Tristan silently cursed his cousin. He would consign Peter to whichever hell was appropriate. He was not ready for the conversation. When they had the conversation, he had planned how it would go and it would not involve his misbegotten cousin. 'He enjoys playing practical jokes. I think he saw the humour in it. I had hoped that it had been delayed.'

'Humour? Sending a large sum of money to a married woman is humorous? Some people would take offence at being given such a gift.'

'Peter knows who Lady Thorngrafton is.'

'And she is? I will send the money directly to her.' Lottie ignored the trembling of her stomach. She had given Tristan an opportunity. She had not accused him, but had given him a chance. Even now, she wanted to believe that there had been some horrible misunderstanding, that he had not attempted to deceive her.

'The wife of Lord Thorngrafton.' Tristan regarded her with dark eyes and an enigmatic expression but the tone of his voice told her that the matter had ended.

It had not. It would only end when she had her answers.

Lottie drew herself up to her full height, squared her shoulders. She would do this. She had a right to know the truth. 'Are you Lord Thorngrafton?'

'You would not be asking the question if you had not already made up your mind. What do you believe, Lottie?'

He reached towards her, but she stepped backwards, away from him. Lottie knew if she went into his arms, she would forgive him, even before he asked her to. She was not yet ready to forgive. He had to suffer. She wanted him to suffer. He needed to learn that she was not to be trifled with in this manner. She had stopped playing his game, had stopped dancing to his tune. He had hurt her. 'Belief has nothing to do with it. It is a simple fact of life. Who is the current Lord Thorngrafton?'

'Do you want me to be?' he asked softly. 'Is that what you desire? A title? Or do you desire your husband?'

'Do not answer my question with another question!' She slammed her fist against her open palm. Her voice broke as anger rushed through her. 'I want the truth! I deserve the truth!'

'I am Lord Thorngrafton.'

Lottie's stomach reeled for instant before righting itself. A wall of ice came down, surrounded her. Not red-hot, but ice-cold fury. He was Lord Thorngrafton. He had deliberately tried to make her believe otherwise. He had tried to make her think that he was a pauper without any prospects. He had made a fool of her. He had lied to her. She had trusted him, and he had lied. 'Then why did you deny it?'

'I have never denied my title. How could I? It is something I inherited. It is something I obtained because of my birth.' He gave a small shrug. 'Can I help what others think? I never said to you one way or the other. You simply assumed.'

'You actively encouraged me to think differently. That was wrong.' Lottie clenched her fist. 'Very wrong.'

'I was not aware that you needed any encouragement.' His eyes were cold hard lumps of black granite. 'You seemed intent on believing that my cousin was Lord Thorngrafton.'

'He told me that he was.' Lottie kept her head straight and her voice even, but inside she wanted to weep. He blamed her for the mix-up. Her! She refused to start screeching. She would behave rationally. 'He told everyone. He presented credentials in Newcastle. I had no reason to doubt it.'

'He lied.'

'But at Shaw's? You were there. You should have taken steps.' She pressed her fingers against her temple. This time she would not forget what she was going to say. She would discover the truth. She had to. 'This whole misunderstanding is your fault. Do not attempt to twist the truth.'

'I did what I thought I had to do.' Something flared in Tristan's eyes. 'I wanted to protect myself. I feared if your mother knew about our earlier encounter as well as my title…'

'So instead, you seduced me.'

His mouth fell open.

'You have no ready answer for that.' Lottie tapped her foot.

'I am no cad.'

'Did your uncle leave you money?' She forced her voice to be hard. 'Did you mislead me about that as well? Did you?'

'My uncle sought to leave me an empty title and a broken-down estate.'

'That is no answer!' She lifted her foot and then stopped, slowly lowered it. She was not going to start stamping like an overgrown child despite her fury at her husband.

'It is the best you will get for now!'

'I want an answer, Tristan. I demand an answer! Did your uncle succeed?'

'Look around you.' Tristan gestured to the house. 'It is a shadow of what it once was. Gortner Hall was the grandest house in the district once. It is a ruin.'

'There is more to it.' Lottie crossed her arms as anger surged through her once again. 'Even now, you seek to twist my words. It was your coachman who gave me money at Gretna Green, wasn't it? He was acting under your orders, I presume, when he handed me the money. You wanted me to go. You had no intention of marrying me.'

'I found you! I rescued you!' He stretched his hands out to her, a gesture designed to placate her.

'Only because you abandoned me in the first place!' She crossed her arms tighter, held them in place. Refused to be manipulated. 'Why did you look for me, Tristan?'

'You are only asking because you want to pretend to be angry with me.'

'There is no pretence about my anger, Lord Thorngrafton.'

A huge great crater opened up in her middle. She met his gaze measure for measure. Did not look away. His shoulders sagged. He ran a hand over his face. 'Do we have to stand here, arguing like fishwives? I have been up all night, Carlotta. Allow me some sleep and we will speak. We have much to discuss. But later, sensibly. I can explain everything, if you will let me. I had to be certain.'

'No!' Lottie kept her head high. Inside, her heart had shattered into a thousand shards. She doubted that she would ever feel whole and secure again. She had loved him. Trusted him. It would be very tempting with him here to allow everything to be postponed. She could feel the tug of attraction, but she knew what was right. And what he had done to her. How he had treated her. 'We have nothing to discuss later, Tristan. We discuss this now.'

'No?' He took a step towards her. His hands were outstretched, but she moved away from him and his hands fell to his sides. 'We are married.'

'Are we even married? You never said your title.' Hot tears sprung to her eyes. She blinked rapidly. 'Or were you going to discard me when you'd had your fun?'

'Yes, we are married. You were there. We married over the blacksmith's anvil. I gave my full name. It is a legal marriage, Lottie. You are my wife.'

'You decided to test me.' Lottie stared at him. The full horror of what he had done sinking in. 'You did those things to me deliberately. At the inn. Those men who attacked me.'

'You did those things yourself. You paid no heed to my advice. You would have come to no harm.'

'You left me there!'

'I was going to tell you the truth, Lottie.'

'When? You had ample opportunity. It is not as if we have never spoken.'

Tristan's lips became a thin white line. 'Once I was sure. This was our wedding trip. Our chance to get to know each other before the world crowded in.'

'You never even attempted to get to know me.' Lottie picked up her satchel. 'I am leaving you, Tristan. I am going back to my world. This was a false world. What we shared was false. You tricked me.'

'There is an explanation.'

'You only think there is an explanation.' Lottie's stomach ached and she knew the lump in her throat was growing beyond all proportion. And if it became too large, she would burst into noisy floods of tears. She refused to cry in front of Tristan and to show how deeply he had wounded her. She wanted to be strong. 'I have gone over and over in my head the possibilities and have come to the conclusion that you thought me proud. That I needed to be punished. You had no right to do that, Tristan.'

'I had every right!'

'The man I thought I married would never have done that,' Lottie replied quietly, in control of her emotions once more. 'He had integrity.'

'What are you going to do about it? I can't change the past.'

'I am leaving you, Tristan. You can stay in this ruined hall with your memories, but I am going back to my world, the world where I belong, the world where people love me. If this is marriage, it comes at far too high a cost.'

'I thought I pleased you.' He pulled her into his arms, lowered his face, but she turned her head and pushed at his chest. His hands let her go. He stood stock still, chin lifted high, a remote expression on his face.

Lottie swallowed hard. He was seeking to manipulate her. Again. This time it was not going to happen. This time she would win.

'Physical attraction vanishes, Tristan, when you betray someone. And you betrayed me in the worst way.' She picked up her satchel and held it in front of her like a shield. If he made another move towards her, she would be tempted to melt and she was determined not to do that. She wanted him to understand what she had gone through. 'You decided that I was a blank slate to write on, to mould and shape however you wanted. You never asked me if I wanted that.'

'I may have been highhanded, but it was for the best. I needed to know.'

'May have been? Definitely you were.' Lottie composed her features. She had made her plans in that long dark night. She was not some desperate woman, intent on having her man at any cost. Tristan had to want her and her alone. 'Goodbye, Lord Thorngrafton.'

'Goodbye? We have not yet begun!' The roar of his words resounded in her ears. 'You are not going anywhere, Carlotta. I forbid it.'

'I have always hated that name, Lord Thorngrafton.'

Lottie held out her hand briefly. She saw that he ignored it, preferring to stand there glowering at her. She composed her features and refused to show any sign of weakness.

'I thought our time together would show me who you really were. And it has!' Tristan turned on his heels and closed the door behind him with a thundering crash.

Lottie waited for a moment, head tilted. She heard the sound of heavy footsteps mounting the stairs. A great feeling of loss welled up inside her. Angrily, she brushed away her tears. He thought he could end the argument by simply leaving the room and that she would obey him. He had another thing coming.

She twisted off her iron wedding ring and placed it on the marble-topped table by the entrance. Tristan would be sure to find it, if he looked.

'It was so very pleasant to have had this time with you, Lord Thorngrafton. Truly enlightening. I do so hate prolonged goodbyes. I wish you great joy in the future,' she said to the empty hall.

Chapter Fifteen

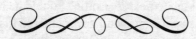

Tristan sat in the empty morning room, turning the tiny iron ring over and over in his hand. The room seemed lifeless without Lottie's presence. It was surprising how in a few short days, he had come to rely on her being there, hearing her excited chatter and listening to her latest scheme. It was as if a large part of him had gone with her.

Lottie would return. This was a grandiose gesture on her part. She would not even get as far as Hexham station. All he had to do was wait.

'Mrs Elton,' he called. 'What train was Lottie leaving on?'

'The express. For Newcastle.'

Tristan glanced up at the clock. A great emptiness opened inside him. If she was going to return, she would have been back by now.

She had gone. Left. Without a backward glance, without waiting to hear his explanation.

This was not how it was supposed to have happened. He had calculated that she might be slightly angry with him, but that she would have been pleased to have all her dreams come true.

He took one last look at the ring and placed it in his pocket. He would lock it away somewhere, keep it in a box and never take it out again. And he would go far from here. Never to return.

He pressed his hands against the mantelpiece. Was this what his uncle had felt when Suzanne had left him? Was he only seeking to possess Lottie? Should he just go about his business as if Lottie had never entered his life?

Tristan gave a wry smile. It was almost as if his uncle had set a trap for him, one that he had blindly walked into. Had he become his uncle?

Instantly Tristan rejected the notion. He did not want to possess Lottie. He wanted her in his life. His life would be an empty place without her. And he had never even asked her to stay.

His fingers went to his other coat pocket where her Claude glass resided, had resided ever since he'd found it.

He would get her back. He would fight for her. He was finished with games and riddles. Lottie was too valuable for such things. He only wished that he had realised that before.

He would get her back…even if it took a lifetime.

She did not stand a chance.

He had to be patient and draw on all the lessons he had learnt. Only now it seemed that he was playing for the highest stakes—Lottie's love.

'And is that the end of your tale?' Lucy Charlton leant forward and touched Lottie's hand. Her sister-in-law's face was wreathed in worry lines as Lottie finished re-counting her tale later that afternoon in Newcastle.

'I came here.'

Lottie put her head back against the armchair in the familiar comfort of Lucy and Henry's dining room. It was a place where nothing bad was ever allowed to happen. The walls were painted the most fashionable shade of Dragon's Blood red. White lace hung over the backs of chairs and pincushions with their mottos carefully pricked by Lucy's friends were arranged so that they could be admired. Familiar. Safe, but somehow stifling. All the way back to Newcastle Lottie had thought that if she made it here, everything would be fine. But she had been wrong. Everything was far from fine.

Every bone in her body ached and a great weariness swept over her. She would cry except she believed she no longer had any tears left inside her. She had shed those last night while she'd waited for Tristan's return. Now she felt like a dried-out husk. She doubted whether she would ever feel anything again.

'But surely Lord Thorngrafton tried to stop you.'

'No, Lucy, he made no effort. The journey was quite straightforward. Mrs Elton had arranged for a pony cart. The express arrived swiftly and I caught a cab to your house.'

'Mother Charlton remains at Shaw's. She is hopeful of Sir Geoffrey Lea for herself. She is very proud of your marriage, you know.'

'She knew about Tristan's title?'

'Not at first. I believe Sir Geoffrey used the knowledge to comfort her later.'

'Sir Geoffrey knew? Why didn't he warn me?'

'Who would you rather be married to?' Lucy's eyes danced.

To Tristan, came the immediate answer. *To the man I said yes to. The man I am afraid doesn't exist.* Lottie managed to hold back the words. 'That question is not relevant, Lucy. I would have found a way. Mama was being stubborn.'

'You have your title, Lottie. Isn't that what you said you would always have?'

'Times change.' Lottie rubbed a hand across her face. 'I had very little sleep last night and almost none on the train. I am so sorry for my poor company, Lucy. You must think me dreadfully dull, going on in this manner.'

Lucy reached over and squeezed Lottie's hand. 'But the problem remains unresolved—what are you going to do with your future now that you have left Lord Thorngrafton?'

Somehow the fact that Lucy used Tristan's title made things easier. Lottie knew she had never been in love with Lord Thorngrafton. It had been Tristan she'd loved. And every time she closed her eyes, she saw his face. That one last terrible look he had given her. Cold and unforgiving. Had he even seen her, or had he merely seen the reflection of Suzanne? Deep within her, Lottie knew that she was far from being that sort of person and that was what hurt most. He had judged her and found her wanting.

'I had rather thought to go on as before.'

'You are married, Lottie. There may be consequences…'

Lottie put her hand to her mouth. 'I had never thought about such things as babies.'

'You should do. From what Henry wrote me, you and Lord Thorngrafton have been engaged in an activity that is likely to result in children.'

'Lucy! I never!'

'Well, it is why you married, isn't it?' Lucy folded her hands on her laps. 'One might as well be practical about such things. We are both old married women now. You know what goes on behind closed bedroom doors.'

A small warm bubble built inside her. She would like to be a mother and to hold Tristan's child in her arms. But then it popped. She had stopped believing in dreams. Right now that would be the worst thing for her. Tristan would have complete rights over the child. She would have nothing. Life was cruel to do that to women. It was wrong. She pushed away her fears, composed her thoughts. 'I will cross that bridge when I come to it.'

'If that is the way you feel.' Lucy bent her head and kissed Lottie's cheek.

'And the question remains—what am I to do now?'

'You are quite resolved not to return to Lord Thorngrafton?'

'There is no point. There is nothing in that relationship, Lucy. He does not respect me.' Lottie fought hard to keep her voice calm. 'I discovered that I wanted more from my marriage than he was prepared to give. I deserved more.'

'You, of course, may stay here for the time being. A woman alone in Mother Charlton's house would not be suitable. If you are determined to take this course.'

'I am quite determined, I have done nothing to feel ashamed of.'

'Good, then you will come with me to the At Homes. You always enjoyed such things.' Lucy proceeded to list the ones that were happening the next day.

Lottie shook her head. 'I couldn't bear it. No, not yet, Lucy. Give me a few days. I need to rest after my journey.'

'You did say you were tired.' Lucy's eyes were speculative. 'I will give you some time before you go back into society, but your true friends will stand by you, as I will.'

Lottie turned her head and tried not to think about what might have been, that green and pleasant land shimmering just beyond her reach.

* * *

Lottie sought to hide a yawn. Her fourth conversation about the weather in as many stops. She should never have agreed to join Lucy for today's At Home round. They still had two more stops, including Emma Stanton's first At Home since she'd returned with her new husband from Italy.

'I hear you have married, Lottie.' Mrs Fletcher, one of the leading matrons of Newcastle, advanced towards her, leaning heavily on a cane. A woman who had often shown little regard for her mother.

'Very suddenly.'

Mrs Fletcher peered around her. 'And your new husband, he is not with you? I understand you are making your first calls after your marriage.'

'Yes, I am. It is amazing how many people have remarked on that.' Lottie leant forward, swallowing the annoyance that rose in her throat. 'But enough about me— tell me, how is your bad leg? Has it started to heal? I was speaking with Mrs Elton, my husband's housekeeper, about such matters and she swears by a special ointment.'

Mrs Fletcher started on a long rambling explanation and Lottie breathed a little easier. She would write to Mrs Elton and get the recipe for Mrs Fletcher. It would give her something to do. She would have preferred not to do the calls on her own, but she could. And it was only those people who were not truly her friends who mentioned the lack of a husband by her side. Her friends were either happy for her or concerned that she appeared pale.

'You know my dear…' Mrs Fletcher had finished her story '…I never realised before what a good listener you are.'

'I like hearing about other people. I am interested in

them and tend to want to find a solution to their problems. It is one of my most glaring defects.'

'Hardly a defect and time will curb your impulses. I must have you and your new husband to dinner. You remind me of myself when I was a young bride.'

'That would be lovely.' Lottie pasted on a smile. 'I shall have to consult Tristan.'

'And what does Mr Dyvelston do?'

'She means Lord Thorngrafton, Mother.' Mrs Fletcher's younger daughter came up hurrying up. 'Lucy has just told me that you married a lord!'

'You are a dark horse, Lady Thorngrafton.' Mrs Fletcher inclined her head. 'I do hope we will get to know each other better. I fear I may have misjudged you. You must be ecstatic.'

'Supremely happy in every way.' Lottie forced the words from her throat. 'All of my girlish dreams have come true. And what more could I ask for?'

'And will we see your husband at the summer ball, Lady Thorngrafton?' The younger Miss Fletcher gave a sharp-toothed smile. 'I do so long to meet him and see the man who swept the incomparable Lottie Charlton off her feet.'

Lottie found it difficult to breathe. She had hoped to avoid the subject of Tristan. Each time he was mentioned, it was like a dagger to her heart, opening the wound once more. Someday, it might close, but for now it was physically painful.

'Lottie has no idea when Lord Thorngrafton's business will be finished.' Lucy's arm went around her waist and Lottie regretted every solitary cruel thought that she had ever had about Lucy. Lucy was kind and Henry was lucky to have her as his wife. She could hear the real affection that Lucy had for Henry.

Was affection enough? Was she wrong to hope for more? Was she wrong to want more?

'Lottie, don't you agree?' Lucy was looking at her with a quizzical expression. 'About the ball?'

'Yes, yes, I am positive it will be wonderful.' Lottie firmly but politely changed the subject back to the weather.

'Do you think I can skip the next few calls, Lucy?' Lottie asked as they left the Dresser household. 'My head is beginning to pain me.'

'I never thought to hear you say that.' Her sister-in-law paused as she was getting into the carriage. 'You do not appear to be enjoying today's round of calling. I thought you lived for it and home was dull, dull, dull. Isn't that what you wrote me when you first arrived in Haydon Bridge?'

'It must be some other Lottie that you are speaking of.' Lottie pressed her hand against Lucy's. 'Have I told you lately how dear you are to me? And how much I appreciate the things you have done for me lately.'

Lucy's cheeks turned a rosy pink and she became almost beautiful. Lottie could suddenly see why her brother had married her and why *he* was the lucky one and not the other way around.

'I do declare, Lady Thorngrafton, marriage has been good for you.'

'Sometimes, one learns lessons the hard way, lessons you did not even know you needed to learn.'

Lucy settled herself in the carriage. 'As long as you are rested for the ball tonight. Henry has promised that he will be back in time from Durham.'

'I shall sit on the sidelines and keep you company. Lottie, the very respectable matron.'

'Here, I was looking forward to seeing you dance.'

'I am not sure…' Lottie allowed her voice to trail away. How could she go to a dance without thinking about Tristan and the last time they had waltzed together? She would find an excuse later in the day. She had no desire to go the Assembly Rooms today or any time soon. It was not the pity that she would see in people's faces when she took her place among the matrons. Or the inevitable sitting out of every dance because her husband wasn't there. Her reasons were far more personal. She was not ready to face the emptiness in her heart. 'I wanted to thank you for your intervention back there.'

'Don't let the harridans bother you, Lottie.'

'Mrs Fletcher and her kind don't, Lucy. She is actually very nice once you begin speaking with her. Honestly, I would be a pretty poor person if I based my self-worth on the judgement of a few. It is just…' Lottie gave a small hand wave as her throat closed.

'We can go straight to the Stantons if you wish. I know both Emma and Mr Stanton will be looking forward to seeing you.'

'I hardly think that.' Lottie smiled, regaining her composure now that the danger had passed. She was certain that she could act normally until the next time something reminded her. 'I only hope that Emma has forgiven me for my inopportune comments.'

'Emma and Mr Stanton are very much in love. I for one have revised my opinion of those comments. They were precisely what was needed.'

'Very well, we shall press on.'

The crush at the Stantons was worse than Lottie had anticipated. Everyone who was anyone in Newcastle appeared to have descended on Emma and Jack Stanton's

At Home. Everyone would know that she was making calls without her husband.

Lottie had to admit that she had been wrong about Emma being ancient. She looked so lovely and happy, standing next to her doting husband that Lottie felt a distinct twinge of jealousy. She did not mind the gossip about Tristan not being there. She wanted him to be there for her own well-being. She wanted Tristan to look at her like that. She wanted to feel his hand about her waist and see his eyes fill with warmth and good humour. Not that it was possible. She had been at Lucy's for more than a week now. And with each passing moment, she missed him more. But he had not sent word. It would not be difficult to find her, if he desired it.

A well-upholstered lady moved and she spied a pair of broad shoulders encased in a form-fitting frock coat. Lottie rubbed her eyes. And she was seeing things now. Tristan here? Impossible. Her nerves were becoming addled.

'I wanted to say how sorry I was about my outburst after the skating party,' Lottie said in an undertone to Emma. 'It was wrong of me. I understand now how these things can happen.'

'On the contrary, I am now grateful for it. Jack and I married and resolved our differences. It changed my life.' Emma smiled at her. 'Think on it no more. I understand you have become a lady now.'

'That is correct.' Lottie braced herself for the inevitable question—where was her husband? She had already seen several people pointedly nudging each other. 'I married Tristan Dyvelston, Lord Thorngrafton, a few weeks ago… Undoubtedly Lucy told you the circumstances.'

'Jack says that Thorngrafton is a good and able man. High praise indeed from Jack. I wish you all the happiness.' Emma pressed Lottie's hand. 'I can see a change in you. There is a certain glow that wasn't there before.'

'Thank you,' Lottie said around the sudden lump in her throat.

'And where has—?'

'There you are, Lottie. At last I discover you.' Tristan's voice slid over and around her.

Lottie hardly dared breathe, let alone turn and see him. But he was here. In this room. She had to be hearing things. Tristan would never go to an At Home and certainly not one with her. It was beyond imagining. His fingers grasped her elbow. And she knew this was no dream. 'Tristan.'

'Lottie left before I could accompany her on her rounds,' Tristan explained to Emma. 'I am so pleased that my hunch was correct and that you were so gracious to allow me to wait here for her.'

'Grace and politeness had nothing to do with it. It gave Jack and my father someone to converse with. Jack hates these sorts of gatherings, but even he recognised the importance of the first At Home to a bride.' Emma gave another smile and swept off to greet some more callers, leaving Lottie to stand awkwardly, facing Tristan.

Eagerly her eyes searched his face. His mouth appeared slightly pinched and his eyes hollowed, but that could have been the result of anything.

'You left without saying goodbye.'

'I said goodbye to the empty hallway.'

'That does not count, Lottie. You should have said goodbye to my face.'

'I have no wish for a scene, Lord Thorngrafton.' Lottie made her voice cold.

Tristan's response was to press his lips together. The silence between them grew.

'Tristan,' Lottie said into the silence, striving for nor-
malcy, 'I have told everyone you were away on business.'

'What sort of husband leaves his bride alone so quickly
after the wedding?' Tristan smiled down at her. His eyes
were warm and pleasant. A show for others. It had to be.
'You forgot your ring.'

He held it out. Lottie's heart lurched. She longed to
grab it. Her hand felt too light and empty without it, but it
was impossible. There was too much between them. She
forced her hand to remain still.

'Keep it. It represents a lie.'

'As you wish…for now.' His eyes were inscrutable as
he smoothly returned the ring to his pocket.

'But why come here? Why not to the house?' Lottie
could hear her voice begin to rise as she ruthlessly crushed
any hope. Tristan had shown up at this At Home. He was
in Newcastle and he had not bothered to visit her first.

Several of the more elderly ladies turned towards them.
Lottie saw at least one disapproving glance as they lifted
their hands to gossip.

'Do you want to make a scene?' Tristan asked out of the
side of his mouth. 'I am here. I arrived in Newcastle after
you went out this morning, after you began your round of
calling. I did promise that you would not be humiliated.'

'And you always keep your promises,' Lottie said carefully.

'Always.' His eyes crinkled at the corners. 'You did say
that the first At Homes a woman attends after her marriage
are among her most important.'

Lottie resisted the urge to smile back. She wanted there
to be another reason why he was here. A reason beyond
simply keeping his promise and she wanted the reason to
be her.

Then it hit her like a physical blow to her stomach. Tristan had not attempted to find her earlier. He had appeared at Jack Stanton's At Home, and had been here far longer than propriety suggested necessary. Jack Stanton was the key to everything. He was a business associate of Tristan's. He was here because of Jack Stanton and not because of her. And he had known of her association with Jack when they met at Shaw's. It did not take a genius to see who he was wary of offending. Whose society he wanted to be accepted in. The irony of the situation failed to make her laugh.

'Did you have trouble finding me?'

'Finding you?' He raised one eyebrow and his body stilled. 'Not particularly, I suspected you would be here.'

'Ah, Thorngrafton, I see your wife has appeared.' Jack Stanton came up and clapped Tristan on the back. 'Good, good, Emma will be relieved. She was a bit worried when you appeared earlier without her.'

'Yes, Stanton, Lottie has finally arrived. You know how the ladies are. Stubborn and insistent.'

'I do, indeed. But Emma would have it that I am the stubborn one.' Jack Stanton inclined his head. 'We must compare notes some time.'

'I look forward to it.'

Jack Stanton moved on, greeting other people. Lottie waited until he was out of earshot and lowered her voice. 'Is he a close business associate of yours?'

'A business associate and a friend for more years than I would like to remember. We share an interest in railways and progress.' Tristan's hand caught her elbow, moved her closer to him and out of the way of a maundering matron who was intent on greeting her friends. The brief collision of their bodies caused Lottie's heart to leap. 'He was vastly amused when he learned we had married and the manner of our marriage.'

'Amused.' Lottie shifted uneasily. She could well imagine Jack Stanton's amusement.

'I believe he said something about pots calling kettles black.'

'I explained about that.' Lottie plucked at her glove. 'It was an error of judgement on my part. I have apologised to Emma, but she simply laughed.'

'His wife suits him. I don't think I have seen him look this happy and contented before.'

The pain between Lottie's eyes threatened to overwhelm her. She bit her lip, wondering what she could say. 'My time is nearly up.'

'Time? We have scarcely begun.'

'Fifteen minutes is the proper length for a call. Enough for a cup of tea and a conversation about the weather.' Lottie tilted her head. 'I have no wish to trespass on the Stantons' hospitality.'

'I will take you home.'

Home. The word echoed through her body, conjuring so many memories. But she knew that she could not simply go with Tristan. Nothing was settled between then, and she refused to go back to what they had. It was an infatuation, that was all, and it would pass in time.

'I came with Lucy.'

His eyes clouded and then cleared. 'I understand.'

He did not move away from her.

'Oh, Lottie, Lady Thorngrafton, Lord Thorngrafton. Your prediction from last summer came true after all.' Martha Irons came up, giggling, and Lottie wondered if murder was ever justifiable. 'Do you realise that you will have to lead the quadrille at tonight's dance at the

Assembly Rooms? How does it feel to have your dreams come true? All your predictions?'

'I am very happy and looking forward to the ball,' Lottie replied woodenly as she resolved herself to a crashing headache.

'Are we going to the ball tonight?' He raised an eyebrow, looked down at her.

To go to the ball with Tristan. On his arm. Did he want to go? Lottie hesitated. The lure of waltzing again with Tristan was powerful, if only for a few moments. She would have to guard her heart, but she knew she would be unable to resist. 'I suppose we are. Everyone will be there.'

'It does seem to be the talk of the At Home.'

Lottie's smile froze. She had forgotten about Jack Stanton and the need to be correct. The formality of being titled and keeping up appearances. She wanted to throw down her gloves and stomp off. She wanted Tristan to waltz with her because he wanted to, not because it was expected of him.

'Balls and the like always excite the gossips.'

'And do they excite you, Lottie?'

'Sometimes.' Lottie examined the handle of her reticule. Then she glanced up into Tristan's face. There was a wariness about his expression. 'I believe I shall enjoy this ball after all.'

'I will take you in my carriage. We do not wish to cause talk.'

'If you wish…'

'I positively insist.' Tristan raised her hand to his lips and turned it over. His tongue briefly found the gap in her glove and touched her bare skin. Heat seared up her arm and she gave a brief gasp. His eyes took on a cynical look. 'Not indifferent to me, then, Lottie.'

'Lucy is signalling, Tristan. I must go.' Silently Lottie cursed her wayward body. She would forget her passion for him in time.

'I will bid you *adieu*, then.'

Lottie forced her legs to carry her to Lucy's waiting carriage and did not look back.

Chapter Sixteen

'Why has he done that?' Lottie frowned as the carriage returned to the Charltons' home. 'Why has he sent the carriage so early?'

Outside the Charltons' drive, with his arms clearly emblazoned on it, stood Tristan's carriage. On the ride back from the Stantons', Lottie had sat stone-faced, concentrating on tonight. What she would wear and how she would show Tristan that she was indifferent to him.

'Done what?' Lucy leant forwards and gave a pleased smile and a little clap of her hands. 'I thought he might do that! Emma said that he had arrived early to the At Home. I am certain that he wants to mend this quarrel between you two. Quarrels often happen in the early part of a marriage, Lottie.'

'This was why you insisted we make the small stop at the milliner's.' Lottie's heart sank. Lucy had decided to meddle and fix the quarrel. She had tried to keep most of the trouble to herself, not wanting to overburden Lucy, but now it appeared that Lucy considered the chasm between them to be a mere tiff and had encouraged Tristan to call

at the house. It wasn't. It was something far more fundamental. She was not some sort of blank slate to be written
on, to be shaped and moulded as Tristan saw fit.

'I wanted to see the new bonnets, but I also wanted to
give your husband time. I hoped he would be here when
we returned after I hinted at it. I am so pleased he understood.' Lucy reached over and patted Lottie's hand. 'You
have spent long enough hiding in your room. Even Henry
remarked on it two nights ago.'

'Remarked? He positively bellowed.' Lottie attempted
to peer around Lucy and discover exactly where Tristan
was and in what sort of mood. 'A rogue elephant would
have had more subtlety and tact.'

'You do your brother a disservice. He simply feels that
you should have given your marriage a chance. He does
care about you. He is willing to provide a home for you,
if that is what you require.'

'Thank you. I know this is your doing.' Lottie placed a
kiss on Lucy's cheek. 'You can move mountains in your
quiet way. I never quite appreciated how well you manage
him.'

'Sometimes, one accomplishes more.' Lucy reached
over and straightened Lottie's bonnet. 'Now, enough of
this. You have a husband, standing there waiting for you.'

'Will you stay with me?' Lottie asked, suddenly
nervous. What more could Tristan have to say to her?

'It is far better to speak to your husband in private
before the ball.' Lucy's eyes turned grave. 'It saves scenes.
It is better for all concerned this way.'

'There is really very little to speak about.' Lottie
climbed down from the carriage. Her insides trembled.
'Our marriage is over.'

'Is that you want? Or are you going to fight?'

'There is nothing to fight for.'

'Ah, Lottie, you return at last.' Tristan came up and put his hand on her shoulder.

'Have you been waiting long?' Lottie forced her voice to be normal.

'I decided to bow to your expertise on At Homes and left.'

'Are you staying somewhere in Newcastle?'

'I arrived this morning, but have arranged for lodgings at the Royal Hotel. I felt you might prefer it that way.'

Lottie's heart twisted. Rooms without her. There was no indication that he intended that she should live with him. They would maintain separate lives and establishments, how many in the aristocracy behaved. 'Are you planning on staying long in Newcastle?'

'It depends on how long my *business* in Newcastle takes.' His jaw tightened and his eyes became hooded. 'We will have to appear as husband and wife, Lottie. Society will demand it.'

'I hardly intend on cutting you, Lord Thorngrafton. We are married. There would be talk and I have no intention of causing unnecessary scandal. It would reflect badly on my family.'

'You relieve me no end.' He inclined his head. 'Now, do we continue this discussion on the pavement or do you wish to take a ride in my carriage?'

A ride in his carriage. Lottie's head pounded. She was not ready to be alone with him. It brought back far too many memories of the other carriage ride out to Gretna Green. 'I am tired, Tristan. Anything you need to say can be said in Lucy and Henry's drawing room.'

'If that is what you wish…' He inclined his head.

'I do,' Lottie said firmly. 'Our marriage is of great

concern to me. We need to determine how best we go on from here.'

'Yes, you wouldn't want anyone to think anything was amiss.' Tristan stared at his wife, drinking in her form. Not a hair was out of place. It was as if she was encased in armour. There had to be a way of reaching Lottie, of making her understand that he had never intended to hurt her.

'Appearances can be deceptive, Lord Thorngrafton.'

A muscle jumped in Tristan's cheek as her barb struck home. He had hoped that she might show some signs of missing of him. Had he inadvertently destroyed everything between them? 'Indeed they can.'

Lottie led the way into a drawing room that groaned with knick-knacks and pincushions. Every chair leg was carefully hidden. Up-to-the-minute good taste and sensibility, but somehow, despite its fussiness, it also seemed comforting.

'Your sister-in-law provides a comforting home,' Tristan said to fill the silence as Lottie removed her bonnet and gloves, handing them to the butler.

'Henry and Lucy are proud of it, but it is too cluttered for my taste.' Lottie began straightening the cushions and moving the figurines.

'You would decorate differently?'

'I shall have to see when the time comes.' Her eyes twinkled. 'There again, perhaps I will develop a sudden affinity for neatly picked-out mottos and shell pictures.'

'Mottos and shell pictures.' Tristan was unable to stop the brief shudder of horror as Lottie's eyes twinkled.

'As I am unlikely to have my own establishment, it is not a problem.'

'There is Gortner Hall,' Tristan said quietly and waited.

'That belongs to you. You may reside there if you wish.'

'But you are my wife. You should be making my house into a home; while I may not care for the decoration of this house precisely, it does exude a homely atmosphere.'

He went to close the door, but she held up her hand, stopping him. 'Leave the door open, please.'

His hand lingered on the doorknob. Not as indifferent as she might pretend. He had something to work with, something to build on. 'Who is it that you don't trust, Lottie, you or me?'

'That sort of teasing is obvious, Tristan.' Lottie wrapped her arms about her waist. 'And unworthy of you.'

'I merely asked the question.' Tristan took a step closer, invaded her space. She had called him Tristan. It was the tiniest sliver of hope and he found his mind clinging to it with all its energy. 'You refused a ride in my carriage and now insist on the door remaining open.'

'I should not like anyone to think that you are taking advantage.'

'I promise you that I have not come here to ravish you.' Tristan adopted his most innocent face. Not here. Not until he had her on his own, without fear of being disturbed. He wanted to show her that he intended to devote his life to her.

'Why have you come?' She toyed with a Dresden shepherd.

'Because our conversation at the Stantons' was unsatisfactory,' Tristan said, looking at her and trying to think beyond kissing her mouth. He had missed her more than he thought it was possible to miss anyone and she appeared not to have missed him one bit. 'I wanted to speak to you about more than the weather.'

'This morning has been very enlightening to me.'

She placed the china dog closer to the shepherd,

arranged them in a pleasing tableau, taking her time, concentrating on the figurines instead of him. Tristan watched her long tapering fingers. The memory of how they felt against his skin swept thorough him, nearly destroying his sanity. 'Has it? I am afraid I found the whole proceeding deadly dull.'

'Yes, it has now become clear to me why we married. I was blind before.' She widened her eyes and gave him a brilliant smile.

'Pray enlighten me, Lottie.' Tristan leant against the door frame with crossed arms. Exactly how much had she guessed? And, more importantly, how could he show her the true reason? 'Why did I marry you?'

'You are a business associate of Jack Stanton's.' Lottie began ticking the reasons off on her fingers. 'You had no wish to be outside his society. It could be bad for business. You were very unsubtle today, Tristan.'

'You are very blind.' Tristan clung on to his temper. How dare she think that!

'Not blind now,' she retorted, her voice becoming chips of ice. 'Once, definitely. I have stopped believing in fairy tales.'

Tristan stared at her in amazement. He had thought to show her that he was willing to meet her halfway and she had twisted it! He gritted his teeth. His plan was not going the way he had intended. 'This is what you have decided. Irrevocably.'

'Yes, and, as such, I can see why you feel that we need to show our marriage is a success.' Lottie pressed her hands together. 'Why we need to show a united front. Why you are here in Newcastle, rather than staying on the estate or wherever you wanted to be.'

'And you are willing to accept this sort of marriage?'

Tristan asked as every fibre of his being strained to hear her response.

'Yes,' she whispered and then her voice grew firmer. 'It is the only solution to the problem. An annulment is not possible.'

'Why not?' Tristan felt the tension drain from his shoulders. She wanted to stay married. It was a small straw. He had to have patience, despite the desire of his body. He could not force her. She had to come to him, to forgive him.

'Because I am unwilling to lie. I am no longer a virgin.'

'And this is what you want. A formal marriage.'

'For now.' Lottie kept her head high. 'I will make a good hostess, but I have no wish to be buried alive in the country.'

'I can see that.'

'We will lead separate discreet lives.'

'If that is what you wish…' Tristan clenched his hands. Refrained from shaking her. There had to be a way of getting her to see that it was not what he wanted. This interview was going much worse than he had planned. This was her territory, her bolt hole. He had to hope the surprise he had planned worked. That she would realise what he wanted.

'It is the only solution.'

'I can see that there is nothing to speak about. You have decided everything.'

'It is the way it has to be.'

'For now.' Tristan put his hand in his pocket and withdrew a slim box. 'I would ask you to wear the Dyvelston pearls, even if you don't want to wear my ring. Every Dyvelston bride has worn them. I retrieved them from Peter's pawnbrokers.'

'They do not appear to have brought the Dyvelstons much luck.' Lottie held the box with two fingers.

'Nevertheless, wear them. It is expected.' Tristan replaced his hat on his head. 'I will take you to the ball, Lottie, and then we will discuss our exact marriage arrangements.'

Lottie touched the pearls that hung about her neck as she waited for the first quadrille of the Assembly's Summer Ball to begin. She did not like the pearls any better now than when she had first seen them, but she had worn them, determined to show Tristan that she could play her part. She wanted to be his wife. Her rose silk with its décolleté neckline did set them off, but she made sure the lace was properly tucked and that she looked more like a matron than a debutante.

Her stomach clenched slightly as she struggled to remember the intricate steps. She had always thought that leading the dancing must be the pinnacle of success. Now she knew it for a hollow sham. It had nothing to do with what sort of person she was.

'What are you doing in Newcastle, Tristan?'

'Waiting for the quadrille to begin, standing next to my wife.'

'You did not even know this gathering existed before Martha said something.' Lottie gave a little laugh. She tried to ignore how handsome Tristan looked in his evening clothes. How, without him even touching her, every bit of her was aware of him. 'I don't need the pretence, Tristan. I have had enough of that.'

'You are wrong there. I knew about this ball before this morning,' he said firmly. 'Do be quiet and let the man start the ball, Lottie. The sooner the speeches are over, the sooner the dancing can begin.'

And the sooner they would be finished. Lottie heard the unspoken words. With every breath she took, this charade of being happy became more and more difficult. The candles blazed down on them, throwing heat into an already crowded room. It appeared everybody who was anybody in Newcastle was there, and all eyes were turned towards her and Tristan. She wanted to run screaming from the ball. This was all fake, all shadows and mirrors without any real substance. This was not life.

The master of ceremonies began speaking. Lottie listened with half an ear and then froze as the man proceeded to thank Lord and Lady Thorngrafton for their generous support.

She glanced up and saw the amused twinkle in Tristan's eye. 'But why did you do that?'

'I was determined to force you into the first quadrille. It is what you want—to be a social success.'

'I wanted it once.' Lottie began to dance and was grateful that the steps led her away from Tristan, away from danger. She had considered her heart immune this afternoon, but here she knew it was not. She had pieced it back together, determined to keep it whole, but within a few hours of seeing him again, she was making castles in clouds.

'Did you miss me?' he asked when they next joined hands.

'How can I miss someone I don't know?' Lottie tilted her head and peered up at him. 'Lord Thorngrafton is a stranger to me. We have never been formally introduced.'

He missed a step, Lottie noted with satisfaction, but his bland mask remained firmly in place.

'I asked you to call me Tristan,' he said finally. 'It is the name I want to hear from your lips.'

'But which one are you?' Lottie's steps faltered and his hand went to hold her up. 'Lord Thorngrafton or Tristan?'

'I am your husband.'

The dance swept them apart again and Lottie made pointless conversation with the other man in the set. Then the music stopped and the quadrille ended.

Lottie stood there, ready to begin the long march over to the side to join the other matrons, but Tristan's hand closed about her wrist, held her there. Imprisoned.

'The dance is finished.' Lottie gave a slight tug on her hand, but his fingers slipped down her palm, held it gently.

'The newlyweds' waltz is about to begin.' Tristan gave a brief smile. 'I have made my enquiries. Everything has been carefully explained to me. Jack and Emma Stanton are on the floor. You would not want to give people cause to comment.'

Lottie pressed her lips together. She remembered how once she had dreamed of dancing with her titled husband, being the envy of all the unwed women. How she had boasted that she would do that at this very ball. It seemed so childish now. Titles and money were not as important as the person. She knew that if Tristan had neither, she would still be proud of him, still want to be here in his arms.

She wet her lips and held her head high. She could do this. She could waltz with Tristan, without remembering exactly what it meant to be in his arms. And why it could never happen again.

'If we must keep up appearances, then I will.'

She put her hand into Tristan's, felt his other hand touch her waist. Immediately her head reeled. It was one thing to dance a very formal quadrille with him and quite another to dance an intimate dance like a waltz. The music rose up and surrounded them. All the air whooshed from her lungs and she struggled against her corset to take a deep enough breath to replace it. A coincidence, it had to be that.

The orchestra were playing the same Strauss waltz that they had first waltzed to.

'Do you like it?' Tristan asked, and his body seemed tense.

'It has a beautiful melody,' Lottie replied carefully as the memories swamped her.

'It has become one of my favourites.' His hand tightened on her waist. 'Since that evening at Shaw's.'

'Did you know they were going to play it?'

'I was consulted.' A faint smile touched his lips as he inclined his head.

Her heart began to pound in her ears. He had been consulted and had chosen this waltz, a waltz that had recently become his favourite.

What exactly was he doing? Was this another game? Another lesson she had to learn? She had finished her lessons.

She wanted to hope that he cared something for her but she was too scared. How he had cynically treated her was too raw.

Distantly she heard the sound of clapping hands as they circled around the dance floor. She forced her feet to keep moving, but it became harder and harder. Her head became light. When she thought she must fall down, the music stopped. And with it, she knew that she could not be in a loveless marriage. She could not participate in a sham. She had no use for games.

She slipped out of his arms and fled, not caring about the shocked gasps that echoed after her.

Out in the corridor, she pushed past people until she reached an empty room, one that would be used later for cards. She sank down on a chair and put her face in her hands. Everything was over. All her dreams were gone. She was never going to find love because the man she loved did not care about her. She allowed the tears to fall on to her gown, creating large red blotches.

'Lottie?' Tristan's shadowed figure loomed in the doorway. 'Are you ill?'

'I can't go on.' She raised a tear-stained face to his. 'I have tried, Tristan, but I can't. It is all pretend and make-believe out there. It has no meaning beyond the music and the twinkling lights of the chandelier.'

'Many people enjoy such things.'

'But I don't…not anymore. It feels false. Everyone clapping and me pretending to be happy, when I am miserable, utterly miserable.'

'You look pale, Lottie. Have something to drink.' Tristan thrust a flask into her hand. 'It will do you good. Restore your confidence. It was bridal nerves. When you are ready, we can go back.'

'My head is spinning enough as it is.' Lottie shook her head and waved the flask away. 'You are being very kind.'

'It is my job to take care of you. Let me.'

He put an arm about her shoulder and Lottie indulged herself by leaning there, drawing strength from him. If she closed her eyes, she could pretend…then she discovered that she did not want to pretend anymore. She had to explain to Tristan her feelings for him.

'Did the crowds give you a funny turn?' He came forward and caught her hands in his. Warming them. 'You could be breeding.'

'It is far too soon to know such a thing.' Lottie withdrew her hands. Ice encased her. He was looking after her because she might be bearing his child. An heir, and he was the last one. She should have thought. 'I will let you know if I am. I understand how much you must want an heir.'

'I am not my uncle, Lottie. The getting of an heir became an obsession with him. In the end, it destroyed him. I have no wish to follow in his footsteps. I intend on living my life, my way.'

Lottie closed her eyes. She had to know. 'What happens if I am pregnant?'

'For my part, I hope you are not…not yet,' he amended with a smile.

He wanted to end everything. A quick break was probably best. 'Have you found a way to end our marriage without a scandal?'

He knelt beside her. 'Lottie, very selfishly I want to have more time with you, to get to know you far better before we have children.'

'But you wanted a sham of a marriage.'

'It is you who wants that. I agreed because if that is the only way to have you, I will, but I want more than that. I will always be praying for more than that.' Tristan paused and brushed her hair from her forehead, allowing his words to sink in. A small fluttering of hope built within her breast. Did he want more from the marriage? Did he actually care for her? 'And I hoped tonight that I showed that I wanted anything but. Lottie, I need you in my life.'

'You care for me?'

'You are determined to have your pound of flesh.' Tristan gathered her into his arms. He was vulnerable in a way she had never seen before. Naked with longing. 'I love you, Lottie Dyvelston. I want you in my life as my wife in truth. I want you and not some reflection of you. I want you to be you and not try to twist yourself into someone you are not. You are my world and I need you to be with me to make me complete.'

'What are you saying?' Lottie breathed, afraid that this might be some sort of cruel dream.

'I was wrong, Lottie,' Tristan said humbly. 'Utterly and inexcusably wrong. I have come here to beg your forgiveness and to ask if we can begin again. If there is any hope for me. Can you care for me?'

'Tristan…' Lottie tried to let his words sink in but her heart was pounding far too loudly and her limbs were trembling. He was asking her to forgive him. Her! 'But why? Why did you do this?'

Tristan reached into his coat pocket and drew out a small oval object. He placed it in her hand. 'This might help you to understand.'

'My Claude glass? How did you…? When did you…?' Lottie stared at it in astonishment. 'Why are you giving it to me now?'

'Because it is the only way I can explain.'

'Explain about what?'

'I found it that first day after you had gone from the graveyard.' He curled her finger around it. 'Lottie, I accused you of looking at life through a mirror and not really living it.' He paused. 'It was not you who was doing that, but me.'

'You?'

'I had made sure that I was self-sufficient, that nothing and no one could hurt me again.' Tristan stood and moved away from her. His eyes became shadowed, and Lottie could see the pain etched on his face. 'I was wrong. It wasn't really living. But I arrogantly thought it was. That I knew better than anyone else how my life should be lived. I was determined not to repeat my uncle's mistakes. But without realising it, I was slowly becoming him—bitter and twisted, thinking of no one but myself.'

'I think you are being too harsh on yourself. I know the sort of man I met that day in Haydon Bridge.' Lottie moved over towards him, knowing that she had to go to him. She had to show him that she cared.

'You think far too highly of me.' His fingers touched her cheek. 'I began living again when you became upset about the state of my parents' graves.'

'It was a little thing. It was wrong of me.' She squeezed his hand.

'It was utterly right of you. And then when we met again at Shaw's, I knew that I could not let you marry anyone else. I knew you were the right woman for me.'

'You did that to save me from Sir Geoffrey Lea, because you did not want me to be tied to an old man… like Suzanne was.'

'You think so little of my abilities that I could not find another way of saving my reputation, besides marrying you.' He gave a slight laugh, but his hand went about her waist and pulled her close. Lottie laid her head against his chest and listened to the steady thumping of his heart. 'I wanted to secure you for myself and not have to worry about anyone else taking you away from me.'

'Is that why you married me?' she whispered, unable to trust her ears. Tristan had married her because he desired her.

'Yes, and selfishly I wanted you to want me too. I wanted you to care for me, not just my title or my wealth.' Tristan tilted her chin so she gazed up into his deep black eyes, burning with an intensity and desire that she had not seen before. 'Can you? Can you forgive me for what I did?'

'There is nothing to forgive,' Lottie said and knew it was the truth. She could understand now why he had done it. She could forgive him now she knew that he loved her.

'I want to spend the rest of my life making it up to you.' There was a humble note in Tristan's voice that she had not heard before. 'Please tell me that there is a little bit of your life that you are willing to share with me. That it is not all duty for you. Please take my ring back.'

'With pleasure. My hand has missed it so very much.'

He took off her glove and slipped it on her finger. She gave a contented sigh as the weight settled once again on her hand. 'I love you, Lord Thorngrafton.'

His response was to lower his head and claim her lips. She brought her arms up and arched her body towards his, savouring him. Wanting him. Demanding him. Here. Now.

The door clicked and Lottie jumped away from Tristan, hurriedly tried to straighten her gown, but knew she looked thoroughly kissed. Tristan moved to shield her.

'Excuse us.' Emma Stanton's musical voice floated from the door. 'We thought to find a quiet room, but I see this one is otherwise occupied.'

'I thank you for that,' Tristan said, and started to draw Lottie into his arms again.

'And you need not worry, Lady Thorngrafton, our lips are sealed.' Jack Stanton gave a laugh as the door closed once more.

'Tristan,' Lottie whispered.

'I am afraid your reputation is ruined, Lottie. It is just as well we are married.'

'That is true.' Lottie laughed as she reached up and

pulled his face next to hers. 'They already know what a hopeless pair we are.'

'And do we go back to the ball?' he asked against her temple. 'This room is not exactly secure. I have no desire to be interrupted again.'

'I was hoping for a little more.' She peeped at him from under her lashes.

'Shall I take you home?'

'But you are in lodgings.' Lottie attempted to keep the disappointment from her voice. She could not imagine taking him back to Henry and Lucy's. It would be unbearable.

'I have a small confession.' Tristan laced his fingers with hers, and pulled her close. 'I think that the principal suite in the Royal Hotel would be suitable for you… for now.'

'And for later?'

'We can live in Newcastle if you wish. I also have homes in London, Paris and Rome.'

Paris. Rome. London. Places that had she once dreamt of and had boasted she would see, but they held little appeal now. The only place she wanted to be was in Tristan's arms.

'But the estate?' Lottie paused, thinking of that once-loved place and how much it mattered to Tristan. 'What about Mrs Elton? And the rest of the servants? You wanted to restore it, or was that another ruse?'

'I will restore it in time, but we will live where you want to live.'

'Let's go home to Gortner Hall, Tristan—tomorrow. I find I am weary of society and long for my bed. And my husband in it.'

'Done!'

Their mutual laughter rang off the walls of the little room. Lottie smiled up at her husband and knew that somehow, despite all the misconceptions and mistakes they had both made, all her dreams had come true.

* * * * *

A Question of Impropriety

MICHELLE STYLES

For Lydia Mason, whose unerring eye for plot problems,
challenging questions and enthusiasm for my stories
continually inspires

Chapter One

September 1813—the Tyne Valley, Northumberland

Diana Clare fought the overwhelming temptation to swear violent, inappropriate oaths, oaths of the type that no one would even consider a spinster such as she would know.

One tiny scream of frustration and the merest hint of a word passed her lips. Jester, the piebald mare, turned its head and gave her a disgusted look. Diana shifted uneasily in her seat on the gig. Jester was correct. She had given in to her anger, and had broken one of her cardinal rules—a lady never allows passionate emotion to overcome her sensibilities.

She drew a breath, counted to ten and concentrated hard on a serene outlook. But the gig remained held fast in thick oozing mud and the tug of pain behind Diana's eyes threatened to explode into a full-blown headache. Adding insult to injury, Jester began to munch another clump of sweet meadow grass, daintily choosing the last few remaining daisies. Diana tucked a stray lock of midnight-black hair behind her ear and peered over the side of the gig. It was her fault that it had become stuck. No one else's. She accepted that, but accepting, and wishing to admit it to the general populace, were two entirely separate matters.

Diana knew she ought not to have been reading and driving at the same time, but she had needed something to erase the full horror of visiting Lady Bolt's At Home as the congregated gaggle of gossips had blithely torn another woman's reputation to shreds.

That the third and final volume of *Pride and Prejudice* had been waiting for her at the circulating library she took as providence, a way to restore her temper. Normally she scorned novels as frivolous and refused to open them, but Mrs Sarsfield had insisted she read the first page, and Diana had discovered that she'd had to read on and on. She had not bought the book, but done things the proper way—waiting her turn for each volume. And finally it was here, on the seat beside her in the gig. As she often joked to her brother Simon, Jester knew every step of the way home.

And what possible harm could come to her in the country?

Slack reins and the temptations of late-summer meadow grass had proved too great for the mare and Jester had pulled the gig into the mud pool just as Diana reached another scene between Miss Elizabeth Bennet and Mr Darcy.

Diana straightened her straw bonnet and measured the distance from the gig to solid ground.

She could do this—easily, with dignity and in a ladylike manner. One long leap. She pushed off from the gig and hoped.

Her half-kid boot caught in the oozing mud, several feet short of dry land. Diana gave a small cry as her bonnet tilted first one way and then the other before sliding off into the mud, taking her cap with it. Gingerly, Diana picked the bonnet up by one ribbon and stuffed the cap inside. Mud dripped from it, splattering her dress.

'Beauty in distress,' a low voice drawled behind her, cultivated, with more than a hint of arrogance. A masculine voice. A stranger's voice.

Her throat constricted and every particle of her froze. Her situation had suddenly become a thousand times worse.

'Distress fails to describe my predicament.' Diana refused to turn. Spoken to in the correct manner, the stranger would depart. Nothing untowards would happen to her as long as she behaved like a lady. She had to believe that, otherwise what had been the point of the last few years? 'My gig has become stuck, and I am solving a problem with calmness and fortitude. There is a difference.'

Diana concentrated on finding the next halfway decent place for her foot, rather than glancing over her shoulder at the owner of the voice. If she ignored him, there was a chance that he would depart and everything would be fine. Her ordeal would end. It was her actions that mattered. Her balance altered slightly and she was forced to make a windmill motion with her arms in order to stay upright.

'As I said—definite distress.'

'Nothing of the sort. I am finding my way out. It is simply proving trickier than I first imagined.' Diana put her foot down hard and heard a squelch as brown liquid spewed up. Her feet slipped. An involuntary shriek emerged from her throat. She flailed her arms about, trying desperately to regain her balance, before the mud sucked her down and destroyed all her dignity and decorum.

Her fingers encountered a solid object and she grabbed on with all her might. She rebalanced and looked, hoping for a branch. But instead her hands clung to the sleeve of a white travelling cloak. It was a choice between two evils—the indignity of falling into the thick black mud and the impropriety of clinging to an unknown man's arm. Impropriety won.

'It would be a shame to stain your dress, I believe.'

Without waiting for a reply, the man's hands moved to her waist, and lifted her up. Her breast and thigh grazed his broad chest. Her senses reeled, then righted. She refused to give way to panic. She kept her body rigidly still and willed him to release her, but the arms stayed strong about her.

'You may let me go.' Her voice resounded, high and shrill, in her ears as she glanced up into deep grey eyes. A strange sensation stirred, deep within her, curling around her insides with insidious slowness. She swallowed hard and beat it back. 'Please.'

'After I have had my reward.'

'Reward?' Her tongue seemed to be three times thicker than normal. The day was rapidly becoming a nightmare. Surely this man, this gentleman, had to understand that she was a proper lady? She was not going to be punished. Again. 'Why do you insist upon a reward?'

'For rescuing you. Surely my gallant action warrants the merest trifle.'

He lowered his lips and his mouth skimmed hers—a brief touch, but one that sent a blaze of fire coursing throughout her body. Panic engulfed her. She turned her head and beat her fists against his chest.

'Put me down this instant!'

'If that is what you truly desire.'

Diana gulped and struggled to hang on to some sense of dignity. It was the only thing that could save her. A truly worthy and refined woman was never in danger. Ever. 'It is.'

'Never let it be said that I do not accommodate a pretty wench's wishes.'

Her rescuer withdrew his arms and she was unceremoniously deposited on a green knoll. Her skirt flew up and revealed her legs up to her calves. Diana hurriedly pushed it back down and hoped that the man had been gentlemanly enough not to look. Silently she promised never to read novels again, never to utter oaths, if only she would be delivered from this nightmare. It was all her fault. She had broken her rules of ladylike behaviour and this was what happened to women who behaved inappropriately.

Diana forced her breath in and out of her lungs and regained some small measure of control. She could not show that she was discomforted. Exhibiting emotion only made situations like this one worse.

'I did not mean quite so quickly.'

'But I did as you requested. Beauty, thy name is perverse.'

'You have rescued me. Now you may depart.'

His black boots remained still. She glanced up at her rescuer, praying that he was a stranger, someone she might never encounter again. Broad shoulders filled out the finely cut white coat with fifteen capes and two rows of pockets. Tapered down to buckskins and the pair of black Hessian boots. He sported a white neckcloth with black spots, immaculately tied. Diana's gloom deepened. It was the sort only worn by a member of the Four Hand Club, the premiere carriage-driving club in the country.

She studied his dark features again and recognised the distinctive scar that ran from his forehead to his cheek.

Her insides twisted. That little place inside her that she normally kept locked and barred cracked opened. The man was Brett Farnham. Had to be. Diana pressed her hands into her eyes. She slammed the door of that place shut and willed the terror to go.

'Is something troubling you, Beauty?' The warmth in his voice lapped at her senses. 'Forgive me if I have offended, I merely sought to assist you.'

'Nothing, nothing at all.' Diana forced her face to relax and her lips to smile. Politeness must be her shield. A lady was always polite. 'Why should anything trouble me? Today has been without blemish or stain.'

'Aside from becoming stuck in a pool of mud.' A smile crossed his features.

'Aside from that.'

Diana resisted the temptation to bury her face in her hands. She had allowed herself to be carried and kissed by one of the most renowned rakes in the country, a man who had founded the notorious Jehu driving club at Cambridge University and who had set the fashion for speaking cant, tying neckcloths, a close confidant of both Brummell and Byron. Her late fiancé had revered him, and ultimately that reverence had been responsible for his destruction.

After all the years she had spent here, trying to forget that London had ever happened. Then Brett Farnham appeared and everything came crashing back as if it were yesterday. But whatever happened, she had to remember that it was *her* actions that decided her fate. If she held fast to her rules, she would be safe. If she had learnt one thing in London, it was that. 'Please, I beg you—go and forget about my predicament.'

He continued to stand there, looking down at her from a great height. 'I am no fool. You disliked being rescued.'

'Normally a gentleman waits to be asked.'

'A gentleman acts when he sees a lady in distress. He attempts to prevent greater harm.' His gaze roamed over her body. And Diana was fervently glad that she was wearing her dark brown gown with its high neck. 'It would have been a shame if your dress had become mud-splattered.'

Diana forced her eyes from his face. She struggled to breathe as her throat constricted again. It was nothing more than polite words, the sort that rolled off his tongue a dozen times a day. She was a fool to worry. This encounter would not happen again. London remained in her past. All was safe here. Her place in society was secure as long as she maintained her poise.

'Thank you,' she said quietly. Polite. Calm. She had to banish any hint of emotion and behave as if they had encountered each other at a tea party or some other social function. It was the only way.

'Remain here and I will free your gig.' A dimple showed in his cheek. 'You may thank me properly...later.'

'You do not need to do that. I am perfectly capable of freeing my horse.' She struggled to stand and started forwards, but he blocked her way, preventing her from reaching the gig. She cleared her throat, and tried to ignore the sudden trembling in her stomach. 'If you would kindly move, I have no wish to be in your debt.'

He lifted one eyebrow. 'Ah, so you intend on ruining your boots after all the trouble I went to. And your...uh... pretty dress. I wouldn't let a Beauty do that.'

'I am quite capable of getting myself out of the difficulty.' Diana crossed her arms, ignoring his flirtatious tone. A Beauty, indeed. She was no pretty farmer's daughter or green girl ripe for the plucking. No doubt in another moment, he would give his dishonourable intention speech and steal another kiss. This time, longer, deeper. The thought of the consequences made her blood run cold, even as a tiny piece of warmth curled around her. She regarded her hands. This was all her fault. She should have been paying attention to the road. This is what happened when she forgot her rules of ladylike behaviour.

'It looked different to me. It appeared as if you were heading for deep water and sinking fast.' He put his hand on his heart and made an exaggeratedly contrite face, no doubt expecting her to smile. 'Consider my reputation as a gentleman. How could I allow a Beauty such as yourself to meet with such a fate?'

'I am hardly a fainting violet who does not know how to handle the ribbons. I can free the gig…in time.'

He cleared his throat and looked pointedly at the vehicle with its wheels half-submerged in the mud. The position made it perfectly clear that she had driven straight at the puddle. She hated to think how long it would take to clear it. Or the difficulties she would have with Jester, who appeared intent on devouring every last speck of meadowsweet grass.

'I like to have my roads free from hazard. It could have been worse. I intend to rattle down this road today at high speed. If a carriage had encountered the unexpected obstacle, there would have been an accident. A bad accident.'

'It is a public road.' Diana lifted her chin a notch. His road indeed. Arrogant. Concerned with only his pleasure and comfort. Her heart rate slowed. She was back in control. Brett Farnham and all his kind were in her past. She was immune from such men now. She knew what danger they represented. But they also understood the code. Ladies were to be respected.

'I have never driven into a mud puddle, intentionally or unintentionally.'

'You think I intended on driving in?'

'As I am not privy to your thoughts, I remain unable to discern them. Mind-reading is, alas, not one of my talents. Dealing with horses is.' But within a moment, Brett

Farnham had moved around the gig and with a few whispered words coaxed Jester back towards the road.

The pool gave up its hold on the gig with a great sucking sound. Diana reluctantly admitted that he had done it far more efficiently than she could have. And except for the splashes of mud on his gleaming black Hessian boots, Brett remained spotless.

'I must thank you for that. Very neatly done.'

'You climb back in and then we will depart.' He gestured towards the gig. 'I will drive.'

'Go? Where?' Her throat closed around the word and she was suddenly aware how deserted the road was, how far she was from any cottage. Alone with this man. Vulnerable. 'I refuse to go anywhere with you.'

'I am taking you home. You drove into a mud pool. Anything could happen.'

'My competence as a driver has never been questioned before.'

He pursed his lips and his face assumed a sceptical expression. 'We have a difference of opinion on competence, I fear. Your horse is a placid and serene animal. Easily managed.'

'It is not what you think. I can control Jester.'

'And now you know what I am thinking? Mind-reading *is* a talent of yours. How marvellous.' His eyes pierced her. 'Do let me in on your secret some time. But for now, I will settle for your explanation.'

'I failed to pay attention.' Diana hung her head and her cheeks grew hot. 'I was reading a…a book.'

'Indeed. There is no book in the gig.'

'But it has to be there,' Diana said in dismay. 'The last volume of *Pride and Prejudice*. I left it on the seat when I jumped. I had to know the ending. The author writes so well. I shall have to search out more of his books.'

'I have it on good authority that the author is a woman.'

'The author's identity is a closely guarded secret, but I understand from Mrs Sarsfield that it is a man.'

'Shall we wager on that?' His grey eyes twinkled. 'A simple wager. With a suitable reward.'

He held out his hand. Diana kept her hand firmly at her side. No wagers. Ever. A simple enough rule to remember. She raised her chin and stared directly at him. 'I suspect you would not offer unless you knew the truth. I accept the author is a woman.'

'It does help to know the publisher and his habits.' He gave a small laugh. 'Never wager on facts you are uncertain of or have not independently checked. It helps keep people honest. But I shall agree with you—*Pride and Prejudice* is well written.'

'I had assumed that members of the Jehu club disdained reading and education, Mr Farnham.'

'How do you know I have anything to do with the Jehu club?' His eyes changed instantly and became cold slate.

'My fiancé was an admirer.' Diana spoke around the sudden tightness in her throat. 'Algernon Finch.'

He drew his eyebrows together before shaking his head. 'I have no recollection of the name.'

'He was younger than you at Cambridge, but he used to speak about the doings of the Jehu club.' Diana clenched her fist. The man who had done so much to encourage Algernon's folly and ultimately his death had forgotten his existence. 'He even introduced us five years ago.'

'Five years ago is a long time. I regret that I cannot remember the occasion.' Brett's voice held the faintest note of hesitation. A smug satisfaction swept through Diana. It was beneath her, but she did enjoy the feeling of wrong footing a rake. 'I look forward to renewing my acquaintance.'

'He died five years ago, Mr Farnham.'

'My condolences. But people will talk, and they do sometimes exaggerate the acquaintance.' He gave a slight shrug of his perfect shoulder, once again every inch the arrogant gentleman. 'You must not believe everything you hear. Remember that the next time. The Jehu club disbanded years ago. And it is no longer *Mr Farnham*. I am now the sixth Earl of Coltonby. Have been for the last six months.'

'My mistake. Lord Coltonby.' Diana inclined her head. 'I am sorry for your loss, but my answer remains the same. A title does not give one licence to seduce.'

'I can only apologise for the gross ineptitude of my sex.' A faint dimple showed in the corner of his mouth. 'It is lucky that I was not intending any such stratagem.'

'I am relieved to hear it.'

His eyes slowly travelled down her body, lingered on her curves. Diana reminded herself that this was a simple round gown, nothing too flattering. Suitable for visiting the Bolts and others in the neighbourhood, but it would appear dowdy and misshapen in Newcastle, let alone under the bright lights of London. Demure. Modest. Unassuming. His fingers trapped hers, curling around them and holding them fast. He brought them to his lips as his eyes watched her with a steady gaze. 'You will take driving lessons. I insist. Public safety demands it.'

'The public make no such demand.' Diana withdrew her hand and ignored the faint tremor that ran up it. 'I doubt our paths will cross again.'

Brett Farnham stared at the woman in front of him. This interview was not going the way he had planned when he'd glimpsed her ankle and the slight curve of her calf as she'd drawn her hideous dress up to avoid the mud. 'And if I say that the stories about me are exaggerated?'

'My answer would remain the same. In any case, London is your natural habitat. Your stay here will be a short one.' The Beauty's bee-stung lips were turned down. They were the most exquisite colour of rose pink and Brett wondered what it might be like to taste them again. But he decided against the notion. He would be a fool to try such a thing without knowing her antecedents. She claimed an acquaintance. Brett took pride in being discerning. He had never toyed with a woman whose thoughts might legitimately lean towards marriage; women who understood the nature of the game were infinitely preferable.

'It may be longer than you expect,' he said, keeping his eyes away from the swell of her bosom. Until he knew the exact nature of her status, he refused to risk any consequence. Silently, he prayed that she might be a legitimate pursuit, rather than one who was off limits. 'I recently won a highly desirable piece of Northumbrian property.'

'Did you, indeed?' Her blue-green eyes became cold. Her eyebrow arched. 'It appears to me that you play for very high stakes. Far too high.'

'Cuthbert Biddlestone had had rather too much port and challenged me to a race. I am hardly one to back down. I held his vowels, you see, and it was double or nothing. Now I hold the title to Ladywell Park.'

'You raced a noted drunkard? That must have been challenging.'

Brett brushed a speck of dust from his travelling coat. 'He was the one who insisted. He was the one who became a vice-admiral in a narrow ship. I did warn him what would happen. He chose not to believe me. I do warn people of the consequences.'

'And do you intend to keep this estate or will you wager it again on another race?'

'I never drink too much port. What I have, I hold...

Miss…' Brett held out his hand and prepared to recapture her fingers.

She smiled and managed to sidestep him. 'You will not achieve my name by such stratagems.'

'You claimed acquaintance earlier.'

'You denied all knowledge.'

'Perhaps I spoke too hastily.' Brett dropped his voice to a husky rasp. 'Enlighten me, O Beauty of the wayside, so that I may worship you properly.'

'I shall wait until we are properly re-introduced—' she tilted her chin and her eyes became glacial '—when the proper order has been restored, if indeed you have won the Park.'

Brett smiled inwardly. One of the local gentry. Unmarried as she did not bother to correct him. He had anticipated, given the ugliness of the dress, that she was a farmer's daughter, rather than a social equal. But now that he listened to her tones, he conceded that it was a probability. Annoying, but true. There again, she had mentioned a former fiancé—perhaps there was a stout husband in the background? Or, better yet, she could be widowed. Brett smiled. Possibilities remained. He would play the odds. Five years was a long time. A woman who showed a zest for life like this one would not have remained unmarried.

'I believe your book has tumbled into the mud.' Brett reached down and picked the mud-splattered volume up.

The lady held out a hand. 'My book, if you please.'

'I would not want you to be distracted.' Brett pocketed the volume. 'I will arrange for it to be delivered if you will divulge your name.'

'For propriety's sake, stop this funning and give me my book back…' Her lips became a thin white line, but her cheeks coloured.

'I much prefer impropriety.' He gave a half-smile at her outraged expression.

'My book, Lord Coltonby, if you please. I have tarried here long enough.'

Brett ignored her outstretched palm, and placed the volume in his pocket. 'I have no intention of keeping it any longer than strictly necessary, but for now I feel it would be a distraction.' Brett made a bow as she opened and closed her mouth several times. 'Your servant, ma'am. I look forward with great anticipation to our next encounter.'

Her response was to twitch the carriage ribbons. Brett stood and watched it. She would find an excuse to come to him. It was only a matter of time.

Chapter Two

'Rude. Arrogant. Impossible.' Diana threw her gloves down on her dressing table and finally gave vent to her frustration. Passion and emotion were permissible in private.

Lord Coltonby actually thought that she would seek him out! And the worst thing was that he possessed the same sort of lethal charm that Algernon had oozed from his every pore. But she had learnt her lesson about how quickly such things vanished. Her rules had kept her safe since then. Diana concentrated on taking deep calming breaths.

'Who?' Rose, her maid asked, looking up from her pile of mending. Rose coming into her life was the only good thing that had happened in London. Sometimes, Diana felt that the world would have gone entirely black if not for Rose's practical approach to life and her sense of humour. 'What edict has the master issued now? You were displeased with him at breakfast. I could tell by the set of your mouth when he went on about you going to visit Lady Bolt. Why he should be interested in the Honourable Miranda, I have no idea. The woman is a menace. She is the sort who considers every cold a lung fever and faints at the merest hint of anything untoward.'

'It is not the Honourable Miranda's charms that interest my brother, but the possibilities of using Sir Norman's landing on the Tyne if he makes an offer. Business, always business with Simon.'

'Your brother should make other things his business. That son of his needs a mother. You do your best, Miss Diana, but you ought to have a life while you are young enough to enjoy it.'

Diana gave a short laugh as she gazed with fondness at her maid who sat sewing by the window. 'I have discovered someone worse than my brother—an unadulterated rake who goes by the name of Brett Farnham, the sixth earl of Coltonby. He thinks all he has to do is click his fingers and women will fall at his feet.'

'And do they?' Rose laid her mending on her lap. Her placid face crinkled up. 'I have often longed to meet one and to see if such a thing is really possible. What was he like, your mysterious rake?'

'He is no rake of mine. He will have forgotten my existence by the time my gig turned the corner, and certainly once he encounters the next skirt.'

'You judge yourself too harshly. You have done so ever since you returned from London.' Rose made an impatient motion with her hand. 'And what do you know of rakes and their doings? You resolutely refuse to read the Crim. Con. papers.'

Diana gave a small shrug as she stared into the large mirror that hung over the mantelpiece. Her features were ordinary: dark hair, reasonable eyes and an overgenerous mouth. They had not been what had caught the eye of Algernon Finch. He had been attracted to the size and newness of her fortune. And his determined seduction and easy manner had dazzled her. She had never thought to question his stories until it was too late, far too late. But she had learnt her lesson. 'Brett Farnham is a rake, Rose. His exploits with gaming, carriage driving and women were the talk of London five years ago. But simply because *other* women fall at his feet, there is no need to think that I should.'

Rose made a noise at the back of her throat. 'How has he behaved? Tried to flirt with you a bit? You never used to mind such things, Miss Diana…'

'That was a long time ago, Rose.' Diana tucked a tendril of hair behind her ear as she tried not to think about the girl she had once been. 'I am no longer a green girl, ready to believe the lies that drop from a man's lips, particularly not when he appears sophisticated and charming. And I have better uses for my fortune than buying a bankrupted title.'

'Is Lord Coltonby bankrupt?' Rose's eyes widened. 'You know a great deal about a man in whom you profess no interest, Miss Diana.'

'The state of Lord Coltonby's finances fails to intrigue me. I simply know what sort of man chased after me in London. Bankrupt. Let in the pockets. They saw only my fortune and not my face or personality.'

Rose shook her head so that her ribbons bobbed. 'You should judge each man on his own merit. And stop seeing yourself as a plain old maid, an ape-leader who is on the shelf. Abandon your caps and embrace life. There, I have said my piece, Miss Diana, and it has been a long time coming.'

'Please, Rose. You have it all wrong.' Diana briefly related what passed between her and Lord Coltonby. Her voice faltered briefly when she neared the kiss, but she pressed on, avoiding any mention of it. If she did not think about it, it would be as if it had never happened. 'I shall enjoy seeing his face when he realises who I am.'

'Why would you want to do that?' Rose finished darning a stocking. 'I thought you were not interested in the man's opinion—good or otherwise.'

'I can hardly allow Lord Coltonby's arrogance in the matter to continue.' Diana pressed her palms against her eyes, trying to think straight as Rose's lips turned up into a smug smile. 'I do have my pride, Rose. Simon is a man of consequence in this county.'

'It is a start.' Rose shifted the mending off her lap and smoothed out the wrinkles in her apron. 'You should borrow one of those lady magazines and see the latest fashions. One of Mrs Sarsfield's daughters-in-law is sure to be willing to lend her copy of this season's *La Belle Assemblée*. I could easily alter one of your London dresses.'

Diana shook her head. She had lost count of the number of rules she had broken today. Wearing clothes that made her fade into the background was vital, a constant reminder of what happened when one let one's guard down. 'My clothes suit the life I have chosen.'

'It is such a pity. All those lovely silks going to waste.'

'They stay where I put them—in the attic.'

'You have mourned your fiancé for too long, Miss Diana. No one expects it. Not after the manner in which he died.'

Diana froze. How could she explain to anyone that she went down on her knees every night and thanked God for her lucky escape? That she had no intention of being caught out again. Ever. There were things about the past that even Rose did not know. Diana forced her fingers to pick up a pile of letters from the dressing room table. 'The post has arrived. You should have said.'

Rose tightened her lips and showed that she remained

unmoved by Diana's sudden enthusiasm for her letters. 'Doctor Allen has written. Already.'

'What has Robert done now? It is barely a week into term.' Diana tore the seal on the schoolmaster's letter. 'He promised me when we said goodbye that there would be no repeat of last year. He would attend to his studies. Simon will be so cross.'

'It would be better if—'

Rose's words were drowned out by a door being flung open. The noise resounded throughout the substantive house. Diana gave Rose a startled look and hurried out of the room.

'He's gone and done it! Lost everything! On a horse race!'

'Who has gone and done what, Simon?' Diana regarded her brother's thunderous face as he strode about the entrance hall, his black coat flapping and his neckcloth wildly askew. 'You will make yourself ill, if you continue in this manner. Be calm and collected.'

Simon gave her a disgusted look.

'Cuthbert Biddlestone has wagered his fortune on a carriage race. And lost.' He handed the cane and top hat to Jenkins, the butler. 'He lost his entire Northumberland estate, everything that was not in the entail.' Simon Clare shook his head as his dark green eyes flashed emerald fire. 'He wagered the whole thing on his ability to handle the ribbons against one of the best horsemen in the country! His father would be turning in his grave if he knew.'

'I suspect he did know. It is why he put off Sir Cuthbert's majority until he was thirty.' Diana forced her lips to turn up, but saw no answering smile in her brother's face. If anything, his face became darker. 'You always predicted such a thing would happen. What was it that you called Sir Cuthbert—a witless fop?'

'He was a fool. He claimed in his letter that it was my fault as he wanted the money to invest in the travelling engine.'

'That is complete nonsense!'

'But it is exactly like Biddlestone. And he did not listen to what I said. I only wanted a bit of his money…for my new engine. Then with the proceeds from the investment, he would have been able to build that new Italianate manor he was always on about. I was even prepared to sell him that parcel of land overlooking the Tyne—you know, the one where the old wooden wagon-way used to run—at a knockdown price.' Simon ran a finger about his collar.

'But what does this have to do with the new owner?'

'He wants to buy the land. Says Biddlestone and I had an agreement. Goodness knows what arrangement he will then strike with Sir Norman Bolt. Bolt's been after that land for years. About the only spark of intelligence Biddlestone showed was his loathing of Sir Norman.' Simon's lower lip stuck out. 'Is it any wonder that I am furious? Get me the latest copy of *Debrett's,* Jenkins, I want to know the measure of this Earl of Coltonby.'

Diana reached down and gave Titch a pat on the head. Lord Coltonby had told the truth—he was their nearest neighbour. The terrier looked up with big eyes. The simple act eased her nerves. She would be practical and she would not give in to her fears as Simon appeared to be overwrought enough for the both of them. Calmness and tranquillity were the keys to an orderly life. 'Why should it affect us? Why shouldn't we be able to go on as before? The colliery is profitable.'

'Everything has changed, Diana. Everything.' Simon's lip curled back slightly and his eyes became even greener. 'The bloody Earl of Coltonby now demands that I dance attendance on him and listen to his scheme for improving the area. I dare say that he will tap me for money. These aristocrats are all the same. Jenkins, I want my copy of *Debrett's* now, not in a month's time!'

'I am trying, Mister Clare.' The butler's voice echoed from the library. 'It does take time.'

'I know of Lord Coltonby,' Diana said quietly as Simon looked about to explode and the butler wore a hurt expression. The last thing she wanted was to have to find yet another butler. Jenkins was the third butler they had had in a year. 'He was there when Algernon died. One of the seconds…for the other man. It was all in Algernon's last letter. Then Brett Farnham…'

Diana hated the way her voice trembled. She swallowed hard and steeled herself to explain about today, but Simon held up his hand, preventing her from speaking further, from telling him about her earlier encounter with Lord Coltonby.

'By all that is holy! Brett Farnham…' He made a disgusted noise in the back of his throat. 'I never realised your fiancé knew him. I would never have listened to Jayne and agreed to the match if I'd known that.'

'You never wished to know much about him,' Diana replied carefully. She refused to speak ill of the dead—neither Algernon nor Simon's late wife, Jayne. 'Perhaps it would have been better if you had. How do you know Brett Farnham?'

'Farnham and I were at Cambridge together. He with his drawling voice and oh-so-smooth manner as he threatened to dunk me in the Cam for wearing the wrong cut of coat.'

'It was mostly likely a joke, in poor taste, but an idle boast.'

'The water was ice cold, but I swam to the other side while he and the rest of his cohorts stood braying on the bank.' Simon's eyes flashed a brilliant green. 'The man is debauched, Diana. He bragged about his gambling prowess and how well he drove carriages. And the women. You should have seen the parade in and out of his rooms. He and his kind are one of the reasons I detested Cambridge.'

'It may not be as bad you fear. Rakes are ever in need of money.' Diana kept her head high and her voice expressionless. She wanted to shake Simon. He should have questioned her chaperon in greater detail before entering into negotiations about her marriage.

'Why me? Why now when the engine design is beginning to show its true potential? Why am I being punished in this way?' Simon slammed his hand down on the mantelpiece, making the Dresden shepherdess jump. 'I should have insisted on the agreement being formal, but Sir Cuthbert hemmed and hawed about being honourable gentlemen. Honourable! Him! My great-aunt Fanny! He wagered his entire estate on a daft horse race. How can that be considered honourable?'

'He was not the man his father was.' Diana closed her eyes. 'The ways of the aristocracy are very different from ours. They always honour their debts to other gentlemen.'

'And never to their tailors. Papa finished being a tradesman before you were born and I am no tradesman's son.' Simon waved an impatient hand. 'I do not need the lecture, Diana. We both know what they are like, despite our dear papa's desire to become one. Coltonby is the worst of the lot. Mark my words. He will be up to some deviltry.'

'You don't know that.' Diana laid a hand on her brother's arm. She had to get Simon out of his black mood. A fit of the blue devils was not what anyone needed. The entire house's routine would be upset for days on end. 'Think logically, Simon.'

'You are against me as well! My own sister.' Simon slammed his fist against the table, narrowly missing the alabaster lamp.

'Simon Clare. Do not pick a fight with me, simply because you are cross with Lord Coltonby and his treatment of you years ago. You will find the finance for the engine. Perhaps Lord Coltonby is keen on all these new machines. Maybe he, too, sees the possibilities of steam and iron. Ask him. Maybe he will want to invest.'

'Ask? You never ask Farnham anything. He always declined politely to remove his boots from the stairwell, to not hold drunken parties, to stop fraternising with coachmen. He simply curls his lip and laughs at you.'

'You could try. People do change. You have.' Diana regarded her brother with his expensive frock coat and well-tied neckcloth, the very image of a prosperous landowner. 'You are no longer a student at Cambridge with little consequence. You do have a name and standing in Northumberland. You have a reputation for innovation and resourcefulness. The earl will listen to reason in time. You are under no obligation to sell that parcel of land.'

'I hope you are right, sister.' Simon's face closed down. 'Is there a method you would like to suggest?'

'Yes, wait and see.' Diana popped the final bit of toast into the terrier's mouth. 'Time has a way of solving problems.'

Brett paced the library of Ladywell Park, side-stepping the boxes of books that needed to be re-shelved and the portraits of Cuthbert Biddlestone's ancestors that needed to be sent on their way. The Beauty of the road invaded his thoughts, preventing him from learning more about the estate and how mismanaged it was, from planning his new house overlooking the Tyne, one which would be free of damp and mismatched rooms. He had had plans drawn for one years ago, something he had promised himself when he finally succeeded in restoring the family's fortune. And the outlook here was perfect. Biddlestone had been correct about that.

Who was she? Her eyes haunted him. Blue speckled with green, fringed with dark lashes. He had seen them before. He idly took down a book. 'Finch, Finch. Should I know the name?'

'You won't find songbirds there, begging your pardon, sir,' Hunt, the butler, put down the tray of port. 'Birds and natural history have always been kept at the other end of library. Shall I fetch you a book on the subject?'

'Songbirds?' Brett snapped the book and turned to face his new butler. 'Admirable insight, Hunt. You must tell me how you do it some time. Songbirds, indeed.'

'I do try, my lord.'

Brett waved a hand, dismissing the butler. Then in the stillness of the room, he poured a glass of port from the decanter and swirled the ruby-red liquid.

Songbird. Finch. Algernon Finch. Son of Hubert Finch, Viscount Whittonstall. He'd died in the duel. That dreadfully pointless duel over a disputed Cyprian. How could he have forgotten the name of Bagshott's opponent? The man who had unwittingly changed Brett's best friend's life and his own. A stupid boorish man who'd got everything he'd deserved.

It bothered Brett that the detail of Songbird's name had slipped away. He had been so sure that he would remember everything. The mud, the mist and the absolute horror of a life ended in such a way. Bagshott had already been up to his neck in debt, but it had not stopped him from quarrelling with Songbird. Standing on the dock after he'd bundled Bagshott into a ship, Brett had vowed that he would make a new start, that he would succeed and would restore his family's fortune. That he would not waste his talent, waste his life; but would use it wisely. But he had forgotten Finch's first name. And that of the man's fiancée.

How much else had he forgotten? Brett pressed his knuckles into his forehead.

Now all he had to do was remember her name, and why she was off limits to him.

'A man approaches,' Rose said the next morning as Diana sat re-trimming her straw bonnet in the dining room. 'He is driving one of the smartest carriages I have ever seen.'

'Since when were you interested in carriages, Rose?'

'I have an eye for a well-turned carriage, same as the next woman. My uncle used to work at Tattersalls. You should have seen them come in their carriages.' Diana's maid gave a loud sniff. 'Which admirer of yours drives such a thing?'

'I have no admirers, as you well know.' Diana bent her head and concentrated on the bonnet. A large silk rose now hid the mudstain and the ribbons were a deep chocolate brown instead of hunting green. More sombre. Less noticeable. By following her rules, her life was returning to its well-ordered pattern. 'It will be someone coming to see Simon.'

'The master is at the colliery. Where he always is these days. Why would a man not call there?'

Diana stood and went to stand by Rose. Her breath stopped. Lord Coltonby neatly jumped down from the high-perch phaeton and handed the ribbons to his servant. Diana drew back from the window as his intense gaze met hers. Her heart skipped a beat, but ruthlessly she suppressed it. She began to pace the drawing room. 'Lord Coltonby, Rose.

He has come to call. What has Simon gone and done now? I told him to wait.'

'Shall I inform his lordship that both you and the master are not at home, Miss Diana?' Jenkins asked, coming into the dining room.

'No, no, Jenkins. I will see him. I want to know why he is here. I can only hope that Simon has not done anything rash.' Diana's hands smoothed her gown and adjusted her cap so it sat squarely on her head. Although some might have argued that at twenty-two she was far too young for a cap, Diana had worn it ever since that dreadful day in London when she had received news of Algernon's death. There was a safety of sorts in caps. 'You may show him into the drawing room if he asks to see either one of us. Else you can take his card if he asks to see Simon.'

'Should I stay with you, Miss Diana?'

'That won't be necessary, Rose. I believe I have the measure of the man,' Diana dismissed the maid. The last thing she wanted was some subtle interference from Rose.

Diana forced herself to wait calmly and to rearrange the various vases on the mantelpiece as she strained to hear the conversation between Jenkins and Lord Coltonby. Why had he appeared today and what would he say when he realised who she was? Diana gave a wry smile. She doubted that he would call her Beauty any more. She would be proper and hold her temper—the very picture of a spinster, an ape-leader.

Brett followed the butler into the Clares' drawing room. The house exuded new money, rather than old. The drawing room, with its multitude of alabaster lamps, Egyptian-style chairs and green-and-gold striped walls, was the height of fashionable elegance, even though the colours were enough to make a grown man wince in pain. He could well remember Clare revelling in his wealth at university, always going on about his latest acquisition or his father's newest business. A man who knew the price of everything and the value of nothing. A man without bottom. He had not changed.

'I wish to speak with…' Brett arched an eyebrow as his gaze took in Diana Clare. Even her badly fitting dress in a green that rivalled the chocolate brown she had worn the other day for sheer horror and the oversized cap with ribbons did little to diminish her memorable eyes. Their almond shape and the curve of her mouth had plagued his dreams last night. Clare's sister. And a woman with a delectable bottom. 'How pleasant to renew your acquaintance, Miss Clare. I believe we once had correspondence on a less happy occasion.'

'I thought you had no recollection…' Miss Clare's pale cheeks flushed.

Brett inclined his head. 'I regret that it took me a while to connect you with Songbird's demise. I had quite forgotten that his fiancée was from Northumberland. Forgive me.'

He watched her intently. The aftermath of that day lived with him still. His determination to do more than simply chase skirts and play at gaming tables stemmed from the moment he'd seen Finch breathe his last. He had seen how quickly the dead and the departed were forgotten, not even a ripple on time.

'Songbird?' A puzzled frown appeared between her brows, marring her perfect skin. 'I am afraid that you are now the one who holds the advantage, Lord Coltonby.'

'Algernon Finch, as was. I only recalled him by his nickname, more's the pity. I had thought every detail to be emblazoned on my mind and now find that certain details had slipped from my grasp. A thousand pardons.' Brett tightened his grip on his cane and prevented any words from slipping out. The irony of the situation did not escape him. The whore had taken a new man within hours of the duel, despite her protestations of undying devotion to Bagshott. And yet, Miss Clare, the innocent fiancée, who had had no party in the action was here, alone, apparently living a retired life. 'A sorry business that day. Totally unnecessary. Both men were insensible to reason. They paid a high price.'

'You do remember.' Her blue-green eyes widened slightly.

'It took me until the early hours of this morning to recall the precise identity of the fiancée,' Brett explained smoothly. 'It was a nag at the back of my mind that prevented me from sleeping. I then felt compelled to apologise for my behaviour. It was unforgivably rude of me to question your source of information. Although I would contend that Songbird was not the most reliable of men when alive. And people change over the years. You should not judge me on his tittle-tattle.'

'I am surprised that you troubled yourself with the recollection.' Miss Clare gave a bright smile, but her hand played with the ribbons of her hideous cap. 'It was most impertinent of me to bring the connection up. I was out of sorts from my difficulty with the gig. Please accept my apology for referring to the matter.'

Brett stared at her. Today all the life seemed to have gone out of her. The vibrant woman of yesterday had vanished and in her place was this shadow. How long had she been like that? And which was the true Miss Clare? He knew which one he preferred.

'It is I who must apologise,' he said at last. 'That particular duel has long played on my mind. It should never have happened and I most sincerely regret that it did. Hopefully, it does not impinge upon your present circumstances.

And although I once presented them in a letter, again let me offer my sincere condolences on your most grievous loss.'

'Five years is a long time. I have quite recovered from the shock of it all, Lord Coltonby. You do not need to allude to the matter in oblique terms. I know my fiancé fought the duel over a courtesan. I had friends in London who took great pleasure in explaining it all. And I see no point in pretending that the duel did not take place.'

'I regret your choice of confidants, then. It was supposed to be a private matter.' Brett cleared his throat. It was all too easy to imagine. And even though this woman was innocent of any connection with the duel, people would have drawn their skirts back and whispered behind their hands. 'Those concerned with Songbird's death did everything in their power to keep the affair hushed. You must believe that. I know I never breathed a word.'

'A death such as Algernon's was never going to be private, Lord Coltonby.' Diana kept her head erect, but her insides trembled. She had never spoken of the hours that had preceded Algernon's death and she did not intend to start now, particularly not to a man such as Lord Coltonby. 'Whatever was said about me years ago is long forgotten. The wags and the wits found fresh victims to flay.'

'I can only recall pleasant things. You were quite right in thinking that we had been introduced before. I particularly remember Vauxhall Gardens. You commented on the brilliance of the fireworks.'

'I did?' Diana's feet felt rooted to the ground. Ice crept down her spine. Had he been there as well? That fateful night before the duel? How close had he been? Had he heard her cries and mistaken them for pleasure? And what would he say if he knew the full truth behind that night? She pressed her fingers to her temple. She would have to hope that he meant some other night. 'I have no recollection…'

Brett's eyes became a soft grey as he shook his head. 'Songbird was a scandal waiting to happen. He would never have done for a husband.'

'I didn't ask for anyone's pity.' Diana pressed her hands together. Privately she agreed with Lord Coltonby. But she could not make any excuses for Mrs Tanner, employed to keep fortune hunters away from her. The chaperon had failed miserably. 'My only excuse was that I was naïve and unused to the ways of the world. No doubt most young women saw him for what he was. I only regret that my chaperon did not.'

Lord Coltonby's mouth turned down at the corners. 'What a pity *your* friends did not speak up. His situation was no dark secret.'

'The *ton* is not so forgiving when one is only clinging to the edge.' She kept her head high and refused to allow the old feelings to swamp her. Calm. Tranquil. Her rules had protected her ever since that night at Vauxhall. She forced her mind to clear and then continued. 'I much prefer the peace of Northumberland. Society here may be an altogether duller affair, but the quality and quantity are at least known.'

'Why go to London in the first place?'

'My father had his heart set on brilliant matches for his children. My late sister-in-law's mother advised him to send me down there. I was to share the Season with her niece. Unfortunately the girl became ill and was forced to abandon the project. My father determinedly pressed ahead.'

'Did your father take the disgrace well?'

'My father died of lung fever, in the same epidemic that took Jayne. He never knew. When my brother's letter

arrived, my duty to return to Northumberland was clear.'
Even as she said the words, she knew they were a half-truth
at best. Simon's letter demanding her return had been a
godsend, a chance to lick her wounds and to dedicate her
life to being sensible and calm. It was wrong of her to think
that their deaths had been providence, however much it
felt that way. 'I learnt my lesson the hard way, and have
no regrets.'

'No regrets.' His eyes swept down her body, lingered on
the neckline. 'That is good. I had worried. Songbird would
not have wanted it.'

She paused and smoothed out the lines of her green
round grown. 'Is there some other reason you called,
Lord Coltonby? Surely it is not to reminisce over departed
friends. I have turned my face towards the future. Life has
been good to me.'

'Your book, Miss Clare, as you did not call for it. I
felt certain you had need of it now that you were safely
home.'

'My book.' Diana stared at the volume and then back
Lord Coltonby. 'Of course, my book.'

She reached out to take it and their fingers touched. A
small shock jolted her arm and she fumbled with the book,
sending it tumbling towards the ground. Brett smoothly
caught it and placed it gently on the small table.

'I had expected you to send a note, as you held the
advantage,' he said into the silence.

'I had no wish to trouble you or your servants with such
a trifling matter,' Diana breathed.

'And here I thought you would want to see me again.'
His eyes became hooded. 'We have unfinished business,
you and I.'

'We have no business.' Diana cleared her throat, ready
to send him on his way, before she asked him to stay.

With every breath she took, that little reckless piece of her seemed to once again grow stronger. She had to slay it before it led her back down the road to ruin and scandal, a road she had blithely trod before. Her heart pounded in her ears.

'I intend on teaching you to drive, Miss Clare. I have no wish to discover the roads cluttered with all manner of gigs and carriage simply because of your inattention.'

'It will not happen again, I can assure you. In any case surely you will not remain in the neighbourhood for long. A few weeks at most.'

'You know my schedule? Intriguing. Is this some party piece of yours? Or do you wish me ill?'

'Sir Cuthbert always complained of being buried in the countryside,' she said quickly to cover her *faux pas*. 'He only spent a little time here each year.'

'I am hardly Sir Cuthbert. His figure is far more rotund than mine. I do not think there is any danger of anyone mistaking us.' Lord Coltonby smiled. Diana found it impossible not to answer his smile with one of her own. 'I find the air very agreeable here.'

'On that we hold the same opinion.'

'Shall we be friends as well as neighbours? Put the past behind us?'

Diana drew in a breath. Friendship? Since when did a man like that seek friendship from a woman? 'We are neighbours.'

'And how shall we celebrate this neighbourliness? How shall we seal our friendship?'

Diana licked her suddenly parched lips. Sealed. The back of her neck prickled as a distant memory woke. Warned her. She held out her hand. 'As a gentleman and a lady.'

He regarded her hand, and then his gaze lifted to her mouth, made it tingle under his gaze. A smile transformed his features. He reached out and touched her hand. Held it for a moment longer than strictly necessary. 'A pleasure as always, Miss Clare.'

'Welcome to Northumberland and the neighbourhood, Lord Coltonby,' she said gravely, trying to ignore the sudden pounding of her heart, and withdrew her fingers.

'I look forward to discovering everything Northumberland has to offer. To deepening our friendship.'

'There are neighbours, and then there are friends.'

'I trust we can be both.'

Diana adjusted the ribbons of her cap so it sat more squarely on her head. 'My brother will be sorry he missed your visit.'

'It gives me an excuse to come by another time.' Lord Coltonby's deep grey eyes met hers.

'If you wish,' Diana replied and made a mental note to add another rule—Lord Coltonby represented danger and was to be avoided. Her survival depended on it.

Chapter Three

'Have you heard about the exciting development, Miss Clare?' The tinkling tones of the Honourable Miss Miranda Bolt assaulted Diana's ears as she left the circulating library the next morning.

Pride and Prejudice had been safely returned to the library, and Diana had no reason to even think about her new neighbour. Her well-ordered life would go on as before. She would be able to concentrate on things like needlework and visiting the houses of the colliery's employees, tasks that today held about as much appeal as getting her teeth pulled. But good tasks, worthwhile ones.

'What news? What has happened?' Diana asked cautiously as she turned to greet the impeccably dressed Miranda Bolt. Already she could feel a distinct pain behind her eyes. 'Is it anything untoward, Miss Bolt?'

'Positively the most important thing that has happened in the district for the last century.' Miss Bolt gave a toss of pale yellow curls. Her tiny mouth quivered with excitement. 'My parents are to give a ball in honour of our new neighbour. I fainted when I heard the news. Mama had to call for the smelling salts. Papa has agreed to the ball.'

'You mean the most important thing to happen to the district since the Napoleonic War.'

'War is utter tedium and boredom.' Miss Bolt gave a tiny shrug of her shoulders. 'The only good part is the number of men in uniform. Both Carlisle and Newcastle are full to the brim with soldiers. Lovely, lovely red coats and gleaming buttons. They add such colour to a party.'

'We received our invitation yesterday.' Diana forced her face to stay bland. Penning her regrets was a task for this afternoon. Simon might go if he liked, but she would find a reason to avoid the ball. She always did.

'You and your darling brother must come. You missed the St Nicolas Day ball in Newcastle last Christmas and you must not miss this one.' Miss Bolt gave a clap of her hands. 'I knew if it was in the neighbourhood, all the eligible bachelors would come. I shall be quite in demand. I told Mama that. A woman who is in demand soon attracts the eye. It is only a matter of time before I make a brilliant match, one which is well suited to my station. Forgive me, Miss Clare, if you think me proud, but I only speak the truth.'

'Indeed.' Diana's jaw tightened and she forced her smile to remain in place.

'It would be so lovely if we had more entertainment in the district. Then, we should not have to venture quite so far afield in search of culture.' Miss Bolt stuck her chin in the air. 'Culture is very important to me. It is the foundation of society.'

'You are forgetting about the Grand Allies routs. And the Sarsfields' *musicales*.' The idea that the Bolts were the final arbiter of culture in the Tyne Valley grated on Diana's nerves. They had only arrived here when Sir Norman's great-aunt had died and he had finally come into his inheritance. 'The elder Miss Sarsfield plays the spinet beautifully.'

'True, true, but I thought her Chopin was a bit sharp last week. It laid waste to poor Mama's eardrums.' Miss Bolt tapped a finger against her mouth. 'There again, you were absent, weren't you?'

'Unavoidable. One of the servants had come down with a chill.' Diana forced her lungs to fill with air. The excuse was threadbare, but she had discovered it was far easier to keep to her rules if she avoided entertainment wherever possible. 'It sounded pleasant enough to me when I heard the dress rehearsal.'

'Dear Miss Clare, if you could but hear what passes for music in the great drawing rooms of London...'

'I have been to London, Miss Bolt.' Diana held back a stinging retort. A lady must be polite, but Miranda really was insupportable. 'I even managed to attend several *musicale* evenings there when I had my Season.'

'The London Season. I have tried and tried to convince Mama of the necessity of a London Season. A proper one, with vouchers to Almack's.' Miss Bolt put her hand to her mouth. 'My dear Miss Clare, I nearly forgot how trying the mention of London and the Season must be to you. Mama has warned me and warned me, but my tongue goes flippety-flop.'

'Why should the mention of London be trying?'

'You know *the disaster*.' Miss Bolt lowered her voice and her blue eyes shimmered as she put a hand briefly on Diana's elbow, a show of false concern. 'Every time I think about it I want to weep. Mama remarked on it the other day and how it should be a lesson for me, a lesson I intend to take to my heart. Dear, dear Miss Clare, when I go to London, I shall be a success. I will not be a wallflower.'

'I wish you every opportunity.'

'And I will take every single one, I can assure you of that. I am meant for a viscount or an earl at the very least. It is too bad that the royal dukes are so very old.' Miss Bolt gave her curls a little pat. 'With my looks, breeding and Papa's fortune, a title should be within my grasp.'

'One should always aim for the attainable.'

'How very witty of you. The attainable, not the unattainable. I will remember that. I collect witticisms so that I can repeat them to my friends.' Miranda Bolt gave another trill of laughter. 'There again, did you?'

'Did I what?' Diana stared at Miranda Bolt. Was Miss Bolt entirely without reason this morning? The young woman seemed intent on ignoring all of Diana's attempts to end the conversation.

'Aim for the attainable,' Miranda Bolt replied with maddening complacency. 'Is that why it was a disaster?'

'My situation hardly compares to yours.' Diana gritted her teeth. 'I returned to Northumberland for family reasons.'

'It must be so hard getting old.' Miss Bolt tilted her head to one side and gave her parasol a twirl. 'Every broken sleep shows. Mama told me. It is why I take such care with my complexion.'

Diana counted very slowly to ten. Passionate emotion was the enemy of reason, but the thought of Lady Bolt and her odious daughter pitying her after all these years was insupportable. 'I believe your mother will be looking for you.'

'Mama is always searching for me. It is part of our little game.' Miss Bolt gave a gasp and a tremulous giggle as she lifted her reticule. 'Is that…? Can it be Lord Coltonby's carriage?'

Diana felt a prickling at the back of her neck and turned

to see a smart yellow curricle. A tiger held the heads of two sleek bay horses. The lines of the horse proclaimed speed and the need for a firm hand on the ribbons. 'It may be.'

'He made his own fortune, you know,' Miranda Bolt continued on, her cheeks becoming infused with pink. 'Papa said that all he inherited when his brother died was a bankrupt title. Luckily Lord Coltonby had already won his fortune. He apparently has an eye for the horses. Papa is very much hoping to persuade him to support him in a business venture.'

'Lord Coltonby is a force to be reckoned with.'

'Have you met him? He is your nearest neighbour, after all.' Miranda Bolt clasped her hands together. 'I do think he is the most handsomest of men. He called on Papa the other day and we were introduced. Mama is most hopeful.'

'How pleasant for you.' Diana tapped her finger against her mouth, determined to make her voice sound casual, but to gently lead the subject away from Lord Coltonby. 'The horses have good lines as well.'

'How can you tell?'

'It is the way they hold their heads and shift their feet. They have a bit of spirit. In the right hands that curricle would fly over the ground.'

'I knew you would know about carriages and that sort of thing. I have heard Papa converse with you about them before.' Miss Bolt gave a little wave of her hand as if discussing the speed of carriage and horses were somehow slightly *outré*. 'I will confess that they bore me senseless. All a carriage does is get you from one place to another and wild horses scare me. But if they are Lord Coltonby's passion, I suppose I must assume an interest. It will be expected.'

'Horses are noble creatures. They deserve better than the conditions they are currently subjected to.' Diana tightened her grip on her reticule. Rules. An accepted mode of behaviour. She must not give way to her anger and keep within the bounds of society. It was the only thing that protected a lady. Why did she always come so close to forgetting the basic precepts of etiquette in Miss Bolt's presence? Diana strove to keep her voice light and bland. 'Do you know how many horses are lost because of the mail coaches each year?'

'Mail coaches, Miss Clare, are a necessity.' Miss Bolt looked down her nose. 'How else would I know which regiments were in Newcastle?'

'How, indeed?' Diana hid a smile and felt the tension ebbing from her shoulders. She would now bring the conversation to a close and everything would be well.

'I do believe he has glanced this way.' Miss Bolt rapidly smoothed her skirt and readjusted her bonnet. 'Mama says that his fortune exceeds that of Lord Allendale and Lord Carlisle combined. Mama is always right about such things. Marriage is not something that should be left to the young. She is singularly determined.' Miss Bolt gave another trilling laugh. 'But I forgot, dear Miss Clare, you are unlikely to marry. The ever-so-sensible Miss Clare. Does it pain you when other people speak of marriage?'

'It does not affect me in the slightest, Miss Bolt. I take little notice of such things. If you will forgive me, Robert requires a few sweetmeats from the grocer's. He particularly asked for candied peel in his last letter.' Diana started to move away from Miss Bolt, but the young woman clutched Diana's arm.

'Wait, please, Miss Clare. Your dear sweet nephew can have his things later. My need is at present the greater one.'

'Miranda Bolt, kindly contain your gesticulations.' Diana stared in astonishment at the young woman. And slowly Miss Bolt released her vice-like grasp. Diana rubbed her arm, trying to get the blood to flow again.

'If I have given offence, I most humbly beg your pardon, but please remain here with me.' A faint glimmering of tears shone in Miss Bolt's eyes. 'Do not desert me in my hour of need!'

'Why? What is so urgent? What disaster can possibly befall you on Ladywell's High Street?' Diana struggled to contain her temper. She started to fumble in her reticule. 'Are you feeling unwell? Do you need smelling salts?'

'Lord Coltonby is going to acknowledge me. I know he is. He is coming towards me. We met the other day when he called on Papa. It was a very brief meeting, but somehow I knew.' She gave a huge sigh. 'It is in the way he says hello. And he is attainable, I know he is.'

Diana's hand stopped halfway out of her reticule. Someone had to warn the girl before she did something foolish, before she made a life-altering mistake. Rakes only brought scandal. 'Miss Bolt, Lord Coltonby is definitely not one of the attainables. You will have to trust my judgement on this matter.'

'We shall see.' Miss Bolt nodded towards where Lord Coltonby had emerged from the livery stables. His black coat contrasted with the cream of his breeches. He appeared every inch the gentleman, but there was something more in the way he moved, something untamed, something that called to her. Diana forcibly wrenched her gaze away and filled her lungs with steadying breaths. She tried to remember all the reasons why Lord Coltonby was dangerous, and found she could only think of his smile.

'It does appear that he is coming towards us, but it could be that he wishes to visit the circulating library.' Diana prayed he would nod, acknowledge them both and move on. A civilised way out of her predicament.

'My knees grow weak. Mama will be ecstatic.' Miss Bolt hurriedly pinched her cheeks and straightened her gown. 'To be favoured in this way by Lord Coltonby. Do you know how far his lineage stretches back? Mama had me learning it the other night. Fortune favours the well prepared.'

'You hardly need me here.' Diana prised Miss Bolt's fingers from her sleeve. 'Your mama has brought you up properly. Eschew the vulgar and you will prosper.'

'I have heard of his reputation and do not wish him to say anything untoward,' Miss Bolt whispered. 'Mama insists that there always be a witness. A woman of quality cannot be too careful, particularly when she means to catch an earl.'

Diana pressed her lips together, holding back the words of warning. Poor foolish Miss Bolt. She had never expected to feel pity for the young woman. Someone needed to explain about the consequences of trying to capture a rake. Someone—but not her. Miss Bolt would dismiss her as a jealous spinster. And what could she say without betraying her own experience?

Diana wrinkled her nose and looked again at the figure striding towards them. His top hat shrouded his expression. The only thing she could do was to try to subtly protect Miss Bolt. It was her duty.

'You always have a choice, Miss Bolt. Your mother will not be the one married to him.'

'But will I make the right decision? My future husband needs to be someone special, someone who will put me on a pedestal.' She shook her head. 'It is a matter that vexes me nightly. I must marry well, Miss Clare. A title or a fortune, preferably both. It is expected. Mama will not have it any other way. And sometimes I dream of dashing redcoats and faraway places.'

'Sometimes, the unexpected happens.' Diana kept her voice carefully neutral, but felt her throat tighten around the last words. Suddenly she wanted Miss Bolt to experience happiness. 'Hold fast to your dreams, Miss Bolt. Never settle for second best.'

Miss Bolt gave a small squeak in response and grabbed Diana's arm again.

'Ah, Miss Clare, how delightful to see you again.' Lord Coltonby captured Diana's hand and brought it to his lips. He held it there for an instant longer than was proper. Diana gave a little tug. His thumb lightly caressed her palm as he released it. She was grateful that the shadow of her bonnet hid the sudden flame of her cheeks. She regarded his black boots, counted to ten and regained a measure of control.

'Lord Coltonby. I have returned the book to the library. It will trouble you no further.'

'I can only hope you enjoyed the ending as much as I did.' His rich voice rolled over her. 'I enjoy a happy ending.'

Miranda Bolt gave a soft cough and pointedly held out her hand. Her eyelashes fluttered and her soft blonde curls quivered. 'Lord Coltonby, it is marvellous to see you again. Such an unexpected pleasure.'

'Miss Bolt.' Lord Coltonby inclined his head, but made no move to take the outstretched fingertips. 'I trust your mother is well. The fruit basket she sent over was such a thoughtful, welcoming present.'

'Mama will be so pleased.' Miss Bolt swept into a deep curtsy. 'She told me to ask specifically after your health if we should meet. She has several tonics that you might wish to try if the Northumbrian air proves to be too chilly…'

'How kind of Lady Bolt. I have no need of attention at the moment.'

Diana breathed a sigh of relief. Perhaps Miss Bolt was

not in his sights. She could safely take her leave, if Miss Bolt would let her have a word.

As Miranda twittered on about the weather, Lord Coltonby languidly reached into his pocket and withdrew his snuffbox. Diana's eyes narrowed and her body tensed as she remembered Algernon had once used that stratagem. Should she intervene? She could see Miss Bolt at war with herself over whether or not to take the proffered snuff. Diana gave a pointed cough and shook her head. Miss Bolt's face fell, but she made no further move towards the snuffbox.

'You do not approve, Miss Clare. I can tell from the set of your eyebrows,' Lord Coltonby said and a faint smile touched his lips. 'The ever-so-faintly censorious Miss Clare. Always so determined to do what is right and proper.'

'Whether I approve or not is immaterial as you appear intent on taking snuff.' Diana kept her chin up and made her gaze meet his, forced herself to ignore her natural inclination to walk away as quickly as dignity would allow. She would protect Miranda. She refused to allow an innocent to be drawn into his web. No true lady could ever do that.

'But I desire your good opinion. Your smile is so much prettier than your frown.' Lord Coltonby slid the snuffbox back into his pocket. 'I bow to your knowledge of the local situation as I do in all things. What is permissible in London... And it was a gift from Brummell.'

'The rules of society seldom change that much, Lord Coltonby.' Diana drew a deep breath and tightened her grip on her reticule. Protecting herself had to come second when she was faced with a situation like this. Miss Bolt stood poised on a precipice. She did not understand the danger. Surely a small sacrifice on Diana's part was worth preserving Miss Bolt's reputation. 'I find if one exercises common sense and courtesy, most situations resolve themselves.'

'What sound and estimable advice, Miss Clare. Is it any wonder I hang on your every word?' A dimple flashed in his cheek.

'Insincere flattery does you no favours, Lord Coltonby.'

'How do you know it is insincere?'

'It was the upward twitch of your lips that gave me the final clue,' Diana said with crushing firmness. All she wanted was to end this exchange, to get back home where she was safe.

He gave a barely suppressed snort of laughter. His grey eyes shone like opals. 'As ever, Miss Clare, I find it difficult to disconcert you…but it is so much fun to try. I can't remember when I have been so amused.'

'My existence does not revolve around your amusement.'

'It could be arranged, if you desired it.' His voice lowered to a purr, one that played on her senses and made promises of sensual delights, if only she'd accept. As if she were some naïve débutante to be led astray during a visit to Vauxhall Gardens.

Diana shook her head. She'd never forget. She knew him for what he was—a leader of the Jehu club, the prince of rakes. Such men spelt trouble for the unwary woman. They were only interested in their own pleasure, and took rather than gave. But a tiny piece of her wanted to believe that he was different.

'Ignorance is bliss, as some say.'

'But I thought you enjoyed being educated, Miss Clare. A denizen of the circulating library?'

Diana struggled to contain her temper. He delighted in provoking her.

'I was unaware that you were familiar with Lord Coltonby, Miss Clare. That you were *intimate* friends.' Miss Bolt's voice held an edge to it and her tiny mouth turned down, giving her the appearance of having swallowed a particularly sour plum.

She elbowed her way so she was standing between Diana and Lord Coltonby. The feathers on Miranda's bonnet tickled Diana's nose and she fought against the urge to sneeze. She stepped to one side.

'Intimate? Are we?' Lord Coltonby raised an eyebrow, regarded her with a faintly sardonic look. 'You must inform me of the Northumbrian definition of *intimate,* Miss Clare. I wish to see if it coincides with mine. As you know, I never like to disappoint a lady.'

'She hasn't said anything. She simply let me make a fool out of myself,' Miss Bolt cried. 'She has been keeping secrets!'

'Miss Bolt, Lord Coltonby and I were acquainted in London,' Diana replied, swallowing hard, scarcely able to believe it was her own voice. 'Lord Coltonby was good enough to call on me the other day as he happened to be in the neighbourhood and we renewed our acquaintance. He seeks to tease. It is his way. You must ignore him.'

'I always like to renew acquaintances where I can.' A bright light appeared in Lord Coltonby's eyes. 'Particularly when they are as charming as Miss Clare. It was one of the bonuses of coming to reside in this neighbourhood, to be able to renew an acquaintance that was cruelly cut short.'

Diana tilted her head and peered at him from under her lashes. This time his face, save his dancing eyes, was a mask of sincerity. No one would guess that it was an act. Her heart thudded in her ears. She played with the button of her glove, wishing she knew why he seemed determined to play this game.

'Lord Coltonby seeks to flatter, but one must never believe insincere flattery.'

'You sought Miss Diana Clare out? Deliberately?' Miss

Bolt gave a little stamp of her foot. Diana noted her face did not appear nearly as angelic. 'You went to visit her? But I always understood her time in London to have been a complete and utter disaster.'

'You were misinformed, Miss Bolt.' Lord Coltonby made a deep bow. 'She was one of the highlights of the Season that year. Unfortunately, duty called her home and the capital became a little greyer, a little less pleasant.'

'Duty...yes, I suppose.' Miss Bolt tapped a finger against her folded arms. 'Poor Mr Clare's wife died, leaving him that...that boy. I had never considered. It makes a great deal of sense now that I think of it. Dear Miss Clare was truly selfless.'

'Every time I have encountered Miss Clare, I have noted her quality. It is only increased if she also manages an impossible child.'

'Robert is far from being impossible,' Diana protested. 'He's lovely, if a little high spirited. I am very proud of my nephew.'

'High spirited? He put beetles in your sugar bowl and frightened poor Mama half out of her wits.'

'He had thought the bowl empty.' Diana stifled a smile as she remembered the incident from earlier that summer. Robert had sworn that it was a natural history experiment, but neither of the Bolts had been amused, particularly as one of the beetles had found its way on to Miss Bolt's new straw bonnet. Simon had claimed he'd been able to hear the shrieking all the way from the estate office. 'He did apologise.'

'Only because you demanded it.' Miss Bolt gave a loud sniff. 'I can never look at that particular bonnet without a shiver going down my back. If you hadn't plucked the beetle out!'

'It is good to hear that Miss Clare had the situation well

in hand. Quick thinking and a calm head are qualities to be admired.'

Diana lifted her gaze and met Lord Coltonby's steady one. She nodded her thanks. She bit her lip. She had been so quick to believe the worst of him. What if she had made a mistake? What if he truly sought only friendship?

'I must confess to having never given it much thought. A cool head in a moment of crisis. You could describe it that way.' Miss Bolt drew her top lip over her front teeth, giving her face the expression of a startled rabbit, and brought Diana back to reality. 'Mama can be wrong in her assessments of people sometimes.'

'I consider it best to judge people as individuals. To eschew cant and hypocrisy whenever possible.'

Miss Bolt's smile vanished as she looked quickly from one to the other. 'I don't listen to gossips.'

'You have a wise head on your young shoulders, then, Miss Bolt. Discover the true person. That is the key to success.'

Diana knew the words were for Miss Bolt's benefit, but to her surprise a tiny piece of her wanted them to be true. She wanted him to think well of her despite the long-ago gossip from London and Lady Bolt's pronouncements.

Diana put a hand to her face and mentally shook herself. Soon she would wish to believe in impossible dreams again. There was safety in the everyday world. Its strictures and structures prevented impulsive action. Impetuosity had led to her downfall before. It would never do so again. She had conquered it.

'It was lovely to meet you again after so long, Lord Coltonby,' she said, inclining her head. 'And to know that your feelings remain the same.'

'My feelings towards you have never changed since the

day I first glimpsed you,' he murmured, capturing her hand again and bringing it to his lips.

Diana forced her body to stay still as his mouth touched the small gap left by her undone button. Heat washed through her. Rapidly she withdrew her hand and did the button up. When she glanced upwards, she discovered he was watching her with a sardonic twist to his lips.

'Oh, oh, I see Mama. She will need to know…to know…' Miss Bolt hurried away.

A smile tugged at the corner of Lord Coltonby's lips as they watched Miss Bolt run to her mother, obviously bursting to impart the bit of gossip she had learnt.

'That went delightfully well. Now I look forward to exploring your Northumbrian definition of intimate.'

'I have no idea what sort of game you are playing, but I don't like it.' Diana took a long steadying breath. 'We are not having and never will have a flirtation. How dare you imply otherwise?'

'Did I? You must be reading too much into my words. A very bad habit, Miss Clare. I always mean precisely what I say. I find it saves trouble.'

'I have shopping to do. I do not have time to discuss the precise meaning of words with acquaintances on the High Street.'

'And here I had anticipated that we might become friends.'

'I fear, Lord Coltonby, that we are destined for ever to remain acquaintances.'

Diana straightened her back and, with a sigh of what she convinced herself was relief, walked away from him. She refused to look behind her even when she thought she heard the word—coward.

Brett swirled the amber liquid in the crystal glass and gazed at the darkening landscape through the study's window. All the land the eye could see—his, and unencumbered by a mortgage or debt. He had kept his promise, the one he had made on that windswept field and on the dock as he'd waved off Bagshott's ship. He had turned his fortune around. He had not sunk into the mire like his brother, and neither had he needed to run to the Continent. And he had achieved it in his own way. And yet, the victory seemed hollow in some fashion. He pushed the thought aside. It was a victory, and that was all that mattered.

All things considered, today had gone well. He had enjoyed crossing swords with Diana Clare, far more than he ought to have.

She might not have conventional beauty, but it was her prickly exterior that intrigued him. Why was she so set against him? What had he ever done to her?

'Simon Clare to see you.' The butler had barely uttered the words when the tall man brushed past him. The cut of the coat might be better and the boots shinier, but Brett felt he would recognise the intensity of Clare's eyes anywhere—and the feebleness of his manners.

Brett pursed his lips. The days when all he'd had was his name and a good eye for the horses were long gone. He refused to be intimidated by a man wearing the latest of everything and boasting about it. Clare always assumed that having money meant you could forgo the niceties of polite society.

'Ah, Clare,' he said, reaching for the decanter. 'It has been a long time.'

'I have come to discuss your latest demand.' Clare ignored the decanter and waved a piece of paper. 'I assume it is why you called at my house yesterday.'

'To see if things could be settled satisfactorily without calling in the lawyers.' Brett paused. How to say it? How not to antagonise Clare? 'Between landowners. Disputes have a terrible way of getting out of hand.'

'You mean amongst the aristocracy.' Clare snorted. 'Don't worry. I know where I fit in. And I can guess what flim-flam Biddlestone said, but I have no intention of selling that piece of land. I might have use for it sometime in the future.'

'Doubtful.' Brett swirled the brandy. Clare was the same jumped-up *arriviste* with his eye on the main chance that he'd been at Cambridge, lacking in bottom. Dog in the manger. The land was lying derelict. 'You have not used that wagon-way since you built the new staith. You have no use for it. I have offered a fair price in the circumstances.'

'You know all about coal mines as well as horses now, do you? Once I have a travelling engine up and running, that old wagon-way could be highly desirable.'

'I can tell when a man seeks to take advantage. Travelling engines are notoriously unreliable.' Brett regarded Clare. At university, Clare had gone on and on about this investment and that investment, always seeking to further his own ends. 'I want the land for the view over the Tyne. Not that you would understand that. The pursuit of pleasure is nothing compared to the pursuit of wealth. Wasn't that what you proclaimed on the staircase? That first day at Cambridge?'

Clare made a disgusted noise. 'You have a better memory than I. Is this derisory sum your final offer?'

'It is a fair sum. Consider it. That is all I ask.' Brett reached for the brandy again, preparing to pour Clare a glass. He and Clare were neighbours after all. They would have to put Cambridge behind them. 'I enjoyed speaking with your sister when we met at your house.'

'And spoke to her again on the High Street.' Clare crossed his arms and glowered. 'What sort of game are you playing at, Coltonby?'

'We were introduced in London. I had no idea at the time she was your sister. She is somehow much more…'

'Refined? Is that the word you were searching for? My sister was educated at a ladies' academy. She is young enough not to remember how my father had to scrimp and save for every penny.'

'Convivial was the word I was looking for.' Brett permitted a smile to cross his face. 'It would have been vulgar of me to cut her. Don't you agree, Clare? I do despise vulgarity.'

A muscle in Clare's cheek twitched. 'I know what you and your kind are like. You are trying to use her.'

'Am I?' Brett managed to hang on to his temper. 'Pray tell me how.'

'My sister is a lady. Remember that.'

Brett stared at the man in astonishment. 'Tell me how I have behaved inappropriately.'

'I know what you're like. I remember you and your deeds from Cambridge.' Clare leant forward. 'Your business is with me. Keep away from my sister. You are not fit company for her.'

Clare stalked out. The door slammed behind him.

'And what will you do if I keep company with her? How will you stop me? What price will you be prepared to pay?' Brett asked quietly in the empty room. 'Will you sell me the land? No, you will give the land to me, Clare.'

If ever there was a woman who needed a bit of romance and flirtation in her life, it was Miss Clare. All Ladywell society would thank him if she abandoned her hideous caps.

He would do it. It would prove a challenge. But in the end, Simon Clare would surrender.

Brett raised his glass. 'To this week's quarry—Miss Diana Clare.'

Chapter Four

Diana balanced the empty basket on her hip. When she had started out this morning, it had been full to the brim with gifts for the sick, and hard to carry, but after visiting the miners' cottages down by the wagon-way, it weighed hardly anything. It had been a productive morning concentrating on other people's problems and once again her mind was free from outlandish thoughts.

'Miss Clare, wait a moment and I will walk with you.' Lord Coltonby called from where he stood, chatting with one of the farm labourers. His hat was slightly pushed back and his cane dangled from his fingertips. The cream of his breeches outlined his legs perfectly. He seemed so entirely different from the men who surrounded him and yet he appeared perfectly at ease.

Diana shielded her eyes. She could hardly cut him now that he had called out. She attempted to ignore the sudden thump of her heart. She had nothing to fear here, not with all the children running about the lane and playing in the dust. 'Lord Coltonby, what a surprise. I did not think to find you here. That is, Sir Cuthbert never came here if he could help it.'

Lord Coltonby covered the distance between them in a few strides of his long legs. 'I believe you and my tenants will discover that I am a very different sort of landlord. Crop rotation, corn yields and stock breeding excite my interest. I vowed a long time ago that I would not be an absentee landlord when I came into an estate, but instead would nurture it. The land responds to care and attention.'

'Then you plan on doing the repairs to the east cottages?' Diana asked, unable to disguise the scepticism in her voice. The answer was far too pat and too easy. Care and attention indeed. Sir Cuthbert had never given a jot about his tenants. 'A number of the miners and their families rent rooms there. I quizzed Sir Cuthbert about the repairs, but despite his assurances, nothing was done.'

'Repairs cost money.'

'Having unlivable hovels costs even more in the long run—the landowner has a duty towards his tenants.'

'Quite so.' He lifted an eyebrow. 'And I am here to see my buildings. Please judge me on my own merits, Miss Clare.'

'And have you? Have you seen what needs to be done— the holes in the roofs and the smoking chimneys?' Diana asked quickly before her courage failed. She had seen the conditions that the people lived in. Concern for other people and their welfare had been her salvation. She knew that.

'I have never shirked my responsibilities, Miss Clare.' He held up his hand, preventing her from saying anything more. 'Sir Cuthbert was not overly concerned with his estate and his manager was incompetent. We can agree on that. It is in far worse shape than he led me to believe.

Give me time to put things right and I am certain you will be pleasantly pleased with the situation.'

'Are you saying that you would not have taken the estate if you had known?' Diana shifted the basket to her other hip. A shiver ran down her back. She was not sure why the thought alarmed her.

'I always enjoy a challenge, Miss Clare. It saves me from getting bored.'

'And boredom is undesirable?'

'You are only leading a half-life, if you have a safe existence.' His eyes flashed steel. 'In order to live, you need to take risks.'

'Ah, does that mean you will be leaving soon?'

'I believe that Ladywell Park offers me enough challenges for the present.' Lord Coltonby stopped by an apple tree. He picked two apples off the branch hanging over the road, and offered one to her. Diana took the fruit with trembling fingers and held it while he took a large bite of his. 'I dislike predicting the future. It can change in an instant.'

Diana rapidly placed the apple in her basket, resisting the temptation. 'Sir Cuthbert always hated being here after he had had a taste of London. The attractions of the city can exert a strong pull.'

'Sir Cuthbert and I are not alike.' He took another large bite of his apple. 'My primary interest is racing, Miss Clare, the breeding and the running of horses. It is how I earn my crust of bread. Northumberland grass is sweet. The air is clean. The purses and plates are rich because the local landowners have the coin from coal. It is a simple equation.'

'Everyone in the village will be glad that something is being made of Ladywell Park. It was once a prosperous estate.'

'It will be again. Better than before. I intend to build a

new house overlooking the Tyne. I have had plans for such a house drawn for a very long time.' Brett finished his apple and tossed away the core. 'I made a vow once.'

'Which is why you wish my brother to sell you the land?' Diana inclined her head. The reason for Lord Coltonby's attention was now clear. He thought she could exert some influence over Simon. She should have guessed. The knowledge made her both relieved and vaguely disappointed. 'I am very sorry, Lord Coltonby, but I have no say over what my brother does.'

His eyes widened slightly. 'How did you know I was going to ask you?'

'It stands to reason. Simon was in a frightful temper when he returned home last night.'

'I would consider it a great personal favour if you would at least speak to him.' He paused. 'We shared a landing at Cambridge and it was not successful. I fear he holds my youthful indiscretions against me.'

'My brother keeps his personal feelings out of business.'

'Does he?' Lord Coltonby's lips twisted upwards. 'I wonder if that is a good thing, or not.'

'He never consults me on such things.' Diana tightened her grip on the basket. The conversation was meandering down an unexpected path and she had no wish to repeat the High Street incident. 'Now tell me, is the grass really that much sweeter than Warwickshire? Does the location give you that much advantage? Everyone in Ladywell will want to know.'

'Much.' His eyes grew grave. 'Racing horses is my passion. When I race, I race to win. And I want to be where the biggest purses are.'

'I will remember that.' She gave an uneasy laugh. 'I

doubt we will have the occasion to race or even to pit our wits against each other.'

'You never know. You might enjoy it.' The words poured out of him, smooth as velvet. She could almost feel them stroking her skin. 'Are you issuing challenges now, Miss Clare?'

'No.' Diana forced her chin to rise and refused to let him see her discomfort. He was trying to unsettle her, that was all. She tried to ignore how silent the track had become and how the sounds of the children playing were now quite distant. 'If nothing else, London taught me caution. I found it hard to credit how many inappropriate suggestions were put to me before Algernon was cold in the ground. Good day to you, Lord Coltonby.'

She took several steps and then felt his hand on her elbow, preventing her from leaving. His breath fanned her cheek, warming it. Diana kept her body still and concentrated on a stone in the road. 'Let me go.'

'I can only apologise for the crassness of Songbird's brethren, but you mistook my meaning.' His voice became clipped, his eyes chilled. 'I would never use such a stratagem to force a woman to do anything that she did not want to do. You have nothing to fear from me, Miss Clare, with or without your spinster's cap.'

She knew the combination of her current gown and cap made her look bilious and forty. Even Simon had remarked on its ugliness. She had been pleased with this before, but suddenly she wanted Lord Coltonby to look at her in a different way. A faint tremor went through her. It was as if she had opened Pandora's box and all thoughts and desires she had tried to suppress or hide rushed out in one fell swoop. Maybe she was wonton after all. Maybe all this attraction was coming from her. Maybe her cap no longer protected her. Maybe it never had. No, it had to. It was just further back on her head than she would wish.

Diana jerked the ribbons of her cap hard. The right-hand ribbon and half the cap came away in her hand. Her insides turned over and the stain of humiliation flooded on to her cheeks as she saw the gleam in his eyes.

'It still does not suit you. Heed my advice, Miss Clare— get rid of the cap. Better yet, burn it. A truly determined suitor would take no notice in any case. It only gives the illusion of protection.'

The man was insupportable. How dare he say such things! Her cap was important. It kept her safe. It showed the world that she was a lady, that she was not in the market for a husband. She would have to repair the cap immediately. 'Illusion of protection?'

'I once knew a man who swore that a certain rabbit's foot would keep him from illness and ruinous debts. He paid a tremendous amount for it. He even cajoled me into returning to a nest of thieves and cut-throats to retrieve it after he had been injured in a fight and could not leave his bed. I tried once and was beaten back, but the pleas of the man only increased as he begged me to help him. Bagshott had suggested caution and to forget it, but I opted for the bold approach and retrieved the item. I had promised, you see.'

'And what happened to the man after…?'

'My brother died of typhoid with the rabbit's foot clutched tightly between his fingers. And he was in the process of removing to the Continent to escape his creditors.'

'I am so sorry.'

'Don't be. I merely sought to illustrate what happens when one puts one's faith in objects. Actions are what counts, not objects, Miss Clare.'

'Good day to you, Lord Coltonby.'

'And you, Miss Clare.'

Brett watched her go—her skirts swung about her legs, revealing a well-turned ankle. The encounter had gone better than he had dared hope.

A light suggestion. Friendly banter. Nothing too overt. Miss Clare in the end would do as he wished.

He smiled. And there was very little Simon Clare could do about it, except fume and fret. He looked forward to seeing Clare's face, but mostly he wanted to see what *Miss* Clare would do next. The chase in many ways was far more satisfying than the final surrender.

'I had expected you to be at home.' Simon's annoyed tone greeted Diana before she had even had time to put the basket away.

'I was out visiting the colliers' families. Mrs Dalton is confined with her third child and the Widow Tyrwhitt has taken to her bed.' She paused and removed her bonnet. 'It is my afternoon for making the rounds. You agreed on the importance of this. It is our duty to make sure they are looked after.'

'Yes, yes, you do a fine job. God knows that I cannot see the point. People always have complaints and they fail to understand the virtues of business.'

'Simon.' Diana pressed her lips together. They had had this argument several times over the past few years. It bothered her that Simon appeared to care more about the machinery rather than the people who made it work.

'Later, sister. There is something you need to see.'

'What have you done, Simon?' Diana's corset suddenly felt too tight as she looked at her brother. He was swaying back and forth like Robert did when he'd found a new bird's nest. He was up to something.

'You need to come with me to the colliery. Straight away. There is no time to change.'

'To the colliery? Now?' Diana glanced out of the window at the lengthening shadows. 'It will be nearly dark by the time we get there. Can't this wait until morning? I can then take a basket to the Widow Bosworth. You know how she likes company now that her boys are working down the mine.'

'There is something I want you to see.' He put his hand on hers. 'Please, Diana, say you will come? For me.'

When he looked like that with his dark green eyes, Diana was forcibly reminded of how her brother had been before he had married Jayne, before he had become obsessed with order and control. Before business had ruled his life. Whatever new thing he wanted to show her, it would take her mind off Lord Coltonby and that could only be a good thing. 'I will come.'

'Behold the future!' Simon proclaimed when they arrived at the colliery.

Diana stared at the huge black machine on wheels. A gigantic smokestack was at one end and at the other, a place for someone to stand. Her mouth went dry. 'What is it?'

'A travelling engine based on adhesion rather than pulling or ratchet.'

A travelling engine. The holy grail of every coal owner in the district. Besides William Hedley at Wylam and the viewer at Killingworth, she doubted another man in the whole of England could make a travelling engine work.

'Where did you get it?' she asked, coming to stand by Simon. 'Who drew up the plans?'

'I acted decisively.' Simon's expression was that of a rapt schoolboy. 'Isn't it a thing of beauty?'

'But how did you get it? Only last week, you said that you could not find one. Or even obtain the plans for one.'

'I have ways and means, Diana.' Simon hooked his thumbs into his waistcoat. For the first time in months, Diana saw him smile, a genuine smile instead of the tight-lipped one that did not reach his eyes. 'I had to take the opportunity. All the other masters would have given their eye teeth. Once it is up and running, whole vistas will open out in front of us. I can start up Little Ladywell again, run wagons along the disused wagon-way. Then no one can claim that the land is worthless and redundant.'

Diana sucked in her breath. The disused wagon-way. The land Lord Coltonby wanted to purchase. While she did not doubt Simon's dedication, she wondered how much he was being spurred on by his desire to antagonise his old rival. 'And you discussed this with Lord Coltonby?'

'They delivered it today. I could hardly discuss it before I had the engine.' Simon advanced towards the big black machine, and ran his hand down its side. 'Hedley is right. The only way an engine will work is to be free running, not on a ratchet system.'

'And how much will it cost? Who are the other inves- tors? You have to be practical, Simon.' Diana crossed her arms, and refused to let her brother divert her attention.

'Not if I run it along the old wagon-way. I worked it all out in my mind. It can be done. The old staith can be reopened. And I will have no over-privileged aristocrat telling me how to run my business.'

'Simon!' Diana said through gritted teeth. 'You are behaving in a high-handed fashion. You will antagonise him. I remember the quarrels you had with Sir Cuthbert.'

'But he had learnt the errors of his way. Common sense prevailed.'

'Only because he needed money.' Diana drew a breath.

She would have to explain about her encounter earlier and what she had seen. 'Lord Coltonby is different. He isn't intent on drinking the port cellar dry and gambling away his inheritance.'

'What on earth are you talking about Diana? I knew Coltonby at university. Gaming and drinking are the man's life. He was a seven-bottle man. And I could not count the number of card tables he graced, how many brawls he was involved in.'

'University was a long time ago. It strikes me that he is someone who you would want to have as an ally, not as an enemy.'

'He was the over-privileged son of an earl. He threw his weight around. Humiliated me. And I refuse to bow to his wishes and desires. He is not getting one inch of my ground until he has sweated blood for it.'

Diana stared at the large black machine. She had never realised how deeply Simon's experiences at university had affected him. But she had also heard the passion in Lord Coltonby's voice when he spoke of his estate and his desire to do something with it. There was more to the man, if only Simon would see it.

'Simon, you need to grow up and think beyond what happened to you all those years ago.'

Brother and sister glared at each other. Finally, Simon looked away. He loosened his stock. 'Once I get The Duke to run properly, I will see whether I need that strip of land. If not, I will sell it to him for the going rate, not some paltry sum. I only offered it as a sop to Biddlestone when he said he might invest in the engine. Does that satisfy you?'

'It will have to.' Her stays seemed to pinch more tightly than before and a pain developed behind the back of Diana's eyes. Simon had decided to set himself on a collision course with Lord Coltonby and that did not bode well for anyone.

She concentrated on the engine. 'But why are you calling it The Duke? After the Duke of Northumberland? One of the royal Dukes? Are you hoping for investment?'

'No, because it is noisy and belches quite frequently.' Simon gave a brilliant smile. 'The steam pressure needs to be high. Nearly to the breaking point of the boiler.'

Diana watched her brother with a sinking heart. Stubborn and unwilling to listen to reason. There were times when she wanted to shake him. He thought he could ride roughshod over everyone and everything in his path. He did not mind the enemies he made as long as the business prospered. Some day, he would realise that there was more to life than proving his business acumen. 'Simon, there are those who doubt that anyone can make a reliable travelling engine.'

'I will do it. When have I ever failed with machines?' He caught both her hands. Simon gave a lightning quick smile, transforming his features and making him more like the boy she remembered from childhood, rather than the embittered man she'd discovered when she returned from London. 'Trust me to do the right thing. It will work, Diana. I know it will. Have faith in me.'

'I do have faith, Simon. How could you ask that of me?' A shiver went down Diana's back. 'I hope you are right. I don't think Lord Coltonby is a good man to cross.'

'Neither am I, Diana, neither am I.'

Diana offered up a silent prayer that it would not come that. She glanced one last time at The Duke, sitting there black and brooding. How much was bravado on Simon's part?

Chapter Five

'Is it true what Miranda Bolt says?' Charlotte Ortner asked Diana, leaning over her tea cup, her face alight with excitement.

'What does Miss Bolt say now?' Diana regarded the candlesticks on the Ortners' mantelpiece. Her weekly round of visiting had proved more tedious than she'd thought possible. Everywhere she went hummed with whispers of Lord Coltonby and his arrival in the neighbourhood, endless questions and speculations. One would be forgiven for thinking nothing else had happened recently in Ladywell or the Tyne Valley. She had only a few minutes left before she could make her excuses and leave. She always stayed precisely a quarter of an hour—no more, no less. 'What new entertainment for the ball has she devised?'

'Miranda says that Lord Coltonby singled her out for special attention and it is merely a question of time. She said you were a witness and saw his preferential treatment at close quarters.'

'Charlotte!' her mother called. 'Modulation!'

Charlotte lowered her tone and glanced over her shoulder,

but, seeing her mother was actively greeting new arrivals, she continued in a low voice, 'I thought I could ask you as you weren't in the running, so to speak. Mama will be livid if Lady Bolt beats her in this marriage stake. And you are the only person who knows the truth. Does he have a penchant for Miranda Bolt?'

'I am really not able to indulge in idle speculation or gossip.' Diana folded her hands on her lap. Trust Miranda Bolt to twist the encounter. There had to be some way of rectifying the situation without calling attention to her own part.

'But Miranda said you were there and would confirm everything.' Charlotte's eyes danced and her mouth quirked upwards. 'Mama's eye is very firmly fixed on Lord Coltonby at the moment. Miranda is planning a stratagem for the ball, and so naturally I wanted to know. Does Miranda tell a tale that is too good to be true?'

Diana shifted on her seat. She needed to stop Miranda Bolt. If she continued in this fashion, the result would be heartache—or worse. Everyone appeared to have little understanding of a London rake's methods. Lord Coltonby would only be caught when he chose to be and not before. 'I have no reason to believe any wedding bells will be ringing for Lord Coltonby in the near future.'

'Wait until I tell Mama.' Charlotte placed her tea cup down with a bang. 'Miss Clare has made one of her pronouncements: Lord Coltonby is destined to remain a bachelor.'

'Please, don't say anything… My acquaintance with Lord Coltonby dates from London. I know what he is like.' Diana's cheeks burnt with a sudden heat. Why did people insist on reading too much into things? She had merely wanted to protect Miranda and ensure her reputation was kept safe, not begin an *on dit* of her own. Her hands went to straighten her cap, but instead encountered her hair. Hurriedly Diana placed them in her lap and made her face assume a beatific expression.

Charlotte's eyes narrowed. 'Why, Miss Clare, I do believe you have abandoned your cap. I cannot see it peeking out from your bonnet.'

'It...it did not suit the dress.' Diana stood up, hoping against hope that her meaning would not be twisted. The rent in the cap had been too great to be quickly repaired and she had hoped no one would remark on it as her status as an ape-leader was widely known. And how could she begin to explain the circumstances in which it had been ruined?

'But Lord Coltonby remembered the acquaintance and he sought you out, practically the day he arrived in the neighbourhood.'

'There are reasons for it.' Diana shifted from one foot to the other. She wanted to avoid mentioning the encounter in the lane. It would only add fuel to the fire. 'Simple reasons. Reasons that have nothing to do with Lord Coltonby.'

Charlotte leant forward. Her eyes gleamed. 'He is the most excitingly attractive man to come into the neighbourhood for ages. Not only titled, single and pleasing to the eye, but with sufficient income to support a wife. Is it any wonder you are tempted?'

'I have no plans to marry. Ever.' Diana pasted a smile on her face. 'I have no wish to join the circling hordes. Your mama's matrimonial plans are safe.'

'Oh, is that how it is?' Charlotte gave a coy little smile. 'You are full of secrets, Miss Clare. I shall have to tell Miranda that she has a rival. You are planning on going to the ball, aren't you?'

'I believe, Miss Ortner, that my time here is at an end. It would be impolite to stay longer.'

However, Diana noticed with a sinking heart that Charlotte had already turned from their conversation and was whispering in excited tones to one of her newly arrived friends.

'And will that be all, Miss Clare?' The shopkeeper stood with his quill poised.

'I believe it will be sufficient.' Diana gave her head a shake. She should have behaved more rationally at the Ortners. The sensible thing would have been to nod and exclaim about the audacity of Miss Bolt. She should never have tried to put the story right. Miranda didn't need Diana's protection.

It was most disconcerting. Normally, she had more control. She did not add to the gossip. But today it seemed to her that everyone was staring and whispering behind their hands. She had made a fool of herself. Their gazes remained friendly, but she knew how quickly such looks narrowed in disapproval...

'Miss Clare?' the shopkeeper said again, bringing her back to the present. Her cheeks burnt slightly. 'I need to know how much of the green velvet you want. Sufficient is a very expansive word.'

'Two lengths will be more than enough.'

'Very well, Miss Clare.' The shopkeeper retrieved his scissors and began cutting the material.

Diana breathed more easily, and studiously ignored the slight jangle of the bell behind her. She refused to turn around and see who had entered the shop. Refused to see if it was him. Life would return to normal now. This instant. She was a mature sensible woman, not given to flights of fancy. She behaved with decorum at all times. She had learnt the value of restraint.

'Here you go, Miss Clare.' The shopkeeper held out her packages.

She gathered up her brown-paper parcels and narrowly missed colliding with Lord Coltonby. His face appeared as black as thunder. His large hands reached out and steadied her, closing around her forearms. A tide of heat washed through her body and her fingers grew lax on the parcels. She forced them to curl back around them, and her body began to regain its composure. She stepped away from Lord Coltonby and nearly tumbled over a bucket. His fingers came very firmly under her elbow.

'You appear flustered, Miss Clare,' he said as he led her out of the shop. His eyes twinkled down at her. 'Something I have done, I hope?'

'No, not flustered, Lord Coltonby, merely in a hurry.' Diana reached up one hand to straighten her bonnet. She longed to ask him why he had gone into the haberdashery. It was not the sort of place she assumed he would frequent. French modistes maybe, if he was outfitting a mistress, but a simple haberdashery, never. 'It is one of the worst of my faults. I spent far too long at the Greys'. And the Ortners'.'

'One can be so busy noticing one's faults that one forgets to notice one's virtues, Miss Clare.'

She tilted her head to one side and prepared to sweep out of the shop with dignity. 'You turn a phrase very charmingly.'

'Sometimes, the truth is charming.'

'I prefer my truth to be unvarnished, without adornment. It is an irritating habit, I am told, but it has held me in good stead these past five years.'

'Or merely prevented you from living?' His eyes slowly assessed her. 'I see you have abandoned your cap. It makes you look years younger. I must congratulate you. Now, perhaps, you will consider wearing a more becoming colour.'

'My life is quite full enough, Lord Coltonby, and I have not yet had the time to repair my cap. I have no need to be made into an enthusiasm, a project to amuse your days. A pleasant attempt, but I know how quickly enthusiasms fade.'

'You truly do not believe in the veracity of that statement.'

'It is what keeps the *ton* fashionable and exclusive. You have to know which is the right tailor, or the correct box at the theatre, which authors to read and which are beyond mentioning. The dances and figures change constantly.'

He blocked her way. 'I ask to be judged on my own merit, Miss Clare, not some poor unfortunate's. It is a small request.'

Diana's cheeks grew hot. It pained her that he was correct. She had been judging him based on someone else. 'There are books waiting for me at the library. I received a note this morning.'

'Minerva Press? Another novel by the author of *Pride and Prejudice?* What excites your fancy today, Miss Clare?'

'Improving tomes on agriculture and crop rotation,' Diana replied in a crushing tone.

'Why do you feel the need to avoid novels? To keep from driving off the road?' He arched a brow. 'I would have thought putting them in a basket behind you would have sufficed.'

'You are an aggravating man.'

'I do but try.' He inclined his head. 'You pique my interest, Miss Clare. Will you truly take out an improving tome?'

She started towards the library and he fitted his steps

with hers. Rather than create more of a scene, Diana ignored him. The librarian gave a nod as Diana headed for the stacks. Randomly she picked up a manual on agriculture and the need for efficient crop rotation. 'You see—an improving tome.'

'I never doubted it, and that one is particularly dry.'

'You have read it?' She stared at him. 'Crop rotation?'

'I do my research. It makes for an easier life.' He took the book from her and placed it back in the stacks, standing so close she could see the precise folds of his neckcloth.

She nodded to several library patrons who stopped to acknowledge her. She had thought that Lord Coltonby would make his excuses and depart, but he continued to stand at her elbow, surveying the variety of books. A silent sentinel. 'Are you going to the Bolts' ball? Or do such things frighten you?'

The unexpectedness of the question made her blink and nearly drop the book of sermons. 'I think it is best if I choose my books now. We are beginning to be remarked upon.'

'Clearly something you wish to avoid—which is why you made remarks while visiting this morning.'

'How did you know?' Diana closed her eyes and the full horror washed over her. How people—and Lord Coltonby—must be laughing at her and her pretensions. 'I had forgotten how quickly rumours can pass from lip to lip. Can I assure you, Lord Coltonby, that I merely wanted to protect an innocent. You are not and never have been the marrying kind. Women who wish to marry should be wary of you.'

'But you have no wish to marry. Does this mean you are not wary of me?' His eyes gleamed. 'What an interesting proposition, Miss Clare.'

'That is not what I meant, and you know it,' Diana said

in a furious undertone. 'Certain things have been taken out of context. I merely sought to put a stop to gossip. I do prefer the truth.'

'The truth has many guises, Miss Clare.'

'It was wrong of me.' Diana swallowed hard. 'But I simply had to say something. Otherwise certain women might have given your words and actions a different connotation. I have no wish to see any young girl ruined for the sake of a few pie-crust promises.'

She kept her head high and hoped he would understand.

'You appear to have already made your decision, Miss Clare.' He moved a step closer to her, reaching behind her to pluck a volume from the shelf, his hand skimming her bonnet. 'I am only trying to understand our positions, and to make sure that the rules of engagement are precise.'

'You make it seem like a battle.'

'Oh, it bears some similarities.' His eyes became hooded. 'Certain campaigns must be planned strategically and all eventualities considered.'

'I know your reputation, Lord Coltonby. Your many seductions. I am simply trying to avoid having innocents seduced.' She gave a little laugh and moved away from him.

'You do me a great honour, but I assure you I am human. My exploits have been exaggerated. I have never dallied with an unwilling lady.'

She stared at him in astonishment. She found that she wanted to believe him, that his exploits were not as bad as they had been painted. She wanted to trust her instincts, but they had failed her so miserably before. She could not risk it.

'This is hardly the sort of the conversation one has in a library.'

'I am always open to suggestions, Miss Clare.' His voice was as smooth as silk, reasonable, as if it were she who had proposed something outrageous. The cheek of the man!

'Lord Coltonby, you are being outrageous. Deliberately!'

'No, I am enjoying our conversation and wish to prolong it.' He lifted his eyebrow. 'Would you please explain your objections to this? We are near neighbours.'

Diana tapped a finger against a book of sermons on the shelf. 'And when I do, will you leave me alone?'

'If I consider them valid, of course. I am a reasonable man.'

Diana gestured about her as the rational objections seemed to have completely drained from her mind and the only thing she could think about was the way his long fingers held the books he had chosen. 'For one we are in a library.'

'That can be remedied, presuming you have discovered all the improving books on agriculture that you need. Reading should be a pleasurable experience, Miss Clare. Why do you close yourself off to such things? If you cannot enjoy your reading, why read?'

'The sort of easy words I'd expect from a member of the Jehu club.' Diana shook her head slightly; it seemed to be growing lighter with every breath she took. The only thing that appeared to be keeping her on the ground was the book of sermons currently pressed against her chest.

'And it does not matter how tightly you hug that book, or how many times you repair your cap, life will still happen to you.'

'I am not afraid of life.' Her voice rose sharply. 'Can I help it if I am wary of your reputation?'

'And if I promise to be on my best behaviour?' His voice lapped at her being. 'Will you then continue this conversation? I did so want to hear more of your views on my estate and what actions I should take.'

Diana glared at him. He was insensible to reason. But it also seemed like life had taken a sudden unexpected turn. A little voice in the back of her mind warned about the dangers of becoming involved, however briefly, with a known rake, but she quashed it. But Lord Coltonby's interest was surely only neighbourly. A tiny tug of disappointment wavered within her.

'As it appears that I cannot get rid of you, you may escort me back to my gig.'

'I am delighted that you have seen sense, Miss Clare.'

'Miss Bolt and I were admiring your curricle the other day,' she said firmly, directing the conversation towards more impersonal topics as they started down the High Street towards the livery stables. For once she would indulge in speaking about horses to an expert. 'Or rather *she* was, and I was looking at your horses. Are they from Tattersalls?'

Brett regarded Miss Clare. Her long eyelashes had swept down over her ivory skin. Her dark gown with its high neckline hinted at her curves rather than revealed them. Had he not held her in his arms, he would have been tempted to say that the curves did not exist. But he had, and his body knew they were there. Each tiny step she took was a victory. Slowly. Slowly he'd lead her where she needed to go. She was like a frightened bird and he looked forward to gentling her. However, it was not proving to be as easy as he had first considered. How to get under her defences? That was the question.

'Do you like horses?' he asked, tucking the books she had chosen under his arm and guiding her progress along the street.

'My brother despairs of me. He swears I will break my

neck one of these days. With him, they are an imperfect mode of transportation only.'

'Your brother is not fond of horses? That makes sense. I never trust a man who does not have a passion for horses.' He forced his voice to remain smooth. 'A man who has no time for horses has no time for life's pleasure.'

'He has his reasons. Valid ones.' Miss Clare waved a vague hand. 'I understand it, but I disagree. I have loved driving ever since my father first let me hold the ribbons. It was his first proper carriage and I was about four.'

'Ah, that explains a great deal.' Brett gave a short laugh, remembering her indignation at being caught in the mud. His shoulders relaxed. He would use his new-found knowledge to his advantage.

'Does it?' She tilted her head to one side. The shadow of her bonnet brim pointed directly to the fullness of her bottom lip.

'Your annoyance when we first encountered each other.' Brett tucked her arm in his and began to stroll towards his curricle. Not too fast. She gave him a startled look, but he noted with inward pleasure that she did not draw away or find an excuse to depart. He would break down these barriers she had erected. 'I thought it was directed at my rescuing you, but in reality it was directed at the situation. You hated being caught out, not being perfect. And when you are, you retreat.'

'It was arrogance rather than inexperience that led me into that mud pool.'

Brett watched the sunlight kiss her cheeks. There was a passion within this woman, as much as she tried to hide it. He could sense it. But she had repressed it, hidden it even from herself. He would reawaken it and see if the woman she was now bore any relation to the quicksilver girl he had met in London. A memory of her laughing and pointing at the fireworks in Vauxhall Gardens suddenly surfaced and he knew he wanted to hear her laugh like that again. 'Your eyes were spitting mad that day by the mud pool. They shone brighter than the fireworks at Vauxhall. Surely you remember those.'

Miss Clare's face became clouded as the life drained from it.

'I try to forget London.' Her long lashes swept down over her cheeks, hiding her eyes and her shoulders hunched ever so slightly. It was as if she expected to be beaten for it. An impotent rage coursed through Brett at his simple error. She had been at Vauxhall with Finch. He longed to have Finch in front of him, so the man could see what havoc his carelessness had wrought. Brett had disliked his superficial charm and easy manner years ago. He had seen the way the man whipped his horses and his careless disregard for their welfare after outings. No matter what the weather, or the time, horses had to come first.

'Do not judge all men by the failings of one.'

He waited. A breeze blew a tendril of hair across her face. With impatient fingers she brushed it away, but still she said nothing. He willed her to understand.

'I thought it was my love of horses that made him notice me.' Her voice was low and her fingers toyed with the string of her parcel. 'I thought...that we had something in common. Rather, my money and his need for ready cash.'

She gave a hiccuping laugh, as if she had practised the words a thousand times.

'I am sure there were other reasons why he was interested in your hand.'

'That is a backhanded compliment.'

'But sincerely meant,' Brett said gently. 'Take a chance. Trust me to be different.'

Her eyes twinkled, transforming her face, back to the woman of the mud pool. He relaxed slightly. The mood had passed. He could reach her. Somehow he wanted to transform her back to the woman who had been delighted by Vauxhall's fireworks. If he could do that, he would be well pleased.

'Sincerity is always to be welcomed.'

'Shall my horses meet you? However briefly?'

'I would like that. I would like that very much.'

As they approached the curricle, Brett signalled to his tiger. The bays arched their necks and pawed the ground. Brett half-expected Miss Clare to behave like other women and clutch at his arm. Or possibly to turn her lips down in disapproval. Instead, she gave a delighted smile, one that reached her eyes, and advanced towards the horses. She reached up and touched their necks, speaking to them in a soft crooning voice. His tiger nodded his approval.

'It is good to see that you are fearless, Miss Clare.'

She gave the bays one last pat and then stepped away from them. 'They are high-stepping beauties. I would love to be able to sit behind them...' she finished whistfully.

'Now, come driving with me now.'

A strange light flickered in her eyes and he wondered if he had lost her. He willed her to say yes.

'To drive or to watch you drive?'

'You would have to prove your worth before I would allow you to handle the ribbons.' Brett gazed into her eyes. They were changing again.

'Many more people claim to be able to drive to the inch, than can actually achieve the feat.' Brett shrugged.

'And how does one prove this, if you refuse to let them drive?'

He regarded Miss Clare's gloved hands. They looked

strong and capable, but small. He shuddered to think what could happen if the horses bolted. The bays took all of his strength to control. 'Before I allow my horses to be driven by anyone—man, woman or child—I make sure that I know the driver is up to the mark.'

'Caution? Hardly a word I would have associated with you.'

'Practical. It prevents accidents.' He touched his hand to his hat.

'Why? How difficult are they to handle?'

'They are a challenge. I enjoy challenges. They fly when I let them, but in the hands of an inexperienced driver, I would not like to be responsible for the consequences. Are you tempted, Miss Clare?'

She gave the brim of her bonnet a tug, shading her face, deliberately hiding it from him.

'I came to town in the gig.'

'My tiger can return it.' He held up his hand and took a deep breath. It felt as if he were playing a very high-stakes game of whist. One final try, then he would be forced to resort to another gambit. But he would win. She wanted this. He could sense it in his bones. 'I promise to be on my best behaviour. Are you prepared to take a ride behind the horses? To feel the wind against your face? They have a turn of speed that is almost unequalled. Of course, if you prefer to return home in the company of your staid mare, I understand completely. Do not complain you were never asked.'

'I am no coward.' Diana fiddled with a button on her glove, weighing her options. Did she dare take the risk? Lord Coltonby had already made it abundantly clear that any attraction was on her part and her part alone. She was not risking her reputation. She was simply going for a drive with a neighbour, an entirely different thing. 'I should like to feel the wind against my face.'

'A drive home, nothing more.' A faint smile played on his lips. His eyes held a distinct gleam. 'I wish to be neighbourly, Miss Clare.'

Diana wet her lips, took once last glance down the High Street and nodded.

Chapter Six

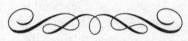

Brett concentrated on the horses and the taut reins, rather than on the slim woman sitting next to him, but every so often he glanced over to where she sat, face entranced, watching the horses' every move. He had half-expected her to cling to his arm, the instant he allowed the horses to leap forward, but her back remained resolutely straight and her hands folded. She showed no inkling of screaming, but every aspect of enjoying the ride.

Colour had flooded back into her cheeks and her eyes shone with a blue-green intensity. She leant forwards slightly as if she was urging the horses to go even faster. The wind caught her bonnet and sent it flying backwards.

'I had quite forgotten what it was like to have the wind blow throw my hair,' she said with a laugh as she struggled to replace the bonnet, holding on to it with one hand.

'And do you like it?'

'I like it very much. It is exhilarating.'

'Good, I am glad. If I have made you remember joy, then it pleases me.'

'Oh, yes, joy.' She leant forward. 'Can you make them go faster?'

Brett flicked the reins and the horses sped away. He knew in that instant that he had never seen a woman more alive. Her love of carriages and fast horses shone from her—but it also made her dangerous.

He pulled on the ribbons and the horses came to an abrupt halt.

'Why have you stopped here?' A furrow appeared between her brows as she turned in her seat, looking up and down the deserted road. Her hand clutched the side of the curricle and the bright colour faded from her face, draining all the life from her features. 'Have I been foolish in the extreme? You gave your word, Lord Coltonby. Straight home.'

'We are going back to your house, but I wanted to stop here for a moment. I wanted privacy for our conversation. We need to get the parameters in order.'

'Take me back,' she squeaked. 'Now! I command you! I beg you! Do as I ask.'

Brett resisted the urge to curse. He had misjudged the moment. He had to gain her trust, but certain things needed to be said before they went further. He always conducted his romances in this manner. It made things less messy when the time came to part. He wanted Diana Clare to have no false expectations, no excuse to claim breach of understanding.

'I have my code, Miss Clare. You are as safe here as you were in the library. I merely wanted to speak with you privately. Forgive the slight deception.'

'Privately?' Her eyes widened, much as a horse's did when it was spooked.

'To make sure you understand that I have no intention of marrying.' Brett made sure his words were said very slowly and unhurriedly, almost singsong. 'My attention is not to be perceived as a courtship. Marriage does not figure on my horizon.'

'Am I supposed to swoon at this earth-shattering news, Lord Coltonby? You are not telling me anything that I don't already know.' She gestured frantically towards the road. 'You may drive on, having said your pretty piece. Allow me to reassure your vanity by saying that I have no intention of marrying you.'

'It is well we understand each other. I would hate for a miscommunication.'

'As would I.' She turned her face away.

He reached out and his hand covered hers. Brett felt it tremble slightly and let it go. He would accept the strictures of their relationship for now, but he intended to have more. There was a passionate woman under her frosty exterior. He was certain of it. Brett silently cursed all who had made her this way. She was like some nervous wild thing, intent on camouflaging herself so that she could escape unnoticed. London gossip had badly scorched her, but he could see the woman inside trying to escape. 'You are a welcome distraction from the necessary business of sorting out the estate, and I value your friendship. I enjoy getting your perspective on the problems I face. Biddlestone nearly ran it into the ground.'

'It was lucky you acquired it, then. It is an estate that begs to be loved.'

'But seems unlovable to the casual observer.'

'And are you a casual observer?'

'I pride myself on my keen eye, Miss Clare.'

Diana shifted uneasily on the curricle seat, increasing the space between her and Lord Coltonby. With his thigh pressed against her leg, she found it difficult to concentrate on anything but his physique. He was speaking of more than the estate. It terrified her that he might be speaking of her. 'I need none of your flummery, Lord Coltonby. If you are going to persist in this sort of behaviour, we will have to return to being the barest of acquaintances. We need to decide which of the cottages you should…'

'Brett.' His voice positively purred. And the look he gave her was pure male. A look that sent her pulse racing. The look of a rake, a practised seducer, she reminded her heart. 'I really must insist you call me by my Christian name, if we are to be *intimate*.'

Intimate. Diana felt her cheeks grow hot at the picture it conjured up in her mind. She banished it, locked the thought away in that little part of her mind where she never permitted herself to go. Forced herself to remember the pain and humiliation she had suffered and to silence the little voice which protested that Brett was different. Diana took a deep breath and regained control. She would hold true to her promise. She would never be seduced again. She had learnt her lesson.

'Acquaintances implies no intimacy.' She tilted her chin in the air and focused on the horses' ears. 'Lord Coltonby or Coltonby will surely suffice. I cannot address you by your Christian name. Think of the scandal.'

'I must disagree with you. The word said in private will have no effect.' His eyes danced with an unholy mischief and Diana began to wonder what precisely she had agreed to. She should never have behaved impulsively and agreed to the drive. She should have contained her temper. When would she learn not to give in to temptation? Reason was what was important. Brett's hand slid down her shoulder and his fingers curled around hers, held them in a light but gentle grasp. Diana resisted the urge to tighten her fingers about his. 'Try it. Once. Here and now. No one but me will listen.'

'But I...' Her tongue became thick in her mouth and she turned her head away. It seemed there were two of her—the lady she had promised over and over again to be on her journey from London to Newcastle, and then her true self, the one who could not resist temptation. She had thought the latter gone, but she had only been slumbering, waiting her chance. But was Diana ready for heartache? For the pain, for the scandal?

'Give it a try. You will find it quite simple. Allow my name to flow from your lips.'

'Brett,' she whispered, her voice barely audible. Her lips ached as if they had been brushed by his. She touched her fingertips to her mouth. Concentrated hard. 'There, I have said it. Are you satisfied?'

'Say it like you mean it. Roll the R's.'

'Brett!' Diana said, through gritted teeth. 'And I never roll my words.'

'I would have preferred honey-sweet seduction, but I will take the tartness of vinegar for now.' He clicked his tongue and the curricle began to move. Diana felt a sigh escape her throat. Of regret? Of disappointment? She refused to ponder the emotion.

'You are incorrigible.'

'So my nurses used to tell me.' His laughter rang out, startling the wood pigeons in the trees.

'You had more than one nurse?'

'My brother and I had a succession of nurses. It depended on whether my father was in funds. My mother used to despair. The worst was that the roof leaked. In many ways, I was pleased to be rid of the Abbey after my brother died. Constant repairs and a house so riddled with damp that one should start anew.'

Diana absorbed the knowledge. 'But your father was an

earl. Surely he had the money to fix the roof and to keep the damp out.'

'My father was also a poor gambler. He gave in to impulse and failed to do his research properly. Inclined to rush his fences. Neglected to ensure the settlement before his death.'

'You are wealthy now. Or is that something else Lady Bolt has mistaken?'

'My wealth is my own, Miss Clare. In that I have proved more adept than my brother or my father. The title I share with my forebears. There is a difference.' He clicked his tongue and the horses stirred, obeying every flick of his ribbons. There could be no doubt that the beasts knew who their master was. *Their* master, but not hers. She refused ever to have a master.

'Stop! Stop!' A young girl stepped out in to the road and waved her arms wildly. 'Please stop, I beg you.'

Brett pulled hard on the horses and brought the curricle safely to a halt.

'Jenny Satterwaite, what sort of mischief is this?' Diana asked before the girl had the chance to say another word. 'I know about the tricks you and your brother played on Widow Tyrwhitt.'

'No trick, Miss Diana.' Jenny drew a line in the dust with her toe. 'And I did clean out her house, like. Mam said it were proper, like.'

'Then what is the difficulty? Is it your father again?'

'No, Miss Diana. He's back at the mine.'

'Is some hazard up ahead?' Brett asked smoothly.

Jenny shook her head. 'It's me mam. She's stuck. Stuck in the stairwell and there ain't none that can help. Me and Jimmy have pulled and pulled, but she ain't moving.'

'How did it happen?'

'The stair boards were loose, but no one has fixed them.

We've been waiting for the new lord to come. Me mam said he would put it right.'

Diana shifted uncomfortably, not daring to look at Brett. She could not bear it if he refused this child.

'He is here and he will help if he is able.' Brett leapt from the curricle. 'Do you have someone who can hold the horses?'

Jenny's brow puckered. Then she nodded. 'Jimmy can. He loves horses. Da is hoping to get him a job at the mine as soon as there's an opening.'

She ran off back in to the house, shouting. Diana stared at Brett in astonishment. What did he plan on doing? 'Shall we send somebody out?'

'Forgive me, Miss Clare but you will be slightly delayed. I believe this woman has the greater need.'

A small boy, a year or so younger than her nephew Robert, came out of the house. His eyes widened when he saw the horses. 'I thought Jenny was funning me.'

'If I give you a penny, can you hold these horse? Tight, mind, and don't let them move.'

'I will do it, sir.' The boy stood straighter.

Brett held out his hand to Diana. 'Right, shall we see about this woman in distress?'

They followed Jenny into the cottage and immediately were greeted by a series of moans. Diana's heart twisted. She had half-expected it to be another one of Jenny's tall tales, but Mrs Satterwaite was lying half in and half out of the stairwell, her face creased in pain.

Without hesitation, Brett went over and lifted her out. There was a great cracking as the board gave way, but the woman emerged to great squeals of delight from Jenny.

'Thank you, sir.' Mrs Satterwaite gave a tired smile. 'I had no idea how I'd have kept going till them that lives next door came home.'

'Is there somewhere you can rest?' Diana asked. The cottage with its narrow stairs was even darker and danker than she remembered from her visits.

'Bed's upstairs. We had to let the downstairs room go and move upstairs now that money's tight.'

'Look after this.' Brett took off his coat and handed it to Diana. Her fingers curled around the warm cloth and held it close. 'I believe I can fix this—temporarily. Boards, nails and a hammer, if you please, young Jenny Satterwaite.'

The girl ran off and quickly produced them. Diana watched as Brett nailed the boards in place, covering the rotten patches. Then he tested each of the other stairs. 'Not perfect, but it will suffice for now. I will send the workmen to fix it properly tomorrow.'

'Yes, my lord.' Mrs Satterwaite's eyes grew big. 'If you please, my lord, I've been telling me man about those boards for an age. He is a good man, Miss Diana. It were just the accident that turned his head.'

'It will be sorted now. I intend to look after my tenants properly.' The words echoed in the small cottage. Before, she had thought his words were easy, but now she could see that he meant them. He cared about these people. 'I trust you have no objections, Miss Clare.'

He took his coat from her unresisting fingers and they returned outside. Jimmy Satterwaite held the horses. His face was screwed up into an intense look of concentration. At Brett's approach, the horses pawed the ground but Jimmy clung on with dogged determination, preventing the curricle from moving.

'I doubt my tiger could have done better.' Brett handed the boy a coin. 'Come to my stables. I can always find a job for a boy who's good with horses.'

Diana watched the boy run back into the cottage, shouting the news. 'You are not what I expected.'

'Neither are you,' he murmured as the curricle started moving once again. 'And do I have your leave? May I call you Miss Diana like the Satterwaites do?'

'If you must.' She took a deep steadying breath and willed the ride to last a little longer, but already the gates to the Park were looming ahead.

'Diana, named after the huntress goddess of the moon.' His voice purred her name, doing strange things to her stomach. 'Have you been to Italy or Greece, Miss Diana? Have you seen how large and yellow the moon can be as it rises over the sea?'

'I have only once been away from Northumberland—to London.'

'A pity. Italy is beautiful, but with the war, Greece is more accessible.' He slowed the horses to a steady walk. His arm came over the back. 'I should like you to see Greece with its hidden glades and moonlit beaches.'

Diana ignored the slight tremor inside her. Words flowed from him as easily as water slipped down the Tyne.

'I doubt that will be possible. I have too many responsibilities here.'

'Will you go to the ball?'

Diana hesitated for a heartbeat. She could readily imagine dancing a cotillion with him. It would be so easy…then she shook her head decisively. 'My mind is made up there as well. Balls and I are not a happy combination.'

He reached out and touched her cheek. It took all of Diana's willpower not to turn her face into it, to press her lips against his palm. Her being shivered. 'But attempting to change it could be amusing.'

'I am not here to provide you with amusement.' Diana moved her face away from the delicious torment.

'Ah, the proper Diana Clare.' His hand fell to his side.

'You did promise—friendship.' Diana kept her back

ram-rod straight. 'Surely you are not going to break your word? Or was it simply a rake's promise, one designed to lull me into a false sense of security?'

'It is you who holds the reins. We will proceed at your pace.' He put his hand over his heart. 'On my honour as a gentleman.'

'And your honour as a renowned whip?'

He sighed and rolled his eyes heavenwards. 'That as well. You are perfectly safe with me, Diana, even if you persist in challenging me. Confirmed ape-leader that you are.'

'Should I be flattered with your assessment?' Diana asked in a tight voice.

'That is a matter for you to decide.' His face betrayed no emotion and he appeared utterly absorbed in handling the reins.

Diana breathed easier when she arrived back at the Lodge. Brett had obeyed her wishes. He helped her down and his touch was impersonal rather than the searing one of earlier. A vague disappointment washed over her body. She realized she had wanted more.

A wisp of hair blew across her face, reminding her how the wind had felt in her hair and she brushed it away with thoughtful fingers. Diana knew in that moment that she could never wear her caps again. She had remembered the joy that came with experiencing life.

Another spray of roses needed to go in the garland, Diana decided as she regarded her sketch with a practised eye. She had spent the afternoon sketching out a new mural for the summer house.

She had begun decorating it five years ago when she'd needed to forget Algernon, pouring out every passionate impulse until it seemed like her soul was on the walls and her body was only an empty shell. It had seemed complete six months later, but now she realised it could do with another garland or two of painted flowers. It had worked once. It would work again.

'I understand you made an exhibition of yourself this morning,' Simon said, glowering in the doorway of the dining room. 'I would have thought you'd be the one person I could trust not to invite scandal.'

Diana looked up from her sketch. Simon's face bore traces of grease and the stock at his neck was askew. Her hand trembled slightly. She had considered that there might be some talk, but not that Simon would hear it—not so quickly, at any rate. Nor be upset about it. He had to realise that she was a grown woman and could be trusted to behave sensibly.

'Hardly an exhibition, Simon. Lord Coltonby offered me a lift in his curricle. It would have been churlish to refuse.' She tucked a stray lock of hair behind her ear and made her voice sound firm. 'It has been a long time since I have ridden in a racing curricle. The bays flew down the road with their heads held high and the wind whipping all around us. Truly magic.'

'I know how they flew.' Simon's frown increased. 'Maurice Bolt challenged Coltonby to a race this afternoon. He wagered his best mare against Coltonby's boot-blacking receipt.'

'What happened?' Diana pressed her hands against her thighs, and silently prayed that Brett had done nothing foolish. Maurice was the apple of Lady Bolt's eye and thoroughly spoilt. According to Mrs Sarsfield, he had been sent down from Oxford last term for some unspecified misdemeanour. And Rose had decreed that no maid ever wanted to be caught in a corridor with him. Diana knew she ought to be neutral, but she did hope Brett had won and won decisively.

'Coltonby won by a length. He is a menace. What sort of man claims a horse when he has only wagered a receipt?'

'Maurice should not wager what he can ill afford to lose. And for that matter, what sort of man wagers his horse against a receipt?'

Simon's face turned beet red and his mouth opened and closed several times. Diana forced her hands to remain in her lap and her back to stay straight. Surely her brother was not so blind to reason that he could not see whose fault it had been?

'I only speak the truth, Simon. And Maurice probably only challenged Lord Coltonby because he thought the bays were tired. He deserved everything that he received.' She leant forward, and was relieved to see an answering smile on Simon's face. Crisis averted. She searched her mind for a more appropriate topic, one that would not include Brett Farnham and his exploits.

'But why did you need a lift?' Simon asked before she had fixed on a good subject. 'You took the gig in. I distinctly remember you saying at breakfast that you were taking the gig.'

'Lord Coltonby's tiger returned it. Jester is in the stables, munching away at her manger of hay.'

'That is by the by.'

'Do you really think I would pass up the chance to go behind a team like that? The speed, Simon.' Diana clasped her hands together. Willed him to understand. 'You know that I liked to drive curricles once upon a time.'

'But Lord Coltonby…' Simon's mouth turned down at the corners. 'He has a certain reputation with women. I worry, Diana.'

'I hardly think he would be interested in me, Simon. Ever since we renewed our acquaintance, he has behaved perfectly properly,' Diana replied, looking her brother steadily in the eye. 'Are you saying that you don't trust your sister?'

She picked up her drawing pencil and sketched another leaf.

'He won't marry you, Diana.'

'Good. I have no intention of marrying him either, Simon.' Diana tightened her grip on her pencil. 'I am quite resolved on the subject.'

'You are not considering…' He cleared his throat.

'Simon! What you are suggesting is infamous.'

Simon's face brightened. 'I was worried. It was the talk of the reading room this afternoon. How my sister had brazenly wangled a ride with the notorious Lord Coltonby and then how he'd triumphed over poor Maurice Bolt.'

'Who has spread the rumour?' Diana saw the confirmation in his eyes. Her stomach churned. She had failed to consider that Lady Bolt might act out of spite. 'Since when have you put any credence in her pronouncements about me?'

'Women sometimes take strange notions into their heads. I have no wish for this aristocrat to break your heart. I know what that Finch fellow did.' Simon slammed his fist on to the table. 'Dammit, you deserve better than that, Diana. When Coltonby was at university, I lost count of the number of women he sneaked into his rooms. My sister will not share that fate.'

'Simon, stop it. You are spinning fancy.'

'Diana, you must be careful. The man has deliberately singled you out. There will be more to it than meets the eye. He will want something in return.'

Diana held back her words. She knew all too clearly

that Simon's late wife had had her heart broken and had married on the rebound. Simon, blinded by her beauty, had not realised what was happening until it had been too late. It was one of the reasons Diana had been pleased to escape to London. Jayne had faded over the years, becoming a pale shadow. Diana knew that even now Simon refused to believe that Robert was his, refused to accept the evidence of his own eyes.

'I learnt my lessons years ago.'

'But you are no longer wearing your cap,' Simon protested. 'It suits you, but I wondered why. Are you seeking to enter the marriage market again?'

'I may have little interest in marrying, but I do not have to conduct myself as a dowd.' Diana carefully sketched a rosebud. 'The two are unconnected. I grew tired of the caps. They made me feel old.'

She bent her head and redoubled her efforts at drawing the rosebud as Simon's eyes bore into her neck. He had to believe her. 'Diana, I will trust you, but may I ask you a favour, a little trifle?'

Diana's hand stilled and she regarded her brother's suddenly intent face. 'A favour. What sort of favour, Simon?'

'I want no distractions, Diana. I do not want to be worrying about you making a spectacle of yourself again. Let me concentrate on my engine.'

Diana pressed her lips together. He was not concerned about her or her reputation—or her protection—rather the distraction it represented. All her brother wanted to do was to work on that engine. 'I have no plans to make a spectacle of myself, as you put it. I am not even planning on going to the ball. You may go alone.'

'You know what I mean—today. You and him. No more fodder for the gossips.'

Diana fought to keep her voice calm. 'Nothing happened, Simon. Nothing at all. He is our neighbour. I hardly wish to start a feud with a neighbour.'

'Diana, be reasonable. I need to concentrate on the engine. How can I if you will persist in parading down the High Street with Lord Coltonby? It is distracting.'

'I did not parade, brother, but I will assure you I have no intention of doing anything of that nature again. As you know, I only went to town because you insist I socialise with the local gentry. I am far happier here—painting and reading, visiting our workers' families and the sick.'

'I will have to accept that.' Simon stuck his thumbs into his waistcoat, every inch the superior brother.

'You will.' Diana jabbed her pencil down and broke the point. How dare he put strictures on her as if she had no more brains than a feather duster? 'You may find that you have much in common with Lord Coltonby. You should take the time to be neighbourly yourself.'

'I have nothing in common with that…that arrogant fop. I have worked for every penny we have, Diana.'

'I only meant that you were both men of intelligence. I am well aware of the sacrifices you have made, Simon. You do not need to detail them for me.'

'Then you will understand.' Simon leant forwards, so that his face was level with hers. His green eyes burnt with a fierce intensity. 'I will do what is necessary to make sure Ladywell Colliery not only survives, but thrives. The travelling engine will be my legacy to the world. And no one is going to stop me.'

Chapter Seven

Diana looked back over her shoulder at the line of painted flowers and leaves. The morning's work had sped by and she now could see the outline of the garland taking shape. It would work, this plan of hers. It had worked five years ago when she had done the first few. Her mind needed a focus, an outlet for her creativity, rather than sitting there, dreaming about things that could never happen.

A leaf was slightly off centre on the first sequence of roses. She wrinkled her nose and stared at it, the mistake in the shading growing more obvious by the breath. Diana bit her lip, considered her options. Did she really want to reposition the heavy ladder for one bit of shading? She could reach it, if she stretched. She glanced down at Titch. The little terrier wagged her tail and shook her head before giving a low bark and covering her nose with her paws.

'I will be careful, I promise.'

She dipped her brush in the paint and began, balancing precariously. Her knees trembled slightly as she reached out a little bit further. Her mind circled back to the problem. Brett Farnham with his money and title had his pick of women. He always had. She didn't need Simon's university tales to tell her that—she had the evidence of her own eyes from London. Why would he be interested in her, an acknowledged spinster? She sighed as she added one final line of dark green. Eventually if she repeated it to herself enough times, maybe her heart would believe it. Maybe she would stop listening for the scrunch of carriage wheels on the gravel.

'Do you always take risks like that?' Brett's low voice resounded in the room.

She turned quickly and the ladder rocked violently. A small shriek escaped her throat. She made a wild grab for the top rung. Missed. Her body fell backwards through the air. Slowly. Strong arms closed around her, and held her.

The stillness of the air was shattered with the thump of the ladder hitting the ground and the splintering of glass. She shivered and tried not to think about what could have been. Looking up, she noticed the dark lashes that fringed Brett's grey eyes. Short, perfect for a man.

'You are safe.' His voice caressed her ear. Their breaths mingled, more intimate than a kiss. His mouth was mere inches from hers. All she had to do was lift her head the merest fraction.

She swallowed hard and resolutely turned her face away. 'Let me go, please.'

'You should take more care. You could have been hurt.'

His arms loosened and her body slid down his, his hand on her back guiding her descent. Soft curves met the hard muscular planes of his chest and thighs. Slow. Sensuous. Creating a burning ache within her. She stood there within the circle of his arms, her body arching closer, seeking him. His hand tightened slightly, burning through the thin cloth of her muslin gown.

Then reality intruded. She realised what she was doing—practically begging for his kiss. She stepped away from him, filled her lungs with air and determinedly changed the subject. 'How...how did you find me?'

'I happened across your maid, sewing in the garden. She thought you might be here.' His voice was silk across her jangled nerves.

Silently Diana cursed the perfidy of Rose and her match-making tendencies. She would have to speak to her maid. She gestured towards the fallen ladder, and spilt paint. 'If you had knocked first, all this might have been prevented.'

'What were you doing, risking life and limb like that?'

'I was painting.' Diana rocked back on her heels and peered up at him over her shoulder. Her pulse raced as the shifting colours in his eyes mesmerised her. She had forgotten the exact curve of his lips and the way he had faint smile lines about his eyes. She pressed her fingertips together. Strove for a normal tone. 'It is one of my pastimes. An enthusiasm. An important one.'

'The ladder was not steady. It was an accident waiting to happen. You could have been seriously injured.'

Diana regarded the wreckage. Water and paint mingled with broken glass and crockery. The ladder, which had seemed sturdy, was now on its side, a pile of sticks. A shudder went through her. She tucked a stray lock of hair behind her ear, a small act, but one which steadied her. 'I had missed the green shading on a leaf. It seemed the easiest way.'

'You ought to have taken the time to move the ladder. You could have overbalanced at any time. If you are going to take risks, you should have someone watching over you.'

'Titch is here.' She gestured towards where the traitorous terrier wagged her tail.

He reached down and gave the dog a pat. Titch wagged her tail furiously at the attention. 'As sweet as the dog might be, she does not inspire confidence.'

'I am fine, truly fine. Nothing untoward happened.' She clenched her jaw. 'I have no need for a protector.'

'Allow me to be the judge of that.' His eyes darkened again, becoming deep pools.

She forced her gaze away and stumbled over to the small table where the teapot and cups sat, waiting for her to take a break from her painting. She concentrated on the fine porcelain and tried to regain control of her pulse.

When she decided she could risk it, she turned, half-expecting him to have followed her. But he stood where she had left him. A large solid presence that had invaded her sanctorum. She knew she would not find the peace she had craved here, that the image of him standing there would be for ever engraved on her mind. Her way of banishing him had failed. She picked up a porcelain cup, but her hand trembled and she set it down with a bang. All she felt capable of doing was staring blankly at the table.

'Did you do all of this?' Brett walked over to the far wall and examined the earlier garlands. His voice was calm, soothing, as if he were speaking to a skittish horse. 'The flowers are very intricate. At first glance, one would almost believe them to be real.'

'It is something to occupy my days. I try to avoid going into the village.' Diana crossed her arms over her breasts, and stared stubbornly at the wall. 'It amuses me to get it correct. I have recently returned to these murals. It needs another garland around the walls. Around the ceiling as well as at chair level. I can't think why I had not realised before.'

'You should be more careful. Your maid should keep you company.'

'I generally am, but I also require solitude when I am painting. Ask anyone. Miss Diana Clare is exceedingly sensible, they will say. An uninteresting life.'

'Except when she drives into mud pools and falls off ladders.' A faint smile played on his lips as he took a step closer. The tiny room appeared to shrink. Diana's hand wanted to stretch out and touch his white shirt front. Instead, she twisted it around her apron. 'It was providence that I arrived when I did.'

'I understand you won a race yesterday.' Diana gestured about her, tried to retake control of the conversation as her heart thudded in her ears. 'When I first heard that you had raced, I was worried that the horses might have been tired out.'

'I wanted Bolt to think that. He was mad to think I would even consider racing if my horses were not up to the job.'

'You tricked him. You wagered your blacking receipt against a mare.'

'He made the challenge. I accepted. There are many who wish to discover the secret of my black boots. My valet has been offered numerous bribes, but, thus far, he has proved a loyal servant.' He gave a short laugh and put a boot on the chair. 'My boots remain as black as ever and now I possess a decent brood mare. I really must go driving down the High Street with you more often.'

Diana resolutely ignored the sudden flush of warmth that went through her. The words flowed naturally. Smooth. Elegant. And all the more deadly for it.

'I can offer you a cup of tea.' She picked up the pot and held it in front of her like a shield. 'Rose only left it a little while ago. I covered it with a towel.'

He pulled out his fob watch, checked it. 'We have no time to spare. We are going driving and I hardly think you want to be seen with paint flecks in your hair.'

'And you think I will go driving with you? Down the High Street again? My brother was livid.'

'In the country.' His eyes danced and his voice became a low purr. 'Your brother can have no objection to my current scheme.'

'Why would I want to do that?'

'I thought you might want to take a basket of food to Mrs Satterwaite. You appeared concerned about their welfare.' He paused. Each word became slower and more seductive. 'Think of the possibilities, Diana.'

'I can easily drive the gig. I will have the cook pack some calves'-foot jelly. It is a quick journey. You really must not think about troubling yourself.'

Brett took a step closer. His smile became more enticing. 'The offer to drive my curricle may not come again for some time. And my cook has already made a meat jelly and a rice pudding.'

'You mean to let me drive?' A shiver of delight ran through her. The bays! And the curricle! 'As reckless and foolhardy as I am?'

'I wanted to see if you can handle the ribbons. However, it is your choice. We can stay in the summer house if that is your desire.' He reached out and covered her hand with his for a heartbeat. A brief touch, but one that promised much… 'Is that what you want? To remain here in the summer house with me discussing the weather?'

Diana withdrew her hand as she gazed up into his eyes. It was strange how quickly the planes of his face had become familiar. Even his scar seemed pleasant, rather than foreboding as she had first considered it. The walls of the summer house seemed to push inwards, making the space between them shrink. Diana swallowed hard. 'We could have a cup of tea.'

'I am quite amenable to taking tea in whatever form you care to offer it.' His voice dropped on the word—*tea*—lengthening it, giving it a connotation she had not considered before.

Silently she cursed her wayward imagination. She forced her breath in and out several times and willed her shoulders to relax.

His eyes sparkled. 'But I think you would prefer the drive. Think of it. The wind rushing past you, the ribbons taut under your hands, the road opening out in front of you.'

The words curled around her insides, causing tingles to run through her.

'You mean to torment me until I give into your request?' She tilted her head to one side, trying to assess his mood.

'To remind you and, I will admit it, to bribe you. I thought you would enjoy showing me your skills.'

'You mean I am to drive the bays?' Diana clapped her hands together. 'They are not nearly as difficult as you made them out to be.'

Brett shook his head. 'I want to be sure you can handle the ribbons. The bays may come in time, but for now the black gelding is harnessed to my curricle. He is steady, but not for the novice. Then I will know…if we should *progress* further.'

Diana bit her lip. He was offering an olive branch to a neighbour. He was willing to give her a chance to prove she could handle the ribbons. And a chance to observe Mrs Satterwaite's condition, to do her duty, rather than simply drive for pleasure. Temptation shimmered in front of her. She could do this. She had given Simon her promise not to go to town, but the proposed drive in the country was an entirely different matter.

She glanced down at the enormous apron that covered her round gown. It was paint splattered and all enveloping. Hardly clothes suited for being seen in public. It would give her a chance to regain her reserve, to forget what it was like to be in his arms. 'If you will allow me a moment to change, I would be delighted to show that I can handle the curricle.'

'Diana.' His hand reached out, held her as she attempted to move past. Her feet skittered into each other as his scent enveloped her.

'Yes?' she breathed. Her mouth ached and she barely recognised her voice.

He brought his finger to his mouth and then touched her cheek. 'You have green paint, just there.'

A little impersonal touch, but one that made her insides turn over. A warmth grew within her but she resisted the urge to explore where his hand had made contact. 'I do?'

He nodded. 'It is gone now.'

All she could do was to stare at his forefinger. Surely he would kiss her. Her tongue wet her lips and she waited, but he merely arched an eyebrow. 'The curricle awaits its driver.'

'I will make sure I scrub my face, then. Make sure every piece of paint goes.'

'It looked quite sweet.'

'I have no wish to disgrace you when we are out on the drive.'

'I doubt you will do that.'

'But I must be properly dressed.' Diana hated the way her voice caught. But she knew once she was in her most severe riding habit, she would feel less off balance, less tempted to make a spectacle of herself. She had spent five years going over the mistakes she had made, and the lessons she had learnt and she refused to throw that all away. Brett Farnham was dangerous. She had to remember that.

'In your own time.' His voice floated after her as she hurried away from the summer house. 'I am a patient man.'

Brett was prepared to admit that Diana could handle the ribbons as well as most men by the time they left the Satterwaites. Mrs Satterwaite was recovering from her ordeal nicely and had asked if her Jimmy's tale was true, would Lord Coltonby be prepared to employ him? When he confirmed it was, she'd called on all the angels to bless and keep him. Brett had smiled. The day was turning out to be far more enjoyable than he had thought possible.

Under hooded eyes, he watched Diana's profile and saw the intent but happy expression on her face. She had changed out of her paint-splattered clothes into a very severe riding habit. But rather than hiding her charms, it only enhanced them. After holding her in his arms earlier, he knew what must lie under the high-necked collar and artfully placed lace at the base of her throat. His fingers itched to unwrap her and lay siege to her hidden desires.

She reminded him of one of his more nervous horses, one which had been badly abused by a former owner and was disinclined to trust. He would handle her reins very carefully; gently but firmly he would lead her in the direction he wanted to go. He would teach her and she would trust him. Each step towards intimacy had to come from her. If he gave the slightest indication that he desired more, she would shy away as she had done yesterday.

'Does your brother let you drive?' he asked to distract his thoughts from the agreeable way her bosom filled out her dress.

'Simon considers horses to be a means of transportation rather than a way of life. He grumbles about the cost. And how if horses could eat coal, we would save a great deal of money.'

'For me, horses are a way of life.'

'That does not surprise me.' Her merry laugh rang out. 'You appear to have a way with them. I had despaired of ever getting Jester out of that mud pool.'

'Is the piebald your only horse?' Brett kept his voice carefully neutral, but watched her face for any sign of hesitation. She might not want to go into the village with him, but she *would* go to the ball. It would be the final act to push Simon Clare over the edge. Clare would learn a very important lesson. The best part was that Brett was having a far more enjoyable time than he had presumed possible. Miss Diana Clare was entirely unexpected.

'Jester is good for generally driving about the country. Simon keeps a pair for the carriage, and I have a chestnut for riding. Robert, of course, is still on ponies. He keeps begging for a proper horse and I hope to convince Simon that he is old enough. But all that will have to wait until he returns from school.'

'How old is Robert?'

'Nine.'

'Surely he could move on to proper horses? What is your brother thinking about?'

'My sister-in-law was thrown from a horse. She took too high a jump because my brother had dared her and spent the last few years of her life in pain.' Diana's face became shadowed. 'She eventually caught lung fever and died, but Simon has hated horses ever since.'

Brett regarded the horse's ears. He had no wish to feel sorry for Clare. But for the first time, he had a small glimpse of what the tragedy must have done to him. For a long time, the only sound was the steady turn of the wheels and the clomping of the horses.

'I had wondered about riding,' Brett said into the stillness. 'Do you feel the same way as your brother?'

The torment of sitting next to her was growing with every breath he took. She was not his usual sort of fare, but there was something about her. He kept finding reasons why he had to see her, and couldn't help but think about the way she held her head or her hands.

He would make her want him, would make her forget about everything but her desire for him. She would come to him.

'I generally ride out every morning. Early. Sir Cuthbert's father used to let me use the Park's grounds as well as our own, but now...' She made a little gesture with her hands. 'I had not wanted to disturb you. Or for you to feel that I was taking advantage.'

'Please do not let the change of ownership stop you.' He put his hands over hers on the reins, and they quivered beneath his. 'You do take someone with you?'

'Generally, I have a groom, but really, if I am riding on the Lodge's grounds, there is no point.'

'Is there anywhere in particular you recommend for riding in the neighbourhood?' His eyes were intent on her mouth. 'What is your favourite ride? Where is the best place to exercise a horse?'

Her fingers curled tighter around the ribbons and for an instant he was sure he had gone too quickly. 'If you ride up the hill and past the spinney, the view over the Tyne is very good, particularly in the morning when the mist hangs and it has an otherworldly look. It always makes me feel as if life is worth living.'

'It is a good view to know about.'

'Yes it is. You should go up there sometime.'

'I intend to.'

Her eyes had turned a deep turquoise. Brett fought against the temptation to cup her face in his hands. They would meet there, one day, he promised himself, but not yet. She had to want it first.

'Tell me about your nephew, the one you left London for.'

'He goes to Dr Allen's Academy in Newcastle. He boards there.' Diana paused. How could she explain Robert? He wanted his father's attention, but Simon refused to pay any notice. 'He gets into scrapes, but he means well.'

'I should like to meet him. I enjoy speaking with children.'

Diana started and the horse began to move more swiftly. She grasped the ribbons and rapidly brought him under control. Brett raised an eyebrow.

'Now there is something unexpected,' she said with a laugh. 'It will teach me not to be surprised when I am driving a curricle.'

'The horse—or the fact I enjoy other people's children.'

'You and children.' Diana gave a smile.

'Why?'

'I would have thought as a founder member of the Jehu, you would be immune to the joys of such things. Drinking, gambling and debauchery—wasn't that the creed?'

'People change and grow.' His eyes became hooded. 'Children provide a respite from the strictures of the society. Some day, I should like my own. I like to think I will do a better job of it than my father. I swore I would on his deathbed.'

'And I wish you well with it.' Diana disliked the slight quaver in her voice. No doubt, he would marry some Diamond of the Season. She had to remember that theirs was an acquaintance, a friendship, not one destined for the altar.

She refused to even consider dreams of what that might be like. And yet, it refused to go away.

'You seem perturbed, Diana.'

'I think the paint fumes were rather stronger than I expected.' She gave her head a shake and banished the image of Brett holding a baby. 'But driving has revived me.'

His fingers closed over hers, a warm firm grip, but one that did not allow for refusal. 'Then would you care for another challenge and a wager?'

'What sort of wager?'

'A simple one. I will wager you driving the bays whenever you want against a dance at the Bolts' ball.'

'But I am not going to the ball,' Diana replied quickly before she could give into the temptation. Wagering with him could only be dangerous. How could she even be contemplating such a thing?

Brett raised one eyebrow. 'Are you not confident of winning, Miss Diana?'

'In order to dance with you at the ball, I would have to be going to the ball. I am not.' She clenched her fists. 'In any case, I do not make a habit of wagering.'

'And the thought of going to a ball is so dreadful that you are not prepared to risk it for the pleasure of driving my bays... whenever you want to.' He rubbed his hand across his chin. 'It appears to me that you do not consider yourself an expert driver, and this is why you have no wish to take up the challenge. It has nothing to do with wagering and everything to do with you not feeling confident.'

Diana bristled. Not confident? She could tackle anything. 'What do you want me to do?'

'I have set up a little obstacle course. Something to test my reflexes. It occurs to me that if you can complete a clear round, you will prove to my satisfaction that you can drive…unless you are afraid of losing.'

'I am not afraid.' Diana drew a deep breath and ignored the sudden warning voice in her mind. This was not a wager per se. It was about proving him wrong. But she had to think strategically. 'I have doubts that you can complete this course.'

He pursed his lips and she thought for a moment he would refuse.

'How sensible you are, Miss Diana.' As he took the reins from her, his voice became liquid honey. 'The rules of the course are that you do it as quickly as possible and the curricle does not hit any of the hurdles. I shall demonstrate.'

The curricle went through a gate into a harvested field. Bits of stubble and gleanings still lay about, but the ground was firm. Five sets of hurdles were placed at odd angles to each other, providing a series of quick turns.

Diana wrinkled her nose 'The hurdles seem to be set awfully close together.'

'It can be completed…if you know what you are doing.'

Brett clicked his tongue and the black gelding set off at a fast pace. Once the curricle tipped on to one wheel and bounced back down, but he managed to make it through all the openings.

'Well done.' Diana clapped her hands.

Brett gave a boyish smile. 'It is your turn, Miss Diana. At a trot, if you dare…'

'Of course I dare.' Diana spat on her gloves and took the ribbons. She regarded the first opening, went over the course in her mind, trying to remember how Brett had done it. It was the fourth set of hurdles that was the most difficult. Once she got past them, everything would be straightforward.

'Whenever you are ready.'

She flicked the reins and the horse set off. The first set of hurdles flew by. The second and the third. Diana reined in tightly and felt the curricle slip a little. She corrected her grip and aimed for the fourth set, held her breath and heard the carriage wheels slide through.

She let out a breath. Risking a glance up at Brett's face, Diana could see it had become set.

The last hurdles loomed in front of her. An easy set, slightly narrower than the others, but her line was true. She would do this. She could imagine the bays in front of her, responding to her every moment. She would drive out every day. She flicked the ribbons, urged the horse forwards, to complete the final obstacle.

The curricle started to go through. Diana winced as she heard the slightest crunch of the wheel against the left hurdle. She pulled back, trying desperately to change the angle as the hurdle seemed to hold. The curricle went through and she pulled the horse to a stop and prayed.

She released a breath.

'I have done it! I have done it!' She raised her hand in triumph.

Behind her, a distinct thump resounded. She glanced back and saw the hurdle down on the ground. 'I...I...'

Brett lifted one eyebrow and his lips twisted upwards in a sardonic smile. 'I believe you will be going to the ball after all, Miss Diana, but a solid attempt all the same.'

Chapter Eight

Of all the idiotic things she had done in her life, yesterday's wager with Brett Farnham was one of the worst. She should have known that the course would not be easy. She should have yielded to caution. She'd made her rules for a purpose, not to be bent or disregarded. But it was done and she would abide by the terms of the wager. The next time, she would turn a deaf ear to his blandishments.

Luckily she still had the very modest ball gown from two years ago when Simon had forced her to go the Grand Allies rout at the Assembly Rooms in Newcastle. Rose had reluctantly agreed to alter it slightly, grumbling that either the blue-green or the deep rose pink would have been a better choice. After insisting on the brown, Diana retired to the summer house and painted furiously.

'I thought I might discover you here,' Brett's low voice slid over her skin. 'I am pleased to see that you took my advice and your feet are solidly on the ground.'

'The garlands are nearly completed.'

'Hopefully they give the effect you want.'

'Not entirely,' Diana admitted. 'There is something missing.'

'A perfectionist. Is this the only summer house that you have painted?'

'I painted the Bolts' summer house four summers ago when the Dowager was still alive.' Diana kept her gaze on the flowers. 'She insisted that no one else would do.'

'You did those murals?' His eyes widened. 'Now I am impressed. Sir Norman showed me them the other day when I picked up my winnings.'

'Thank you.' Diana bowed her head as warmth infused her body. 'In the end, I was very pleased with them, but the Dowager was a hard task master—always changing her mind.'

'Of course, you have completely ruined my stratagem for getting you out into the garden during the ball.'

Diana looked up at him and saw a small smile tugging at his lips. 'I never go into gardens during balls.'

'A wise policy, but you will go to the ball and you will dance with me.'

'I have not danced for years.' Diana gave a strangled laugh. 'Some of the newer dances were nearly beyond me. All the twists and turns. It was a nightmare at the Grand Allies ball. I was so nervous that I would be asked to dance, but thankfully only Simon bothered and that was only out of duty, so I excused him.'

'Your steps might be slightly rusty but you have natural rhythm. I can see it in the way you move, the way you walk.'

'Thank you.' Diana took a quick glance up at him. The sunlight from the door gave him a halo, darkening his face, but highlighting his broad shoulders and well-formed legs. What would it be like to be in his arms? She quickly dropped her gaze and studied her hands. A paint blotch marred the right one. Something real and solid to cling on to. He was being kind.

'I do mean it. I seem to recall you dancing beautifully in London.'

'You will find me a poor partner unless it is the Roger de Coverley at the end. The last time I took lessons was five years ago and I am certain the figures will have changed.'

'I have a plan to deal with your lack of knowledge.'

'You do?' Diana started to rearrange the brushes in the water pot—smallest on the left, largest to the right. Everything correct and in its place. Simply because she had abandoned her caps did not mean she had abandoned her reason or her rules.

'I shall teach you to waltz. You and I are going to dance a waltz together at the ball.'

'A waltz?' Diana swallowed hard and concentrated very hard on the middle brush, the one she had used for the red of the final rose. 'I have no idea how to waltz.'

'I suspected that. It is why I am here.' He held out his hands. 'I plan to educate you on the finer points of the waltz.'

'You must be joking. I won't waltz.'

'But you agreed, Miss Diana. You agreed to dance with me at the ball.' His voice was smooth, but there was a steely determination. 'Unless you want me to choose another forfeit, a forfeit more suited to a wager between a man and a woman. You were the one who lost the wager. It is up to me to name the terms.'

'You wouldn't dare.'

'Try me.'

Diana backed away, looking about her. 'But where are you going to teach me to dance?'

'Here will prove adequate for my purposes.' He held out

his hands. 'My expertise is at your disposal. You do not want to look foolish in front of the Honourable Miranda and the Ladywell gentry, do you?'

Diana put her hand to her throat. 'With you? Alone? In the summer house? There will not be space for more than a few steps.'

'A few steps will be all you need.' He quickly moved the table out of the centre of the room before placing his coat, hat, gloves and cane on it. 'There, you see—lots of space.'

'There must be a thousand reasons why I should refuse. It is a highly improper suggestion.' Diana squared her shoulders and took a deep breath of air. Tried to think something else besides how Brett looked clad only in his shirtsleeves. 'I would be dancing unchaperoned.'

'And one reason to do it.' Brett's voice became the merest whisper.

'What is that reason?'

'The very best.' He paused. His bare hand touched her shoulder. A shiver went down her back at its warmth. 'Because you want to. Because you desire it.'

'I think it is probably the worst reason.' She backed away.

'It will be perfectly acceptable. Have I done anything untoward? Behaved improperly?' He inclined his head. 'Come with me, take a risk.'

Diana kept her hand firmly at her side, concentrated on filling her lungs with air and then releasing it. The action appeared to steady the muzzy feeling in her head. 'I fail to see when I would need to know how to dance the waltz. It is a pointless exercise.'

'The dance is all the rage on the Continent.'

'Napoleon is all the rage there as well,' she returned

quickly, ignoring the tingling that ran through her body. 'Does this mean we shall have him here as well?'

His face sobered. 'He will lose. His reign will come to an end—sooner or later. But I speak of dancing, not politics—an infinitely preferable subject when conversing with ladies. You will not get around me that easily. To the matter at hand—your waltzing lesson.'

'Sometimes, dancing and politics appear to be the same thing.'

He laughed, a rich deep laugh that circled around her and lapped at her senses. '*Touché,* Diana Clare, I know why I like you. You always argue your corner and counsel the sensible action. You are...unexpected.'

'And this is a bad thing?' Diana tilted her head, trying to assess his mood. He seemed intent on teasing, rather than seducing. She breathed slightly easier.

'When taken to extremes, but I think there is hope for you yet.'

'I shall take it as a compliment.'

'Will you take your lesson like a well-brought-up lady?' He leant towards her and lowered his voice. 'Or do you wish to display your ignorance in front of Miss Bolt and her mother? I overheard Miss Bolt proclaiming that there would be a waltz at the ball. She seeks to prove a point, I believe.'

Diana pressed her lips together. The scheme sounded like one of Miranda Bolt's. And no doubt she and her cronies would be the only women on the floor who could actually dance it correctly. She could hear the giggles and the small pitying sighs. He was right. It would be fun to wipe the smirks off their faces.

'I have trusted you this far. I will trust that you waltz like a gentleman.'

Brett looked down at the pale oval of Diana's face and

willed her to stay. It was not deception. He would not do anything that she did not want to, but she *would* waltz with him at the ball and he was determined that she would not make a fool out of herself. Then he would take her out into the garden. And when the kiss happened, it would seem to come from her. He would simply give her the opportunity. And there would be nothing Simon Clare could do about it, except give him the land. A perfect, fool-proof plan.

'Shall I demonstrate the steps first?' he asked, moving away from her and her teasing scent—a hint of vanilla, lavender and something else. It lingered in his mind and he found himself thinking about it at odd times, wondering about her and what she was doing.

'It is probably best. How long can learning to waltz take? A few basic steps. Once around the summer house?'

She moved away from him, crossed her arms and watched him with a sceptical expression. It would be easy to capture her and to tilt her face towards his and make it change. He took a step forward, stopped and regained control.

'Oh, it will take several turns. I think the tea can wait until we are finished. You don't want the servants gossiping.'

'I suppose you are right.'

Brett heard the slight tremor in her voice. Silently, he cursed Finch and all those who had harmed her with careless actions or words. He could see flashes of the woman behind the mask she wore.

'Solid preparation is always the foundation of a good campaign.'

'Ah, yes, a campaign, I can see that.' Diana clasped her hands in front of her, lacing the fingers together. In another moment, she would find an excuse and flee. The moment would be lost for ever. Brett was certain of that. He willed her to stay. To trust him and her instincts. His plan required her to dance the waltz beautifully.

'I generally get my way in the end,' he said softly, watching the way a curl of hair kissed her cheek.

'Your way?' She put her hand to her throat and took a step backwards as her eyes darted about the small room. 'Are you certain of that?'

'Which is why I am going to teach you to waltz. Now pay attention.' Brett picked up a chair, held it in front of him. 'Pretend you are this chair. Keep your eyes on my feet. You will be following my footsteps in reverse. It is terribly bad manners to step on your partner's toes.'

He quickly executed a few steps. A burst of laughter came from behind him. He stopped. Frowned. 'What is wrong with my dancing?'

'You look…ridiculous. Waltzing with a chair.'

'Then dance with me.' He placed the chair down and turned to face his quarry. 'It is easier if I have a woman in my arms.'

Brett waited as her tongue flicked over her lips turning them a deep red. He held his body still. Suddenly, like the sun breaking out from the clouds, her face transformed and she held out her hands. Brett released his breath.

'You have convinced me. What do I do?'

He stepped closer, allowed her perfume to envelope him, savoured it. Then he forced his mind to attend to business. 'Place one hand on my shoulder.'

'Like this?' She raised her hand and grabbed. 'Do I have it right?'

'Lightly. A caress. Not a death grip.'

She gave a nervous laugh and loosened her grip. 'I am not used to such things. Perhaps we should forget it. There must another dance, an easier dance, you could teach me. What else is fashionable in London?'

He placed his hand on her waist, lightly. Held her there. 'No, I want to teach you to waltz. I came here today for that purpose. Now allow me to help you.'

She trembled slightly at his touch, but did not move away. He concentrated hard as his fingers itched to draw her close and to feel the way her soft curves met his body. Suddenly he longed to undo the tiny buttons that held up her dress and to reveal more of her creamy flesh, but he pushed the thought aside, wondering where it had come from. And why it seemed to block out any other thought.

'You only have yourself to blame if I step on your toes.' She smiled up at him.

'You won't.' He allowed his hand to increase the pressure. He started to hum slowly. 'It is one, two, three and turn. Listen to the tune.'

He began to hum a waltz. She stood rigid in his arms, head cocked to one side.

'Very pretty, but I doubt that Lady Bolt will allow such scandalous behaviour in her ballroom.'

'The Honourable Miranda has her dear papa wrapped around her little finger. It will happen. Now stop trying to find excuses and start moving your feet.'

He forced his feet to move, stepping carefully, keeping the proper distance, resisting the temptation to pull her closer and to breathe in her scent. Hesitantly she followed his steps, but rapidly grew in confidence. He moved faster, feeling her limbs move in time with his.

'I keep thinking I will stumble or fall. Are you sure it is the right tune?' She looked up at him with a tiny frown between her brows. 'We seem to be moving awfully quickly.'

'I know what I am doing.' He took a step and changed direction. Her skirt swirled out, grazing his shins. She gave a breathless laugh and he spun them around the narrow confines of the summer house again. 'Follow my lead. You are doing well. We shall make you an expert at the waltz in no time, and then no dance shall hold any fears. All will say what an up-to-the-minute miss you are.'

Her footsteps slowed and he cursed his wayward tongue. She started to pull away, but Brett tightened his hold on her waist.

'I doubt I shall ever be able to dance this in front of others. I have no idea what folly possessed me to agree.'

'Relax your shoulders. It is not folly to learn new things.' Brett smoothly turned her again, her skirts billowing out again. He wanted to keep on dancing with her, around and around.

'Sometimes, it is. I learnt the hard way. I know what I am doing now. The lesson should end.'

'Stay.' He kept hold of her hand. 'Please. You are nearly perfect. Once more around the room. I wish to be certain.'

Her footsteps faltered, slowed. He sucked in his breath. His body felt as if wave after wave of molten heat had hit it. His control began to slip as her lips were inches from his...

'Please,' she breathed.

Brett took it for an entreaty and gave into his desire. He lowered his lips to hers, sliding across their lush softness. He pressed his hand against her back, drew her closer, drank from her lips. A moment suspended in time and space, having no beginning or end, just the sweet temptation of her mouth. His tongue traced the outline of her lips and then the tiny parting, a gentle persuasion.

His arms went around her waist, pulled her closer, felt the melting warmth of her. He adjusted her body to his and his lips moved against hers—asked rather than demanded.

There was an innocence about her kiss as if she did not fully understand the passion that could exist between a man and a woman, the passion that threatened to overwhelm him. Brett couldn't resist deepening the kiss, flicking his tongue against hers, teasing her. She gave a little moan in the back of her throat and then she stiffened, pulling away. With his last ounce of self-control, Brett allowed her to go. Forced his body to take a step backwards and his ragged breathing to slow. It was harder to do than he imagined, but necessary. He would not force her.

The lesson was over.

This was not the time, nor the place. When she came to him, he wanted to be able to take his time and savour every inch of her. She would come to him, he was certain of that. It was only a matter of time.

'I believe that is enough for now.'

'For now?' Her fingers explored her mouth and her sea-green eyes were dilated, wide and alluring, surrounded by dark spiky lashes. He gazed up at the ceiling, trying to concentrate.

His hand reached out and lifted a curl from her shoulder, tucking it back into place. 'A lesson in waltzing was all I promised. One new thing a day.'

'I think you ought to go.'

'I believe that would be a good idea.'

Every particle of him longed to pull her back and kiss her, make her beg him to stay, but it would cause more problems than it would solve. She was far too tempting a morsel for something rushed. And they had been lucky. It was only a matter of time before her maid came searching or one of the servants found a reason to visit the summer house. No, the situation was far from ideal. Right now, right now, he needed to think, to clear his head.

He ran his thumb over her lips. 'So beautiful, so beautiful.'

Brett turned on his heel and strode out of the house and away from temptation.

Diana sat, regarding the toast and tea on the breakfast table with a distinctly jaundiced eye. This morning, she had taken pains, dressed in her best blue riding habit and had gone for a gallop, fully expecting to see Brett as she reached the top of the hill. Nothing. It bothered her that she had succumbed, that she had eagerly anticipated seeing him. Bother Brett Farnham and his flirtation!

'Mind where you put that.' Diana moved Simon's plans away from her coffee cup.

'The answer is in here, Diana. A bit more steam, a bit more pressure, and the engine will go.'

'But will the boiler be strong enough?' she asked, turning her mind forcibly away from Brett and his lips. 'I heard one blew recently at Wylam.'

'You know nothing about engines, Diana. Don't even start.' Simon snatched up the drawings, knocking over his tea cup. He gave a low curse and then apologised.

Diana spied several letters as well as Simon's copy of the *Newcastle Courant,* half-buried under his massed papers, pens and ink. 'You should have said something.'

'I am very busy with the engine.'

Diana reached for the letters. She had recognised Robert's childish scrawl, but frowned at the bold masculine hand of the second letter. With impatient fingers she broke the seal. Her heart dropped further. 'Lord Coltonby has had to depart for a few days. He hopes to be back soon, but makes no guarantees.'

'Why would Coltonby be writing to you?' Simon's green gaze narrowed.

'He and I have become friends, after a fashion. I told you that we both like driving.' Diana opened Robert's letter. 'Robert has written from Dr Allen's. He is doing Tacitus and Cicero this term. Hates them both.'

'I refuse to be distracted with Robert's news. Did Coltonby say why he was departing or where he was going?'

'Is it important, Simon?' Diana regarded her brother and willed the sudden hollow feeling inside her to go. 'He has left the neighbourhood.'

'It means that I have the measure of the man. Lord Coltonby will be no threat to us. He is much the same as Biddlestone.' Simon bent his head and made a few more notations on the plans. 'And it was far easier than I dared hoped it would be. If you will excuse me, sister, I have work to do.'

'But don't you want to read Robert's letter?' Diana held the missive out. 'He has mentioned Henry again, the lad who gave him so much trouble last term.'

A pained look crossed Simon's face. 'Later, when I have time to answer it. Or, better yet, you answer it. You know what he wants to hear. I am no good at such things.'

Diana stared after her brother. A great feeling of hopelessness swept over her. There had to be something she could do to help Simon and Robert, but the one person she felt instinctively would give her some advice had gone away. It bothered her that within a few short days she should come to value his opinion. She tapped the letter against her mouth, pondering.

She had to go to the ball, even if Brett was not there. She was tired of hiding in the house. Tired of wearing browns. Tired of running from life.

'I have changed my mind about the brown silk, Rose,' she said when the maid came in answer to the bell.

'Yes, miss?'

'You were right after all. It is only fit for the rag-and-bone man.'

'You are not going to the ball?'

'Do you remember the gown that I was going to wear to Vauxhall Gardens, but decided against? The deep rose silk?'

'Yes, miss, it complimented the colouring in your cheeks.'

'It came home with me, didn't it?'

'Yes, miss. It is in the attic.' Rose's eyes widened and she clapped her hands. 'You want to wear that.'

'It is a bit out of fashion, I know, but I think it will suffice.'

'It could be altered…' The maid screwed her face up. 'I mean, the ball is less than a week away, miss, but it could be done.'

'Do it, Rose.' Diana caught Rose's hand. 'Do it for me. I am through being overlooked and disregarded.'

The white waistcoat he wore for Almack's or the patterned one he wore for other balls? Brett checked his appearance for the fourth time. The white one. He wanted everything to be perfection. Diana Clare would keep her part of the bargain and dance with him. To waltz in anything but his best would not do.

Over the past few days as he had travelled to the various stock markets in Northumberland conducting business, Brett had found it difficult to banish Diana from his mind. The temptation to taste her lips again nearly overpowered him and his mind had wandered. In Rothbury, he had ended up missing the one horse that he had wished to acquire. Not a fatal error, but disturbing nevertheless. Normally distance made him forget, but it had only increased his longing. Her eyes and her mouth had invaded his dreams.

Brett fumbled with his neckcloth, swearing at his own incompetence. He then took up another piece of starched linen and began to do the intricate folds. Concentrated. This time, the neckcloth fell into its accustomed shape. All was right with the world.

Tonight he would put the final pieces of his scheme into place, and he would strike. It would be the end of it. A pang of something went through him. Regret? Sorrow? Brett did not stop to analyse. He had enjoyed Diana Clare's company. That was all. Her wit and her refreshing conversation. He frowned. The neckcloth was slightly skewed to the right and looked as if he was still at Eton. His hands went to straighten it. Spoilt it. He tore it off and began again.

'The neckcloths appear not to be holding their shape this evening, sir, as well as they normally do. Shall I ask for more starch next time?'

'They are fine as they are.' Brett ignored the growing pile on the ground. Seven at the last count. 'I was…attempting a new fold.'

'And, my lord, if you do not mind me saying, a woman is not worth fretting over. Fickle, they are. Changeable.'

'I have never fretted over a woman, Vrionis.' Brett lifted his chin, and completed the last precise folds. He stepped back, slipped on the black tail coat. 'Ever. Remember that.'

'I know that, sir. I was just saying, like…in case you had forgotten it. The air up here in Northumberland.' His valet brushed a speck of dirt from the coat. 'Only the other day, I caught myself looking at a piece of skirt, wondering, like, what it would be to have little ones with her. Nearly frightened me out of my breeches. I have given the woman in question a wide berth since then. A very wide berth.'

'The air has nothing to do with it. I know what I want.

I know why I am going to this ball.' Brett closed his eyes. His first glimpse of Miss Clare at Vauxhall Gardens all those years ago rose before him. A vision in white, her eyes sparkling as she looked around her with great eagerness. Her laughter as the fireworks had sparkled overhead. A woman in love with life. Innocent but with promise. He shook his head, willed the image to be gone. 'I am only going tonight to ensure Miss Clare carries out the terms of our wager. She failed to negotiate the last set of hurdles. I will not have her going back on her word.'

'As you say, sir, you never fret about a woman.'

Chapter Nine

Everyone who was anyone in the Tyne Valley and Newcastle—from the Grand Allies who owned the coal mines and ran the north of England to the various serving officers and their wives—appeared to be at the Bolts' that evening. From joining the queue of carriages to reaching the Bolts' door had taken the Clares' carriage a half-hour, a journey that normally took but a few moments.

Diana adjusted the neckline of the deep rose ballgown. Thankfully her figure remained unaltered from London and Rose had been able to work miracles with her needle and thread.

Lady Bolt's mouth visibly tightened when she and Simon greeted her. However, as Diana took her customary place at the side of the dance floor, she knew that it would take more than an elegant dress to make her the belle of the ball. The men's eyes slid over her and she became invisible as time after time she saw the bright goldenness of the Honourable Miranda being led out on to the dance floor. It was foolish to even hope that Brett might be attracted to her. He had merely sought her out as a distraction from the boredom of being buried in the country. Simon had been correct. She had been foolish even to hope and even more foolish to allow that kiss to happen.

Obviously he had removed himself in order to allow the situation time to resolve. Sensible but ultimately disappointing.

Diana forced her mind to concentrate on exchanging pleasantries with various neighbours. Hopefully, after tonight's disappointment, he would stop invading her dreams, filling her with an intense longing, a longing so great that when she woke, her lips ached and her body burnt. It was an affliction, but one from which she would recover in time.

Diana clenched her hand and redoubled her efforts to listen intently to Mrs Sarsfield's explanation of how she had managed to cure her grandchildren's fever with little more than a cold compress. Mrs Sarsfield's cap with its many ribbons positively quivered as she related each detail with increasing animation. Diana felt her eyelids begin to slide shut and struggled to contain her yawn. It would be hours before Simon would want to leave.

A shadow fell across her face and her nerves instantly became awake. Without even looking, she knew who approached. Even Mrs Sarsfield fell silent and her withered cheeks pinkened.

'Miss Clare, how delightful to see you again.' The purr of Brett's voice flowed over her. 'I had wondered if you would be here.'

Diana turned her head. She had forgotten how devastating he looked in evening clothes. His broad shoulders neatly filled out the black tail coat, his pristine white neckcloth was tied to perfection and his black breeches clung to his thighs.

She remembered when Algernon had once pointed Brett

out at the masquerade they had attended the evening after they had become engaged. He had been surrounded by a bevy of beauties, but had lifted a glass of something in her direction and she had looked away, cheeks glowing with heat, desperately confused by her reaction. The same sort of nervous anticipation filled her now. Only this time, she knew it for what it was—desire—and knew what it was like to be held in his arms.

'Lord Coltonby.' She kept her voice cool, but tightened her grip on her fan and forced her gaze upwards to where the many crystals of Lady Bolt's imported chandelier twinkled. When she felt she had regained her sense, she looked directly into his ever-changing grey eyes and discovered that she had forgotten the multitude of colours therein. She swallowed hard and strove for a normal voice. 'I see you have returned from your journey? Did you discover everything you desired?'

'Most things, but I hurried back for the dance. The evening festivities have been on my mind constantly.'

'Constantly?' She ignored the sudden fluttering of the butterflies in her stomach.

'I even let several farmers believe they had got the better of me in order to be here.'

'Hopefully, that does not mean you made any mistakes in purchasing your horses.' Diana attempted to keep her voice light, to remember that this conversation was purely for show, but she wanted to believe that he had returned to see her. 'I would hate to think that, in your haste, you had mistaken the horses' form.'

'My eye for line and form remains undiminished, even when attempts are made to disguise them.' His eyes travelled slowly down her face and came to rest on her neckline. 'Definitely undiminished.'

Diana forgot to breathe as she resisted the urge to pull

her lace higher up. She should never have let Rose alter the bodice this low. Her only hope was that he would think the pink of her cheeks was down to the warmth of the room.

'Are you two acquainted?' Mrs Sarsfield enquired, raising her quizzing glass. 'I am not sure I have had the pleasure…'

'Lord Coltonby,' Diana said quickly in an undertone. 'He has recently acquired the Park.'

'Oh, I have heard about him. And you. Old friends, Miss Ortner said. And I said that there was more to it than that, but my daughter-in-law refused to believe it.' Mrs Sarsfield gave a distinct nod and smacked her lips together as if she had chanced upon a particularly juicy piece of gossip. 'Wait until I tell her I have actually met the man in question.'

'But Mrs Sarsfield…' Diana began.

'The introductions, if you please, Miss *Diana,*' Brett commanded.

Diana swiftly made the introductions as Mrs Sarsfield beamed and her ribbons quivered. The elderly woman gave a little titter as Brett bent over her hand, treating Mrs Sarsfield as if she was the most important personage in the room. Two bright spots appeared on her cheeks.

'I had the pleasure of meeting Miss Clare in London many years ago and made it a point to renew our friendship when I moved up here,' Brett said smoothly as Mrs Sarsfield's effusive greeting died away.

'My daughter-in-law dismissed my notion out of hand as fanciful. She swore that you two could not possibly have met. And that…well…never you mind.' Mrs Sarsfield stood up. 'If you will excuse me, I am going to enjoy this.'

Without giving Diana a chance to protest, Mrs Sarsfield hurried away, moving more quickly than Diana had thought possible in a woman of her stature, pausing only to hurriedly whisper to another group of elderly ladies.

'I believe you have made a stir,' Diana commented. 'One smile from you and she melted.'

Brett merely lifted one eyebrow. 'It is you have made the stir in that dress. All I hear is the men asking themselves who the vision in deep rose is and how can they beg an introduction. I came over to stake my claim before there was an insurmountable queue.'

'And pray, when will this queue develop?' Diana gestured at the empty space in front of her. 'I have yet to see any sign.'

'After we dance.' He held out his arm. 'Shall we? One small cotillion?'

Diana let out a little breath. So it would not be a waltz after all. It was probably safer this way, but she had wanted to feel his arms about her again, however briefly. She refused to let idle compliments turn her head. She was the sensible Diana Clare. The débutante who lived for parties and who had hoped to make a splash in the *ton* had vanished long ago. Her dreams had turned into a nightmare and it was only her rules that now kept her safe.

'I might step on your feet.'

'No one will be watching my feet. All eyes will be on my partner.'

'I had not realised that you had returned,' she said. In another moment, she would follow Mrs Sarsfield's example and melt under his gaze. 'I had wondered if your business would keep you out of town.'

'My note said I would appear. Trust me when I say that I keep my promises.'

'I would have understood.' Her hands curled tighter around her fan, waiting for the signal that they should go out on the dance floor. 'I would have understood if you'd thought better of our rash arrangement. It seems foolish now that I think about it. This dance will certainly fulfil the terms of our wager.'

Brett's jaw tightened and he slowly looked her up and down. 'You only think you understand, Miss Diana, but I wonder if you actually do.'

'Like you, I keep my promises, but I am glad that I came.' Diana dropped her voice. 'Miranda Bolt gave me black-daggered looks as I entered, but she soon cheered when it became apparent that I was in my customary place, speaking with Mrs Sarsfield.'

'There is to be a change to your customary place.'

'You need not worry about that.' Diana made a little gesture with her fan. 'Simon will look after me once he has finished speaking with Mr Hedley and some of the other Grand Allies. They are discussing the merits of engines.'

'I promised you a dance. I have come to claim it.' He held out his gloved hand, beckoned to her as the orchestra struck the first notes. 'A waltz. I did guess correctly after all.'

'Mrs Sarsfield considers the waltz to be immoral,' Diana said quickly to banish the thoughts of Brett's hand on her shoulder and their bodies moving in time together. 'She predicts it will never be accepted by society. Her daughters-in-law all agree. She has been most vocal on the subject.'

'And I predict that it will be danced at Almack's in the very near future. Its popularity is growing on the Continent.' His fingers curled around hers, pulled her towards the dance floor. 'The time for speaking has ended. Now you can show me how you practised in my absence.'

'I know the theory from our lesson.'

'But as in life, the practice is very different. Relax and let the music be your guide. I shall go wherever you wish. Even out into the moonlight, if that is your fancy.'

'I believe I shall decline at present.' Diana drew a deep

breath. This was flirtation for the benefit of others. She had to remain calm and offhand, no matter how much the feeling of warmth was enveloping her.

'When the opportune moment arises, you must try it.' His hand tightened on her waist, burnt against the silk. 'I believe you will find the experience quite rewarding.'

A warm shiver went down her spine. Ruthlessly, Diana suppressed it. She was never going to dance with Brett in the moonlight.

'Shall we concentrate on this dance, rather than speculate on others?' Diana nodded towards the dance floor where several couples, led by Miranda Bolt and a red-coated officer, were assembling. At the sight of Diana, Miss Bolt's face took on a petulant expression. 'Miss Bolt does not appear at all pleased with the turn of events.'

'Wait until she sees how you dance.' The corners of his mouth twitched. Diana swallowed hard and attempted to remember the intricate steps as she placed her hand on his shoulder. Her whole being was aware of him.

She managed to get through the first few steps without treading on Brett's toes. Gradually her feet appeared to remember the steps he had taught her and she grew in confidence. His hand seemed to burn a brand on her waist and his fingers gently held hers. Their limbs moved together in time to the music.

'Your mastery surprises me, Miss Diana,' Brett said as they slowly circled the room. 'I fear your days warming a chair will have ended with this dance. Already I see several soldiers lining up to usurp my place. You will have to be careful to keep your feet on the ground.'

'Not all of my life was spent as a wallflower, Lord Coltonby.' Diana kept her chin up. 'I know the perils of giving credence to compliments.'

'We agreed—Brett.'

'But Lord Coltonby feels safer,' Diana returned, and concentrated on a point over his left shoulder rather than the intent expression in his eyes.

'Does he?' Brett expertly spun her around so she was once again forced to look him in the face. An unholy light danced in his eyes. 'Would you care to wager on this, Miss Clare?'

Before Diana could think of a suitably crushing reply, the music stopped. Diana breathed deeply and smiled. Before she could escape from the floor, a queue of officers had formed, all begging for the favour of a dance. Diana found she had little option but to accept. And all the joy and pleasure she had once had in music and ballrooms came back to her. Once or twice as she circled the ballroom floor, she was certain Brett's eyes were on her, but each time that she looked, he appeared deep in conversation with someone else.

'Ah, Lord Coltonby, you are here. My sister thought you had departed from the district.' Simon Clare blocked Brett's view of the dance floor. 'But I knew you would not miss this dance.'

'Clare, it is good to see you again.' Brett kept his eyes on Diana, who was dancing yet another cotillion, laughing up into the face of some red-coated soldier for a moment longer than was strictly necessary. A surge of white-hot anger coursed through him. 'The ball is very pleasant.'

'Quite a change from the fare you are used to in London, I would imagine.'

'A welcome change.'

'As you may have heard, I have been working on a travelling engine. It is showing real promise. But it is an investment that I cannot miss.' Simon Clare pulled a tightly folded sheaf of papers from the inside pocket of his coat.

'I have some papers here, if you wish to glance at them. A number of the others have expressed an interest. Of course, Sir Norman proclaims that his will go better, but I fear he is mistaken. It will never run.'

'In the middle of a ball? Are you mad, man?' Brett swung around to face Diana's brother. The man would never change. Business, always business. 'You may send the papers over in the morning.'

'If that is what you wish…if you think you cannot make sense of them tonight.' Clare returned the papers to his pocket. 'I naturally bow to your wishes.'

Brett regarded him through narrowed eyes. Exactly what was his game? Was he simply inept at social conversation or was there something more sinister? He would give Clare the benefit of the doubt. 'My head is perfectly clear.'

Clare's cheeks flushed slightly. 'Sir Cuthbert always encouraged me to bring the papers to any function we might be attending. It saved time. He preferred the hurdy-gurdy of the dance for pushing the pen.'

Brett thinned his lips. The look in Clare's eyes said it all. He considered Brett to be a fop, a macaroni like Sir Cuthbert. It was time that he learnt they were different. Very different. He looked forward to delivering the final blow tomorrow, to seeing Clare crawl.

'I conduct my business in the proper venue. Balls are for pleasure, not negotiation.'

'Never let it be said that I didn't offer. I thought we could discuss the land at the same time.'

'See to it that you do not make the same mistake again.' Brett turned on his heel, shaking with anger.

'My sister appears to be enjoying herself on the dance floor,' Clare called after him.

Brett halted. What new game was Clare playing? Why was he bringing his sister into this? 'She does, rather. I was lucky to discover her sitting amongst the widows. It would appear I have inadvertently brought her to the attention of some others.'

'I know and I wanted to thank you for it. She took the notion somehow to wear a new ballgown. Dressed up. More fancy than I have seen her for...for years. I had thought it was going to go wrong and then you stepped in and danced with her.'

Brett stared at the man, astonished. He was actually thanking him. His shoulders tensed and the muscles in his arms clenched—the same reactions he always had before the start of a race or a high-stakes game of cards. He should say something, start the process of explaining to Clare what he had done and why. But the words refused to come. 'I was pleased to help. We are friends.'

'There is now a queue twenty deep for the honour of dancing with her. Some of them have come to me, begging to hear about the engine. I do worry that it will go to her head, but she does deserve some happiness.' Clare pointed towards where Diana was laughing at some sally a red-coated officer made. Brett forced his shoulders to relax. 'I trust her implicitly, of course, but as one Cantabrigian to another, I do worry.'

'Your sister is most assuredly a lady, Clare. I believe we can agree on that point.'

'Quite.' Clare blinked at him, and he looked surprised. 'I am so glad you agree.'

'I will endeavour to ensure that no harm comes to her,' Brett said as he watched Diana start out once more for the dance floor. He wanted to rip the officer's head from his body for even daring to put his gloved hand on her bare shoulder.

'Thank you, Coltonby. I appreciate it.'

Brett's mouth thinned as he watched Simon Clare disappear into the throng. He knew then that he could not use Diana in the way he had planned. He wanted her. He would have her, but he would not use her. He wanted to protect her. And the thought scared him far more than facing a team of runaway horses.

Cheeks flushed and feet throbbing, Diana was forced to admit defeat and retired to a chair. It had been so long since she'd properly danced that she was determined to enjoy every moment. Seeing the Honourable Miranda's slightly shocked countenance as she had realized that Diana was not a wallflower was the added spur she had needed.

The major with whom she had been partnered for a quadrille left to get her some refreshment. Diana stared ruefully at her dancing slippers. In her excitement at dancing again, she had forgotten how much they could pinch. She had also forgotten the sharp burning sensation when drops of wax fell on to the back of her neck. It was a hazard of dancing under chandeliers, but as far she could tell none of the wax had landed on her gown. She craned her neck and tried to inspect the point where her sleeve joined the back of the bodice.

'It is good that you are sitting down,' Brett purred. 'You appear to have danced without a break since our waltz.'

'I have had years to catch up on.' Diana blinked up at Brett. She had spent the better part of the last six dances trying to forget that he was in the room and failing. She had finally managed to convince her wayward mind that he would not speak to her again tonight, but then he had appeared, glowering. His brow was darker than Simon's. She clutched her fan tighter. That was it—Brett had decided to play an older brother. The thought should have brought a feeling of relief, but she knew he meant more to her than that. She would get over it. 'It is interesting how much of the excitement and the sheer thrill of dancing that one forgets. Have you enjoyed the cotillions and quadrilles? I noticed you led Mrs Sarsfield out. It was thoughtful of you.'

'I have danced enough, but your cheeks are over-bright. Are you sickening?'

'Hardly.' Diana waved her fan in front of her, carefully hiding her expression from Brett. He had noticed. It would be far too easy to develop a *tendre* for him. It frightened her that her body became more alive when he was near. 'Merely tired from my exertion.'

'Shall I get you a cup of punch?'

'Major Spence has gone to fetch me some punch.'

'How good it is to know that Spence is looking after you.'

'Like you, he seemed concerned. He suggested a turn in the garden, but I explained a sip of punch would be enough.'

Brett's face looked as if he had swallowed something distasteful. 'And you believe the punch will revive you?'

'Lady Bolt's punch is considered to be the finest in Northumberland. She keeps the receipt a closely guarded secret, but it is reputed to have wonderful restorative powers. Mrs Sarsfield thinks it is to do with the amount of rum and gin Lady Bolt adds.'

'I shall have to try it…but later. Is there anything else you require? Shall I take you into supper?'

'A cup of punch and a sit down is all that is necessary at the moment.' Diana rearranged her skirts. 'Lieutenant McGowan has already requested the honour of accompanying me into supper.'

'He is not here now. I believe he is dancing with Charlotte Ortner.'

'But I agreed.'

'Do I detect a certain mulishness to your tone?'

'A certain decidedness, yes.'

'It is something to be admired, but not necessarily welcomed.' He held out his arm. 'Shall we stop this silly quarrel before it begins? Come have a stroll with me around the room.'

'I did promise Major Spence that I would wait here. Like you, I keep my promises.' Diana saw the man in question advancing behind Brett. She had to admit there was no comparing the two. Major Spence was weak chinned and possessed a nervous tic in his eye whenever she asked him about when he was going to join his regiment in the Peninsula. 'And he has gone to the trouble of getting me a cup of punch. A gentleman by all accounts. Lady Bolt assures me on this point.'

'Jeremy Spence is not to be trusted.' Brett's voice held more than a hint of menace. 'Not even with a glass of punch. Remember that.'

'He was involved in a gallant action in the Peninsula. Apparently he is noted for his gallantry. It was something to do with a convent, but he refuses to say. It appears to me to be more than natural modesty, but Mrs Ortner and Lady Bolt find him charming.'

'There is gallant and there is *gallant,* Diana, as I am sure you know.' Brett lifted one eyebrow. 'You did, after all, keep company with one of the Jehu. You know the language we use. Spence drove with the crowd as well.'

Diana's cheeks burnt with an even greater intensity. She had forgotten the *double entendre* of gallant. A gallant action was one involving a mistress. Her hand began to tremble and she concentrated on not snapping the slender ivory leaves of her fan. 'In a convent?'

'Nuns are women as well. And it involved more than one convent, or so Spence boasts in male company.'

'I bow to your expertise.' Diana shifted uneasily. She had thought Major Spence safe despite her slight unease. All her rules told her he should be, but now it seemed that she had no compass to guide her. She had to trust in luck. She swallowed hard. Not luck. Brett. She had to trust Brett. And surprisingly the thought brought her comfort.

'Thank you for allowing me to handle this.'

Brett smoothly took both cups of punch from Major Spence. 'It was so kind of you to fetch Miss Diana and me some punch.'

'There are to be three of us?' The major's pale blue eyes blinked rapidly and his prominent Adam's apple bobbed up and down. 'I had hoped for a quiet word with Miss Clare, Coltonby. You do understand my meaning.'

'Miss Clare explained that you would be giving details of your gallant action and I do so love tales of heroics.' Brett smoothly took the cups of punch from the major. 'She did urge me to take a sip of Lady Bolt's punch. I trust you won't mind. After all, I should hate for you to be accused of anything underhanded.'

'No, no, not at all. I will fetch another cup.' Major Spence's lip curled slightly. 'After all, one never likes to upset an earl and particularly not one with a reputation like Lord Coltonby's.'

Diana glanced quickly from the major to Brett. Brett merely straightened his cuffs and took a sip of the punch. 'An excellent concoction. I do believe Lady Bolt is to be complimented. You must try some, Major Spence, before it is all gone,' she said.

'I shall, dear lady.'

'Have this one.' Brett held out the other cup. 'Miss Clare will be going into supper shortly in any case. I believe Lieutenant McGowan has that honour.'

Diana gritted her teeth. Brett was behaving far worse

than her brother. He was truly insupportable. 'I did ask Major Spence for a cup of punch.'

'I will get another one for myself, dear lady.' The major handed her the cup. 'I am used to making sacrifices for the ladies.'

Diana took a sip and nearly choked. The punch appeared to have twice the alcohol that it normally did. Brett lifted an eyebrow.

'Precisely how many convents were involved in your gallant action, Spence?' Brett said, drawling the word gallant. 'I am very interested in learning the unembellished truth.'

'Well, naturally I hesitate to give the full details because of Miss Clare's sensibilities. War is not for the ladies.'

Diana regarded Major Spence over the rim of her glass. His cheek was flushed. Brett's surmise had been correct. His gallant action was Jehu gallant. 'I must assure you, Major, that I do not give way easily to fainting.'

The major tugged at his collar and his florid face grew even redder. 'I wish to state…' he began, but then stopped. His eyes darted from Diana to Brett and back again and his Adam's apple bobbed up and down several times 'The fireworks are about to begin in the garden, Miss Clare. I overheard Maurice Bolt telling another lady. If you would be so good as to join me on the terrace, we can find a good place to watch the display.'

Diana froze. Her hand trembled slightly and the punch threatened to spill. Brett's fingers took the cup from her as she struggled to regain her composure. Fireworks. Gardens. Darkness.

A black hole opened inside her and threatened to swallow all her happiness and joy, sucking her into the past and its nightmare.

How could she have forgotten, even for one instant?

'I believe Miss Clare is very comfortable here. She and I are looking forward to your tale of derring-do.' Brett's voice appeared to come from a long way away, calling her back to the present.

Diana smiled up at him and he nodded slightly.

'We are waiting, Spence.' Brett tapped his fingernail against the rim of his glass. 'Indulge us.'

'I see Sir Norman quizzing Simon Clare on his new engine. I believe Sir Norman is keen to acquire one of his own. If you will excuse me. I truly must hear more.' The major rapidly retreated.

Diana forced her shoulders to relax and her breath to come naturally. She was not in London, but Northumberland. The events of five years ago were in the past. She was safe in the light. With people. Nobody knew. Nobody guessed. Everything was behind her.

'If you wish to go and hear about the travelling engine, I won't keep you. It is Simon's pride and joy.'

'There are other things to interest me.' He raised a casual shoulder. 'I am not overly enamoured of machines—filthy necessary evils that thankfully stay still. My horses always shy around pumping stations and wheel houses.'

'Then you have not caught the infamous Loco Motive fever?'

'Thankfully, no.'

'Perhaps you have not been in the north-east long enough, then. Everyone from the Duke of Northumberland on down seems obsessed with the idea.'

He curled his fingers around hers and drew her to her feet. 'Now, most everyone has gone to see the fireworks. I seem to recall that you enjoyed them. The punch of Spence's has done you no good, perhaps the cool air will help.'

The faint screams and the whistles of the rockets penetrated the room, but they were far away. Bearable. Slowly she shook her head and pulled away. 'I find they are not to my taste. They...they...that is to say, I dislike the bangs.'

His eyes grew troubled. 'But I have a clear memory of you laughing up at them. Once at Vauxhall Gardens.'

'It must have been some other girl,' Diana said firmly. 'I have never liked them.'

Silently she prayed he would accept her lie.

'Shall I remain here with you?'

'No, you go. I will go and keep Mrs Sarsfield company.'

He made a bow. 'As you wish.'

Diana's shoulders sagged. She had done it. All would be well. She had survived.

Chapter Ten

The morning sun shone directly in Diana's eyes as she lay in her bed, gazing at the curtains. Every time she'd closed her eyes, Brett's face had appeared and her body had relived the waltz and the pressure of his hand against her waist again and again. Her body had ached with an intense longing. Finally as the first cocks had begun to crow, she had fallen into a dreamless sleep.

'Your brother left hours ago, up at the crack of dawn, muttering about the impertinence of the aristocrats, or so his valet proclaimed.' Rose said, bustling in with fresh tea and toast. Titch followed at her heels, looking hopefully for a dropped crust. 'I took it to mean that he did not have a pleasant time at the ball. Did you have a good time? Was the gown remarked on? You never really said last night.'

'Your gown made me the belle of the ball, Rose, but I had forgotten how tiring they can be.' Diana reached under the counterpane and gave the base of her foot a rub. 'And how much they can make your feet ache. Luckily I remembered to put on that cream—you know, the one the stableman uses to keep horses' hooves soft—and do not have blisters.'

'The master appeared quite surprised at the amount of time you spent dancing.' Rose gave a loud sniff. 'Why he should be surprised, I have no idea. You looked a picture in that dress.'

'My brother was his usual early-morning self, then.' Diana pulled the covers up and snuggled further down into the bed. 'I am pleased I slept in.'

'You are avoiding my question, Miss Diana. There has been talk. Who played you court? Your dress was fit for a princess. How many soldiers? How many titles? And what about your Lord Coltonby?'

'Has anyone paid me court for the past five years, Rose? Stop teasing me.' Diana kept her gaze resolutely on the bed curtains, but at Rose's clucking she turned over on her side. 'Out with it, what news have you heard? What am I supposed to confirm?'

'There is talk about Lord Coltonby and he did come to call.'

Diana's hand paused. Her feelings about Brett were too new and fragile. She had no idea what she wanted to do. The only thing she did know was that marriage was not possible. For either of them. He seemed to have only brotherly concern for her. He had left after they'd kissed and only returned because he had promised to dance with her at the ball.

When he did marry, he would undoubtedly go back down to London and find a suitable wife, a Diamond, rather than a Disgraced Has-Been with a modest fortune.

'Rose, Lord Coltonby is an old acquaintance. He was a friend of my former fiancé. He took me under his wing and re-introduced me to society. He has done so, and there it ends.'

'If you say so, Miss Diana, but why has he sent this note? First thing, by special messenger?' Rose produced a missive from her apron pocket. 'It is the second time in under a week that I have seen that handwriting. And the under-housemaid had it from the stable hand who had it from the Bolts' footman that...'

Diana resisted the urge to snatch the missive from Rose's hand. Instead she leant down and fed Titch some toast. The terrier gave a soft snuffling bark. 'The servants' network never ceases to amaze me.'

'It is a good thing we have it, too, since certain people will not bother to inform other people of what's happening.'

'Rose dear, there is nothing to say. You would be the first to know. Have I ever kept secrets from you?' Diana kept her eyes firmly on Titch's ears. There was one secret that she had kept from Rose. They had never spoken of that night more than five years ago. She had often thought it providence that Rose had left to visit relatives before Diana had returned from Vauxhall.

'Humph. I do worry about you, Miss Diana. I want to see you settled.'

Diana stared at the heavy cream-coloured paper and resisted the temptation to immediately break open the seal. 'Has any other post arrived?'

'A letter from Master Robert's headmaster. The master glanced at the handwriting and then said that you would handle it as you were so good with the headmaster last time.' Rose shook her head. 'The lad doesn't mean any harm. It is a bit of fun. Boys will be boys. My younger brothers were always trying to put handfuls of beetles and spiders down my back. One is a clerk in a shipping office now and the other's joined the navy.'

'He does it to get Simon's attention.'

'You know that. I know that. The man in the moon knows it, but will the master listen?'

Diana drew in a breath. Perhaps Robert and his troubles at school were the distraction she needed. Another way to remind her of her duty. Her time was better spent on this rather than on thinking about castles in the air and things that could never be. Her treacherous mind kept returning to Brett's kiss and ways in which it could be repeated.

'Any guess on what he has done this time? I only hope it is spiders down some poor boy's back.' She opened the letter and quickly read the complaint. The corners of her mouth twitched. 'Robert has let off a stink bomb in the headmaster's study. Doctor Allen quite rightly points out that he cannot tolerate this sort of behaviour. Simon will have to contact him and persuade him otherwise, if Robert is to stay at that school.'

'Are you going to tell him about the last time? You know what he was like.'

'Robert must learn that he has to obey rules.' Diana tapped the letter against the table. 'I will write to Robert and explain. If he is expelled, his father will never let him have a horse.'

'Young master Robert will not take any notice of the threat. The times I have told him not to take the softening cream off your dressing table…horses have their own, I said.'

'You are right, Rose, I shall have to write to the headmaster and beg him to reconsider his threat. Robert takes such threats as a challenge.' Diana put a hand to her head. 'With Simon in his current mood, the combination of the two would stretch my nerves unbearably. They may deserve each other, but do I deserve them?'

'He has a good heart, Robert does. He picked me a bunch of daisies before he left.'

'Both of them do, Rose. However, I do get tired of being the one to enforce discipline, of being the sensible one, while my brother immerses himself in his work.'

'If Robert is thrown out of this school, where will he go? The master won't have him here. Remember the ink incident.'

'We solve that problem if it arises, Rose.' Diana put the letter to one side and reached for the tea pot. She became aware that Rose still stood there, regarding her with a strange expression. 'Is something amiss?'

'There's a letter from Lord Coltonby and you are seeking to distract me with tales of young master Robert,' Rose said. 'I heard from Lady Bolt's housekeeper you danced a waltz with him. A waltz, Miss Diana. Where did you ever learn such a thing?'

'Yet more gossip, Rose?' Diana lifted her cup to her lips and hoped Rose would ignore the sudden flaming of her cheeks. 'The tongues have clearly been busy this morning. When shall I be informed of the engagement?'

'There is something between you two. Why write to you? And come calling? Twice. And all this fuss to get the ball dress altered. A body wants to be prepared.'

'You may put the patterns away, Rose.' Diana swirled the tea in her cup. 'There is no wedding in my future.'

'But, miss...'

'He has become a friend. He is being kind. He sees me as no more than a younger sister.'

'Then your *friend* has sent you a note. One which you refuse to open. You should read it immediately.' Rose crossed her arms. 'He is unmarried and an earl. He will be looking for a wife, it stands to reason. You should stop doing yourself down, Miss Diana.'

Diana's throat closed. She refused to explain the how and the why, not after all these years. 'I have sworn never to marry. There is Robert to think of. Stop attempting to matchmake, Rose.'

'You get the strangest notions in your head, Miss Diana. Not marry? The women who say such things do not have an earl as a suitor. Nor a sizeable fortune. You are not thinking straight, Miss Diana.'

'I enjoy my independence. Once I was delivered from a disastrous alliance, and I do not want to risk it again.' At the sound of Rose's disgusted noise, Titch began howling. Diana gave a sigh. 'I suppose you will not give me any peace until I do open the note and respond to it.'

'What do you have against the man?'

'He had a certain reputation five years ago,' Diana said slowly, drawing out each word. She bent down and picked Titch up, placated him with a corner of toast. 'He would pursue anything in a skirt. I am a challenge to him. He finds me an amusement. He will soon tire of the chase and find other prey. It is what men do.'

'Who are you trying to convince—me or you? I looked through my magazines. You know, the ones Mrs Sarsfield sends me. They go on about his horses and the purses that he was won, but he hasn't been involved in the Crim. Con.'

'He is infinitely discreet.'

'Or maybe you underestimate your charms.'

'I know what my charms are, Rose.' Diana buried her face in Titch's soft fur. The little dog gave her a disgusted look and leapt off the bed.

'I know what they are as well, Miss Diana. And you are doing yourself a disservice. You are frightened of living. Any time a man comes sniffing around your skirts, you put up shields and blocks. Excuses.'

'There is no need to be vulgar.'

'But I am right.' Rose gave a decided nod. 'You have

piqued his interest. You should capitalise on it. You never know where such friendship might lead.'

'I am being realistic, Rose.' Diana knew her cheeks were glowing as the maid's beam increased. 'Try to understand.'

'Oh, Miss Diana, you can be such fun to tease. Think nothing of me. I am so pleased you have decided to wear pretty clothes again.'

Diana broke open the seal and read the note. A few words leapt out at her and her breath stopped.

A matter of urgency has arisen.

'Is there a problem, Miss Diana? You have gone ashen.'

'I think I will be going out after all.'

'And you are still positive that he wants nothing to do with you?'

Diana brushed the crumbs from the bed. 'Ask Jenkins to get the gig ready.'

'I am coming with you.' Rose moved her ample bulk in front of Diana. 'You are not without friends, Miss Diana— should you need them. You are far from being alone. This isn't London. You have a certain standing in this community. People know and respect you.'

Diana reached out and clutched Rose's hand, relief flooding over her. She had dreaded the thought of travelling there on her own. This way it was somehow more respectable. But she kept wondering—what had Simon done now? Why did Brett need to see her? 'Thank you.'

'You wished to see me urgently?' Diana held the crumpled note aloft when Brett entered his drawing room. She had spent an uncomfortable few moments alone after the butler had shown her into the room.

Annoyingly, Brett appeared remarkably unruffled in

his black morning coat and buckskin breeches. Even his neckcloth was impeccably tied. He gave no sign that he was under mental distress or that anything untowards had happened. She was aware that her bonnet was slightly at an angle and that her old burgundy gown and pelisse had been the first ones to hand. And her hair was pulled back in a simple knot. Now she wished that she had taken more time, rather than starting out like some mad thing.

'You are later than I'd thought you would be,' he said finally. 'I had expected you before noon. It is a shame, but there we have it. A few hours of daylight remain.'

'You expected me to come here?' Diana's fingers curled around the note, twisting it beyond recognition.

'Why else would I have sent the note?' He tilted his head to one side as his eyes assessed her. 'Asking you to visit.'

'Demanding.'

'Definitely asking.'

'A polite note would have sufficed. The whole tone was alarming in the extreme.' Diana swallowed hard. Since the moment she had first read the note, various possibilities had gone through her brain, each more dreadful than the last. 'What has happened?'

'I had no wish to alarm you. A situation has risen and I would like some advice.'

'You have a funny way of going about it. I was certain some terrible disaster had befallen you, that something was dreadfully wrong.' Diana crossed her arms.

'Nothing is wrong. There are things I wanted to discuss with you. Reasons to have you visit.' Brett gave an unrepentant smile.

'But I thought…Simon had been and there was trouble.' Diana stumbled over the last few words.

The corners of Brett's lips twitched. 'Can I help it if people choose to leap to illogical conclusions?'

'You knew I would think that!' Diana gritted her teeth, refused to give in to his increasingly engaging smile. 'You are insufferable! I care about my reputation, even if you do not.'

'Have no fear. I will not use it as some sort of bargaining counter. What has passed between us, stays between us.' His face sobered and a muscle twitched in his cheek. 'Harm comes to reputations when people are indiscreet. No one has ever accused me of being indiscreet.'

'I know the value of discretion.' She pressed her hands together. She wished she knew exactly what was in his mind—but how to ask the questions when she feared the answers? 'I know how the world works. One may do much, if it is not flaunted before the censorious eyes of society. Men have far more licence than women. Hypocrisy reigns.'

'An advocate of Mary Wollstonecraft?'

'The scales had dropped from my eyes before I read her work, but, yes, I see much to admire in it.' She waited to hear his mocking rebuttal.

'It is the way of the world. However much we might hope to change it.' He lifted an eyebrow. 'I, personally, loathe hypocrisy.'

'I...I am pleased you feel that way.'

'Sit. Please sit.'

'I would prefer to remain standing.'

'The sofa will be more comfortable than your dance-worn feet, but if it is your pleasure...'

Diana concentrated on the room rather than on his mouth or his hands. The furniture had changed very little since the Biddlestones' occupancy, but Diana noted the other changes. Silver cups from various horse races now lined the tables and, instead of the long line of Biddlestone family portraits, the drawing room was full of portraits of horses, each labelled with the rider and winning races. A few simple changes but enough to exude a masculine rather than feminine touch. Diana waited for him to begin speaking.

'Why did you summon me here? I have a right to know,' she asked in a small voice when she could bear the silence no longer.

'Are you interested in another commission?'

'Commission?' Diana tilted her head to see if she could detect a hint of laughter in his eyes, but he appeared serious. 'What sort of commission?'

'I need your help, your painterly eye, and it struck me that given today's beautiful autumn weather, why wait? A man can achieve much if he acts. We are friends after all.'

Friends? Eyes? He was about to say his goodbyes. A great lump rose in Diana's throat. She did not want to say goodbye. With the greatest effort, she kept her face as neutral as she could.

'I do value your friendship, Brett,' Diana said quickly before she had a chance to regret it. 'I shall be disappointed of course to see you quit the neighbourhood. Your being here has added a certain colour to my life.'

Diana found she had no desire to think about what might happen when this friendship came to an end. That was all it was, she told herself firmly—an unlikely pairing that must inevitably come to an end and one that she would treasure.

What had happened in the summer house was solely her fault. It had been a light kiss that had meant nothing in the grand scheme of things. He must have bestowed a thousand such kisses in his lifetime. She would not let him know what it had meant to her. What dancing in his arms last night had meant. And how the hours in front of her seemed to stretch out unceasingly.

'Diana, are you attending me? You have a faraway expression in your eyes.'

Dimly she realised that he had been speaking, gesturing with his hands, an excited expression on his face. 'Yes, yes, I agree. It will be the best thing.'

'You miss the point entirely, Diana. Are you quite the thing?'

She put a hand to her head and sank down on the sofa. 'I fear last night's unaccustomed festivities made my head throb this morning.'

'Too much of Lady Bolt's punch?' He stopped and reached for the bell. 'I can remedy that. Lightly browned toast and copious amounts of tea. I was hoping for a stroll in the gardens, but your health is far more important. We shall have to do this the next fine day.'

'You were explaining about your commission. What do you want me to do? I will pay attention now, I promise.'

'There is a folly—a grotto—on the estate. It is rather plain and unadorned.' He leant forward, his eyes shone silver grey. 'I think it could be more. It should be more.'

'I know the one you mean.' Diana glanced at the wall behind him, which boasted a stain from a leaking roof. The grotto. Of course the grotto. He had seen her work and knew she had done the painting for the Bolts' summer house. It had nothing to do with his imminent departure. She placed her reticule carefully in her lap and berated her mind for leaping to inappropriate conclusions.

'How long has the grotto been there? Do you know?'

'The late Sir John Biddlestone, Sir Cuthbert's grandfather, had it put in.' Diana breathed easier. It was a topic they could discuss and the strain would become easier. She wanted to get back to their easy friendship, the one they had had before the kiss, before her mind became filled with him. 'He wanted pleasure gardens to ramble in and for his wife to paint, as she was a keen water colourist. Unfortunately she died a few years later and not much more was done. I suspect it has not been cleaned out properly for years. Sir Cuthbert was not overly fond of the estate, but neither did he want to let it out.'

'I intend to change that. This estate is to be my principal seat. It must have a garden worthy of an earl.'

Diana stared at him. How was she going to go on facing him, meeting up with him when their liaison had ended? She was like an addict, craving more. 'Why is it to be your principal seat? Surely you must have more estates down in Warwickshire.'

'My father and brother did not manage their affairs correctly and neglected to ensure a settlement. All the historic Coltonby lands were sold to pay my brother's debts.' Brett's face became shadowed. 'It has fallen to me to restore the family fortune. And luckily, I proved adept at making money. I want a new beginning. The shadows of the past can be long and inharmonious.'

'And you want me to paint the grotto?' Diana bit her lip. Painting the grotto would be fun. She could already see the shells and pictures that she wanted to put on the walls. She knew she could do an excellent job. It would give her an outlet for her passion. 'My painting is…well…floral and I think the grotto would need shells, something in keeping with the water.'

'I agree.' A sardonic smile twisted his lips. 'Stop throwing up obstacles where there are none. Let me judge your work on its merits. Indulge me.'

'I indulged you with the waltz lessons and I know where that led.' Diana kept her voice steady. She had said the unmentionable. She had brought it out in the open, but it had needed saying. 'We are both adults, Lord Coltonby.'

'Nothing happened that you didn't desire.' His grey eyes seemed to pierce her soul. 'Or do you seek to deny what happened when you were in my arms? Do you need reminding?'

Diana tightened her grip on the letter as images danced in front of her. Her lips ached at the merest thought, the faintest look. She wiped a hand across her mouth and concentrated on the various pictures of horses and their jockeys.

'What happened in the summer house is best forgotten and never spoken of again. Ever.' Her voice sounded high and strained to her ears. She prayed he'd understand. 'I trust you will heed my wishes on that. It is the most sensible course of action.'

He snapped his fingers. 'Consider it in the past as it is the most sensible course of action. Far be it from me to ever suggest that you act in a reckless manner.'

'You are laughing at me now.'

'Not at all. I am very serious. I do want you to see the grotto, Diana.' His fingers reached out and took hold of her elbow, caressed her there. A warmth seared through her. She moved her arm and he let her go. She put her hand over where his fingers had been.

She took a deep breath, plunged onwards. He had to understand what she was saying, why she could not allow such a thing to happen again. 'What could have happened doesn't bear thinking about. And it would have been entirely my fault, I asked you to kiss me.'

'Are you quite through with being noble?' His cold voice cut through her, chilling her to the bone.

'Yes,' she said steadily. 'Although I consider it to be practical, rather than noble.'

'Nobody will ever force me into marriage.'

'Nor I. I promise you that.' She lifted her chin and ignored the knots in her stomach.

'You?' His eyes widened at her words. 'Whatever are you speaking of, Miss Clare? Why would you be against marriage?'

'I plan never to marry.' She kept her head up and refused to flinch despite his incredulous expression. 'I made that vow after Algernon Finch died. Nothing has ever happened to make me change my mind.'

'Was that because you buried your heart with him?' His voice was barely a breath, so low that Diana wondered if he had even spoken.

'Nothing so melodramatic. He was after my money.' She waved a hand and tried to make her voice sound calm and reasoned. How could she begin to explain about the perfidy of the man? Of the letters she had discovered, mocking her? Of that last horrible night when he had ensured that she could never break the engagement? Of the hours she had spent scrubbing his touch from her skin? 'I realised how close I came to losing everything. A woman's property is only her own if she is unmarried.'

'If she is a widow, she has control of her property. You are not a widow unless the Northumbrian definition is different from the rest of England's,' Brett corrected after a long silence. 'Your brother or your guardian must control your estate as you have never married.'

'I trust my brother. He has looked after my money well. The colliery and the other businesses thrive. He has built on the solid foundation that my father left.'

'Yes, no one could ever accuse your brother of not being devoted to his business interests.'

Diana released a breath and resisted the temptation to crumple Coltonby's note further. Simon had sent the papers to Brett. They were much alike, her brother and this earl, possibly too much alike. Both were determined. 'Simon does keep his word. At the moment, the colliery consumes the vast proportion of his time. He worries about it failing to keep pace with the other Grand Allies, particularly now that Mr Hedley has developed a travelling engine for Wylam Colliery.'

'Mr Hedley guards his secrets well, and it is unlikely that your brother will be able to get one for the Ladywell.'

'My brother can be very resourceful when the occasion demands. He searches for more investors.'

'I saw an example of his resourcefulness last evening.' Brett's level gaze met hers. 'Does he often do business at balls?'

Diana regarded her hands. 'My brother swears the age of the travelling engine will arrive sooner than people expect. He wants to convince people his ideas are right.'

'If it does, I shall make a proper assessment of the risk. But enough of this talk about Loco Motion and collieries.' He inclined his head and reached out to take the paper from her hands. 'The grotto awaits if you feel capable of walking. I am most anxious to hear your thoughts on its possibilities.'

'We could discuss it here.' Diana met his level gaze with hers.

'But the possibilities are there, out in the grounds. How can you begin to advise if you have not actually seen what needs to be done?'

She picked at the button of her glove. 'I will call Rose. She can accompany us.'

'You hardly need a maid to go walking with you. I am sure she is quite safe in the kitchen conversing with staff. Allow her to have a good long gossip and a chance to rest her feet. I asked the cook to prepare a picnic for beside the grotto.' His eyes became hooded. 'I thought after walking out there, we might need a little light refreshment while we discussed my requirements.'

'Surely it will not take that long.' Diana looked at her reticule as her insides trembled and a flood of warmth went through her. Out there. Alone. This time, she would not behave irresponsibly.

'I wish to go over my scheme in depth. We are friends, Diana. I value your opinion. You may think of possibilities.' His voice was smooth. Diana glanced up, but his expression was bland. However, she could not rid herself of the feeling of being caught up in a current that was heading for somewhere unknown. 'And remember, Diana, you are free to return to the house whenever you wish.'

'I know that.' She took a deep breath, concentrated. The only thing she knew was that she wanted to be with him. 'Shall we go?'

Chapter Eleven

Brett resisted the impulse to support Diana's arm or guide her hand as they walked along the overgrown path towards the grotto. The red pelisse with white lace at the collar complimented her bonnet as the skirt of her dress billowed out, slightly revealing her slim ankles. The colour suited her far more than the browns and greens he had seen her in before. But she was the very picture of demure femininity. It belied the woman who had danced with him last evening and who had once again invaded his dreams. He tightened his jaw and kept his steps moving towards the grotto.

Patience and careful planning were the keys to success. Her words about never marrying had been an unexpected blow. It had not occurred to Brett that Diana might not be seeking marriage, but it bothered him that she had rejected the notion out of hand.

Was it her polite way of rejecting him? Or just the institution?

His fingers curled around his cane. He would discover her reason in due course, but today's plans revolved around other pursuits. He wanted her to feel comfortable with him and to begin to understand that she and he were intimate friends. That her head was not to be turned by the red-coated officers who had pursued her at the ball.

'What are you planning for this area?' she asked, stopping suddenly and gesturing towards a heavily wooded area where scrub and brambles vied with a few good specimens of trees. Brett forced his thoughts back to the garden and away from his plans for the afternoon.

'It will have to be cleared. The cedar of Lebanon will be happier standing on its own. The pleasure gardens will be restored to their former glory.'

'That will take a long time.' Diana's head was turned resolutely away from him. Her shoulders were set. 'It takes years to make a garden. It is not a harum-scarum thing accomplished in a few weeks and then off to London.'

'Time I have. I intend to live here once the new house is built. There is an aspect overlooking the Tyne that I particularly favour.' He touched her elbow, supporting her over a rough patch of ground. 'It will be done properly. I want your advice about the grotto and which motifs should be painted on the inner walls.'

She gently moved her arm and her body away. He fought his instinct and allowed her to go. 'I think you will need to do more than slap paint on the rock to restore this garden. That is all.'

A small gasp came from Diana's throat as she scrambled over the last few remaining boulders to reveal the grotto. A small weed-choked stream emerged from the mouth of a substantial cave. Nettles and brambles formed a curtain over the entrance.

'It has possibilities. Surely you must see that.' Brett mentally cringed. He hated the pleading note that had escaped from his throat.

'Possibilities, hmmm.' She walked away from him,

tilting her head from one side to the other. 'Certainly it does want love and attention. The whole estate is crying out for it.'

Brett regarded the tumbled stones and muddy stream. He wanted her to see it as he saw it—the possibilities, rather than the depressing reality. A test of sorts. Could she look beyond the practicalities? Could she taste the dream? Her blue-green eyes became even deeper pools that Brett wanted to drown in. He shook himself and forced his voice to remain bland.

'You have a talent and an artistic eye. I merely seek to use them for my own ends.'

'And I merely do it for the pleasure of it. I claim no expertise.'

She tiptoed closer to the edge and peered into the cave. The thin material of her dress clearly outlined her bottom—round, tight. Appetising. Brett allowed his eyes to wander over it, to linger as she peered first this way and that. 'You do yourself a disservice. What I have seen is entirely satisfactory.'

'You are right. It could do with painting, or maybe an actual shell border. I have heard of several houses with shell-patterned borders. Little shells, carefully placed.'

'It sounds time consuming.' Brett forced his mind from pondering the exact shape of her bottom and how it would feel in his hands. He had to remain casual. She seemed more nervous than ever today as her hand straightened and re-straightened her bonnet, an overblown confection of silk flowers and ribbons and straw. Fashionable, he supposed, but it hid her glorious dark hair.

'Time consuming? Yes, but it does have the most marvellous effect—a sort of jewel-like quality with the water and the light.' Diana waved a hand towards the grotto. 'Shells would make this spot very romantic.'

'Would you be placing the shells?' Brett kept his voice steady. Willed her to answer yes. Willed her to agree to having reasons to visit him.

She regarded the cave walls for a long time, her finger tapping against her mouth. He could almost see the pictures painting themselves in her mind. Waited with bated breath for her verdict.

'I could do it, but it would take some time,' she said finally, breaking the silence. 'Perhaps it would be better if you employed someone, someone who knew what they were doing.'

'I have faith in you. You can do anything you set your mind to. You waltzed beautifully last night.'

'Easy words.' Her laugh spilled from her throat.

'Perhaps you don't have faith in yourself.' His fingers closed around her upper arm and he breathed in her scent of lavender and soap. A far more intoxicating combination than other women's perfume. He willed her to remain there, close by his side. 'Trust your instincts.'

'I am not sure I can.' Diana's words were no more than a breath. 'Brett, help me, please.'

Diana felt his hand rest lightly upon her shoulder, the merest whisper of a caress, but she knew it was there. He stood inches from her. Waiting. The urge to turn around became a compulsion.

All her admonitions of last night and this morning, all her promises and resolutions faded like mere wisps of morning cloud. She needed this. She was born for this—out here next to this grotto with its impossibly choked stream and hidden romance. She was drawn to him like a moth to a flame despite the certainty of being singed. It only mattered that he was here and he wanted to kiss her. She wondered if she dared to take a risk. She knew she wanted to, knew that she could not live with the thought that it only might have been.

Abruptly and without warning, his hands turned her. She met his mouth full on. Warm, soft and seeking. His lips roamed over her face, pressing small kisses against her mouth and her eyes. Each touch sent a tremor along her body, stoking a fire within her.

Finally, his mouth returned to hers and his tongue traced the outline of her lips. First around the outside, delicately, and then along the crease, demanding entrance. A slow but thorough exploration. Her lips opened under the onslaught and she drank from his mouth, lifting her hand to curl around the back of his head to bring his lips and tongue closer. She needed them closer.

Cool, sweet languor filled her as his tongue penetrated her mouth. Slow and lazy, but then with an increased urgency. There was a difference from the last time. In the summer house, the kiss had a finite quality, but today, it promised secret glades along pathways of pleasure. Paths that beckoned and urged her forward. Unhurried and leisurely exploration.

Her body arched towards his, moulding itself against the hard muscles. His hand fastened on to her waist, crushed her to him. He pressed small kisses along the corners of her mouth, her eyes and her temple, small nibbles that sent little pulses leaping throughout her body, warming her, making her yearn for something more. His mouth recaptured hers, devoured her. This was what it was like to be thoroughly and utterly kissed.

Diana shifted as he fitted their bodies together. Pressed against her and ignited a fiery hail of sparks that leapt and danced. Her world had come down to this—his mouth touching hers, his hand, his body. Him. Only a few thin layers of material separated them. She shifted again and his hand slid over her backside, held it there. Firmly. The point of her meeting him.

She gasped and clung on to the one straw of sanity she had left, wrenching her mouth away from his.

'You see what you do to me,' he growled in her ear.

She drew back slightly and looked up into his hooded eyes. Slate grey, now alight with a fire burning deep within. And she could feel an answering fire build within her. 'We are friends. Friends.'

'We went past friendship days ago.' Brett's voice was ragged and his breath came fast. But he stepped away from her. 'I'd be lying if I said differently. You would be lying if you denied it. You knew what would happen if you came out here. You wanted this as much as I did.'

'And what do you want?' She brushed a hand across her mouth, tried to ignore the aching points of her breasts. Tried to ignore the burning inside and found the task too hard.

His hands reached for her again, pulled her against him, the apex of her thigh meeting him. 'You.'

The word sent a delicious shiver down her back. Diana discovered she could not think beyond the shape of his mouth or the pressure of his hand on her waist. Her limbs appeared incapable of moving. Her tongue flicked over her suddenly dry lips wetting them, anticipating another onslaught of his mouth. He lifted an eyebrow and blew a cool stream of air across her lips. The coolness contrasted with the fevered heat of her skin and made her yearn all the more.

She swallowed hard and tried to concentrate on something other than the growing tide of heat that built within her. She had to be sensible and consider what could happen. She forced her feet to move.

'And I have no say in this? You are simply going to take?

To plunder like a pirate?' She barely recognised her voice. Husky, breathless.

He placed his finger under her chin and raised her head so she was staring into his deep grey gaze. 'We stop when you say stop. I wish to bring you pleasure. No force. Never force. But be warned, once you say stop, it ends. All this ends.'

He withdrew his hands from her. Her body howled in protest. A great longing grew within her. She needed to have his lips against hers again. She wanted him to kiss her with that hunger.

'I understand.' She forced her gaze to meet his. A peace settled over her. She could do this. She trusted him to keep his word. They would kiss and that would be all.

'We go at your pace, Diana. But once we stop, we stop. I do not play the tease.'

'But the servants…what if we are discovered?' Diana tried to step away but his fingers twisted around hers and held her still. Gently, but firmly. A hot molten surge coursed through her, far more potent than anything that had gone before. She willed him to understand. It was not simple for her.

'We won't be. I gave orders that we were not to be disturbed.' His voice was low and slid over her like velvet. She tried to tell herself that he was a master seducer, but her body paid no heed. His look was for her and her alone. It had to be.

'Rose will pay no attention to your orders.' She pulled her hand away and kept her head high. 'She will come soon, worried.'

'She will not trouble herself. She will be drinking and sitting with her feet up.' His hand caught hers, his thumb circling on her wrist, distracting her. 'If she disapproved, she would have never told me you were in the summer house that day. She has done her best to foster this.'

'She had no call to be so brazen.' Diana felt her cheeks begin to burn. 'I never asked her to be. You must believe that.'

'I thanked her for it.' His words stroked like silk over her skin. 'And I will thank her again if she remains tucked up in the kitchen.' He paused, tilting his head to one side. 'Or we could go back and ring for a cup of tea. My cook won't thank you for interrupting their gossip, though. After all the trouble she went to, to prepare the food. You could at least take a glimpse.'

'I…' Diana's voice trailed away. One by one he had demolished her arguments. The first time she had truly put her resolutions and rules to a test, and they had failed her. Maybe she hadn't wanted to try very hard. Maybe she was wicked and wanton and all those things that people had called her five years ago. But she worried that if she went back, she might never sample his lips again. 'I could stay for a while longer. Explore the cave. Measurements should be taken. I will have to know the approximate number of shells that will be needed and the types you might prefer.'

Brett waved a hand. 'The picnic is here and the servants set it up. They brought the table from storage and the under-housemaid raided the garden for the last of the Michaelmas daisies. I was most particular. Come and take a look and see if it does not whet your appetite.'

'You seem awfully certain that I would come out here.'

'Hopeful. There is a difference.'

Diana bit her lip. Reason warred with desire. She wanted to be with him.

'It would be a shame to waste it. The servants will talk

if we don't eat. You should try the seed cake. One little taste.'

Diana attempted to think of a coherent answer, but his fingers had recaptured her wrist. They swept tantalizingly along her skin, caressing the underside of her wrist. Soft, silky, sultry, but entirely innocent. The fire that his kisses had stoked seemed to leap up, but she knew if she said anything that he'd simply lift one eyebrow. She pulled her hand away, covered it with her other one. A small smile tugged at his lips.

Diana held back the words asking what precisely he hoped to gain from this. She knew he wouldn't lie. What he offered held no strings. As long as there were no consequences, no one would question. She understood how society rules operated in these cases.

She drew a deep breath, stood poised on the brink for a moment longer and then plunged. 'I should like to see the picnic.'

'You will not be disappointed. I asked Cook to prepare all of the delicacies—pork pies, potted cheese, salmagundi salad and even a rich seed cake.' Brett rubbed his hands together. 'And I must say Cook's seed cakes are delicious. I have become quite partial to them.'

It was a picnic. A real picnic. Not the wild seduction she had imagined. She wanted to laugh. Had she really expected anything different?

'You make it sound tempting.' Diana forced her shoulders to relax. She could control her body and, for this one day, she wanted to be with him. Nothing would happen if she did not want it to. She trusted him. 'I have not had potted cheese since…since before London.'

'You will enjoy the picnic.' His eyes turned serious and his fingers gave hers one last squeeze, then let go. 'And,

Diana, we return to the house when you say the word. You are in charge.'

She followed him around to the side of the grotto. There in a sunlit grass hollow, a table with chairs had been placed. A starched white linen cloth lay over the table protecting it. With a flourish, Brett lifted the cloth and revealed the picnic. As promised, cold meat pies vied with salads and little pots of shrimp. A bowl full of late season fruits sat in the very centre—blackberries, apples and pears. The seed cake stood on its own little pedestal. There was even a crystal pitcher full of lemonade with mint floating on the top. The sort of picnic one might serve a maiden aunt. She gave him a quick glance under her eyelashes. Her stays felt far too tight.

'Does the picnic not please you?'

'I had thought it would be more…' She looked at her hands. She could hardly confess to secretly hoping for a bottle of wine and a blanket on the ground. Maybe grapes. She had thought him the consummate rake, but nothing here screamed seduction. It was all so ordinary. 'It is lovely, Brett. Thank you for thinking of it. Every single detail has been looked after.'

'Everything is done properly.' He pulled out a chair. 'If you would care to take your seat, we can begin. I find walking works up an appetite.'

'It looks perfectly splendid, particularly the seed cake.' A lump grew in her throat. 'I can't think when anyone took so much trouble over my pleasure.'

'It is *my pleasure* to look after you.'

A lock of hair fell across his forehead. Without allowing her mind time to react, she reached forward and smoothed it away. His fingers curled over hers, held them there for an instant, then let go. He undid the ribbons of her bonnet and lowered it to the ground.

'I wouldn't want it to get crushed.' Then he pulled off her gloves, finger by finger. Repeated the gesture with his. 'Nor have these mussed.'

She started to speak, but he put his finger to her lips and drew her to him again.

'Bonnets are a nuisance. And gloves can get soiled.' His breath tickled her ear, sending a fresh wave of heat through her. 'You should not have to worry about the sun. The table is in the shade.'

His hands cupped the back of her head and he lowered his mouth. 'Good enough to eat.'

'Brett,' she whispered as his breath once more touched her lips, made her remember.

'Enough talking for now.'

Hot. Insistent. His lips plundered hers with a carnal desire. No longer seeking, but demanding. Demanding a response, a response her body was only too ready to give. Her arms went around him, held him there. Her body touching his.

His steady fingers undid her pelisse and pushed it off her shoulders. 'You looked warm in it.'

His lips travelled lower, nibbling at the column of her throat and then tracing a line down to her lace fichu. Grazing her skin. A wave of molten heat washed over her.

The lace fell to the ground unheeded as his mouth traced the neckline of her gown. Her breasts grew full and strained against the confines of her stays. He cupped them with his hands, gently rubbed his knuckles over the cloth and smiled as the nipples puckered. Her back arched, seeking his touch. Wave after wave of sensation racked her, leaving her knees weak. Her hands came up and buried themselves in his thick crisp hair. She held on for support. Her fingers traced the outline of his ear.

'May I?' he whispered. 'Please?'

Beyond speech, she inclined her head, wondering what she had agreed to. She only knew that she wanted him to continue. She could not bear it if he stopped. His hands slipped beneath the cloth, stroking her fevered skin. A featherlight touch. And the already tight nipples hardened further.

A gasp came from her throat and she teetered on the brink of an abyss. Teetered and then fell as his fingers explored the outlines of her breasts. Her hands clutched his shoulder for support. Her body sought the comfort of his.

'Do you like this?' She could only nod in agreement as her eyes watched how his hands moved over and under her breasts. He leant forwards. His breath fanned her ear. 'You will like this more. I promise.'

She wet her lips with her tongue and tried to think of a sensible answer as his fingers found her nipples again. Catching them between his thumb and forefinger, he rolled them. Pleasure thrummed through her. And she knew she was powerless to stop. She needed this. Everything. Here. Now.

'Yes,' she breathed and then her body convulsed.

'Shall I stop?' He deliberately withdrew his hands, held them hovering over her breast. Tantalisingly close. If she breathed deeply, they would rise, and graze his palm. She tried and his hands moved upwards. 'To touch or not to touch.'

She shook her head. 'Are you planning on tormenting me?'

'For as long as possible.' His lips traced a line down her throat, stopping where her bodice kissed her skin. They slipped under the cloth and touched her naked flesh. Warm. Hot. Sensuous touches. Slowly he repeated the manoeuvre. Her hands reached up and buried themselves in his crisp hair. Each tiny movement sent shooting sparks through her body.

'I...'

'Hush.'

With one swift movement, he pulled her bodice down and freed one breast from its confines. Nestled it in his palm. 'Perfect.'

His hot breath touched her tightly furled nipple and then his cool tongue traced its edges, sampling. Finally his mouth sucked, taking the whole of the dusky rose areola inside. Her whole body became infused with heat. Her knees gave way and she knew the only thing keeping her upright was his hands on her waist. The ache that had been growing inside her opened into a throb, became insistent and she knew she needed something more than this. And all the while his tongue swirled and suckled at her breast.

An inarticulate noise sounded in the back of her throat. He lifted his head. One hand smoothed an errant curl off her now bare shoulder. 'This is only the first course.'

'There is more than one course?'

'There is always more than one.' He scooped her up and deposited her on the linen cloth that had covered the table and now lay in the crisp grass. He knelt beside her. She lifted her hands and loosened his neck cloth. Her fingers fumbled slightly, but he allowed her to take it off.

'I want to give you pleasure. Always.' He kissed the side of her neck.

She tried not to think that *always* was a debatable term. 'I can't think beyond the next breath.'

His hands stroked down her side and caught the hem of her gown, revealing her white stockings and lace drawers. She was exposed to the cool afternoon sun. His eyes roamed down her body. 'Very prettily arranged. Remain still. I want to savour the feast.'

'Aren't you overdressed?' She hardly recognised her own voice.

'Only if my lady thinks so.' He shrugged out of his coat. The whiteness of his shirt contrasted with the darkness of his hair. He himself propped up on an elbow, regarding her with an amused expression. 'Anything else?'

Giving into instinct, she pressed her lips to the triangle at the base of his throat. Felt the tempo of his heartbeat with her tongue. She withdrew and then tasted again, sampling the sultry smooth skin.

Her hands pulled at his shirt, freeing it from his breeches. She lifted it and ran her fingers along his smooth skin and felt the power of his muscles tremble beneath her fingertips.

He rolled over, on top of her. It felt right, and she could feel the strength of his arousal moving against her hips. She lifted her body to meet the welcome weight of him. His lips reclaimed hers and her body rose to meet the force of his arousal as it hit the apex of her thighs. He nuzzled and suckled until her body was racked with need. Her head thrashed and her hands sought him, but he thrust them away.

'Patience has its own reward.'

His fingers continued inexorably downwards, pushing aside the thin folds of her drawers, weaving between the gap in the material and burying themselves in her nest of curls. She gasped as his finger slid inside her. He stroked one shuddering stroke. Withdrew. Returned again, deeper this time. Her hips lifted.

'Tight. You are so tight,' he murmured. 'I dreamt of this. You, innocent beneath me.'

'Brett…' Her hands pressed against his chest, intending to push him away, but she found her arms had not the strength. A sudden dark panic filled her. He would discover her secret. She should tell him first, but she couldn't bear the look in his eyes when he knew. And she wanted this. This was so very different from... She summoned all her courage. 'I...'

His fingers stilled, lifted. 'Shall I stop? Or do we go on to the next course.'

She wet her lips and tried once more. 'Brett...'

'Hush,' he whispered and his mouth returned to hers. His tongue mimicked the play of his fingers and she felt the hot need grow within her. Consume her.

Her hands slipped under his shirt and found the smooth muscles of his chest. She rubbed her fingers across his nipples and heard his breathing become ragged. He reached down, guided her hand to his erection. Instinctively she curled her hand around it. Hot. Hard but smooth. 'See what you are doing to me? I want to be inside you.'

Desire flooded through her. Was it so wrong of her to want this? She reached up and cradled his face between her hands, looking him directly in the eye. 'Yes.'

He raised his body up and positioned himself between her thighs. She felt a nudge and he slid in a little way. He stopped and his eyes flew to hers. He started to pull away, but she raised her hips, keeping him inside her. Slowly he went further. Then suddenly as if he could bear it no longer, he fully entered her.

She stiffened, remembering the previous horridness. The dark hole of her memory opened up and threatened to swallowed her. She waited for the pain, then noticed he had stopped moving.

'Did I hurt you?'

Silently she shook her head, hating the sudden rush of

shame. He must have guessed. Did he know what she was? What had been done to her? She breathed again.

'It will get better. Relax, sweetheart.'

'I am trying.' Her laugh sounded halfway between a sob and a cry.

His lips brushed her temple. Softly. Beguilingly. Flooding her with warmth at his unexpected tenderness. 'All will be well. I want you too much to stop.'

He began to move within her and she forgot everything as the waves of pleasure increased. Increased and then crested. Her hips began to move in time with his. Inside her, she felt him slide, and knew she had to move faster. A cry was torn from her throat and she heard his answer.

Much later, Brett looked down at Diana. Her long lashes lay dark against the cream of her skin. She had fallen asleep in his arms. He had not known what to expect, but she had exceeded all his expectations.

He made a wry face. From her kisses, he'd expected a virgin, but her response showed she had been inexpertly taken. He could well imagine the lies she had been told. And her reaction to the truth. She had not worn the caps and the awful gowns to mourn the man, but to hide from men. Somehow, he had succeeded in breaking through her defences and unwrapping the passionate woman underneath.

His insides twisted and he hated the way he had seduced her. When she had kissed him by the grotto, his earlier plan of a light romance had vanished, buried beneath the overwhelming need to touch her and to possess her fully. Luckily, she had responded with passion. He wanted to think the passion was for him and him alone.

She would forget other men. He might not have been the first, but he *would be* the last.

Mentally, he rehearsed his speech. He had never been tempted to say the words before and he wanted them to be right. He imagined her joy when she discovered he was prepared to give up the habit of a lifetime to marry her. He would ask, but properly. He wanted her to know that his decision was not spur of the moment, that he had not sought to irrevocably bind her to him. Everything was going to be done properly. He would show her the absolute respect she deserved. He needed her in his life with an intensity that scared him. Earlier, when he planned this picnic, he had convinced himself that if this did happen, it would be enough to break the spell. He knew now that it would never be enough.

He stood up, dressed, planned every move, every word and then placed a kiss on her temple. 'Time to stir, sweetheart.'

Her eyes flew open. She stretched her arms above her head. The temptress personified. His body leapt in response. And he knew he wanted her again, that he would never tire of her.

'I thought perhaps it was a dream.'

'No dream. Reality. Very much a reality.'

'But it remains our secret. Never to be mentioned again.' She brought her knees up to her chest and peeped at him through a curtain of hair. Her voice held a faint wobble of sadness. Her eyes showed a bruised vulnerability, a wariness that had not been there before. They became wild with some emotion that he could not recognise. 'You must promise me that. Swear it, Brett! Swear on your horses and all your carriages!'

'I shall not be telling anyone. I would never treat you like that.' Brett looked at her, perplexed. She gave a sigh and her eyes turned to ice. He ran a hand through his hair. This was not how the conversation was supposed go. He swallowed hard and tried a different tack. 'That is to say, it should remain between us. A happy memory. Something to be cherished.'

'Good.' She scrambled up and began to rearrange her clothes. Rapidly she covered her long limbs, and retrieved her bonnet, tying it with expert fingers. 'No one interrupted us. No one knows. There is no need for anyone to know. We go on as before.'

Brett stared at her. He resisted the urge to run his hand through his hair. He wasn't quite sure what he had expected. Tears, maybe. Recriminations. But not this matter-of-fact attitude. He had no wish to go on as before. What had passed between them had changed everything. She had to understand. They had no choice. They would marry. She would be his wife.

'We shared something more than friendship. I am not adverse to this happening again.' He gave a half-smile and willed her to understand.

'And I agreed.' Her hands stilled on the ribbons of her bonnet. 'I am no green girl, Brett. We are both adults. You are past thirty and I gave up any expectation of marriage long ago. What is between us lasts for as long as it lasts.'

The gods must be laughing at him. For the first time in his life, he was prepared to do the decent thing and she had refused him even before he'd said the words. He narrowed his lips and silently cursed. To say anything now would be churlish. It would sound ungracious.

'What shall we tell the servants? The food is untouched.'

'It is none of their business.' She walked swiftly over to the picnic. With a few deft movements, she had scattered food. 'They will assume we had a pleasant repast. Now, shall we go? I have no wish to worry Rose.'

Brett resisted the impulse to sweep her into his arms. Patience. 'As you wish.'

'I do.'

'And, Diana, next time, it will be in a bed with white linen sheets. Properly and with all the time in the world.'

Myriad emotions crossed her face. Her mouth opened and closed several times. 'I sincerely doubt that.'

'Diana, wait. We need to talk. To plan.'

'To get the details of the story right? As you said, you are an expert at these sorts of picnics. You need not worry. I too know the value of silence and discretion.'

He watched her skirts swish as she walked quickly away, painfully aware that somehow, somewhere, he had lost control of the situation.

Chapter Twelve

What had she done? What had she done? Coward. Coward. Coward. With each turn of the wheel, the gig seemed to speak the words over and over. She had lied to Brett. Diana knew that. She did not want a hole-in-the-corner affair. She wanted something more, but, above that, she wanted him. She wanted him to look at her with favour.

Did that make her wicked and wanton?

She feared it did. But the alternative was too frightening—forcing Brett to marry her, even presuming he could be forced. She could not bear to think of his eyes looking at her with disgust.

She had tried to outrun her fate. She had made promises. She had confined her life to a set of rules, but it had not been life. Merely an existence. And she wanted to live. There was joy in being alive.

Diana laid her cheek against the cool leather and watched the changing leaves of the trees roll by.

'Are you going to tell me about the picnic Lord Coltonby had prepared for you?' Rose asked, settling her basket more firmly in her lap. 'Cook told me of the splendid delicacies she had prepared. Enough to tempt the most delicate appetite. I told her that my lady has a hardy appetite.'

Diana struggled to sit up, every nerve instantly alert. She had managed to keep her secret from Rose before. 'The picnic was wonderful. The cook excelled herself.'

'And you still want to deny that he is courting you?'

'He wanted advice on painting the grotto.' Diana kept her eyes on the passing landscape. The gig had reached the relative safety of the drive and she could see the tops of the chimneys. What happened back at Ladywell Park seemed remote and unconnected to the safety that her house always represented.

'The grotto? Why would he want that tumbled-down heap of rocks painted?' Rose made a tutting noise in the back of her throat. 'The ways of the gentry are a mystery to me.'

'Lord Coltonby wants to restore the pleasure garden. He plans on having Ladywell Park as his principal seat. He believes it perfect for a stud farm.'

'It sounds like a man whose thoughts have turned towards marriage and responsibility. I should wager that he has more on his mind than breeding horses.'

Diana delicately covered her mouth with her hand, deliberately hiding her expression. She did not even want to think about breeding. She had to assume that all would be well. And if there should be any consequences, then she would deal with them sensibly. She knew that coupling did not result in a child every time. She knew that from experience.

'Or perhaps he is simply a man tired for a brief time of London's delights.'

'And London's delights are not so great that they hold everyone. You returned to Northumberland. I remain here with you even though I was born with the sound of the great bell of Bow ringing in my ears.'

'No doubt the lure of London's fleshpots will re-exert their pull. He is a man, and has no family responsibilities.'

'You are being cynical, Miss Diana.'

'Am I?' Diana forced her lips to smile. She was not going to think about what had happened before. She wanted to believe that Brett was different from all the other rakes. Her heart whispered that he was, but she did not dare hope. 'Sir Cuthbert could not bear to be away from London.'

'Lord Coltonby is cut from a different cloth. I said as much to Mr Hunt earlier, I did. He should be grateful for such a good master, instead of grumbling about the extra work.'

'Sweet Rose. You are always quick to defend your favourites, even though I am not sure what Lord Coltonby has done to deserve your regard.' Diana reached out and clutched Rose's hand and gave it a squeeze.

Rose patted her hand. 'You were gone a long while. It stands to reason that Lord Coltonby is not simply wanting advice on where to put his bedding plants. Or painting.'

'We enjoyed the many dishes. Lord Coltonby swears by seed cake.' Diana forced a lightness into her voice. Prevarication would become easier in time.

'I had wondered what was keeping you. Lord Coltonby's valet kept me engaged in conversation. Every time I mentioned you, he had some little quip to tell, or told me that I had to try a little bit more of the seed cake.' Rose patted her stomach. 'He even gave me a glass of the port, the one Lord Coltonby saves for best. Mr Hunt did glower at us, but it was ever so pleasant.'

A trembling overtook Diana. The valet had clearly known what Brett was about. So Brett had enlisted his aid. The whole seduction had been planned down to the last detail! It was five years ago all over again.

She stared determinedly out the window, willing the carriage to arrive at the stables so she did not have to endure Rose's chatter. Then she paused and drew a deep calming breath. She refused to give way to panic. She would never again be the pathetic creature she had once turned into.

'Are you cold, Miss Diana? Perhaps having an outdoor picnic in the autumn was not the wisest of ideas. I will draw you a hot bath when we get to the house. That will soon put you to right.'

A bath. Diana glanced quickly at Rose and then back out at the parkland. A bath. Five years ago, it had been what she had needed. Scrubbing her skin until it was raw. She had felt soiled—inside and out.

This time, it was very different. That great unyielding emptiness that had been part of her for such a long time had gone and in its place was a steady light, growing with each breath she took. For the first time since she had returned to Northumberland, the world appeared to be bathed in a radiant glow. Or was she simply looking at it with new eyes?

She reached over and gave Rose's hand a squeeze. 'Thank you for caring, and for being you.'

Rose gave a sniff. 'Can't see how I could be anyone else.'

'Oh, Rose, you are long suffering.' Diana laughed, loud and long.

'It is good to hear you laugh like that again, miss. I am fair certain that I can't remember the last time I heard that sound.'

'It was a while ago, Rose. A very long while ago.'

Diana listened to the hooves of her horse pound the earth. This morning, she had woken and known she had to

ride. Fast. Furious. Away from the dreams that haunted her
sleep. Away from the knowledge that Brett, having experienced her charms once, was in no rush to experience them
again. It bothered her that she wanted him, that she had
been woken by a nameless longing. It was not merely to
touch him again, but to hear his voice and see his smile.

Her feelings went beyond mere attraction, and it frightened her, just as it exhilarated her. It was as if all her resolutions, all the tenets that she had lived by the last five years
suddenly counted for nothing. The only thing she knew
was that no man would ever hold her in his power again.
She would be the mistress of her own fate. She would never
be forced into a marriage of duty, or one-sided attraction.
She was free.

She urged Merlin forwards, faster.

She had declined the use of a groom, intending to go
no further than the ice house, but it had not been nearly
far enough. Now, she allowed Merlin his head and they
raced past the copse, the home pasture and on up to the hill
towards the gap in the fence that led to Ladywell Park.

She turned Merlin's head and started up the long hill.
At the top, the entire valley lay at her feet, with the Tyne
snaking through like a silver rope. In the distance she could
vaguely make out the buildings of the Ladywell Colliery.
Familiar objects in a familiar, unchanging landscape. Diana
breathed in the cool air, savouring the moment. It steadied
her.

Another horse gave a soft whinny. Instantly her nerves
stiffened. Was she ready for this? How would he react,
seeing her again? All the pleasure in the ride vanished as
if it had never been at all, leaving behind a tight feeling in
her stomach.

'I wondered when you would make it up here.' Brett
came from the spinney of trees, leading his stallion. He

looped the reins about a slender branch and, leaving the horse, started towards her, catching Merlin's bridle with ease.

'How did you know I would come here?' she asked, her breath catching in her throat. Was she that painfully obvious?

'I saw you earlier, riding with your hair streaming behind you.' A faint smile touched his lips, giving him a saturnine look.

'I could have been riding anywhere. It was merely happenstance that I came up here.'

'You described this view to me. You wanted me to be here.' Brett's voice was low. 'It is even more magical than you described, watching the sunrise over the hills.'

'I am flattered that you remembered.' Diana attempted a haughty disdain. She could rebuild the walls around her heart. She could protect that vulnerable bit of her, and ignore the part that kept whispering about his sincerity.

'Some things are worth remembering. Views like the one I had this morning make life worth living. They provide a balm to the soul.'

'Does my soul need a balm?' She tilted her head and glanced up at him through her lashes.

'You were riding as if all the demons in the world were after you.' His face sobered. 'I promise you, Diana, you are safe with me. I am willing to be your champion. Trust me.'

'No, not demons,' Diana said slowly. 'I was revelling in the joy of being alive. It was like I had sleep-walked through my life for years and suddenly I had wakened to find this most marvellous world.'

A silence fell between them, unbroken except for Merlin's quiet chomping. She noticed that Brett's eyes had circles under them as if he had not slept. How long had he been here? Since before sunrise? Waiting for her? She wanted to reject the notion as fancy, but somehow it seemed to grow and take root, refusing to be suppressed.

'You came to see the view. But did you come also to see me?' She hated the way her voice trembled. Hated her need to hear him say the words. Men like Brett scorned ties or obligations.

'I was waiting to be asked.' His voice held an oddly humble note.

'You may consider yourself asked, then. I want to see you,' she whispered. Some day she would have to explain about the past, but not today. She wanted to enjoy this feeling for as long as it lasted.

He took the reins from her hands and looped them around the tree so that Merlin was tethered.

Fastening his hands around her waist, Brett lifted her down from Merlin. Her body slid against his. 'Aren't you going to kiss me good morning?'

He bent his head and Diana tasted his lips. It was gentle and lingering. Her arms rose and fastened around his neck. The kiss rapidly deepened, calling to something deep within her. With all her heart, she wanted to be the girl she had been five years ago. She wanted yesterday to have been her first time. But it wasn't. And she had no idea how he'd react to the truth.

His lips trailed down the column of her throat, placing soft kisses that tantalised her. The embers within her body flared into life and she realised the fire she had thought doused had merely slumbered. Her body arched forward, seeking more contact with his. She attempted to hang on to sanity. The truth lay between them. If she never told him, it would hang there, making everything ugly. She prayed that the disgust would not be too terrible, but she had to say the words.

'Brett, what are you doing?'

'Your skin tastes like the morning dew,' he murmured, cupping her face between his hands. Delicately his tongue traced her lips. Lingered. 'No, I was wrong—sunshine mixed with dew.'

'You spout easy words.'

He moved his lips to her temple. 'What do you want? Shall I stop and go away?'

Go away? Her body protested at the thought. She looked up into his eyes, saw the deep grey pools. 'What are you asking me?'

'I can feel a change in you, and it scares me…'

His breathing was ragged and he placed his hands on her shoulders. She looked up into his eyes. In another instant, he would put her away from him and would return to his horse. It was the last thing she wanted, and she was horrified at her reaction. Shaken to the core. And then, not horrified.

'Diana?'

Her answer was to pull his face back towards hers, her hands digging into his hair, holding him there. 'Kiss me, Brett. Kiss me like you did before.'

He groaned and lowered his mouth. Their tongues teased each other, tangling, touching and retreating only to tangle again. The fire within her flamed into carnal desire. Dark. Dangerous. All the more potent because she knew what would happen, out here with no one about. Knew and wanted it. Her body arched towards his again.

He lifted his head and stared down at her for a long time. This time, his hands pushed her from him, created a wall of air between them.

'Enough.'

'Enough?' she said, and something within her died. She ducked her head. Her lips tingled from the onslaught. She touched a hand to her lips and tried to ignore her aching swollen breasts. 'Enough? How can that be enough?'

'If we continue, I will have your skirts over your head and your back against the oak tree. And that won't do either of us any good.'

'It is a thought. Certainly.' She glanced over her shoulder at the tree. A curl of heat infused her. She knew he intended to make her pause, but pausing meant she would have to confess, would have to ruin this fragile new thing between them. She lifted her arms, held them out to him.

'You are a witch, you know that?'

'No, not a witch. A woman. A woman who has slumbered and now has come alive.'

'Very much alive.' He caught her about her waist and pulled her to him, moulding her body to his. Despite the heaviness of her riding habit, his hard arousal pressed against her thighs, making her wriggle. 'But you deserve more than that. You deserve better.'

She glanced at the oak. 'Would it be so bad, so terribly wicked?'

He gave a low husky laugh that sent ripples along her nerves. 'No, and some day, I promise you, we shall do that. Me filling you, with the rose-gold sunrise erupting all around us. My body worshipping yours.'

'But not today?' Diana bit her lip and tried to banish the pagan image his words had conjured. 'Is the sun too high in the sky?'

'I intend to make this right.' He turned his face away from the oak. 'I promised you a soft bed with linen sheets.'

Diana wrapped her arms about her waist. She knew she was not ready for a small house in some anonymous market town, giving up Robert and Simon. 'I thought we would be discreet.'

'What is indiscreet about a bed?' A smile tugged at his lips.

'That would be far too risky. People might discover us. There would be consequences. Not only for me or you, but for my family.' She forced the words from her throat. 'Servants talk, no matter what. Such things do not remain secrets for long.'

His fingers went under her chin and lifted it up. His eyes searched hers. Then he let her go. 'You don't trust me.'

'I know what happens. It is always the woman who falls.' She gave a little shrug. There were all sorts of trust. 'I desire you, but fear the scandal.'

'And if there was no scandal, what then?' He ran a hand down her back. 'The bed I am thinking of will have no one whispering or withdrawing their skirts.'

Her breath stopped in her throat. She could almost believe that he was speaking of marriage. Her insides trembled and then she rejected the notion firmly. It was beyond the realms of possibility. She gave a small laugh. 'You mean the shepherd's hut in the spinney. I suppose it does have a pallet. I should have guessed.'

His lips thinned and his eyes grew hard. 'I mean the marriage bed, Diana. What happened yesterday may have consequences and I am no cad. It is my duty.'

She went ice cold. The marriage bed. He didn't want to marry, he hadn't professed undying love. Duty. He had made the offer because he felt an obligation. She had to tell him the truth. She steeled herself and searched for the right words.

'We agreed that marriage was not for either one of us,' she said in a small voice.

'Ideas can change.' He reached out and interlaced her fingers with his. 'What would be wrong with a marriage between us? We suit. I must marry at some point to produce an heir and why not you?'

Diana broke away. She crossed her arms about her waist. She had hated the thought of marriage to him when it would have been only duty on his part. Duty provided little comfort in the night. She could not bear it if she had to watch his desire turn to disgust once he saw the awful ugliness that resided deep within her. 'Let's speak no more of marriage in jest.'

His face grew dark. 'I am serious.'

'As was I, when I said that I would not marry.' With each syllable, her voice grew stronger and steadier. She was saying the right things, choosing the correct path. 'You did not coerce me into what passed between us. I knew what I was doing. I had no expectations of an offer. You may rest easy.'

'After what happened, it is my duty. You are a gently bred woman. Cosseted. Cared for. Protected.' Brett stood very straight and pronounced each word with care, as if they had been rehearsed and only emerged with great pain.

Diana winced. The gates of her mind broke open and memories of the other time flooded over her. The pawing hands. The heavy unwelcome breathing in her ear and the pain. All happening while her chaperon had sat, eating and drinking but a few hundred yards from her and the fireworks had burst overhead. She had cried out, but the explosion had swallowed her cries. She forced the gate of her mind closed. Breathed.

She wrapped her arms about her waist, shaking, unable to face the scorn he must have for her. Unable to show the ugliness that she knew must be in her face. 'I was not an innocent virgin.'

'Diana.' His voice was thick, almost unrecognisable.

'You are still an innocent. You possess little knowledge about what passes between a man and a woman. I can tell the difference.' He put his hand on her shoulder. 'Confide in me. Help me to understand.'

'It happened at Vauxhall Gardens,' she whispered. 'One time. I wanted to see the fireworks. I loved fireworks in those days. My chaperon stayed behind. She hadn't finished her supper. He had always been so polite, so correct. He had kissed me once on my cheek. I never thought. We had only gone a short way down a darkened path and a rocket went up, lighting the whole sky. I turned to see it. He kissed me, forced his tongue between my lips, called me a tease. His breath stank of drink. I broke free, but he caught me again with rougher hands. Told me I was a flirt.'

Her throat closed and a deep shudder went through her. She waited to see his disgust, but he squeezed her shoulder, warm steady fingers that somehow cut through the chill. She swallowed hard, regained her composure and then continued.

'His hands were hard. Roaming all over my body. Touching me where no one had ever touched me before. I begged and pleaded, but he seemed to like my fright. It made him more… He threw me to the ground and pinned me there with my skirts over my head. All the while, the rockets were going off. I could hear people's excited shouts and gasps. I yelled, but nobody came. It hurt such a lot.'

She put her hands to her face.

'What were you wearing that night? Your ivory dress?' His voice was cold, deadly. His hands clenched at his sides. 'Was it the night before you became engaged? Is that why your brother agreed to the marriage?'

She shook her head, unable to understand why he had asked. 'I wore my white dress with a lavender net. I cut it up into small bits and fed them to the fire when I returned

home. All except one piece, which became the lining of
my first cap. Why do you ask?'

He released a breath. 'I worried I might have been there.
I could not have borne it to think that this happened to you
and I could have stopped him. Did he do anything else,
anything at all?'

'He said that I had led him on. That I was wicked and
wanton and deserved everything that happened to me. That
a true lady would never have behaved like that, and he
could tell the difference. And he had only done that because
I had wanted to. He said that he had changed his mind
about marrying me and was going to end it that night. But
we would have to marry because of how I had acted and
what we had done and he'd take great pleasure in spending
my money. And my brother would pay dearly for it.' She
gave a little shrug and tried to control the shaking of her
body. 'Two days later he was dead. I prayed he would die
and he did. It makes me very wicked, Brett.'

'It makes you human.'

She turned her face away. She was not going to mention
the blood, or how Mrs Tanner had simply raised her glass
and asked if she had enjoyed the fireworks when they had
returned to the pavilion. How he had smirked. The hours
she had spent scrubbing her skin, until it was raw and
bleeding. The promises she made to God if only somehow
she'd be released from her living hell. Then she had been.
And she had tried to live her life as she had promised. Had
worn the cap until it was rags to remind her. Only it had
not been living, only surviving.

She screwed her eyes shut, refused to let the words
tumble forth. Pity was the last thing she wanted. But it
was vital that he understand that there was no need for his
sacrifice.

'It is good the man is dead or I'd murder him with my

bare hands for putting you through that. As it is, I wish Bagshott had not killed him so cleanly and instead that he suffered more.'

'They said that he didn't suffer. He looked peaceful. I wanted him to experience all the torments of hell.'

'Have you told anyone else your story? Your brother? Your maid? Who knows?'

'It was Rose's night off and she was visiting her family. I had the under-maid draw me a bath. And I have never told anyone. I have been too ashamed. And no one ever guessed.' A bitter laugh escaped her lips. 'They thought it was because he had died that I mourned him. How could I mourn a monster like that?'

'You should never have had to endure that alone.' He put his fingers under her chin and forced her to meet his gaze. 'He was wrong. He forced himself on you to ensure you would marry him. He was deep in debt.'

'But I—'

'You did nothing. Someone should have protected you and I will regret to my dying day that I wasn't there to answer your pleas. That nobody came.'

Hot tears ran down her face. 'You weren't to blame.'

'Neither were you, Diana Clare. Neither were you.'

'But I—'

'The offer stands. It is an honourable offer, Diana. However you were mistreated has no bearing on your future. You are a lady. It is my duty.'

Honourable. Duty. With no words of love. She had no wish for that sort of marriage, even with Brett.

'You feel it your obligation to make an offer. I have refused. That is an end to it.' She forced her voice to become bright. 'Come, we shall say no more of it. You will thank me eventually.'

His cool eyes assessed her. Raked her up and down. 'That is your final word on the subject.'

'It is. I refuse to marry for some sense of misplaced duty. I refuse ever to marry.'

'Why are you standing here next to me?' His lips took on a cynical twist. 'What is it that you want?'

Diana took a long deep breath. Her whole body trembled. She knew she had to do it. She would change the subject and take control again. 'You.'

He swore loud and long, the words echoing across the valley. Words that made her want to curl up into a little ball and die.

'I thought you would have been pleased.' Diana forced the words out. 'A woman who is not looking for marriage. Who is only looking for the pleasure of the moment.'

'How little you know me.' Brett stared at her in disbelief as he struggled to control his temper. He wanted to reach out and shake her. She had to understand what he was offering. He loathed Finch with a passion, but he hated himself for having seduced her, for not having guessed. 'I make the offer for your own good.'

'I have no desire for that sort of marriage. I had a narrow escape from the sort of wedlock you are suggesting. I saw my brother's unhappiness at a loveless marriage. Why is it wrong for me to want a bit of pleasure? Why can't a woman behave like that and a man can?'

Brett was torn between kissing her into submission and shaking her until she saw reason. He took the safe option and did neither, running his hands through his hair. 'Will you listen to reason, Diana? Society will demand it or it will cast you out into oblivion if what passed between us the other day is discovered.'

'Society has no idea about what passed between us.

And you are no cad, Brett Farnham. You will not drag a woman's name through the mud.'

He forced his lips to smile, but his insides twisted. He hated that he had been prepared to use her to get a piece of land. Some day, he would find a way of convincing her she was wrong. He might not love her, but he liked her. He desired her. And surely that was a better way to build a marriage than on some romantic folly. 'Then what do you suggest? I have no intention of giving you up.'

'At the start of our friendship, you made it abundantly clear marriage was an undesirable state.' Her chin tilted upwards and her defiant eyes blazed at him, challenging him to deny it. Brett winced, remembering his arrogant words. 'Some day you will thank me for saving you from this folly.'

Thank him? Brett stared at her blankly. She was refusing to marry him. Not refusing his bed, or to lie with him, but refusing to make it legal. The one woman he had ever offered for had just refused him.

He felt as if he had been punched in the stomach. The ring in his pocket weighed heavy. He had been certain—all he'd had to do was to offer. What woman would refuse an earl?

For a breath, he was tempted to walk away, but that would accomplish nothing. He wanted her. She wanted him. She would want to marry him. He would push her and she'd surrender. He would bind her to him. He would make her his. He would have no hesitation in using any means necessary.

'What more could I have asked for?' he said smoothly. 'You are a rare woman, Diana Clare.'

'Then you agree to my terms.' Her eyes showed a shimmer of uncertainty. 'No marriage and absolute discretion.'

'But of course.' Brett smiled inwardly. They were not finished yet. He would get his way in the end. 'You have agreed to be my mistress, and without preconditions.' He allowed his hand to travel down her arm. 'Some might call you foolish. I would prefer to use other words—generous, giving.'

'I have agreed to no such thing!'

'What other term should I use?' He drew her body to him, felt it mould against him. Soften. 'You know what it is like to be with me.'

He started to lower his mouth, his body already anticipating the sweet surrender to come. But she became rigid and her eyes were fixed on an object beyond his shoulder. Her hands, which an instant before had acquiesced to the onslaught, now fought against him. He allowed her to go. He stared at her, puzzled.

'There is someone there. Someone watching.'

Chapter Thirteen

Diana stepped away from Brett and tried to draw a breath but her stays constricted her. She pointed with a trembling finger. 'Someone is there. He moves in the shadows.'

Brett turned, stared for a moment, before turning back to her, hands reaching out. 'Your eyes are playing tricks. Who would be out here?'

Diana evaded his grasp. He had to see. He had to understand the potential for disaster. 'There was movement.'

'Most likely a weasel or stoat moving in the undergrowth. Think no more on it. If you wish to embark upon a life of sin, Diana, you cannot be perturbed at the slightest wood pigeon's wing clap.'

'No, it was bigger than that.' She shielded her eyes and her body stilled. A small figure moved along the trees, steadily but with great stealth.

'A child is there.' Brett held out his arm, blocking her way. 'Let me go and see. I will deal with the intruder.'

'I know that face!' She pushed against his arm, refusing to be held prisoner. 'I know it! Let me go!'

Diana picked up her skirts and ran towards the copse

at the bottom of the hill. Behind her, the air echoed with Brett's oaths. 'Make up your mind, Diana!'

'Robert!' She reached the bedraggled creature within a breath and had gathered him to her. She kissed him, then held her nephew from her. 'Why, in the name of heaven, are you here? You should be at school.'

'Get off, Aunt Diana.' Robert scrambled away from her embrace and stood facing her. His breeches looked as if he had rolled around in a pigsty and he sported a great rent in his new jacket, the one she and Rose had sewed for hours to get it ready in time for school. A single tear trickled down his cheek. 'I am not a baby anymore. I am nine.'

Diana stared at her nephew, not sure whether she should throttle him or get down on her knees and thank him for being there. With Robert's unexpected appearance, the temptation was gone. It seemed as if in one fatal swoop of his mouth, Brett had broken all her walls. She would have agreed to be his mistress. Her fall would have been complete.

But she had this one last opportunity to change her destiny.

She pushed away all thoughts of Brett and what might have been, grabbing Robert by the arm. She looked at him again. Made certain that he was not some sort of fevered dream.

'Robert Clare, what are you doing here?' she said, kneeling down beside him. 'Why have you left school?'

Robert stood up and stuck his hands into his pockets. 'They punished me for things I didn't do. I had nothing to do with the stink bomb.'

'Doctor Allen sent a note. He believes you did. You should take your punishment.'

'He believes wrongly. It wasn't me. It was some

other boy.' His hands balled into fists. 'They all said it was me.'

'Truly?' Diana crossed her arms. 'And who made a stink bomb in the kitchen this summer? Three times, Robert!'

'That was different. I was experimenting. Once I knew how it worked, it did not matter any more.'

'And if it was not from you, how did the boys get the information? You know what your father will say. You will never have the horse you long for.'

Robert gave a shrug and ran his toe in the dirt, but a single tear gleamed in his eye. Diana's heart squeezed. She wanted to scoop him up and hug him to her, but he had to learn his lesson. He could not simply leave school whenever he wanted. He could not give up.

'Is there some problem, Diana?' Brett came to stand at her shoulder. 'Who is this ragamuffin? One of the colliery children?'

'My nephew.' Diana glanced over her shoulder, up at Brett's questioning face. 'He has run away from school.'

'And I ain't going back…ever.' Robert's voice rose an octave and she could see his muscles begin to bunch. 'I came this way to say goodbye to Rose and Titch. They are the only ones who care about me.'

'Titch?' Brett asked quietly.

'Our terrier.'

Brett nodded and motioned for her to continue. Diana knelt down beside Robert.

'But, Robert, you love school. All this summer you spoke about how you longed to be back.' Diana reached out to hug him to her again.

'I hate school. Stupid school. Don't need it to ride horses.'

'Never underestimate education,' Brett commented in a matter-of-fact tone. 'Without it, you are ignorant.'

'I don't need an education to work.'

'Your father wants more for you then digging ditches or shovelling coal,' Brett said. 'Fathers are like that.'

'I am going to race horses.'

'You need to study. There is much you have to learn,' Brett said. 'There is more to life than racing horses.'

'I won't! I won't!' Robert screwed up his face and stamped his foot.

'Robert!' Diana said, thoroughly shocked. 'Please forgive my nephew. He is normally much better behaved than this. Apologise immediately to Lord Coltonby, Robert.'

Robert hung his head and mumbled an apology. Diana breathed more easily.

'What is the true difficulty, Robert?'

'Greek and Latin are only about dead people.'

The corner of Brett's mouth quirked upwards and Diana fought against the temptation to laugh. Robert was right, but that wasn't the point.

'The Romans were great engineers,' Brett remarked. 'They built bridges and aqueducts that remain standing today. They raced horses and built chariots.'

'I wouldn't know about that.' Robert hung his head.

'Your father sent you to school to learn,' Brett said quietly. 'You should go back.'

'Who...who are you?' Robert backed up against the wall.

'Lord Coltonby—he owns the Park now and he is a friend,' Diana said and prayed that Robert would listen to reason. He was too large for her to pick up and carry back. She had no idea how she was going to get him and Merlin back to the house. Then there was Simon to be faced.

'Lord Coltonby?' Robert's face jerked up. 'Your horses won the Derby and several other plates.'

'You know about the turf?'

'A few of the other boys do and so I joined in.'

'Yes, it was my horse that won. By two lengths.'

'Wait until I tell Rupert and Henry that I met Lord Coltonby and—'

'I thought you had finished with school,' Diana said quietly. 'How can you tell them? And why should they believe you?'

'That's true.' Robert stuck his hands in his pockets and made a circle in the dirt with the toe of his boot. 'I am done with it.'

'Robert, how did you get here?' Brett's voice was low, as if he was coaxing a wild animal.

'Got a lift from a drover. Thought he was nice and kind, like, but he weren't. He beat his horses.'

Diana glanced at Brett. Robert's story did not ring true. 'Robert, who suggested this?'

He drew another line in the dirt. 'Henry,' he whispered. 'Henry was going to come with me, only he didn't appear and the drover grabbed me. Said I owed him money.'

'And then what happened?' Brett asked.

'He threatened to beat me because I didn't have any money. I waited, and waited. Then I saw the Lion and Dove pub and knew I was close to home, so I escaped.'

Diana stifled a cry, and reached for Robert again. Brett motioned for her to be quiet.

'That was very resourceful of you.'

Robert tilted his head to one side. 'Was it?'

'You had a lucky escape and you know it,' Brett said. 'You are a bright boy, aren't you? You know what can happen to children who disappear.'

Robert shook his head—gone was the bravado. 'I do.'

'People will be worried about you.'

'I wanted…I wanted to come home,' Robert whispered.

'I missed it. I wanted to see Papa. He would put things right. A boy's father should put things right.'

'He should do, but sometimes fathers forget.' Brett's face was remote and his eyes faraway. He was speaking of another father. Diana's heart turned over for the little boy that he must have been once. Had he too run away from his school? What dangers had he faced and how had they made him into the man he was today?

'I think Papa is going to be very angry with me.' Robert scrubbed his eyes. 'I should go back to school now, before he discovers what I have done. He will be disappointed in me.'

'No, you face your father,' Brett said. 'You have come this far. You have a responsibility. You were the one to run away. You and you alone must face the consequences.'

'And if he sends me back?'

'I will take you in my carriage with my horses.'

Diana stared at Brett. The offer was so unexpected. Why should he do something for her nephew? Instinctively she knew that he was not making the offer to curry favour with her, but to help Robert make the right choice. He had a way with boys. She had seen that before with Jimmy Satterwaite.

Robert turned to Brett and held out his hand. 'I will consider your offer, sir. But first I must see my father. You are right. I do have responsibilities.'

'He is a good boy, Brett,' she whispered. 'He has had a bad fright. He does not mean to be rude.'

'I can see that. I was a boy like him once and my scrapes were far worse. Luckily his father is there to forgive him. Mine wasn't. His experience has probably taught him a more severe lesson than any punishment could have.' Brett took Robert's hand. 'The pact is made. My horses are at your disposal, should you require it, young Master Clare. You need only send word.'

'And how will we get you home, young man?' Diana regarded Robert, who hung his head.

'I hadn't considered it.' Then his back stiffened and his fists balled at his sides. When he looked like that, Diana could see the resemblance to Simon—the same pig-headed determination. 'I can run alongside.'

'You can ride in front of me,' Diana offered.

Robert gave a half-shrug.

'I suspect he would prefer to ride on Falcon,' Brett said.

'Can I?' Robert's face shone. 'I will be able to tell Henry and Rupert that I rode one of Lord Coltonby's horses. How many plates and cups have you won?'

'Me or my horses?'

'It amounts to the same thing.'

'There is a difference which you will understand when you get older. But for the record I have won two plates and seven cups, while my horses' number in the hundreds. It is the ones I won through my own efforts that I am most proud of.'

Diana's throat closed. She hoped one day Robert would understand what Brett was saying.

The boy's eyes grew round. 'But can I ride with you?'

'If your aunt agrees. She is the lady in charge.'

Diana nodded as her throat closed tight. Brett had known the exact words to say. She had thought to protect herself, but she wondered if it was too late. When the time came for them to part, she knew her heart would be in danger of shattering.

Diana pulled hard on Merlin's reins, forcing the horse to a slow walk. She had given in to Robert's request and she and Brett had raced slightly. But now, she obeyed the rules of the stable and walked the horses back.

Her heart sank as she rounded the corner towards the mounting block. Simon's carriage stood ready in the stable yard. She had half-hoped that he would have left for the colliery before they arrived back. It would have given her a chance to clean Robert up and find out more about his version of events. To prepare a story that would pass for the truth, but give the events in the best possible light.

Behind her, Robert's whoop of delight resounded as Brett made his stallion rear. And at that very instant she saw her brother walk out. He drew his eyebrows together as he jammed his top hat on.

'What is going on here?'

'Isn't it obvious, Simon? I have returned from my morning ride.' Diana kept her voice steady but her stomach clenched. With a few ill-chosen words, Simon could undo everything.

'Why is my son here?' Simon pointed with an accusatory finger. 'Why have you brought him here? Why isn't he at school where he belongs?'

Diana took her time dismounting from Merlin. With Simon in this sort of mood, she had to remain calm.

'I was out for my morning ride and encountered Brett and Robert. It seemed sensible to return here with them. Would you have preferred me to send your son elsewhere?'

'What is Coltonby doing with my son?' Simon thundered, grabbing her arm. 'Why is he riding with him? Why isn't he in Newcastle? At school where he belongs and where I pay good money for him to be.'

'Be civil,' Diana said in a furious undertone and jerked her elbow away. 'Robert ran away from school. I discovered him out by the look-out point. I thought for a moment he might continue to run.'

'Robert ran away from school?' The colour drained from Simon's face. 'Why would he have cause to do that? Dr Allen's has an excellent reputation.'

'And he has had a bad time of it.'

'But why? What is the boy playing at? And where is Dr Allen? I pay him to look after Robert's safety, not to have the boy gallivanting all over the countryside.'

'You will have to ask your son.' Diana nodded to where Robert sat with Brett. 'Go on, call him. Talk to him.'

'Robert Clare!'

Robert slid down from Brett's horse and ran to Simon. 'Papa,' he said with a trembling voice. He stopped and started again. This time, his voice was stronger. 'Father, I have returned home. I was wrong, but I have come back.' He glanced up at Brett. 'Did I say it right?'

Simon did not say anything. He looked solemnly at Robert's bedraggled face. Diana willed him to hug his son, to acknowledge that he was pleased to see him. Anything. Simon placed a hand on Robert's shoulder for a brief instant. 'I will deal with you later, Robert Clare. No doubt your headmaster will be in touch.'

'It wasn't my fault, Papa.'

'Once I know the full facts, then I can make a judgement. I warned you that I would not stand for any more tricks.'

'This isn't a trick, Papa. I will go back now.'

'You should never have left in the first place.'

'I know.' Robert hung his head.

'Were they unkind? Were they cruel?'

'I ran away because I did not want to be punished for something another boy did. I know a man should take his punishment, but only when it is just.'

Simon took out his fob watch, regarded it and then slid it back into his pocket. 'We will discuss this when I return from work, Robert. I am late.'

Diana went forward and caught the carriage door. 'Simon!' she said in an undertone. 'He is your son. Speak to him. He worships you.'

'He ran away rather than face his punishment.' Simon's knuckles shone white against the door. 'I have nothing but contempt for him.'

'He made a mistake. He was very nearly kidnapped.' Diana held out her hands, pleaded with her brother to understand. 'It is but by the grace of God that he is here.'

'Diana, I have a business to run. Allow me to handle him in my own way. You should have forced him to walk. He chose to come here. He should not be rewarded with a ride on Coltonby's horse.' He rapped on the roof of the carriage.

Diana stuffed a hand into her mouth and held back a sob. Who she felt sorrier for—Simon or Robert—she could not have said. All she knew was that this was a tragedy in the making. But she also knew that she could not make Simon do anything. He had to lead his life as he chose to. She glanced at Brett and saw a muscle jump in his cheek. 'Are you not going to thank Lord Coltonby?'

Simon stuck his head out of the window. The two men stared at each other. Neither moving a muscle.

'My gratitude, Coltonby, for returning the boy.'

'As your son has been returned safely to his parent, there is no need for me to remain here.' Brett addressed his words to Simon, but made no move to dismount.

'Thank you,' Diana mouthed. Brett gave a nod and his horse cantered away.

The stable yard was silent until long after his horse's hooves had faded. Simon's carriage, however, remained stationary. Diana went up to the door, opened it and looked at her brother's distressed face. She thought she saw a tiny tear in the corner of his eye, but Simon never cried, not even when he had told her about Jayne.

'Simon,' Diana whispered and willed him to respond to his son. 'You need to do something. He has had a scare. He has agreed to return. I don't think he will try it again. He was nearly kidnapped by drovers. He followed bad advice.'

'I can imagine what risks he took, Diana. It doesn't make it right.'

'You made mistakes when you were that age. I can remember the apple-tree incident. How many saplings did you break?'

'And what did Father do? Beat me! Within an inch of my life!' Simon drew in his breath.

'At least our father cared about your fate.'

'I would never whip Robert like that.'

She offered a small prayer up as the silence stretched again. Simon surely had to understand. Robert was only a boy. She felt a movement at her side and Robert pushed between her and Simon.

'Papa?' he said. 'I didn't mean to be bad. I wanted you to know the truth. I wanted you to think the best of me. I did not make a stink bomb. Henry did. But it was my fault that he knew how to do it. You are right. I should never have left. I should have stayed and accepted the punishment.'

Simon glanced down at Robert. His throat worked. 'Was it very smelly?'

'Terribly.' Robert's nose wrinkled. 'Henry had done the compound wrong. It exploded too early.'

Diana held her breath.

'I will write to Dr Allen. He might be persuaded to take you back, but I expect you to behave like a Clare should—with dignity and honour. It is not up to you to decide if a punishment is just or not. You leave that to your elders.'

'Yes, sir. I will.'

'We will speak about this later.' Simon nodded towards the coachman and the horses began to move.

Diana watched the carriage roll away, painfully aware that there was nothing she could do except hope that Simon would somehow see sense and not brand Robert as being exactly like his mother. There was much in him that was Clare. Simon had changed over the past few years, and she wasn't sure she even recognised him.

'I can't believe Robert did that,' Simon said later that evening after they had finished supper and Robert had gone to bed. 'Left school for such a small thing. He should have taken his punishment like a man.'

'But he *was* punished. He has learnt his lesson.' She paused. 'He is only a boy. Give him time, Simon.'

'But why leave?' Simon held his ruby-red glass of port up to the light. 'All he had to do was to send me a letter. I would have read it.'

Would you have? Diana wondered. Suddenly it seemed after years of not questioning her brother and his motives, she had to break her silence. It was too easy to play it safe. It was as if Brett had awoken some devil within her, and she was tired of taking the sensible course. 'He probably wanted to make sure you understood the whole story.'

'I fear he takes after his mother and you know where her wildness led. Those last years of her life, all that pain and suffering... Diana, how could I want that for Robert?'

'Will Dr Allen allow him to return?' Diana asked. She held back the words explaining that Robert was only nine and could hardly be expected to play a man's part.

'I will write to the good doctor and explain the situation.'

'Why do you think he will agree?'

'I have donated enough money to that school. Dr Allen will hear me out. For the right sum, he will do as I ask. That much was made clear the last time Robert misbehaved.' Simon ran his hand through his hair as he paced up and down in the dining room. 'Robert and I will have a full and frank discussion. He will do as I say. We will have no more of that nonsense.'

Simon had forbidden her to be in the room when he confronted Robert. The boy had emerged white faced, but resolute. Diana longed to hug him to her, but he had clearly grown too old for such behaviour.

'We almost lost him, Simon.'

'I gave my promise to his mother that I would look after him and I have done so.'

Diana pressed her lips together. She knew what Simon believed and why. He had confessed everything about his marriage and his fears for Robert. At the same time she had been grateful that he had never questioned her about London. He'd just been glad that she had returned.

'Does he have to go back? There must be other schools we could send him to.'

'Dr Allen's is the best in the north-east. It is my decision. Robert will have the best, but his mother's tendencies have to be curtailed.'

'And who will take him back when he goes?'

'You can.' Simon waved his hand. 'I am busy with my engine. It is at a crucial stage. It moved two feet this afternoon. Robert will understand. He loved his time there last summer.'

'Simon, it would be better if you took him. You could

speak with Dr Allen. Explain in person. It would mean so much to Robert.'

Simon looked at her and slowly shook his head. 'Please, Diana. You know I would give in. I want to be a different father than ours.'

Diana pressed her hands onto her thighs, regained control of her emotions. 'Very well, I will. I want to see him settled properly. Lord Coltonby has offered a ride in his carriage if it will make things easier.'

'Coltonby seeks to use my son for his own purposes.'

'Why...why do you say that?'

'It should be obvious to you what the man is about, why he is sniffing around here.' Simon's eyes raked her up and down. 'He will never marry you, Diana.'

'Did I say that he would? Why do you persist in thinking the worst of him? Cambridge was finished years ago.'

'He is doing this to get me to drop the price of the land. He will then go and sell the rights to Sir Norman Bolt. Don't think that I am not aware of how much Sir Norman needs that land.' Simon clasped his hand to his forehead. 'My God, to think I nearly gifted it to Biddlestone in exchange for investing in my engine. It was sheer providence.'

'I thought Lord Coltonby wanted the land for the view.'

'Ah ha, he says that, but he and Maurice Bolt have been as thick as thieves. Why else would they have raced? I overheard Bolt boasting about his father's new engine and you know it would give them access. I know Maurice Bolt wouldn't risk his father's prize mare for a boot-blacking receipt. There is more to it.'

'Simon, you are spouting nonsense. Lord Coltonby is not interested in engines. Or wagon-ways. He is interested in horses. You are wrong about him.'

'Then ask him. And while you are at it, ask why he is sniffing around a *tradesman's* sister. What were you thinking about by meeting him, Diana? You are playing into his hands.'

'You are hardly a tradesman, Simon.'

'In his eyes, I am and always will be. Do you really think your charms have beguiled him?'

'You are angry Simon. You seek to hurt someone.' Diana choked back the tears.

'Am I?' Simon whispered. 'Or am I seeing things clearly where you are wilfully blind? He is exactly like your misbegotten fiancé, out to get what he can.'

'I need to see my nephew. He is my first concern, not your ongoing childish feud with Brett Farnham!' She walked with quick steps out of the dining room.

'That's right. Go on, Diana, run away from the truth.' Simon's voice floated after her. 'It is easier that way.'

Diana stopped on the stairs and sank down. She laid her head against her knees as Simon's vile words washed over her. He was wrong. Brett was not using her. He had never sought to use her. They were friends.

Brett surveyed the Ladywell Main colliery from his curricle. The machinery and men were laid out in front of him as the sound of the great pumping engines rang in his ears. The solid ponies pulled the carts along the wagonway towards the landing on the Tyne from where the coal would be shipped to Newcastle and beyond. Prosperous. Clare cared more about his business and his machines than he cared about his son or his sister. He wanted investment in his engine. Very well, Brett would give him the money, pay over the odds for the land as well but, in exchange, he wanted Simon's co-operation with Diana. Together, they could make her understand that his offer was honourable, and why marriage was the only option.

Brett alighted from the curricle and tossed the ribbons to Jimmy Satterwaite. The lad showed real potential as a possible tiger, particularly as Brett's former tiger refused to settle in Northumberland and had returned to the bright lights of London. 'Look after them. They are skittish enough around machines. I'd send them back to Tattersalls but they are high steppers. This will not take long.'

A great roar drowned out the lad's comment. A huge black machine advanced out of the shed, puffing smoke and grinding along the cast-iron rails. Sparks flew up in a massive cloud, showering the machine with red gold. Jimmy cowered slightly and both horses pawed the ground.

'Look to the horses, Satterwaite,' Brett said sharply. 'If they go, there will be no stopping them. You want to be a tiger, don't you?'

'I will, sir, but that thing…' The lad pointed a trembling finger as his horses reared a second time. 'It frightens me. Me da were injured by one of them machines. Spent weeks off work.'

'Hardly a fiend from Hades, boy. Concentrate on the horses. Lead them away from here—slowly and steadily.'

The lad gave a half-nod and clung on to the bridles for dear life. He seemed to be in charge—but barely. Brett turned his attention back to the screaming monster. He started forwards.

A burly man stepped in front of Brett, blocking his way. Brett glared at him.

'You ain't allowed here. No one is allowed here. Not while this here is happening.'

Brett raised an eyebrow. 'I am Lord Coltonby. I have business with your master.'

'I don't care who you say you are. Mr Clare has said no one is to be here. Not today. Today, we are closed.'

'Clare will see me now. Or face the consequences.' Brett regarded the man with a stern eye. Ice-cold fury washed through his veins.

The burly man pursed his mouth and shook his head. 'Mr Clare ain't going to like it.'

'I don't care if Mr Clare likes it or not.' Brett glanced over his shoulder and saw Jimmy struggling to hold the horses as the monster advanced towards him. 'What in the name of all that is holy is that?'

'Travelling engine, sir. That's what they call them. Loco Motives.' The man continued to block his way.

'I do not care what they call them. There is a problem.'

Brett watched in horror as the iron rails began to buckle and twist, splintering under the weight of the engine. He watched as the machine tilted and the fiery coal began to spill out over the wooden blocks that held the rails. The air became thick with oaths and screams as the men realised what was happening.

The foreman stood, stunned, watching in disbelief. Brett saw the flames begin to lick the engine.

'Do something! Get some water,' he yelled, but the man continued to stand there, rooted to the ground.

'He said it was safe.'

Brett ran forwards, shouting orders to the men who gathered around the disaster like fairgoers gawking at the latest marvel. 'Why are you standing there? That man needs your help.'

'We daren't go any closer. The master will have it under control right enough. He always does.'

'This has happened before?'

'Not as bad as this...'

Brett paid no heed to the man and raced forwards. The heat from the engine seared his face. Simon Clare stood propped up at the controls, eyes closed, seemingly oblivious to the carnage happening around him. He had courage, Brett would grant him that.

'This contraption is going to explode! Get out while you can.'

Clare glanced at him. 'Get away from here. You don't know what you are playing at, your lordship. Go back and play with your horses. Leave this to the experts.'

'Neither do you!'

'I am perfectly safe. You will be in danger if you stand there.' Clare leant forwards and twisted a knob. The great machine heaved forward again with a grinding sound. Sparks flew up in greater arcs, covering Brett with a thousand pinpoints of light.

'Not as much danger as you are in.'

Without hesitating, Brett plunged in and pulled the man out. The infernal machine gave one last shudder and then the orange-red flames licked the spot where Clare had stood. He placed Clare on to the ground and turned his attention to the machine and the smouldering rails. The machine continued to puff smoke and steam in to the air.

'How do you stop it?'

Clare lay there, singed, a queer smile on his face. His features were blackened with soot, but his green eyes blazed. He struggled to stand up, stood there swaying back and forth as Brett examined the wreckage. 'What sort of mad man are you, Coltonby? I told you to get away from here. You and your bungling have destroyed everything.'

'No permission needed. No thanks required.' Brett leant closer, made sure that Clare could see his lips. 'You would have died in that machine.'

Clare's response was to land a punch on Brett's jaw. Brett staggered back, surprised.

'I don't forgive a man lightly when he reacts that way,' Brett said, fingering his jaw.

'You had no cause to rescue me.'

'You don't want to be rescued. Very well, then.' He picked the man up by his jacket, started to haul him towards the smouldering machine, then stopped. 'You are not worth it, Clare.'

'Let go of me,' Clare struggled.

The machine's groaning and creaking increased. The men who had been gathered round started to scatter.

Brett kept his grip tight around Clare's arm. In this mood, there was no telling what he might do. And he had no wish for Diana to accuse him of harming her brother.

'Let go of me, Coltonby. If I don't stop it, that boiler will blow.'

'Promise me you will be sensible.'

But Clare twisted and freed himself from Brett's grasp.

Brett gritted his teeth and watched Clare take three steps. With a gigantic roar, the boiler of the engine exploded. Brett watched in horror as Clare was hit. He staggered and fell to the ground. He got up on to his knees and tried to rise, only to fall again.

'I think I might have overestimated something.' He collapsed on the ground and lay still.

Brett leant down him over. Clare's face was pale white against the soot. He gave a funny gurgle and lay still. Brett put his ear to Clare's chest and heard the faint rattle of a breath.

'Get a doctor, quick!'

Chapter Fourteen

'Do I have to do my times table?' Robert looked up from the dining-room table. 'I am not at school, and the sun is shining.'

'You will be learning at home until Dr Allen says that you can return.' Diana regarded her nephew. She wanted to be elsewhere, as well. Not in here, stuck trying to remember how the eight times table went. The weather had turned slightly chillier and the sloes, blackberries and other hedge fruit were ready for picking. There were a thousand other things she longed to do, but her duty was to ensure Robert kept up with his schoolwork. If she concentrated on Robert, she could forget Simon's insidious accusations about Brett. His words kept going round and round in her brain. Why had Brett become interested in her? Why had he started paying her attention? She needed to know the answer, but it also frightened her. What if Simon was correct?

'But…but…'

'Do you want your school friends to see that you have fallen behind? Do you want them to laugh at you? I have always had trouble with my eights, in particular eight times seven.' She swallowed hard. He had to understand how easy it was to fail. 'I know how cruel people can be.'

'But I can already do up to the twelve times table, Aunt Diana,' Robert blurted out, holding out his paper. 'See! It is simple, particularly eight times seven. You write fifty-six equals seven times eight.'

Diana sighed, and reached for the paper. He had neatly written out all the times tables. The pain behind her eyes threatened to become a fully fledged headache. Despite having no expense spared on her education, her grasp of mathematics remained hazy. Abandoning maths might be the best plan. 'Shall we try geography, then? I will draw a map of Northumberland and you can put in the principal rivers and towns. And I want the handwriting legible, not ink stained.'

Robert groaned. Then his face brightened. 'I can hear horses. Someone is coming to visit.'

'Robert. You cannot hear the stables from the house. Sit back down.'

'No really, I can.' Robert rushed to the window. 'They are coming up the gravel path, but it looks like Papa's carriage.'

Diana's hand trembled slightly. There was no reason for Simon to return home so quickly. He had told her this morning at breakfast that he would not make the midday meal as he wanted to have a trial run of the engine. Her mind raced with all sorts of possibilities and she tried to hang on to the most rational—Robert was seeking an excuse to stop his schoolwork.

'What nonsense, Robert. Your father would never come up the gravel path. He always goes to the stables.' Diana pointed to the chair. 'Pick up your pen and concentrate.'

'But he is. I know my father's carriage.'

Diana went to stand next to her nephew. Simon's carriage

was indeed turning up the drive. She pressed her lips together as the back of her neck prickled. 'Robert, I was wrong and you are right. Remain here while I see what is going on. And while I am away, you may recite your eight times table.'

Ignoring his groans, she walked quickly outside, in time to see Brett alighting from the carriage. His face was furrowed and his coat covered in soot. He made no move towards her. She tried for a smile, but he gave a brief shake of his head. She forced her legs to carry her out to the carriage.

'Is this some sort of joke?' Diana asked quietly. 'Why are you in Simon's carriage? Where is yours? You are scaring me, Brett.'

'No joke.' A great weariness hung over him. 'I have been to the colliery. There was an accident.'

Diana's mind raced. Fire damp? An exploding engine in the pump house? The colliery had a good safety record, but that counted for nothing. Pockets of dangerous gas could develop without warning. She had tried to tell Simon that he should find a solution to that problem, but he had only laughed and said that he would, after he'd managed to get the travelling engine to work. She swallowed hard and refused to let her mind wander down that path. 'And Simon? Where is he? What have you done with him? Is he…?'

Her throat closed and she could not ask the final question.

'Your brother lives. You must keep that in your mind. He is alive.' Brett nodded towards the carriage. 'I have brought him back to you.'

'Diana.' A voice croaked from the carriage.

Diana peered in and saw Simon sitting there with his face swathed in bandages. He held his arm awkwardly. His clothes were far more rumpled that Brett's and a distinct smell of smoke and grease hung about the carriage. 'What happened?'

'Coltonby will explain.' Simon closed his undamaged eye and leant back against the carriage seat.

'The travelling engine. Or rather the non-travelling engine. Your brother's attempts at Loco Motion have failed. Spectacularly.' Brett proceeded to explain the morning's events.

Diana listened with growing horror.

'I am grateful you arrived in time.'

'I would have sorted it!' came the yell from the carriage. 'Do not believe Coltonby, Diana! It was a triumph! A triumph! If he hadn't pulled me from the engine, I would have stopped it.'

'Or you would be dead. Nobody could have stopped the boiler from blowing.'

'Coltonby, you have no idea about engines.'

'I know enough.'

'I knew it! I knew it! You want to get that land cheap. You have done a deal with the Bolts. It is why you have been nosing around my sister.'

'I have no idea what you are talking about. I have made no arrangement with the Bolts.' Brett's voice was calm and measured.

'Brett?' Diana whispered. He wrapped his fingers about her hand and gave it a brief reassuring squeeze. Then let go.

'Your brother took a blow to the head, Diana. He is not in his right mind. Ignore what he says. Ignore everything he says about the land.'

She nodded, wanting to believe him, but she had also seen his eyes, seen the way they slid away from her.

'Your brother has been ranting and raving all the way

home. I have paid it no mind. The doctor wanted some-one with him. He is afraid that he might be suffering from shock. People in shock say things that are not to be believed.' Brett reached out and touched her hand. 'He will bear the scars of this day for the rest of his life.'

Diana's brow wrinkled. She knew vaguely of the term 'shock'. She had heard it used before, but had never actu-ally seen the effects. She peered again into the gloom of the carriage. Her brother moved restlessly, irritably.

'Will he recover?'

'He has the luck of the devil. He is alive, Diana. He may lose the eye, but his limbs will heal eventually and the burns on his face will fade. But he will have to spend time resting.'

'Easier said than done with Simon.' Diana attempted a laugh, but it came out as a strangled cry. It was all too easy to imagine what had nearly happened. She had to be thankful for small mercies. Only an eye, when he could have lost his arm or worse. 'Simon hates to be ill. He sees it as a sign of weakness, that it is his duty to get up as soon as possible.'

'Why does that not surprise me?' Brett's lips turned upwards.

'And you are a good patient?'

'Guilty as charged.' Brett touched his hat. 'The doctor has given him some laudanum and it should help make him sleep. He will call later today to check on his patient.'

'I assume you used Dr MacFarlane, the colliery's physi-cian. He is good, if a little old fashioned in his methods.'

'He was quite thorough.'

'And with you as well?'

'With me?' Brett gave a shrug. 'A few bruises and scrapes, but nothing life threatening.'

'I see.' Diana pressed her hands together, to prevent them

from reaching out to him and discovering for herself his injuries. She had to remain discreet.

Diana motioned to several of the servants, who helped Simon from the carriage. At first, it appeared that Simon had fallen asleep, but he eventually rose and stumbled from the carriage.

Simon's face turned black and he pointed his finger. 'That man interfered with my engine. Mine! And the land stays mine despite your sniffing around my sister. I know what you are on about, Coltonby.'

'Simon!'

'We were not all born with a golden spoon in our mouths. Some of us had to work for our fortunes.'

'We will discuss this later, Clare.' Brett turned to Diana, his face stern. 'Get him into the house before he does himself damage.'

Diana concentrated on getting Simon into the house and then settled into his bed. She tried to be efficient and not to cringe at the red welts on his arms and face, burns from the steam. Robert came rushing in, but halted, uncertain, by the door. Diana walked quickly over and shut it, telling Robert that his father was tired.

She had just turned to go when Simon croaked from the bed. 'That Coltonby, don't believe a word he says. Interfering fop!'

'You are overwrought, Simon, and very lucky that Lord Coltonby saw sense not to take offence. Such men settle slurs by duels.'

'I am the equal of him.' He struggled to sit up. 'Bring him on! He has insulted you, Diana. I can feel it. He only paid attention to you because he wants me to give him the land. It is why he came to the colliery. I am not afraid to avenge your honour, Diana. I can shoot straight.'

'I know you can,' Diana said soothingly and forced her

mind from the knowledge that somehow Simon had worked out that Brett had seduced her. How? Had it been only a lucky guess? 'Now lie back down.'

She smoothed the bedclothes, tucking him as if he were no older than Robert. He turned to face the wall.

'You were right, Diana. Hedley did not let me have one that could be easily fixed.'

'I told you the engine wouldn't work. When are you going to abandon this dream?' She waited to hear his scathing remark. He swung his head around and stared at her, his good eye burning with an intense heat.

'It went, Diana. It moved. It is the rails that are wrong. I can feel it in my bones. It is not the engine that is the problem, but the rails it travels on.'

'You sleep now. We can speak later.' She brought the sheets up to his chin.

'You are a good person. Keep Coltonby away from here. He only wants to use you, Diana.'

Diana paused. 'I don't have any say over where Lord Coltonby goes. And you should be on your knees, thanking him for saving your life.'

'I would have had the engine under control, if he had not distracted me.' Simon raised his hand. 'The man's a fop for all his bravery. He is cut from the same cloth as all aristocrats.'

'You are wrong, Simon.'

'I know I am right.'

Diana closed the door with a decisive click. Simon wanted a fight, but she did not. Brett was different. He had to be. She retraced her steps and found Brett entertaining Robert in the dining room. The chairs were drawn up like a coach and four and Robert was perched on the end of the table. 'Robert Clare! Get down this instant.'

Robert slipped down from the table. Both he and Brett

had the grace to hang their heads. Brett had discarded his coat. 'I thought he could use the distraction.'

'But on the table?'

'I needed to have the right perch, Aunt Diana. And Coltonby says that I am a natural with how I hold the ribbons.'

Diana gave Brett a hard look and he shrugged, unrepentant. 'It is all in the proper teaching. How is the patient?'

'Robert, go and see Rose,' Diana said. Robert looked as if he was about to protest, but took one glance at Brett and became quiet.

'We will continue with your driving lesson later.'

'Yes, Aunt Diana.' He left the room.

'I thought it would cheer him up.' Brett began to replace the chairs and restore the dining room to some semblance of order.

'But the dining room table?'

'It is solid.' He lowered his eyes. 'There are many uses a table can be put to.'

'You know them all.'

'One or three.'

Her insides tingled. Ruthlessly she suppressed the feelings. Without even waiting or asking, Brett had set about making himself indispensable. But why? Was Simon right? Did it have to do with the land?

'The fact remains that it should not have been used as a perch.'

'Your nephew is worried about his father. He needed a distraction.'

'And you sought to provide it? How obliging of you.' Diana crossed her arms.

'I do but try. You should see how very obliging I can be.' He made a smooth bow.

'Is that what you are to me—obliging?'

'You are upset, Diana.' He reached for her, but she stayed on the other side of the room. His eyes assessed her for a long moment and he ran his hand through his hair. 'My father was killed in a carriage accident when I was Robert's age. I know what it feels like to have a father who is more interested in machines and objects than in his son. He thought he could make a carriage that could travel on its own. Sheer madness.'

'Is this why you are against engines?'

'I am not against progress, Diana, simply against the all-consuming need to achieve it no matter the cost.'

'What happened after your father's death?'

'My mother remarried quickly, too quickly. My step-father sent my brother and me off to Eton where I was beaten and learnt to make cheese on toast. My mother died in childbirth and my stepfather simply sent a terse note to tell us that we were now orphans. I know what it is like to be miserable at school and what needs to be done to survive. You wanted to know why I understand Robert—because I was once that boy! There, I have said it! Are you happy?'

'Brett, I am sorry.' Diana's throat closed. She could see the boy that Brett must have been. 'I had no idea.'

'I have never asked for anyone's pity. For a long time, all I had was my name, Diana. I had to make my own way in the world.'

'But I am sorry. And I am sorry that my brother said such awful things about you. It was unforgivable.'

'You are upset. Your brother has been injured, but he will recover.' Brett resisted the temptation to take her into his arms. He drew a deep breath. 'Robert will grow up to be a fine young man.'

'Why were you at the colliery? Was it to speak with Simon about Robert?'

'I wanted to put my differences with your brother to one side. Why do you think I went there? I went there to speak to him about you and me, to beg him for his help. I wanted to settle matters between us.'

Diana looked up at him; her eyes had turned a glacial blue and flinched as if he had beaten her. 'You mean the land.'

'That's right, the land. I wanted the problem sorted out... before...'

'And that is why you started romancing me, isn't it? Your feud with my brother?'

Brett was silent for a long moment. He found it impossible to lie to her. And yet in this mood, he feared that she would refuse to understand. 'Do you want me to answer that?'

'Yes. I need the truth. I deserve the truth. Now.'

'Very well, then—the truth. I had planned on using our appearance together at the ball to force your brother to sell me the land. But it all changed once I actually encountered you. You must believe that, Diana. I sought you out because I liked you. The ball was a triumph for you. We came together because I desired you and you desired me. Think about that.'

'I don't want to think about that.' She put her hand to her head. 'I wish I had never met you.'

'And what would you have done if your brother had died in that accident?'

'Survive!' Diana's head came up, eyes blazing.

'Let me help you. Confide in me. I know you must be worried about your brother.' He reached out and caught her chin, forcing her blue-green gaze to meet his own grey one. She had to understand what he was saying. His motives might have been wrong at the beginning, but now he was acting from the best possible motives. 'I want to help. Diana, we are friends. Lovers!'

'You have done enough.' Diana wrenched her head away. She had believed in him and it had all been a lie. 'I think it is best if we part.'

Brett regarded Diana, and was tempted to draw her into his arms again, but retained control. Her head was high and her mouth pinched. It would only make matters worse. She had to understand how ashamed he was. How bitterly he regretted his earlier intentions, but how glad he was to know her now.

'There is much that is unsettled between us, Diana.' He held out his arms and willed her to walked into them and lay her head against his shoulder. She retreated to the window. 'Come away with me. Let us speak privately. We are good together.'

'There is no *us*. Today has shown me what my responsibilities are—my brother and his son.'

'Don't you have a responsibility towards yourself?' Brett continued on remorselessly. 'You were happy with me. I enjoyed spending time with you. You must believe that.'

'I have no idea what I believe any more.'

'We were good together, Diana, and we can be good again.'

'You have no right to say that to me.'

'I have every right! I claim the right...after what we shared.'

She held out her hand. 'Goodbye, Brett, I believe this is where it ends. There are times when one can't follow one's desires. I spent five years rebuilding my life. I do not intend to throw it away on some mistaken moment of passion.'

'It does not end, until I say it does.' Brett clenched his hands at his sides. He wanted to shake her, to make her see that she was trying to erect barriers between them. He had no intention of hurting her. He had never lifted a finger against a woman and he did not intend to start now.

'No, it ends now. I am no wanton woman. I am a lady. And I will not be used in this manner. Did you ever think about what you were doing to me?'

'I only thought about what you were doing to me, Diana. I…grew to like you.'

'You used me and our friendship. I will not be treated in this fashion!'

'And that is your final decision. Is there any way I can make it right?' Brett tried to force his lips to turn up and his voice to purr, but all he heard was the anguish and the despair.

'There is.' She gestured towards the door, unmoving, and unyielding. 'Jenkins will see you out. Go, Lord Coltonby, your presence is not required here. Ever.'

'As you wish.' Brett strode out of the room and did not dare look back.

'If you set the tray down much harder, you will wake the dead.' Simon's voice caused Diana to jump as she tiptoed in the next morning to leave a pot of tea.

'You were supposed to be asleep.'

'I have been awake for hours.' He flashed her a smile. 'Your pacing about your bedroom did not help. You will wear a groove in the carpet.'

'Lord Coltonby made me angry. He…' Diana stopped. Her feelings were too new and vulnerable. She could not explain. All she knew was that he had started his seduction with the express intent of humiliating her. 'It does not matter now.'

'Lord Coltonby saved my life. I have been lying here thinking that. The boiler was already going when he pulled me from the engine. I misjudged the man. He is no fop whose only concern is his clothes and his horses. He risked his life to save me, a man who bore him ill will.' His green gaze pierced hers. 'He is an honourable man. If he says a thing, then he means it. I intend to sell him the land, Diana. I trust his motives.'

'But you said...' Diana stared at her brother in astonishment. He seemed more relaxed than he had in a long time, as he used to be before he had married Jayne.

'I was not thinking straight. Laudanum will do that to a man.' He held up his hand and gave a half-grimace, half-smile. 'Not an excuse, Diana, simply an explanation. I will live yesterday for the rest of my life, but all my men survived. It will be a long time before I touch another engine.'

'All those things you said.' Diana put her hand to her mouth. 'They were a lie?'

'Words of a man driven beyond his endurance. I have no proof that Coltonby and Bolt were in league together. None at all. I have no idea why Coltonby came to the colliery yesterday, but I am grateful that he did.'

'He went to speak to you about the land. You were right, Simon, and I was wrong. He was seeking to use me. He was going to humiliate me at the ball.'

'But he didn't.'

'No,' Diana replied slowly. 'But all the same, it is why he started paying me attention. I have been a fool, brother.'

'Diana.' Her brother held out his hand. She blindly groped for it. 'What has gone on between you two?'

'It does not matter, brother. It is over now. Finished.' Diana slipped her hand from his. She closed her eyes. Suddenly she felt old and tired. With the saying of the words, something within her had withered and died.

'If he ever harms a hair on your head, he is dead. I do

not care that I owe my life to him. I would gladly sacrifice it for your honour.'

'It won't come to that.' A shiver went down her spine. 'I promise you that. Our friendship has finished.'

Chapter Fifteen

'Lord Coltonby promised to take me back in his carriage.' Robert's voice held a distinct whine as Diana attempted to persuade him into the carriage a week later. Doctor Allen had agreed that Robert could return and Simon had decreed that it was vital the boy continue his education. The constant banging of doors and heavy footsteps had made Simon's head pound.

'Your father has decided that you are returning to school today. I don't think we can bother Lord Coltonby again.' Diana kept her voice steady. She refused to think about the fight she and Brett had had.

She wished a thousand times that she could unsay those words, but they were there. She hadn't wanted him to go. She had wanted him to take her in his arms and whisper that he cared about her. And that it did not matter how it had begun, only that he cared for her now. She wanted to have a second chance, but Brett had never sent word and she had her pride.

Sleep had been far from her mind this last week. Simon had even commented on her listlessness. His burns were healing, but his temper was becoming shorter by the day. Nothing anyone did was right.

She had jumped at the chance to return Robert to school and gain some measure of freedom. With Robert gone, perhaps Simon would not complain as much about the disturbances and her life could begin to return to normal. The morning sun shone crisp and clear, a change from the incessant drizzle of the last five days. Diana took it as a sign to get on with the business of living.

Today was all about picking up the pieces of her life. It was better this way—ending before they had really begun. Brett would thank her in time. She knew that she now had a little compartment in her head marked *Brett Farnham* and *what might have been.* Six days ago, she had discovered that there would be no consequences to their joyous afternoon picnic. She knew she should be going down on her knees and thanking God that nothing worse had come of it, but she discovered that all she wanted to do was to forget and forgetting seemed beyond her.

'Please, get into the carriage and stop chattering about Lord Coltonby and his horses.'

'But why? He is an agreeable man. He liked me. I could tell.' Robert's bottom lip stuck out and he suddenly bore an uncanny resemblance to Simon when he had refused to take his medicine earlier that morning.

'You were able to ride on his horse. It will have to suffice.' She knew her voice was far too sharp, but she silently begged him to drop the subject.

'No one will believe me,' Robert muttered. 'And it is all your fault. You could have sent him a note. He said to send him word and he'd come.'

A note? She had the remnants of her pride. He had to apologise first. She looked up at the ceiling of the carriage and composed herself. 'Is that important? You know the truth.'

'Yes.' Robert climbed into the carriage and sat opposite her with a mutinous face and crossed arms. 'He promised, and you have neglected to tell him that we are leaving today. He would have let me sit next to him. He told me so. You made him break his promise.'

'Robert, you must refrain for asking for things.' Diana patted the seat next to her. 'Come, sit beside me and we will be on our way. I am sure the other boys will be anxious to speak to you about your adventures. And even if they are not, school is about more than adventures.'

Just then a yellow carriage pulled into the stable yard, blocking their exit. Brett jumped down from the coachman's position. Diana's heart leapt. Here. After all, as he had said. She wanted to rush out and apologise. She wanted him to scoop her into his arms and whisper words of remorse, of love. She made a face. She might as well ask for the moon. She remained in the carriage, her fingers gripping her reticule.

'I see I have arrived in time.' Brett opened the door to their carriage and peered in. His smile grew as he saw the occupants. 'It is well that word was sent.'

'No word was sent.'

He merely raised an eyebrow. 'This carriage looks to be a bit cramped. Mine will be better suited for our purposes.'

Robert immediately rushed from his seat and pushed past Brett. 'Your carriage, truly?'

'After you, my lady,' he said with an exaggerated bow. 'Your nephew has agreed with me.'

'We are not going with you.' She crossed her arms, but was absurdly pleased she had worn her deep crimson pelisse, the one with two shoulder capes and fashionable trim. 'Robert, we need to leave. I must return you to school today. I have promised your father.'

Robert paid no attention to her, but continued to regard Brett's carriage with awe. He started towards where the groom held the horses.

'It appears your nephew has other ideas.'

'My nephew should learn what is good for him.'

A faint smile played on Brett's lips. 'He reminds me of his aunt—strong willed.'

'You mean pig-headed.'

'You were the one to say the word.' His face sobered. 'I have missed you Diana, more than I dreamt possible.'

'The other day...' Diana paused and wondered how she could explain without betraying her feelings.

'You were upset over your brother. We will speak no more of it.' His eyes hardened. 'I am not proud of what I did, but if I hadn't, we would not have become friends. Thank you for having Robert send the note.'

'I...I never did.'

'Friends?' he asked. 'Can we start again? Properly this time? You and I?'

'Neighbours,' she answered and held out her hand.

His eyes lowered to her lips. 'I believe I will wait for your friendship.'

'You may have to wait a long time.'

'Or very little.' He leant forward and brushed her cheek. 'I have missed you, Diana.'

'Is this your carriage? I mean the one you use for the Four in Hand?' Robert asked in awe, breaking into the conversation. Diana slumped back against the seat back; her lips ached as if he had touched them. 'They are always yellow, or so Henry says. Henry Sowerby is going to be a whip when he grows up.'

'Henry Sowerby is the one who was responsible for the

stink bomb, apparently,' Diana replied at Brett's questioning look. 'I can't tell if Henry is a person to be admired or despised.'

'Probably both in equal measure.' Brett gave a warm laugh and Diana felt her insides turn over.

'You don't have to take Robert. It is a long journey. Simon has agreed that I should use his carriage. It has all been arranged, even down to the coaching inn I should use if I become over-tired on the return journey.' Diana kept her voice firm. She had no idea why Brett was here or who had told him to come. Possibly Rose. But she refused to play his game.

'I gave my promise, Diana. I intend to keep it. It is his choice.' Brett's face became inscrutable. 'You may accompany us if you feel it necessary. I would welcome it.'

Diana stared at Brett. Why was he doing this? What was he asking?

'Aunt Diana?' Robert tugged at her skirt.

'Robert,' Diana said with firmness, 'Lord Coltonby has kindly offered to take us to Newcastle, but your father has lent us the carriage. I know what your father would want us to do.'

'I would like to go in Lord Coltonby's carriage, if you please, Aunt. Papa will be pleased as then he can use the carriage to go out to the colliery. He won't care how I go. He wants me gone.'

'Robert Clare! How dare you say such a thing about your dear papa.'

'But I heard him saying the very thing this morning, before breakfast.'

'His head pains him. He has lost sight in one eye.'

'But it is what he wants.'

'Good lad,' Brett murmured. 'And you will be joining us as well, won't you, Diana?'

Diana drew a deep breath. What exactly was Brett playing at? Go with him? Share a carriage with him there and back? Slowly she shook her head. 'I have promised my brother that I will see Robert safely returned to school. It will have to be in this carriage.'

'There is room in my carriage for you.'

'Please, Aunt.' Robert hung on her arm. 'You did promise I could ride behind them. And it is a coach and four.'

'When, if not now?' Brett's eyes twinkled. 'You know you want to. I will drive and you may ride in the carriage.'

'But—' Diana tried to think of all the reasons why this was a bad idea, except she had missed his company. Going in the carriage while he drove would be no different from riding in the carriage when John drove.

'I will return you by nightfall, I promise. The horses are high steppers. They will easily make it to Newcastle and back. There will be no need for a coaching inn.'

'Oh, Aunt, please, please. You must come with me. It is the only way.'

'Please.' Brett's voice was no more than a breath.

Diana wondered for an instant if she had heard correctly. Was he begging her?

'It is impossible to fight you both. Robert, please inform your father that Lord Coltonby is here and we shall see what he says. I know he will agree with me.'

Robert ran off before she could stop him and they were left alone in the stable yard. Diana pretended interest in the clasp of her reticule as Brett silently watched her.

'What are you looking at?' she asked, feeling the colour on her cheeks begin to rise.

'I was merely wondering if the sensible Miss Clare was coming or if we were going to be treated to Diana.'

'I am always the same person. Miss Clare will suffice.'

'I much prefer Diana.' He lengthened the last word, rolled it in his mouth, giving it sensuous possibilities that she had never dreamt of.

Diana turned her head. Despite what he had done to her, it would be very easy to fall in love with this man. A fatal mistake. The last thing he wanted or desired was love. 'You spout pretty fables.'

'You have not taken to wearing a cap again. I wonder why that is.'

'Robert will be back soon.' Diana kept her voice steady. She refused to let him provoke her.

'He is a pleasant child—a credit to the woman who raised him.'

'I look on him as my own.'

'But he is your brother's.'

'Yes, he is. Sometimes, I wonder if my brother sees it. His wife, Jayne, was wild. It was not a happy marriage.'

'Does your brother's ill-considered marriage mean you are condemned to repeat the same mistakes?'

'I make my own mistakes.' Diana regarded the tassles on her reticule. 'There are some to whom marriage is an aspiration, but not to me. I have seen how easily a woman can be trapped.'

'Surely that depends on the spouse, rather than on the institution itself.'

'I could never marry solely for duty.'

'It is a good way to be.' His lips became a thin white line. 'Sometimes one does not have a choice.'

'One always has choices. It is the consequences that give trouble.'

'This is true. Are you suffering from any consequences?'

'None that I know of.'

'It is good to hear.'

An ice-cold fist closed around Diana's heart. Robert would be back in a few moments with Simon and everything would be over. Only she was not sure she wanted it to be.

'If we are indeed going in your carriage, things will have to be moved.' Diana turned her attention to making sure the basket of food and other essentials for Robert were transferred over into Brett's carriage. 'The sooner everything is properly stowed, the sooner we can leave.'

'I am yours to command.'

'Coltonby.' Simon's voice rang out across the yard. 'My son says that you intend on returning him to school.'

'I made a promise.' Brett glared at Simon. Diana offered up a small prayer that they would not come to blows.

'So I understand.' Simon looked away and his shoulders hunched. 'You sent me a banker's draft.'

'It is for the land as we agreed.'

Diana looked between her brother and Brett. They had been in communication? Her brother had given Brett the land? A niggling suspicion rose within her. The mysterious note sender was standing in front of her, holding the banker's draft aloft like it was some trophy.

'It is twice what I originally asked for.' Simon held up the piece of paper, and tore it into shreds. 'You saved my life, Coltonby and my life is worth far more than a parcel of land.'

'Any man would have done what I did.'

'You hold yourself in too little esteem, Coltonby.'

Diana cleared her throat. 'I will go with Robert and make sure he is settled.'

'You will need a chaperon, Diana,' her brother said, his face becoming stern.

'I can take Rose.'

'Rose is needed here. She makes excellent tisanes. If you are to be gone, who will look after me if my head should pain again?'

'I will return Miss Clare before nightfall. My horses can easily make the journey there and back.'

The men regarded each other and then Simon nodded. 'You bring her back—safely.'

'That is my intention,' Brett replied. 'I gave you my word at the ball, as a fellow Cantabrigian. I see no reason to break it.'

'I will hold you to it then. Diana, you see that Robert is properly settled at school.' Simon turned on his heel and went back inside the house.

Diana stared after him in astonishment while Brett looked at her with a smug expression on his face.

'Are you ready to go, Miss Diana?'

'It would appear everything has already been decided.' Diana started to mount the steps up to the carriage.

'Details can be important.' Brett saluted her with his whip.

'Can I ride on the top with Lord Coltonby?' Robert asked.

'You are too young,' Diana said firmly.

Robert raised both of his hands, but Brett shook his head. 'It would be a brave man who would go against your aunt. You will have plenty of time when you grow up.'

'But you might not be here.'

'I am planning on putting roots down in Northumberland.' He gave a significant look at Diana. 'It seems like a good place to raise children.'

'The fresh air is very good for them.'

'So I understand.'

'I wish you and your bride-to-be every happiness.' She

kept her back straight and refused to think about what Brett's children might be like. She hated the thought of having to meet them and whoever his wife might be. But it would be far worse if she had accepted his half-hearted proposal. Then she would have had to suffer his growing indifference and to become little more than a wearisome burden inflicted upon him by his devotion to some misguided duty.

'Aren't you putting the cart before the horse? I have to marry first.'

'It is usually best.' She forced a laugh from her throat. 'No doubt next season's crop of débutantes will yield an appropriate countess.'

His eyes narrowed. 'We had best depart if you want to return before nightfall.'

'I definitely intend on returning before nightfall. You gave your word.'

'Unforeseen circumstances…'

'Unforeseen circumstances had best not happen. I trust you to do everything in your power to prevent them.'

'Then you will allow Robert to ride up with me.'

'Do I have much choice?'

'No.' Brett lifted an eyebrow, but Diana kept her face composed. She refused to give in. She had put passion behind her. What had happened out by the grotto would not happen again. Today would be a test and she would succeed. 'You are always a pleasure to cross swords with, Diana. No one could accuse you of being boring.'

'I do my best.' Diana climbed into the carriage and sat down on the well-sprung seats as she ignored the sound of Brett's hearty laugh.

The trip to Newcastle sped by. Every so often she would hear Robert's excited voice and Brett's deeper, more gravelled one answering him. Never condescending or hurried, but firm and authoritative. She had to admit that Brett did know how to control the ribbons. He also appeared to have discovered the secret of controlling Robert.

When they arrived at the red brick school, she expected tears or at the very least protestations, but no sooner had the carriage stopped, than Robert climbed down and opened the door for her.

'I have promised to do my best, Aunt Diana,' he said. 'I won't let you down.'

'And remember, my promise,' Brett said, coming to stand by him. 'Be attentive to your lessons, and no more bad reports, then I will instruct you on the finer points of carriage driving.'

Diana looked from Brett to Robert. All through the journey, she had dreaded something like this. What could she say to him? She knew that it was a pie-crust promise. Brett would develop a new enthusiasm and Robert would face yet another disappointment. She kept her chin raised. There would be time enough to explain to Robert later.

'I do mean it, Diana,' Brett said softly. 'How else can I prove to you that I keep my word?'

The timely appearance of Dr Allen and the school's matron prevented Diana from answering.

'Will your horses be all right for the journey back?' Diana asked Brett after Robert had been settled back in school. 'How long do they need to rest?'

'They should be fine. I did not push them too hard to get here. Your nephew was enjoying the feeling of being a whip. You should have seen him holding the ribbons. The boy is a natural. He asked ever so many good questions. He made me think.'

'I saw his face. You have another worshipper, Brett.' Diana pressed her hands together. Simon might not be pleased when he discovered it, but it had certainly made the journey much less fraught. 'I wanted to thank you for what you did. You did not have to.'

'You mean arriving here with a great flourish and the horses going at full gallop?' Brett laughed. 'I can still remember what schoolboys love. I only wish I had thought to bring a mail coach's trumpet.'

'Why did you do it?'

'Because everyone needs someone to make a fuss of them.'

'He has me.'

His gaze travelled slowly down her form. 'You are not a man.'

Diana was grateful for her bonnet. 'I would have had a bad time of it without you and your antics. I thank you for that.'

'I am pleased you see some small use for me.'

'Yes, a small use,' she agreed with a laugh. 'I suppose we ought to go. It wouldn't do for Robert to think we were spying on him.' She covered her hand with her mouth. 'I wanted to apologise for what I said the other day. I had no right to question you like that.'

'Did I say anything?'

'You must understand—I refuse to be used in that fashion.' Her stomach trembled but she had said it.

'Intentions are different from actions, Diana. And my intentions changed, once I began to know you. You must believe that I have every intention of protecting you and your reputation.'

'I will believe that when it happens.'

'Allow me to prove it to you. Will you then admit it? Or are you too proud?'

'Why must we always argue?' Diana whispered. 'I much prefer it when we get along.'

Brett didn't answer. He simply stared down at her with his steady grey eyes, eyes that had nearly turned to silver.

'You are the most provoking of men.'

'I think I enjoy being provoking.'

'Well, I am not entirely sure that I enjoy it.' Diana opened the carriage door. She would end this conversation now, before that little piece of her insisted on continuing their relationship, before she begged for his kiss, before she began believing his promises.

'Which way shall we go back?' Brett asked.

Her hand trembled on the door frame. 'Do I have a choice?'

'We can go back a longer, more scenic route if you wish.' Brett's hand closed over hers. 'I promise to refrain from provoking you, well…not unless you *want* to be provoked.'

A tingle washed up her arm. The scenic route. A room in an anonymous inn. Brett and her. Together. It would be so easy. For a long time, she found it difficult to breathe. 'You promised to return to Ladywell by nightfall.'

'It could still happen.'

Diana gently withdrew her hand, and put the temptation far from her. She refused to do that. She had not sunk so far down into wanton wickedness that she used the return of her nephew to school as an excuse for a liaison with her lover.

The whole idea when she considered it held an unsavoury ring.

She had not sunk that low. She retained her principles. The madness that had enveloped her over the past few days would end. She held on to the thought and let it crowd out all her desires.

'I would like to return home as quickly as possible.' Her

words tripped over each other in her rush to get them out. 'You may spare the horses, but Simon will want to hear about how Robert got on at school. He does care about his son.'

Aware that she was beginning to babble, Diana clamped her lips shut. She willed him to say something. To show that he understood. These feelings inside her were at war with each other. She desired him, but she needed more than desire. She needed more than a half-hearted proposal. She had seen the relief on his face when she had refused him.

Brett regarded her with clear grey gaze. He continued to stand close, too close. She watched the way the sunlight caught his buttons and turned them darker. 'A closed stuffy carriage or up beside the driver in the fresh air—where do you want to ride?'

Diana swallowed hard, turned her attention from the way his buttons looked against the crisp linen of his shirt. She knew if she rode within the carriage, she would not have a chance to speak with Brett. And she had missed him and his teasing tones more than she had thought possible. It would be the end of everything. Irrevocably.

She would end it after today. He would depart for somewhere unknown and, if they ever met again, they would be able to make polite meaningless conversation.

But would it do any lasting harm if she allowed herself to dream for one more afternoon? Within a few hours, they would be back in Ladywell and her life would continue on its preordained path.

'Up in the open air,' she whispered, her voice barely audible to her ears. She blinked, scarcely able to believe she had said the words aloud.

'Diana?' He leant forward and his breath kissed her lips. 'You were impossible to hear.'

'I will ride up beside you,' she said quickly before she

changed her mind. A queer fizzing excitement went through her veins. 'I want to see how you handle the ribbons of a Four in Hand. I may be able to learn something in case I should ever encounter an obstacle course again.'

He gave a half-smile. 'Ever the sensible Miss Clare.'

'Is it sensible to ride up next to the driver?' She peeked up from under her eyelashes. 'It is the first time I have heard that.'

'Oh, very sensible. Quite the best option. You get a whole new view of life when you sit beside the driver.'

'I thought you promised not to provoke me.'

'I said that I would do my best. That is a different promise entirely.'

'Is it? Are you going to twist your words?'

'Can I help it if a certain woman persists in forgetting the exact nature of the words?' His face became a picture of injured innocence.

'And if that woman considered him to be a supreme twister of words?'

'Then she'd be wrong…as she has been wrong about so many things.'

'About so many things?' she whispered and tried to ignore the racing of her heart.

'We need to go if you wish to return to Ladywell before nightfall.'

He helped her up to the perch and then clambered up beside her. Diana had to squeeze over to one side. Brett's leg pressed against hers and all her resolutions appeared to fade away like the mist in front of the sun. He leant forward and his knuckles grazed her breast as he reached for the reins. She drew in her breath sharply.

He said nothing, but gave her an eloquent look before concentrating on arranging the ribbons. Diana bit her lip and decided a dignified silence was her best option.

The coach began to roll away from the school and back into the Newcastle traffic.

The view from up top was entirely different from the view through the carriage window. Tops of carriages, second-floor windows where clerks worked busily at their desks, bonnets covered in flowers and silk intermingled with top hats and flat caps.

She half-turned in her perch. Robert's school was rapidly swallowed up in the traffic of the city. Carts and carriages crowded the streets, suddenly moving forwards and closing spaces where a breath before the road had been clear. Twice Diana was certain they would hit a delivery van or a cart. She sucked in her breath and shrank as the carriage passed through an impossibly narrow gap. Brett put an arm about her shoulders, but she rapidly sat up straight and folded her hands in her lap.

'Impressive driving.' She tried for a calm and measured tone, ignoring his slightly triumphant look. 'There are very few who could make it through that.'

'It is easy once you know the trick. As I explained to Robert, carriage driving is like life. You need to keep your attention focused. And your concentration far enough ahead. It is all about anticipating obstacles. And there are always pot-holes to trip up the unwary or inattentive.'

'I worry that I might get in your way. Perhaps you ought to stop and I will go below.'

'As long as you don't make a sudden lunge for the ribbons, we will be fine.'

He gave a little flick and the horses increased their speed as they left the smoke-shrouded city behind. It seemed as if they were in their own world, up here on the coachman's perch. Diana shivered slightly as the chill of the wind hit her, and wished she had thought to bring her thick shawl as well as her crimson pelisse. That had to be the cause.

It was never a shiver of anticipation, a reaction to her leg nestled against his, her shoulder touching his.

'Are you cold?'

'I will be fine. I thought I would be riding in the carriage and did not bring a shawl.'

'You can go down there, if you want. I will stop the horses.'

'No, I like the view from up here.'

He put his arm around her and drew her into the circle of his arms. 'Is this better?'

She relaxed against his body and rested her cheek on his chest, listening to his heart thump. Warm, comforting and altogether far too enticing. She closed her eyes and sought to hang on to every detail. When this was all over, she would keep the image fresh.

'What are you doing?' he asked when she opened her eyes. 'You have the most intent expression on your face.'

'Making a memory.' She struggled to sit upright. 'I will be fine now. The air is quite pleasant in the sunshine.'

'I am honoured that you want to remember this moment.'

Their gaze caught and held for a long moment. Diana felt the inexorable pull towards him, towards the slippery slope called—falling in love. She also knew the ending and the heartache that came with it. She started to say something, but finally opted for a light tone. 'How many times do I get to see an expert in action?'

'How many times indeed?' He flicked the reins and the horses started moving faster, their hooves beating against the stones.

Diana watched as his hands expertly controlled everything. She knew in the hands of a less-experienced driver, the horses would be running away, out of control, but with Brett, they obeyed the least flicker of the ribbons.

As they approached a village, he pulled the thundering horses back. Immediately they slowed.

A cart loomed ahead, blocking half of the road. A labourer was busy loading barrels. Nothing untowards. Diana sucked in her breath as she saw a bright blue pinafore dart out into the road.

'Brett!' Her hand reached out instinctively to steady herself, but tangled with the ribbons.

Brett cursed long and loud. He pulled back hard. Diana felt her body slam into the railing as the carriage turned sharply, colliding with the cart. Everything slowed down and seemed to take an age.

Images flashed—the little girl in blue, the ball, the lead horse rearing, Brett's arms straining against the ribbons as he struggled to avoid the girl. A piercing scream resounded in the air, followed by the slow crunch of wood. With the noise, the speed started to move double quick and Diana felt the carriage lurch to one side and then the other. Everything hurtled forwards and then stopped. The world became dark.

Diana risked a breath and found her lungs could fill without an ache. She raised a shaking hand and pushed her bonnet back from her forehead.

'Are you injured?' Brett asked, his dark grey eyes peering into hers.

'I am fine, a little shaken.' Diana put her hand to her face. 'I never meant to…'

'It was an accident. You must not think about it.'

'How is the little girl? And the horses?'

'I will see to the horses now, but the child appears unharmed. Her mother pulled her to safety.' Brett lightly jumped down from his perch.

'I still don't know how you missed her.'

'I drive to the inch. There is a practical reason for it.'

A farmer hung on to the bridle of the lead horse. Diana could see a pregnant woman had scooped the child up and was cradling her in her arms. Everything would be fine. It was only objects that were damaged. Not people. The accident could have been much worse.

Diana sank back against the seat, trembling. She heard the farmer's raised voice, the wail of the child and Brett's measured tones. Everything flowed over her as a late butterfly fluttered a few inches from her nose. Silently, she pleaded that everything would be fine and they would quickly continue on their way.

'Everything is solved, Diana, but you need to get down.' Brett reached up a hand to help her down. He wanted to gather her into his arms. The accident could have been so much worse. All he could see was how she had very nearly fallen, but had clung on. The images played over and over in his mind and he knew that he faced many nights waking up in a cold sweat, haunted by what might have happened. Today was not supposed to have been about losing her, but regaining her trust, demonstrating in the only way he knew how that he cared and wanted to start again. He wished to think that friendship was enough.

'Yes, I think I will ride inside the carriage.'

'It won't be possible. Not yet,' Brett said gravely. He gave a wave to the farm labourer. The farmer's cart bore some signs of damage, but it was the wheels of the carriage that needed to be repaired.

'Is the carriage all right? You managed to stop before any lasting damage was done.' Diana's smile faded. 'Will we be able to continue on our journey? We will return to Ladywell today.'

'There will be a delay. The wheels need to be seen to. I will not drive an unsafe carriage, Diana, not even for you.'

'How long of a delay?' Her eyes showed alarm. 'I wanted to get back to Ladywell tonight.'

'There is an inn down the road—the Angel. Respectable, but not fashionable. I will get you a private room.' Brett willed her to understand. He had no desire to compromise her. He wished now that he had thought to bring her maid, someone to make the stay respectable. But he had been certain that time alone would be the correct way to woo her.

'Your version of respectable may differ from mine.'

'Or the farmer's.' Brett reached over and readjusted her bonnet so it was sitting more firmly on her head. 'The mail coach stops there. It is the best the village has to offer. The only place. You will have to brave it, as will I. The village is quiet and so we should be able to get rooms.'

'Can I take the mail coach?' The words tumbled out, tripping over each other in her rush to get them out. 'Rose and Simon will be expecting me home today. They will wonder what has happened.'

'It has departed.'

'Departed?' Her hands went to her bonnet, straightening it and re-straightening it. 'How could it have already departed? It was my best hope of returning to Ladywell. You promised.'

'Are you saying that I somehow planned the accident?'

'No, no. There was nothing you could have done about it.'

He pressed his lips together, feeling a great pit open in his stomach. He wanted her, but he needed her to want him in his life as well as in her bed. This time when he proposed, she would be left in no doubt that his proposal went beyond lip service to duty.

'Your plans will be delayed.' He held up his hands,

cutting off her protest. 'Your brother is aware how long it takes to get back from Newcastle and the hazards on the road. How many times has your brother arrived home later than first anticipated?'

'I suppose you are correct.' Diana swallowed hard. The image of Brett and her together, limbs intertwined danced in front of her eyes. She screwed them up and banished it. He had said rooms—plural. She had to concentrate on being sensible. What had been between them had flared briefly and then vanished. All that remained were the embers of a friendship.

'I know I am correct. It is beyond my control.'

'It seems so pat—the rake and the broken carriage. My brother may fear for my reputation.'

'You were the one who grabbed my arm. Perhaps I should fear for mine.' He gave a half-smile. 'I made a promise to your brother. I will protect you.'

'What exactly has happened to the carriage?' Diana wrapped her arms about her waist. 'Will it take long to fix? A delay of an hour or two will not make too much of a difference. We can still arrive back when it is not too late.'

'One of the wheels has come loose and the horses have suffered a bad fright. It would be folly to continue on today.'

But was it folly to remain here? Somehow their fate had been decided against her plea. She seemed to be drawn inexorably into his arms. And she knew that this time, her heart would go with her.

'I see.' Diana tightened her hold on her reticule. 'It is important to make sure the carriage is adequately fixed. I would hate to be delayed longer.'

'It would be far worse if we set out with it in ill repair.'

Brett's fingers tightened on her elbow, leading her away from the carriage and towards the Angel and its creaking sign. 'There are some risks I refuse to take.'

Chapter Sixteen

'There you go, hinny, a nice cup of tea to restore you.'

Diana gave the landlady a trembling smile. She cautiously took a sip and allowed the hot strong sugary brew to wash through her system. Although the tea was far sweeter than she would normally take it, it had a restorative effect. 'It is very fine.'

'A good cup of tea does a body good, despite what the doctors say.' The landlady smoothed her skirts. 'There is nothing like a singing kettle to put me in a good mood.'

Diana gazed about the room. It was simple but comfortable. Far more than she had hoped for. A small fire glowed in the grate and there was even a mirror over the dressing table. She set the cup down on the small table next to the armchair.

'Yes, I like a cup of tea.'

'You looked like the sort.' The landlady bustled around the room. 'Your man has ordered a private meal for you. He thought you might find it easier. We tend to get a few drovers come through on their way home from the Hexham cattle market. They are harmless, mostly.'

'Thank you.' Diana held back the words explaining that Brett was far from being her man. Neither did she like to think about the few cattle drovers who were not harmless.

'It is good that you have someone like that looking after you.'

Diana took a careful sip of her tea. 'Yes, he has his uses. Were there enough rooms for him?'

The woman gave her a sharp look and Diana cursed her tongue. 'He will be in the stables. It is the proper place for coachmen.' She gave a loud sniff as if she had heard about Diana riding up beside him, rather than within the carriage.

Diana fought the temptation to laugh. It was probably better that Brett had done that. If it became known that Lord Coltonby and she had become stranded, she doubted that anyone would believe the innocence of it. But the landlady's outrage at the merest suggestion that a coachman should have a private room threatened to send her into fits of barely suppressed laughter. No doubt, it would be a story that would be chewed over and over again by Brett's friends. How he had outwitted a landlady and made her believe he was a coachman.

'Yes, it is the proper place for a coachman. Hopefully the carriage will be speedily repaired. I wish to continue on with my journey tomorrow.'

'You should be able to. It didn't sound too bad and Joe the blacksmith is a right good one.' The landlady dropped her voice. 'At first I worried that you and he might be escaping to the Headless Cross at Gretna Green. There are quite a few couples who come this way, you know. And I don't want any midnight knocking on doors. I run a respectable establishment.'

'We were returning my nephew to his school in New-castle, and I am on my way home.'

'You can't be too careful. Still, I could see why you might be tempted with that one. He has a very fine manner for a coachman.'

'I think I am far too old to be contemplating such behaviour.' Diana shifted uneasily. Brett could never come up here to her room. The gossip would spread through the village and from the village to other areas—all speaking about the lady in the yellow carriage who had entertained her coachman. He had promised to safeguard her reputation.

'You're only too old, when you're dead.'

Diana opened and closed her mouth several times. 'I think it would be best if I waited in the parlour. I want to know the extent of the carriage's damage and how long it will take to repair. Please inform him of my request when he returns.'

The woman appraised her. A crafty gleam came into her eye and Diana shifted uncomfortably, feeling the heat grow on her cheeks. She had not made a decision yet. All she knew was that she did not want to wait in her room like some short-heeled wench who only needed the gentlest of pushes to fall on her back. 'Aye, there is one. You can wait there if you like.'

'I would prefer it. It is more seemly, somehow.'

'More seemly. Aye, it is that.'

She followed the woman down to the back parlour. The landlady bustled about the room, straightening the pillows on the sofa. Another pot of tea and plate of shortbread were produced and placed in front of the fire. The landlady held out a claw-like hand as her eyes became crafty. 'I will need extra for the room. For your privacy. You won't want disturbing, will you?'

Diana kept her back straight as she gritted her teeth. Always money. She dug into the bottom of her reticule and held out a few coins. The woman frowned, but pocketed them. 'Once I have spoken to my coachman, I will return up to my room.'

Then she politely but firmly turned the conversation towards the inn and when the mail coach would leave in the morning. If the carriage had not been fixed, she knew she would have to leave anyway.

'And would you like me to send up the scullery maid to help you with your clothes when you are ready?'

'Thankfully, I am wearing a simple gown so I shall manage myself.' Diana kept her chin high.

The landlady gave a nod and tapped her nose. 'I will let your man know where you are when he comes in.'

'I appreciate it.' Diana sat down, and began sipping her tea as she watched the coals burn brightly in the parlour's fire.

The coals had become embers, but Brett had still not appeared or sent word. She picked up the poker and stirred the fire. It erupted into a glorious blaze of colour, but soon burnt down. An indication of her relationship with Brett? A brilliant blaze of intense heat and then nothing?

She glanced out of the window and saw the night had drawn in. To her right, the distant clangs of the bar sounded as more and more men gathered. And even though she knew it was silly to wish it, she felt disappointed that Brett had failed to come to see her. He had to have been finished with the blacksmith by now. The sky only held the few last remaining rays of sunlight. No one worked that late. She dug her nails into the palm of her hand. He was avoiding her. Once again she had misread everything. This journey had been about his promise to Robert, rather than him seeking to repair their damaged friendship.

She lifted the bell, ready to ring for the landlady and to have protection going up the stairs. When she next encountered Brett, she would be distant. Today had taught her the necessity of that. This long agonising wait, this pointless wait—and for what?

Her whole life seemed to stretch out in front of her, grey and colourless, as she grew ever older and eventually even Robert and Simon would stop needing her.

Today's accident had taught her how quickly things could change. How precious life was. It was strange that Simon never saw that. All he seemed obsessed with was creating this engine and making it move. His brush with death had only made him more stubborn, but hers had changed her.

She gave one last glimpse at the dying fire. She wasn't willing to sit there waiting any longer.

Heavy footsteps sounded in the hall. Her hand stilled, waited for the footstep to move onwards.

A discreet knock echoed in the room. Diana tilted her head. The footsteps weren't right. Should she answer the door? The knock came again, this time heavier and more impatient. She opened it a crack and a heavy-set man stood there, swaying and grinning. She went to slam the door, but he stuck his fingers out and caught it.

'You don't have protection.' His words were slurred and the stench of beer assaulted Diana's nose. 'A woman such as yourself should have protection.'

His words sent shivers down her spine. He should have said lady, not woman. What did he take her for?

'I would suggest you return to the bar or wherever you came from.' Diana stood blocking the doorway. She measured the distance from the door to the fire grate and the poker. Did she dare run for it? 'I am waiting for someone. He will not be best pleased to see you.'

'I think you want company.' The man wiped his hand across his mouth. 'Women like you always want company. Mrs Dawkins thought you might, seeing as you was still here.'

Women like her? Diana blinked. He had made a serious mistake, but she had made a worse one. She had thought herself safe in this room.

'You will leave this instant.' Diana used her sternest voice and pointed in the direction of the bar.

'I like them feisty.'

He started towards her. Diana backed away. One step at a time. She would prevail and when she emerged, she would never ever have anything to do with Brett Farnham again. Respectable inn? Hah!

'I am asking politely—go now, please.'

'How are you going to make me, a little scrap like you?'

She reached behind her and her hand closed over the poker. She drew a breath and summoned her courage. She would have one chance, one blow. She lifted the poker slightly, adjusted her handgrip, steadied her legs. 'Go.'

'The lady has asked you to leave. Politely,' Brett's lazy voice drawled. 'I recommend you take up her suggestion.'

Diana felt the poker slip from her hands. Brett was here, lounging against the doorframe. His body appeared relaxed, but his eyes burnt with a steely determination.

'And if I don't?'

'I will not be responsible for the state of your short-term health.'

'You southerners are all alike. You think you can come up here and make a big noise. All wind and no bottle.'

'I wouldn't concentrate on thinking. It is not a drunkard's strong point.'

'Are you insulting me?' The heavy ox turned, balling his anvil-like fists.

'You were insulting the lady.' Brett straightened his cuffs, as a sardonic smile twisted his lips. 'I returned the coin with interest.'

The man pursed his lips and flexed his huge hands. 'Someone ought to teach you manners. You ought not to talk to your betters like that.'

'It is amazing how we think alike.' Brett's fist connected with the underside of the man's jaw, sending him reeling backwards. 'I did warn him.'

'Did I say a word?' Diana kept her eyes on the fight, but tried to grab the poker again.

The man staggered back, shook his great bull-like head and rushed forwards, fists flailing. Brett easily sidestepped him. The man stopped and then turned, meeting Brett's next punch in his stomach. He doubled over. 'Here, there was no cause to do that,' he spluttered.

'We appear to have a difference of opinion about that.' Brett blew on his knuckles.

'I was going. There is only way out of the room, unless I go by the window,' the man protested.

'Do not tempt me.'

'I was only trying to protect this here piece of fancy.'

'Go, please go.' Diana gestured towards the door. 'Do not make it worse on yourself.'

'But this is the room Mrs Dawkins always puts her girls in. Always the parlour when one of them's free.'

'Not tonight.'

The man seemed to sober. His eyes travelled between Diana and Brett. 'I appear to have made a mistake.'

'Do not compound it by remaining.'

The man started towards the door, mumbling.

'Apologise to the lady. And kindly inform Mrs Dawkins

that this lady is not to be disturbed for the rest of the evening.'

'I am very sorry, but she was asking for it.' The man looked truculent. 'Can I go now?'

Brett grabbed the lapels of the man's coat, stared him in the eye.

'You will humbly crave her pardon. You will never do such a thing again.' Then he released the man's lapels.

'I humbly whatever he says.' The man practically ran out of the room. His footsteps could be heard clumping down the hall.

Brett shut the door with a decisive click, locking it behind him.

'Is it over?' Diana whispered and brought the poker around in front of her. Her fingers refused to let it go. 'I was frightened.'

'It is over,' Brett said. 'The man was drunk. He didn't know what he was saying.'

'But do you think that landlady rents out this room as... as...?'

'I didn't enquire.' He ran his hand through his hair. 'You were supposed to be up in your private room, away from this.'

'The landlady seemed disapproving, and I wanted to find out about the carriage.' She was aware that her cheeks were flaming. 'I could hardly ask her to send my coachman up. What would she think? It would not have been seemly.'

'So you came down here to this room.'

'How was I to know? I expected you back long before now.'

Brett came over. His hand closed around hers. Gently he removed the poker. 'You should return to your room.'

'Yes, I should.' Her feet refused to move. 'Will you escort me there?'

He raised an eyebrow. 'If you think it necessary—I doubt your gentleman caller will return in a hurry. Shall I ring for the landlady?'

'I don't think there is any need to bother Mrs. Dawkins.' She ran her tongue over her parched lips and hoped he'd understand. 'The inn appears full tonight.'

'As you wish.'

He held the door open and she went out of the little room. Her heart pounded so loudly that she thought he must hear it. She led the way up the narrow back passage and heard him follow her. She breathed more easily when she had reached her room, opened the door and gone in. A few remaining coals glowed faintly in the gloom.

He bent over the embers, stirred them up and placed more coal on top. The fire blazed into life, sending shadows playing on the walls. 'It will take the chill off the room.'

Diana stood watching him. She noticed how his muscles moved under his coat. 'Thank you.'

'Think nothing of it.' He stood in front of the fire. 'I came back from the blacksmith's to discover this—the entire inn full of drunken drovers. It was not what I had envisioned.'

'You weren't to know.'

'I should have considered.' His mouth became a thin white line. 'How did he get into the parlour?'

'He knocked. I thought it might be you. The landlady said that she would tell you where I was and that I wanted to speak with you.' Diana gave a half-shrug. 'He put his foot in the door, and…this is all my fault.'

'It is not your fault, Diana, you weren't to know.' He made a face. 'I blame myself.'

'Shall we now argue over who is at fault?'

'Has he harmed you?'

She shook her head and crossed her arms about her, tried to banish the image from her mind. The old Diana would have been curled up in a ball. Her days of being timid and scared of life had truly ended. She knew she would have hit the man with a poker, if he had landed one punch on Brett. 'You arrived in time.'

'Thank heaven for small mercies.' He gave a crooked smile. 'I had given up on divine intervention, but I am willing to concede, Diana Clare, that you have a guardian angel looking after you.'

'How is the carriage?'

'Mended. We can leave at first light, and you will be back home before noon.' He pressed his fingertips together and his brow became furrowed as if he was struggling for control. 'I can station myself outside your door if you wish. Regardless of what people might say, it will be safer that way.'

Outside the door. He was about to walk out of her life.

Diana stared up at the ceiling. It had to come from her. The decision she had made before no longer counted. She wanted to be with this man. She wanted to show her desire for him. She had no wish to bind him to her, merely to create memories that would sustain her when she was old and grey, to think that once her life had been a bubble of happiness. 'Please stay with me tonight.'

'I don't think it would be wise.'

'Why think?' she whispered. She ran her hands down her sides and licked her lips.

'You have had a traumatic day.'

'I know what I am doing. Stay here with me.' She took a step forwards, caressed his jaw with her hand and felt the graze of his stubble against her fingers. 'Please?'

His fingers traced the outline of her jaw, featherlight, delicate as if he was memorising it. 'Are you sure?'

Was he going to make it difficult for her? She was no good at seduction. She wanted to show him that she needed to have him in her life, for as long as it lasted. She nodded towards the bed, attempted a joke. 'It has linen sheets.'

'I had not even considered the bed, but you're right, it does.'

'You did promise and you always keep your promises.'

'That I do.' His eyes held a strange light.

'What happens next?' she whispered and stared at the floor, rather than at him. 'I am a beginner at wickedness.'

'Let me watch you undress.' He breathed in her ear.

'Undress?' Her hands went to her gown. She rapidly undid the buttons before she had time to think, before she had time to worry that she was doing it wrong. Tonight was about seduction, and wantonness. It was not about her normal world. It was as if she was trembling on the brink of a threshold. 'Like this?'

He stepped away from her. His eyes became inscrutable. 'Continue.'

'I don't follow.'

'Let me watch you.'

She started to take off her gown, stopped, feeling her cheeks grow hot under his dark gaze. 'It is impossible.'

'Try.' His voice flowed from the shadows.

She did it suddenly, lifting her arms and pulling off the gown, painfully aware that he must have watched other women, women who could make undressing a seduction. And her efforts were clumsy. Her fingers tugged at the stays, and managed only to pull the bow tighter. She gave a little exclamation and tried again.

'You see, I am hopeless at this.'

'Far from hopeless.' His husky rasp wrapped itself around her innards. 'And what would you do next?'

'Plait my hair.'

'Sit down on that stool in front of the mirror, begin plaiting.'

'Are we playing a game?'

'Of sorts.' His eyes crinkled at the corners. 'Indulge me in this fantasy. For tonight.'

She sat down and obeyed, concentrating on her hair rather than on him or the mirror. A simple little action, one which steadied her nerves. If it was fantasy, then it bore no relation to her life. Indulge him? Indulge herself, and the dreams that had woken her over the past few nights and filled her with a nameless ache. 'Am I doing this right?'

'Yes.' The word was no more than a hiss of air.

She glanced in the mirror and saw him standing behind her. The heat from his body warmed her back. 'I want to touch you, Diana. Touch you and watch you watching me.'

She gave a hesitant nod.

His hands came around her, grasped her aching breasts and his lips nuzzled her neck. She watched in the mirror as his hands pressed against her and her nipples stood out, tightly furled and dark rose under the thin cloth. He rolled his fingers over them, increasing the ache. She met his eyes in the mirror, saw her own heavy with passion. Her back arched and she felt his hard body pressing against her, leaving her in no doubt of his arousal.

One of his hands reached inside her shift, found the apex of her thighs. It hovered there as his mouth moved to an earlobe, nibbling, sucking. One finger traced the length of her crease. A jolt of fire went through her.

'Do you like what I am doing to you?' His hot breath teased her skin.

She could only nod. His fingers went deeper, caressing her as his other arm became an iron band holding her in place. She gave her body up to the exquisite torture. The ache within her grew. She twisted against the arm as she felt herself teeter on the brink. Her whole life had come down to this delicious ache. Her hands went up and caught his head, held him there. A mewling cry erupted from her throat.

'Shall I stop?' His hand paused, his fingers skimming her curls, playing in them.

'Continue.' She wet her lips. 'Please continue. Does that make me utterly wicked?'

'Only if you want to be.'

'With you.'

He gave a very masculine laugh. His tongue traced the edge of her ear. 'We are well suited. Think what it will be like to have my mouth there. Warm. Wet.'

His fingers slid inside her, making her buckle. Her hands pushed against the strength of his arm as a deep shudder went through her.

'I need…' she whispered. His finger stroked more and the world tilted.

His hands shifted. He scooped her up and she was held against his chest. She clung to him, regaining a sense of balance.

'I don't even want to think about how close I came to losing you today,' he murmured against her hair.

'You didn't lose me.' Her hand cupped his cheeks and he turned his lips to brush it. 'And I didn't lose you. We have tonight.'

'I know. I am greedy, though.' He bent his head and his lips teased hers. 'I want it all.'

He carried her to the bed and laid her down gently, arranging her limbs. 'I do keep my word.'

She refused to think as his lips sank lower, as they followed the path he had promised. His tongue flicked into her belly button, lingering—circling and teasing. Her body arched up off the bed. He glanced up at her, nodded in approval and moved his lips lower still.

His hands cupped her legs, opening them wider. His hot breath touched her crease, then his tongue parted it, delved deeper. Her head thrashed about on the pillow and little mewling cries came from her throat.

'Please,' she whispered and wasn't sure if she wanted him to speed up or to take his time. All she knew was that if he didn't continue, she'd die.

He took his time, swirling and teasing her until she thought she must surely shatter. Her hands clenched the linen sheets. Then he stopped and swiftly undid his breeches, divested his shirt so that his gleaming body shone bronze in the firelight. He nestled himself between her thighs and powerfully drove inside her.

Diana began to rock, to follow the age-old rhythm. She knew her body was telling him things, and his was answering, driving her to higher peaks.

'Brett,' she whispered.

He paused and looked down at her. 'Yes?'

'This is everything,' she whispered. His only response was to hold her tighter as a great shuddering engulfed them both.

Brett raised his body up on one elbow and looked down at her sleeping form. Gently he smoothed a tendril of hair from her cheek.

It seemed incredible that within a few short weeks, this woman had come to mean so much to him. He wondered how much her declaration was passion and how much was for real. He wanted to feel that she cared for him.

When they returned to Ladywell, he would ask her properly. He would make her understand that it was not duty that drove him to ask. It was his own fault that he had allowed his passion for her to cloud the issue. He had never meant to take her like this here.

She murmured in her sleep and her body sought his again.

'Soon, soon,' he whispered and kissed her temple. He had not asked for tonight, but he would use it. If necessary, he would join forces with her brother; together they would make her see that tonight changed everything. Marriage to him was her only option.

Chapter Seventeen

The cold early morning sunlight shone into the little room. Diana woke to find the bed next to her empty. She looked about her, confused. Then she saw Brett standing in front of the remains of the fire, fully dressed, his black Hessians gleaming and his riding cape immaculate. He was watching her. Her face coloured and she resisted the urge to dive back under the covers.

'If I had not fallen before, I certainly have now,' she said, with a hesitant smile, hoping he would understand. It was one thing to make love in a field, and quite another to make love in an inn. She wasn't quite sure why it was different, but it felt different. She wished that she had woken in his arms. Somehow it would have been all right. But she hadn't and it changed everything. She raised her arms above her head, stretched and tried to show she was unconcerned. 'Truly a pretty wench, rather than a lady.'

No answering smile flitted across his face. If anything, his expression became stern. 'We need to get you home as soon as possible, Diana. I gave your brother a promise.'

'But don't you agree about me being a pretty wench?' She peeped at him from under her lashes.

'I was wrong to call you that when we first met.' A deep frown showed between his brows. 'It was unforgivable and I did apologise. You are no pretty wench. You have always been a lady.'

'But…' Diana concentrated on the remains of the fire. Where had her tender lover gone? She had expected soft words, and instead he appeared cold and distant. She had thought that somehow last night had settled everything between them, but it seemed like everything had been destroyed. He had taken his pleasure and now wanted to leave her. Her passion had led her astray. Again.

'You should get dressed. We have far to go today.'

'The bed remains warm and the cock has not yet crowed.' The pit in her stomach was growing with every breath she took. She knew that she could not play a mistress. Every move she made seemed gauche and awkward.

'I am dressed for a reason, Diana. We need to get you back to the Lodge, back to your life. Inns like these are not made for the likes of you. I made an error of judgement last evening.'

Diana bit her lip. She had said too much. It had been she who had asked him to stay with her. Even her words sought to tie him. She had been the one to seduce him. Thankfully, he had not noted the need behind her seduction. She took a breath and regained her composure. 'Not made for the likes of me. The landlady was happy enough to take my coin last evening. And it was my coin as well. This is *my* room.'

He raised an eyebrow. 'I would have paid for you.'

'She thought you a coachman.'

'Yes, she did, and hopefully that will keep her mouth quiet. Otherwise, her tale will be repeated in every hostelry between Carlisle and Newcastle and up to the borders. And that is nothing to be desired.'

Diana pressed her knuckles against her mouth. 'I gave a false name.'

'That doesn't matter. People will guess.'

'Then you had best go and see to the horses, if you are the coachman. I will dress as quickly as possible.' She paused and swallowed hard. She had not even considered people talking and gossiping. She had thought herself safe. 'I will ride in the carriage. There may be some talk, but not full-blown scandal.' She paused and made sure her voice did not tremble. 'It would be best if you leave me now. I can cope.'

'As you wish…'

'I do wish.'

'Shall I send a woman up to help you dress?'

She shook her head, blinking rapidly. Correct. Polite, but distant. She could not fault him, but she would have preferred the warmth of last night. 'I am reasonably self-sufficient. My gown is easy to put on and my hair simply dressed. Rose despairs. But it is one of the advantages of being an ape-leader—not keeping up with the latest fashions.'

'You were never destined to be an ape-leader.' A faint smile touched his lips. 'You are far too alive for that fate.'

'So you say.' She gave her head a little toss and stuck her chin out defiantly. Inside, her stomach knotted and she felt her heart shatter into a thousand pieces. All she wanted was one word and she'd be in his arms, but she had to know that he wanted her to be there. She needed the security of knowledge. 'I will meet you down at the carriage.'

A muscle jumped in his cheek and his lips parted, but he clamped them together.

'I do not intend to have a sordid affair, Diana.'

'I know how to be discreet, Brett.' She made shooing motions with her hands. 'You were the one who said we had to leave. Now, let me get dressed.'

His boots echoed against the wooden floor. He paused at the door. 'There may be consequences from last night.'

'I will face the consequences when they happen.' She attempted a bright smile, but her stomach turned over. Was it wicked of her to hope for a child? She should be shocked by the thought, but the only thing she could think about was holding a baby in her arms and being able to bestow all her love. She raised her chin. 'Such things are by no means certain. Babies do not happen every time a man and a woman couple. I shall have to hope for the best.'

'You are taking a remarkably forthright attitude.' His eyes had deepened to slate grey and his mouth had become a thin white line.

Diana swallowed hard. 'It is better than weeping and wailing. I knew what I was doing last night, and what the consequences could be. I acted of my own free will with no expectation of being priest-linked.'

'Is that what you want?'

'I want to go back to my old safe life,' Diana lied. She could not bring herself to say the words to Brett, not until she knew how he felt. His derision or indifference would kill her. It seemed she was destined to keep repeating her mistakes. The last thing she wanted was for Brett to be cruel. 'If it makes it any easier, I did not intend for last night to happen. Events overtook me.'

'But it did happen, Diana, and will keep on happening. Think about that. Events will keep overtaking both of us. You must make a decision—do you desire respectability or not? What is it that you want? You need to tell me, for I am at a loss.'

'Not if we stop meeting.' Diana looked at her hands. It was far too soon for that, her heart protested, and her life seemed to stretch out before her. Bleaker. More correct than ever. 'If we stop meeting, become distant friends, then the temptation will be put beyond the both of us.'

'Is that what you want, what you truly want?'

'It is the only way.' Diana kept her head held high. She would not beg him to repeat his offer of marriage. She would not trap him like an animal. She had her pride. 'It is the sensible way. We have never pretended anything more than friendship exists between us.'

He closed the door with a decisive click. And she knew she had lost him, that she had never really had him in the first place. It had been some dream, a dream that she had now woken from.

Diana resisted the urge to throw something at the door. It was her fault for wanting it all. She refused to marry for anything but love. He had to care about her. She had to give him his freedom.

Brett kept his eyes on a point beyond the horses' ears. A steady rain beat down on him, chilling him to the bone and matching his mood. The journey was passing far too swiftly. Normally, driving gave him ideas, but this time his mind was a blank. Each scheme he considered seemed more preposterous than the last. And he had come no closer to solving his problem—Diana seemed implacable. She might desire his body, but she had no desire for his hand.

At the Ladywell crossroads, he had been very tempted to continue on the road to Gretna Green and force her into a marriage over the anvil. He had even started the carriage down the road when he had pulled the horses up and turned them on to the correct path.

For the first time in a long time, he knew he was not in control of the situation. He had allowed someone else to have power over him. Everything he had worked so hard to achieve counted for nothing if Diana was not by his side.

Despite his dawdling, the Lodge's chimneys appeared far too quickly. A carriage passed them on the drive, spraying water and gravel. Brett raised his hat to Lady Bolt. The woman's eyes slid away from him and the Honourable Miranda stuck her nose in the air as their coachman whipped the horses into a faster trot.

The incident had happened so quickly that Brett hoped Diana had been unaware. He concentrated on bringing the horses to a standstill and tried not to think how she would have reacted to the cut.

Brett's innards tightened. He would hold true to his resolve. He would explain to Clare that even though he was the last person he had ever envisioned as a brother-in-law, Brett was going to marry his sister. They would have to set aside their differences for her sake. It was going to be done properly. Together, they could convince Diana where her duty lay. He did not relish the prospect, but it would have to be done.

The door to the Lodge stood open and Clare with his bandaged face gleaming in sun stood, moodily surveying the scene. Brett concentrated on bringing the horses to a complete standstill, before he jumped down from his perch.

'Coltonby!' Simon thundered before Brett had been able to open the carriage door. 'What have you done with my sister? You have ruined her! You promised to have her back before nightfall. On my life I trusted you, Coltonby.'

'There was a carriage accident with a farm cart. We were delayed,' Brett bit out each word. 'Sometimes, these things happen, despite one's plans.'

Diana emerged from the carriage, pale faced but resolute. Brett gave her an encouraging nod but she turned her face from him. He thought he glimpsed the glimmer of tears. He swore softly. She had seen the cut. She knew what was coming. He had wanted to spare her that. He would spend the rest of his life making amends.

'You, one of the most noted whips in the country? Involved in an accident with a farm cart? The truth, Coltonby.'

'Which truth is that?'

'You seduced my sister. You seduced her and intend to let her live a life of sin. You never change, Coltonby.'

Diana's cheek turned bright pink against the white of her skin. 'You have no cause to say that, brother. You have no proof.'

'Your very countenance shows it, Diana. This man will be made to marry you or I will blacken his name from here to the ends of the earth.'

'I have called men out for less,' Brett ground out.

'Name your date and time.' Clare's eyes blazed at him.

Brett stared at him in disbelief. Clare took a step towards him, and raised his fists. 'I will defend myself, Clare. You may count on that, but I have no wish to duel with you.'

'Stop it! Stop it, you two!' Diana came between them, her hands out, pushing them apart. 'I will not have it. I refuse. Simon, you are behaving like a child. Drag your mind out of the gutter.'

'He must be made to marry you, Diana. He dishonoured you.' Simon Clare looked him up and down with a curl to his lip. 'I know his kind. You cannot say that I didn't warn you.'

'No one must be made to do anything.' Diana put her hands on her hips. 'An accident happened. Lord Coltonby swerved to miss a little girl and the carriage was damaged. He has shown me nothing but kindness and consideration. Your prejudice blinds you, brother. Brett Farnham is a gentleman and always has been.'

Brett stared at Diana. Did she intend to brazen out the disgrace? With a word, or maybe even a gesture, he could ensure it. He remained absolutely still. He refused to get her acceptance that way. He could not tell Clare what had passed between them. Just as Diana had refused his earlier offer, he would not have her marry him simply because her brother demanded. He refused to achieve his ends this way. He loved her too much. She had to love him in return. She had to want to marry him.

'The lady has spoken,' he said slowly, almost not recognising his own voice. 'She has done nothing to be ashamed about.'

'Nothing except spend the night with a notorious rake in God knows what sort of hell hole! The disgraceful baggage!'

'You overstep the mark, Clare. Has your sister ever done anything to make you ashamed? Everything she has done has been predicated on you and your business. She is a lady and should be treated as such. She should never have had to live this half-life you condemned her to—reduced to a nurse, caring for your son.'

'I dare because she is my sister.' Simon advanced towards Brett. His hands clenched into fists. 'This has been a long time coming. I tried to ignore the rumours and slurs. But I can't any longer.'

'You wish to drag my name through the mud? Your own sister's?' Diana shook her head. 'Forgive me, Simon, but I don't think you want to do that.'

'I want you to be safe,' her brother whispered. 'I have striven to keep you and your reputation safe.'

'You have done what you did because it was easier than looking for another wife.' Diana held out her hands to her brother, willed him to understand. 'But Brett is wrong. I did enjoy my life. I have no regrets about raising Robert and I love him as if he were my own.'

'Then you will understand why, for the sake of Robert, I have to ask you to leave unless you promise me never to have anything more to do with Coltonby again.'

'Are you asking me to choose?'

'Do not make her do this, Clare.' Brett's voice rang out.

'You keep out of it.'

'Diana?' She heard Simon's voice. 'I need to know. You have brought us to the edge of ruin. Will you give up this man? Or will you destroy Robert's chance in life as well as your own?'

'What do you know about Robert's chances, Simon? You have never bothered to be a father, not properly.' She watched Simon blanch, but knew the truth in her words. She met his green gaze and he was the first to look away. 'He is your son, Simon. Be his father. He has already lost one parent.'

Diana looked towards the house. For so long she had thought it a place of refuge, but, if she allowed it to be, it would become her prison. She looked to where Brett stood, the breeze slightly ruffling his travelling coat. Freedom and life. It was far more important than security. She knew that now. 'Brett, take me with you.'

'What are you asking?'

She held out her hands. Tears streamed down her face. 'Take me with you as your mistress.'

Behind her, she heard Simon's curse and ignored it. She had reached the point in her life at which she had to stop running. Her breath caught in her throat as she waited for his answer.

'No.'

She stared at him in stunned disbelief. 'No?' She swallowed hard. The word had come from Brett. 'What do you mean?'

Brett's lips turned up in a thin smile. 'No.'

Diana felt her world turn upside down. Had he truly meant to end it? Here and now? She had lost everything. She stood there stunned. Unable to take it in.

'Even your lover has more sense than you, Diana.' Simon's scornful words floated on the breeze.

'Please, Brett,' she whispered as her heart broke into a thousand shards. 'Tell me why. Surely I am owed that.'

'Is it me you want, or the idea of me?' he asked in a harsh rasp. His grey eyes had become silver arrows piercing into her soul. 'What exactly is it you want? Love comes at a cost.'

The idea of him? She stared at Brett, confused. She wanted him. Then her mind cleared. She knew what he was asking. She had spent years thinking about him as the prince of rakes, a man around whom scandal and gossip swirled, but that wasn't Brett Farnham at all. Brett was something more—a loyal friend, someone she could depend on, a man who kept his promises. Her idea of him was very different than society's and she knew that she had discerned the true man.

'You,' she said without hesitation. 'I want you. I want my life full of passion and emotion.'

Brett nodded and she knew she had said the right words. He would take her with him. They could go on together, for as long as things lasted. And then when it ended, she'd face the future. She held out her hands. 'I promise to be a good and faithful mistress for as long as it lasts.'

'You cannot have me that way.' His face darkened like thunder and she took an involuntary step backwards. 'I refuse.'

'Why not?' She tilted her head to one side. Her whole being trembled. He could not be planning on repudiating her here, in front of Simon. 'It is what you want. Why are you not agreeing?'

'Because I love you, Diana. I have loved you from the moment you drove away from the mud pool, leaving me standing there with a book in my hand. And then the feeling was reinforced when I met you again, wearing that ridiculous cap and struggling so hard to deny yourself all pleasure. I tried to say that it was simply to spite your brother, but I was fooling myself. I wanted to spend time with you.'

'But if you love me...'

Brett strode three steps to her, caught her hands and went down on one knee. 'I want to marry you and have you by my side for the rest of my life. Please say that you will be my wife.'

'You want to marry me? Out of duty?'

'Duty has nothing to do with it. I don't want you to marry me because your brother insists, or because you think society demands it. I want you to marry me because it is what you desire above everything else. I love you Diana.'

'You love me?' She tugged at his hand and he stood. Her fingers curled around his.

'I have been trying to show you, and now I am telling you. I love you, Diana Clare, with all my heart and all my soul. And I want to marry you for the right reason, the only reason—I need you in my life for all time. Please.'

'Brett, I will. I love you with all my heart and soul and to be parted now would be more than I could bear.' She threw her arms around him and gave herself up to his kiss.

'You will have to bear it for a little while, sweetheart.' His eyes crinkled and he gave a heart stopping smile. 'No midnight gallop to Gretna Green for us. We marry in the parish church with the banns properly read and your brother giving you away. I will have no one speak out about this marriage, Diana.'

'If it must be done that way, then so be it. But let it be a simple wedding.'

'Whatever your heart desires, my very dearest lady.' He lowered his mouth and Diana forgot about everything for a long while.

* * * * *